Julie Shackman is a feel-good romance author and former journalist.

She lives in Scotland with her husband, two sons and their little Romanian rescue pup, Cooper.

julieshackman.co.uk

D0264437

Also by Julie Shackman

A Secret Scottish Escape

A Scottish Highland Surprise

THE COTTAGE IN THE HIGHLANDS

JULIE SHACKMAN

One More Chapter
a division of HarperCollins*Publishers* Ltd
1 London Bridge Street
London SE1 9GF
www.harpercollins.co.uk

HarperCollins*Publishers*
1st Floor, Watermarque Building, Ringsend Road
Dublin 4, Ireland

This paperback edition 2022
1
First published in Great Britain in ebook format
by HarperCollins*Publishers* 2022

A catalogue record of this book is available from the British Library

ISBN: 978-0-00-853896-5

Printed and bound in the UK using 100% Renewable Electricity
by CPI Group (UK) Ltd

Chapter One

"Are you all right, Doug? You've gone very pale."

Douglas Drennan, my editor, lowered his mobile so slowly that for a moment I thought he might be filming a scene for *The Matrix*.

He forced a tight smile from across our bijou newsroom, with its stack of last week's edition of the paper and three walnut desks. There was an assortment of potted plants dotted around, a couple of old black and white photographs of Silver Ness back in the day decorating the walls and a faint scent of percolated coffee. "That was head office. I've been summoned to a meeting in town."

Frances White, a married mother of two in her mid-thirties and our senior news reporter, gave a dismissive flap of her gold manicure from her desk, which was stationed across from mine. "It'll be nothing, Doug. Well, when I say nothing, it'll either be a gold star or a bullet up the arse."

I shot a wary look across at her, before swivelling my chair to face Doug. I was very fond of Frances, but she wasn't known for her finesse. "It will be something about nothing," I assured him. "Probably one of those dreaded budget meetings."

He dragged a hand down his tense, craggy face. "Er. Yes. Sure. That's what it will be. A budget meeting."

I frowned. Something was troubling him. Doug was one of those unstoppable journalists of old, in his sixties, not fazed by anything and convinced that a pint and a packet of pickled-onion crisps could solve the ills of the world. He would always joke that he had newspaper print running through his veins and not blood. Doug glanced down at his watch for the tenth time in a minute, before leaping to his feet and throwing on his crumpled suit jacket.

"Or is it another liquid lunch?" asked Frances with a twinkle. She snapped shut her silver powder compact. "You seem to have been indulging in a few more of those recently."

Doug barrelled round. "I wish it bloody was! I just told you. I've been summoned to some shit-show of a meeting, ok?!"

Frances's hazel eyes grew large and she held up her hands in mock surrender. "Ok! Ok. Bloody hell! No need to get all irate! I was only joking!"

Doug flipped his black and silver tie. He cleared his throat, his attention all at once focused on our beige office carpet. "The meeting is at half twelve, so I'll head off now."

He stalked towards the newsroom door. Then he swung to face me. "And Leonie, can I have five hundred words on that elderly lady in Carbeth Road you went to see this morning?"

"You mean the one whose dog found the message in a bottle on Silver Ness beach?"

My boss gave a stiff nod. He was struggling to concentrate.

"I'm already on it. What a sweetheart she is. She was telling me that cute dog of hers—"

"I don't have time for a cosy chat right now," he snapped, making me blink in surprise. "Just have it sent over to me when I get back. Please."

Good grief. What was the matter with him this morning? He had been a little prickly and distracted recently, but in the two years I had worked here at my local paper, *The Silver Ness News*, I had never known Doug to be like this.

There was an awkward silence as he banged out.

Frances pulled a face. "Oooh! Somebody didn't have their Weetabix this morning," she whispered, once he had gone.

I fiddled with my pen. "Something's bothering him." I shot her a look. "Actually, have you noticed Doug hasn't been himself the last few weeks?"

"Maybe a bit," she conceded. "But I just put it down to him and Cheryl having a few problems."

"Are they?"

Over Frances's shoulder and out of one of the bevelled office windows, Silver Ness beach looked like one giant, golden smile in the hazy October sunshine.

She hesitated.

"Spill, Sherlock. You look like you want to say something."

Frances bit the inside of her lip. "Haven't you noticed the long days he's been putting in here recently? Staying behind well after we've headed home?"

I considered what she was saying. Sure enough, he had still been stationed at his desk well after clocking-off during the

3

past few weeks, his head buried in his screen. "So, you think Doug is having issues at home?"

"It all points that way."

I thought again about Doug barging out of the office. "Do you think we should have a word with him when he gets back? Let him know we're around for him, if he needs to talk?"

Frances nodded her shiny black hair. "You know Doug isn't into all that touchy-feely stuff, but it's a nice gesture."

I flipped open my reporter's notebook and began to rattle off the introduction to my message-in-a-bottle story. At least we could let Doug know we were there to help.

It was my turn to go and get lunch from the seafront deli.

I studied the array of cold meats and cheeses through the panoramic window and let out a frustrated sigh. I didn't know what I wanted. I experienced this dilemma every day of the week, mind you, such was the delicious array of fillings that were always available.

I had worked for *The Silver Ness News* as a junior reporter for two years now and I loved it.

Silver Ness, where I was born and still lived, was a quaint little Scottish seaside town a good hour's journey away from the centre of Glasgow. It was all pretty bed and breakfast cottages and family businesses along the seafront. The shops there sold everything from buckets and spades to dramatic artwork depicting the golden stretch of beach. We also had mysterious historical links to pirates and smuggling, which the day-trippers, tourists, and local children got rather excited about.

Before joining my local paper, I had worked in an uptight advertising agency on the south side of town for three years as a copy writer after graduating from my four-year journalism degree course. I struggled to find a job in journalism after university and remembering Mum's advice of "It's easier to go to a job from a job" (together with the fact that I needed to survive financially) I took the ad agency vacancy.

I hated every minute of it.

Cut-throat; synthetic; stressful; not to mention the grind of the daily commute, which had sapped well over two hours out of my life each day. Everyone at the agency looked every bit as downtrodden as I was.

The term "work–life balance" was treated with derision and even taking a proper lunch break away from your desk was frowned upon. I was twenty-five at the time, but felt like I was ninety-five. I don't know how I managed to stick it for so long. I think the very competitive salary was a large part of why I stayed, until even that palled and I knew that for my mental wellbeing, I couldn't carry on working there.

When my mum tipped me off that she'd bumped into Frances, senior reporter at our local paper, who told her their current junior was leaving to join his girlfriend in London, I knew I had to apply for the vacancy.

I was delighted to hear I had secured an interview and then spent the next few weeks preparing for it, swatting up on my home town. I'm embarrassed to say I had rather taken Silver Ness and its reputedly colourful past for granted.

I read up on everything about the birth of the local paper

too, devouring information on its circulation, regular local correspondents, and previous reporters of note.

It was Doug and a stern-faced character from the Clarity Newspaper Group Human Resources team who interviewed me and I was thrilled to hear a couple of days later that I was being offered the job of junior reporter.

I threw myself into the role, bearing down on individuals with my Dictaphone, notebook, and a wide smile or sympathetic ear. I managed within a matter of months of dogged determination to establish a solid set of contacts in the local police force, the council, and the fire service.

It was a joy, working for a local newspaper that so many members of the community relied upon and which had been a part of their family for over a hundred years. I felt as if I were achieving something; giving something back to the sleepy seaside town where I was born and brought up.

I could smell the sea air from my desk, listen to the gulls bickering over the waves, and I could actually relax and take a breath when I got home.

I inspected the array of tasty breads again in the deli window. Even though it was only the first day of October, the deli owners had enthusiastically placed a couple of small pumpkins in the window, together with plastic bats and a witch's broom.

The idea of Doug being called to a snap finance meeting like that in town niggled me. For the two years I had been working at the paper, Head Office always made sure they gave Doug a clear heads-up on when these meetings were due to take place and on the odd occasion when he couldn't attend or was on holiday, Frances would take his place. I recalled her saying that they were an utter pain in the arse, but that they were well-organised and the minutes and papers were emailed through ahead of time.

Something about this didn't seem right.

I inwardly rolled my eyes and tried to give myself a reassuring internal talking-to as I continued to hover outside the deli window. There was a stiff breeze working its way from up the beach and I huddled deeper into my coat. I caught sight of my pensive expression in the glass, with my smattering of cinnamon freckles across my nose, and pushed my array of spirally, conker-brown hair away from my face.

No. Stop, Leonie. Don't catastrophise. Crikey, I would have myself out of a job in a minute!

I sucked in a sweep of air, clotted with seaweed and salt, and tried to be more rational. That meeting Doug had been summoned to could be about anything. Anything at all. Doug was always a bit on-edge before these sorts of "shit-shows", as he called them, anyway. *And remember what Frances said about Cheryl,* reminded a voice. The long hours and late nights he had been pulling. That would explain his tetchy, barking moods of late.

Maybe it was all to do with him and Cheryl having marriage problems and had nothing to do with work after all.

Yes. That would be it. I was letting my imagination run ahead of me.

I glanced down at my watch. Shit! Frances would start chewing her keyboard if I didn't return with her salmon and cucumber salad bagel in the next ten minutes.

I opted for a salt beef bagel and made my way back along the high street towards the office. Not many people could boast of a view like this from their workplace. The sea was brushing against the rocks in a mirror of turquoise and to the right, the harbour reached out like a gnarly hand towards a couple of creaking fishing boats.

Behind me, the multi-coloured fishermen's cottages and eclectic array of shops were slung like a string of rainbow beads.

This sure beat being stuck on a train an hour each way every day, inhaling other people's armpits.

"Ms Baxter?"

I turned around.

It was Mrs Cooke, an elderly lady I had interviewed recently. She had been swindled out of six hundred pounds by a dodgy landscape gardening company and had come to *The Silver Ness News* for help.

I followed up her story and thanks to the negative publicity and the attention my article attracted, Mrs Cooke was refunded the money these crooks had extracted from her, after claiming they had "recalculated the costs of pruning Mrs Cooke's hedges and realised they had made an administrative error."

"I just wanted to thank you so much for your help."

"Oh, not at all Mrs Cooke," I beamed, putting on a jokey voice. "Just doing my job."

"No, you didn't. You did far more than that. You were so very kind to me." She leant in, clutching her wicker shopping basket. "I have written a letter of thanks to your editor, telling him how wonderful you are, but I'm sure he knows that already."

I felt my cheeks zing with happiness and satisfaction.

"Well, I hope he does but it won't do any harm to remind him. Thank you."

Mrs Cooke laughed and wandered off to inspect some new postcards outside the gift shop.

As I strolled back towards the office, an idea came to me. Maybe we could introduce a consumer complaints page for the local readers? Doug would often ask Frances and me to put forward any ideas we might have for the paper so that he could feed them back to Head Office.

The offices of *The Silver Ness News* were a whitewashed bevelled-window affair that used to be a pub that entertained the weary fishermen after their gruelling shifts out at sea during the early 1900s. It looked out from the high street and onto the moody vista of the beach.

As I drew closer, I noted that Doug's black Hyundai was back and parked round the corner. Wow. If that had been a budget meeting, it had been a much quicker one than usual. They usually dragged on for a good couple of hours.

Doug would return, tie askew, complaining about people loving the sound of their own voices and refusing to stick to the timings on the agenda. Then he would always say he could murder a pint.

If I'd known he was going to return over lunch, I could have treated him to one of his favourites from the deli – a cream horn.

I closed the office door behind me, waggling the brown paper bag embossed with the deli logo. Inside, I was glowing from the kind praise from Mrs Cooke. I bounced across the newsroom. "The hunter-gatherer has returned."

I turned to Frances and my smile withered. She was sitting behind her desk, dabbing at her wet eyes with a tissue.

The usually relaxed atmosphere in our little newsroom was edgy; unidentifiable.

I looked at Doug and then back to Frances. An uneasy feeling gripped my stomach. "What is it? What's wrong?"

Doug shuffled from foot to foot, avoiding eye contact with me. "Switch on the office voicemail, would you please Leonie? We need to talk."

Chapter Two

My stomach plummeted to the floor.

I felt as though I had been punched in the chest. "You're joking. Please tell me you're joking."

Frances dragged her swivel chair round to sit beside me, her suit rumpled and her eyes stinging with more tears.

"I wish I were," managed Doug.

"But closing the paper…"

Doug's words carried more than a hint of sarcasm. "Not closing. Amalgamating."

I couldn't process this. The Clarity Newspaper Group had decided to amalgamate *The Silver Ness News* with one of our sister titles, *The Drummond Post*. Drummond was the neighbouring town to Silver Ness and a friendly rivalry had existed between the two ever since I could remember.

I rocked backwards and forwards in my chair, a rising panic clawing at me. I had been right to be concerned when Doug was summoned to Head Office like that. It wasn't an urgent finance meeting. It was management lobbing a filthy great bomb into our lives.

Frances sniffed into her hankie.

I could guess what Doug was about to say, but I asked anyway. Part of me didn't want to know. "But there must be something we can do," I persisted, my voice dripping with desperation. "How about we try and modernise the paper a bit? Nothing radical, but just give it a bit of an update?"

"Leonie…" started Doug, looking defeated.

"I had been thinking about it before," I carried on, fighting to sound positive. "We could have a few more competitions and get some of the local businesses on board. That could boost the paper's revenue."

Frances sniffed louder and didn't say anything.

"Or we could have a feature such as the Silver Ness Reader of The Week. Highlight a local who's done a lot for the community…" My voice tailed off at Doug's distinct lack of enthusiasm for my ideas.

"Don't you think I've been driving myself round the bend recently, trying to come up with counter arguments against this? I've looked at our advertising revenue, possible feature ideas…" Doug ruffled up his greying hair and left it sitting on top of his head like a wild, petrified animal. "I've been pushing poor Cheryl to the limit at home, doing nothing else."

I slumped in my desk chair. "So, it's definite then?"

"I'm afraid it is."

I glanced at my PC screen, not seeing the text flickering on there. The words were misting over through a haze of gathering tears.

"And what does this mean for the three of us?"

My boss's sullen expression avoided mine for a moment. "HR have said I can take retirement now."

I swallowed. "And what does all this mean for Frances and me?"

Frances squirmed in her chair. She couldn't bring herself to look across at me. "Doug said they've offered me a part-time reporter post on the new title."

"Right. Ok. That's great."

"It's not perfect," she admitted, "but it's something."

There followed a heavy silence.

"And me?" I croaked, my apprehension rising like the tide outside. "What about me?"

Doug looked as if someone were standing on his toes. The words tumbled out of his mouth in one long, apologetic rush. "I'm so sorry, Leonie. I really am. I pushed to have you taken on at the revamped title or at another of our sister publications. I even asked if you could be taken on at another of our papers on a part-time basis, but they kept chucking falling circulation figures and cutbacks at me…"

You're out of a job, hissed a voice in my head. *That's what that means.*

Icy fingers gripped me.

Doug continued to talk. He was saying something about a decision to retain the existing quota of staff on the Drummond title but I was fighting to process any of it. It was just a jumble of sentences he was talking, which all led to the same awful conclusion. I was about to be made redundant.

My stunned eyes scanned our modest newsroom, of which

I was so fond, despite it needing a fresh lick of paint. He may as well have been reciting his weekly shopping list for all the attention I was able to pay.

"But nobody knows their own area like a local reporter," I croaked. "I was born in Silver Ness. I grew up here…"

"I've been pointing all that out," insisted Doug. "I've stressed what a great journalist you are. How embedded you are here in the community and what solid contacts you have—"

Frances jerked up her head. Her flapper-style bob swung onto her cheeks. She cut him off mid-flow. "Wait a minute. How long have you known about all this, Doug?"

Doug blanched.

Frances shifted forward in her chair. "Well?"

He looked like he wanted to slither away under the door. "I've done my best to make them reconsider…"

So, he'd known this might be a possibility? He'd known that the future of *The Silver Ness News* was at risk?

Frances and I swapped electrified looks. "Why didn't you talk about all this before?" I managed, unable to conceal my accusatory tone.

Doug looked wretched as it was, without me piling on the guilt. Nonetheless, why, if he had known about what was to happen, hadn't he told Frances and me? Why hadn't he warned us? He was often calling us The Three Musketeers, for pity's sake!

Could we form a united front together to fight this? To make management reconsider?

Doug swallowed, hurt and shame etched into his anguished features. "I hoped I could do something. I thought I might be able to make them change their minds. But Sir John was adamant that with the general decline in circulation of local papers and so many people accessing news online, they had to make some tough decisions."

Now it was Frances's turn to go on the defensive. "So why the hell didn't you tell us, Doug? Maybe we could have helped."

Doug let out an impatient sigh. "You two had more than enough to contend with at the time." He gestured to me. "You and Miles had just split up."

I flinched at the memory.

"And Frances, your mother-in-law had just been diagnosed with Alzheimer's."

"I appreciate that," responded Frances. Then realisation kicked in. Her mouth dropped open. "But wait… all that stuff with Sarah's diagnosis and Leonie and Miles splitting up… that all happened at the beginning of the year."

Doug paced like an anguished zoo animal behind bars backwards and forwards in front of his desk, which bore his Scottish rugby team coffee mug and a couple of photos of Cheryl – a smiling twinkly brunette.

"You've known for all this time that this could happen?" I gasped. "You've known for ten months and yet you didn't think to warn us?"

He struggled to speak. "Ok. Ok. I'm sorry. I've cocked everything up." We watched him reach into one of his desk drawers and produce a brown cardboard folder. He slapped it down on the desk. "But I haven't been sitting here with my thumb up my arse. I've been trying to salvage this bloody newspaper. I haven't been pulling all these extra hours in the office to do bloody sudoku!"

Frances gave the folder a contemptuous look. "What's that?"

"See for yourselves."

I reached across and flipped it open. It was a thick report and contained everything from projected sales figures and ideas for features, to snippets of exclusive news articles the three of us had managed, at one time or another, to sell to the nationals. There were even a couple of PowerPoint presentations that Doug had compiled.

I raised my stunned, teary eyes to Doug. "You pulled together all this?"

Doug eyed his work with contempt. "Much good it did in the end."

Frances's red suit rustled as she shuffled forward in her chair for a better look. She pointed to one of Doug's flashy-looking presentations, entitled *Alternative Proposals for the Future of The Silver Ness News*. Her watery eyes scanned the print out of the slides. "You suggested to Management that we go online or fortnightly?"

Doug took a rueful sip of his now cold coffee. "I would have suggested us giving away free knitting patterns and flavoured condoms if it meant salvaging this little newspaper." He gave a defeated shrug. "I thought anything was worth a shot."

I aimed a meaningful stare at Frances as I flicked over a few more pages.

"I'm sorry, ladies." A myriad of emotions raced across his

features. "I've been trying to think of something to stop all this, but nothing has worked. Please believe me."

Frances sniffed into her hankie. "I'm so sorry, Leonie."

I whipped my head to look at her. "What are you apologising for?"

"Well, they've kept me on but not you. Just before you arrived back, Doug was telling me that it's all to do with this last in, first out policy nonsense." Her mouth twisted at the corners. "I suppose me being here for ten years has worked in my favour."

My brain felt addled; broken into sharp, jagged pieces that I couldn't sort out into a coherent order. "How long till we close?" The question lodged itself in my throat.

Doug winced. "A couple of months. They've decided to shut this office and use the Drummond one. The rent is a bit cheaper. Staff moving on to the new title are being told today." Great. I was going to be unemployed in time for Christmas.

He pushed his mug backwards and forwards on his desk. "And they've already chosen the title of the new publication as well."

Frances and I raised our brows in unison at Doug. Jesus. They hadn't hung around.

Doug hesitated, as though he didn't want to say it. "*The Drummond & Silver Ness Sentinel.*"

I pulled a face. "Blimey. That's a mouthful."

"I don't like it," ground out Frances.

"According to Sir John, it has an American ring to it."

Frances reached over and grasped my hand in hers. I wished she hadn't. The sensation of her kindness, her fingers clasping mine, made me want to burst into self-pitying sobs.

I thought that, at last, I had got my life into some semblance of order. I had a job I loved and I was pushing forwards after the break-up with Miles.

Outside, the gulls were cackling and hovering and the waters of Silver Ness shimmered, oblivious to the turmoil taking place just yards away.

I felt as though I had taken several positive steps towards the future, only to be turned around and ordered back to the starting line.

Goodness knows how I was going to struggle through the rest of the day.

There was an odd, resentful heaviness in the air for the remainder of the afternoon.

Frances slung on her suit jacket and went out to cover a council planning meeting, while I bashed out an advertising feature for a local bathroom company.

Frances was wearing her guilt like a chain around her neck. She persisted in giving me charged looks whilst still in the office and then couldn't escape to that council meeting fast enough.

Doug, meanwhile, was like a pale, sour imitation of his former self. No dry wit about the day's news headlines or crisp observations about our politicians. He just stalked about like a preoccupied Scottish Jack Nicholson, lost in his own world.

My emotions were skittering from one extreme, fired-up sensation to the next. Fury and anger zoomed towards cold, hard reality. Doug had taken on the arduous task of trying to save the paper, failed, and the weight of not succeeding was pressing down on him.

It wasn't his fault. He had tried his best to salvage the paper's future – and ours. I just wish he had told Frances and me from the start. Perhaps we could have helped. But from what Doug had said, the decisions over our futures had been made months ago, while the three of us continued to provide a much-needed service to our local community in ignorant, innocent bliss.

I stopped typing, my fingers hovering over the keyboard.

My stomach rushed to the floor with the finality of it all. I looked from my PC to Doug's paper-stacked desk. *Oh God.* I was going to be unemployed.

I couldn't wait to finish work for the day.

Five o'clock hauled itself around.

Doug had told Frances not to bother returning to the office after the council meeting.

I slid into my quilted coat and scooped up my bag. Doug was staring into the middle-distance, struggling to come back from wherever he was. "You coming?"

He fired out his legs. "Not yet. I want to get the editing finished on that pottery man piece Frances wrote for next week's edition."

He looked shattered; defeated even. His shoulders slumped under his shirt.

I opened my mouth to persuade him to drop what he was doing and call it a night, but Doug swivelled his attention back to his glowing PC screen. The light emphasised the stubborn smudges under his eyes. "Night, Leonie. See you tomorrow."

I drove the short journey to my parents', inwardly cursing the weather. It had been awful first thing, the rain splattering down my bedroom window. Now, the October evening was splashed with smudges of pale-lemon sun.

I would have much preferred to have walked to Mum and Dad's. They lived ten minutes away from the seafront and just another fifteen minutes from my little cottage. I would have valued the time to breathe in the sea air and attempt to untangle the merry-go-round whirring in my head. To try and reconcile what I was going to do next. How I was going to come to terms with being out of a job. A job that I loved and didn't dread waking up to five days a week.

I negotiated the cobbled streets, fringed with the assorted bed and breakfast cottages and hanging baskets, and drove past the shops, their decorated doorways festooned with everything from postcards to beachballs.

I left behind the swell of the harbour in the rear-view mirror and reached Mum and Dad's on autopilot. I eased into the kerb and sat for a few moments outside their 70s-style detached house. I would now have to tell my parents.

Dread pooled inside my stomach. They would worry, especially Mum. She would deny it of course, but she would be wringing her hands and fretting to Dad when I wasn't within earshot.

My hands gripped the steering wheel. *Get on with it, Leonie. Rip the plaster away from the wound.*

I could imagine my Mum's panic-stricken gaze as she bundled me into her arms. Dad would deliver a torrent of positive, comforting words, assuring me I would find something else in no time.

As I clambered out of my car, it felt as if I were wading through treacle. Putting one foot in front of the other was demanding every ounce of effort I had. The prospect of telling them was making me feel queasy.

With no time to dwell any longer on their reaction, their front door burst open and Harley, my ten-month-old rescue cockapoo puppy, came barrelling down the path towards me.

I swept her plump wriggling mass of toffee-coloured curls up and cradled her in my arms. She lashed my face with her baby-pink tongue. The unconditional love she was demonstrating made me struggle to compose myself. I just wanted to bury my face in her and forget what an utterly shit day it had been. Wipe today from my memory.

A massive bomb had been lobbed into my life, just as I felt like I was getting myself together after Miles. I bit my lip as pictures of him flitted in front of my eyes. I blinked them away.

"Hello darling!" beamed Mum, planting a kiss on my cheek. Her dark-chocolate Italian eyes mirrored mine. "How was your day? Anything hot off the press?"

I nestled Harley closer to me and plastered on a fake smile.

She took a step backwards to look at me. "What's wrong? You look pale and tired." She frowned. "Are you eating properly and getting enough sleep? I bet you're living off next to nothing."

She called over her shoulder. "Ross. Come and see your daughter. You tell me if you think she's eating." She shook her dark layered hair. "Why don't you come in and let me make you dinner. You need feeding up a bit."

Despite my mood, I couldn't stifle a brief snort of laughter. "Are you joking, Mum? Have you seen my arse in my jeans lately?"

"There is absolutely nothing wrong with your arse, young lady. It's a real woman's arse. You have the Carlucci bottom and there is nothing wrong with that. Remember what Sophia Loren said? 'Everything you see I owe to pasta.'"

I rolled my eyes and buried my face deeper into Harley's coat. Why was I standing here on my parents' doorstep, talking about family bottoms and Sophia Loren, when I should be delivering the sobering news that their only daughter was about to join the dole queue?

"Mum," I began, but Dad had now appeared.

"Look at her," pressed on Mum. "You look at Leonie and tell me she's looking thinner. I don't think she's eating properly. Well, Ross, what do you think?"

Dad looked agonised. Either way, he knew he couldn't win.

"*Chi mangia sulo s'affoga,*" said Mum, pulling in her lips and not giving Dad enough time to respond.

"He who eats alone suffocates?" guessed Dad, used to Mum quoting her extensive repertoire of Italian proverbs.

"Well done," I sighed. "Got it in one."

Mum raked me from the top of my head to my toes, scrunching her nose as she scrutinized me for signs of self-neglect. "You could be doing with a good plate of my ricotta and cherry tomato gnocchi."

Dad looked me over, with an intense expression. He broke into a smile. "I think our little girl is gorgeous as she is."

No, it was no use. Those lovely words from my dad tipped

my emotions over the edge, like the penny-falls at a fairground.

His smile collapsed. "Leonie? Leonie? What is it? What's wrong sweetheart?"

I answered my dad's question by erupting into a series of louder, rasping sobs.

Chapter Three

The next week evaporated in a haze of me trawling through various media job sites.

I'd already fired off my CV to several online magazines and tried a couple of the larger regional newspapers in the hope that there might be a vacancy imminent or that they would see my application and decide they desperately wanted to recruit me. Ha!

Every so often I would try to fight – deny, even – my festering panic. I had a mortgage on my little cottage to pay. I knew I was being blinkered, refusing to even consider a short-term job doing something else, but even that idea was beginning to falter. I might not be able afford to be choosy. Needs must.

I pulled my attention back to the present and the lasagne and parmesan in front of me. I plucked a chunk of garlic bread from the bowl and examined it. Beside me, Harley was crunching on her kibble.

I cleared up my dinner debris and called Harley to come to

the front door, by waggling her pink sparkly lead. I felt like someone had tipped me upside down and given me a damn good shake. "Come on, you. Let's go for a walk before I go crazy."

Harley's plume of a curly tail waggled with excitement as I closed the door behind us. I slipped on her harness and glanced around at my modest little garden, with its ceramic pots and flowered hedge.

I lived in an old cottage that was a stone's throw from both my parents' and the newspaper office. I'd bought it for a relative bargain, after securing the junior reporter role at the paper. It had belonged to a frail, elderly gentleman who hadn't been able to maintain it.

When he passed away, his family, all located in the south of England, had been anxious for a quick sale and so I had been able to make them a competitive offer.

It had required a lot of work to knock it into shape and drag it into the twenty-first century. Thankfully, my dad being a semi-retired painter and decorator, meant that he and a few of his contacts had been able to turn it from a tired, jaded house with loud paisley carpets and Venetian blinds suspended from every window into a cosy, modern little home.

I think because I had been born by the sea, that was why I possessed such a love and affection for it. That was therefore reflected in my passion for all things blue, together with my love of rocks and shells. Moody lighthouse pictures adorned my hallway walls and there were sparkly rock and starfish ornaments scattered around my sitting room and bedroom.

I even had a cute little miniature lighthouse on the shelf in my bathroom from one of the local gift shops, which I hadn't been able to resist.

Thanks to the myriad of blue, yellow, and vanilla painted walls through my home, Sea Shell Cottage had been transformed.

I glanced up at the sky. Even though patches of stubborn cloud sat there, I knew I had to get away for a bit. "Let's jump in the car and go a bit further afield, shall we?"

Harley trotted by my side and sat there whilst I ensconced her in her car seat. Without even deciding where we were headed, we took off out of Silver Ness.

Fields soon emerged to the right, the tall grass stirring like exotic dancers. I glanced out of the window. I had to try and think positively. I possessed all that experience from my days working at the advertising agency, plus my freelance credentials. That was without the two years reporting for *The Silver Ness News*.

Then there was my journalism degree from university.

The clouds were giving way to pools of sleepy sunshine as we carried on up a country lane, passing cotton-wool dollops of sheep, huddled together to keep warm. Winter was not far off.

There was another patchwork of fields and a pretty tangle of woodland. The trees were dispensing their leaves now. They rocked to the woodland floor, like dainty amber and claret boats on a tide. I was also concerned about Harley's bladder, so decided now would be a good time to stop.

The next town – Drummond – was just a little further on, but this area – halfway between there and Silver Ness – would be perfect for Harley's walk. Ironic that was the place that was in effect taking over *The Silver Ness News* for this title amalgamation.

I parked up in a deserted picnic-bay and Harley leapt out once I'd secured her lead.

No sooner had we moved away from the car than Harley began to pull on the lead. "Harley, wait up!"

She gazed up at me out of chocolate eyes, her tongue flapping.

"Yes, madam, I'm talking to you."

We set off again, me attempting a brisk pace to keep up with her. She was desperate to take a run in the fields.

I ordered her to sit and she plonked herself down in front of me. "Right, young lady." I rooted around in my jeans pocket and located my dog whistle. "I will let you off-lead, but don't forget that when I do this…" I gave the whistle a hearty blast. "And you come straight back for one of these, ok?"

I fetched a pack of dog treats from the other pocket and her eyes grew.

Mum and Dad said her recall had been coming on well during the week, and the last couple of weekends when I had taken her to the park, she had bounded back towards me whenever I gave a blow of the whistle. I think the allure of more peanut butter and banana treats was the deciding factor.

I gazed around the field, rippling under the sleepy sun, which was definitely beginning to subside in the sky. At this time of year in Scotland it was dark by around seven o'clock. "Ok. Have fun. I'll call you back in a few seconds, so be ready."

I unclipped Harley's lead and she let out a thrilled little bark of freedom. I laughed, watching her podgy bottom disappear into the grass. I followed on behind her, listening to her weaving her way.

Filling my lungs with the zesty woodland air was soothing. I had never brought Harley here before but I strode on, catching sight of her fluffy tail whipping from side to side amongst the grass.

I embraced the rhythmic stride of my walking boots. Out here, it felt like, even for a short time, my worries about my job situation could float away.

Images of my first day at the paper, all keen and anxious to please; the tatty Christmas decorations Doug had strung up in the newsroom before I insisted on going shopping to replace them; seeing my first by-line rippling across the front page; the teasing Frances and I would do of Doug's loud shirts... It all merged into a huge, emotional ball in my throat.

I swallowed and closed my eyes for a moment, letting the sleepy, chilled sunshine flit across my face. *Think positive.*

The sky was beginning to deepen into a delicious raspberry ripple. I glanced down at my watch. "Ok, Harley. Come on girl. Time to go." I raised the dangling whistle around my neck and gave it a short, sharp blow, expecting her to come bounding back to me.

Harley didn't appear.

I blew the whistle again. Still nothing.

An icy, cold panic seized me. I started to stride off, my eyes scanning the distance. "Harley! Where are you? Harley!"

I picked up my steps and blasted the whistle again. I could feel the silvery taste. Harley was nowhere to be seen.

Oh God. Where was she? Had she hurt herself or fallen

down a rabbit hole? I shouldn't have let her off-lead in here. *What was I thinking?!* What a week it had been!

I gulped a ball of worry. No. Stop panicking. She couldn't have gone far. It wasn't that long ago that her tail was bobbing ahead of me.

I snatched up the whistle and gave it another fierce prolonged shriek. "Harley! Come here!"

The birds fizzed amongst the trees, but there was no sign of a cockapoo puppy.

A sickening dread gripped my insides. Where the hell was she?

I scanned the field. Panic reared up again. What if she had run off, made for the main road, and been hit by a car? Or what if she had fallen down a hole and got stuck?

With the cool steel of the whistle banging against my chest, I picked up speed. I continued to scream her name, my voice getting shriller. I couldn't lose her. I just couldn't. I was supposed to be the one looking after her, for pity's sake!

I had adopted her. I was supposed to be the person who was giving her a better life, not losing her in a field, with the darkness descending!

I screamed her name again, racing onwards through the tall fronds of grass, until a flicker of movement to my right made me draw up.

Harley?

I started to run across, but disappointment clawed at me. It wasn't her at all. It was a fox, all sharp-featured and russet-coated.

Then a bark made me gasp. Oh, thank goodness! Harley must have seen it too.

I searched ahead of me, hoping to see her, until my attention honed in on Harley's flapping ears and the fox streaking into the undergrowth. There she was!

"Harley!" I puffed. "Oh, thank goodness. Come here! Stop!" The underarms of my sweatshirt clung to me in patches under my jacket.

I took another ineffectual puff at the whistle. It fell away from my lips as I loped on, feeling increasingly desperate. I couldn't lose her. Where had she gone now?

Darkness was beginning to bleed across the skyline and the air was cooler.

I felt as if I was stuck in slow motion. I picked up speed but Harley was infinitely faster. She was dragging all the energy out of me. *Right. That was it.* I made up my mind to restart my gym membership.

If anything happened to her, it would be my fault. Rescued from a puppy farm in Edinburgh, only to tumble down a well when I was supposed to be giving her a safe, loving, and secure life.

A disagreeing voice argued there were unlikely to be wells situated in the area, but my imagination was streaking ahead of me.

I stopped, bending over to inhale ragged gasps of air. Tears gathered in my eyes. "Harley!" I yelled into the countryside. "Where are you?"

Then came a louder bark. My heart gave a little lift of optimism. This one was closer.

I straightened up in time to see her bomb under a hedge. I let out an agonised sigh and took after her again. The hedge led out onto a woodland floor of twigs, fallen leaves, and bark.

At least it wasn't a main road. Pictures of Harley gambolling in front of a car flashed in front of me again.

My breath was now coming in shorter, sharper bursts.

I was about to give the whistle another blast when I stumbled and almost fell over something. I realised the object was Harley. She plonked down in front of me, her tongue rolling out of her mouth as if she were grinning from ear to ear.

Fright, relief, and then annoyance swept over me. "You little bugger!" I erupted, scooping her up into my frustrated arms.

She lashed my scorching, sweaty face with doggy kisses.

"You're supposed to come back when you hear this." I brandished the whistle around my neck. "This means you don't ignore me and chase off after foxes. More recall practice for you, I think. And no letting you off the lead again until you're five."

She gazed up at me and I nestled my head in her coat, squeezing back a torrent of frightened, exhausted tears. "If I had lost you just now..." I gazed down at her enquiring little face. I'd adopted her from a rescue charity when she was four months old and she'd wrapped herself around my heart from the first moment I happened to come across her photo on the charity's Facebook page. I hadn't been planning on getting a dog but her and her sibling's tragic puppy-farm backstory was heartrending and then when I'd spotted her cheeky expression in her photo, I'd fallen instantly in love. This little toffee-coloured toot needed me and I needed her. Miles and I had broken up at the beginning of the year, and for the past six months Harley had been my little rock. I gave myself an inward talking-to. She was safe and didn't appear to be any worse for her little adventure. I cuddled her tighter to me. "Come on, you. Let's get you home. That's more than enough excitement for one day."

I set Harley down on the ground and snapped her lead back on to her pink and black harness.

We'd only just begun to move away, heading back for the car, when something glinted through the woodland over my shoulder, catching me unawares.

While Harley investigated a snail, I tilted my clammy head to one side, curious. I made sure I had a tight hold of her lead this time.

Straight ahead, through the cross-cross network of tree branches, was an intermittent shimmer of something. I hadn't imagined it.

All I really wanted to do was take Harley home and collapse on the sofa with some dark chocolate, but my journalistic nosiness wouldn't allow it.

I encouraged Harley to abandon her intimidation of the snail and to come with me.

We trampled and crunched over twigs, approaching the area where the shiny glint was coming from.

A sudden break in the trees surprised me. I had expected it to run on for miles. Instead, the branches and trunks parted to reveal what looked like an old, grand house squatting in the middle of a beautiful but overgrown front garden. A high wooden fence concealed the rear of the house.

I realised that what had been shining in the evening light was one of the house's French windows. Surely it wasn't occupied, with a huge garden left to roam like that?

Although unkempt, it had an errant beauty about it, with

its cracked pots struggling to contain a throng of creamy tea roses and purple heather.

A couple of naked cherry blossom trees were in situ, standing to attention in the front of the acid-green lawn. It looked as if it hadn't seen a lawnmower in years. If that was the condition of the front garden, goodness knows what the rear garden was like!

Harley sniffed behind me. The air carried earthy undercurrents of moss and damp woodland.

The house itself was impressive, all solid brick painted white with black beams and windowsills. The angled roof glided downwards towards a porthole hall window.

The front door consisted of ebony wood and a long, slim panel of frosted glass, but the net curtains hanging limply at the windows were faded.

I moved a little closer to where the sitting room window was located. I noticed it was smudged with dust.

Harley sat by my feet and observed.

The curtains were closed, although not completely, so I was able to squint in through a chink. Sunset was splashing through the rear sitting room window, illuminating heavy, ornate furniture. There were two sofas opposite one another in creaky, dark leather. The claret patterned carpet added to the dated aura of the place.

There was no television, but a series of family photographs scattered along two shelves running along the side walls. I couldn't make out the features.

A single painting of Silver Ness beach adorned the left wall.

I was about to step backwards when something bright

drew my eye. It was set to the right of the window I was looking through, on top of an occasional table.

I let out a surprised gasp. It was a Christmas present, wrapped up in red shiny reindeer paper.

Good grief! How long had that been sitting there? Had the person who owned the house died and nobody knew? Could they be lying in there? What if they had no family and were in trouble? Perhaps they were hurt in there and unable to call for help?

I gulped and gripped Harley's lead. "Come on, sweetheart."

I moved to the side window to take a look into the kitchen. There was a patchwork-style blind tugged halfway down. Again, everything carried an air of quiet abandonment. The fixtures and fittings consisted of a bright amber sink unit and cupboards and a long-beaded curtain in the kitchen doorway. It was 1970s kitsch.

I moved with Harley to the opposite side of the house, negotiating the crazy-paving path that was fighting to be seen through the grass. There was a narrow bathroom window through which I glimpsed an avocado bathroom suite.

I guided Harley away and round to the front entrance. On closer inspection, I could see a stack of mail piled up against the frosted glass of the front door.

The light was fading faster now. I debated what to do. What if someone elderly and reclusive did live there and had suffered a fall? Or perhaps they were languishing on that dusty-looking carpet and needed urgent medical attention?

I pulled my mobile from my back jeans pocket and

switched on the light. It spotted against the smudgy windows of the sitting room again.

The sky was deepening and the surrounding trees, with their bare, twisted branches, were transforming into ghostly silhouettes.

I was reaching for the letterbox to give it a rattle in the hope that someone might answer and assure me they were all right when I realised there was the sound of someone – or something – moving behind me.

I spun round, my heart whizzing up to my throat. Harley let out a nervous growl.

A silhouetted figure stood there. "And what do you think you're doing?" barked an aggressive female voice.

Chapter Four

S he shot a frozen look at Harley and me and repeated the question. "What are you doing?"

I was struggling to make out her features. Every so often, strands of light would slip across her pointed face.

I arranged my mouth into what I hoped was my most winning smile. "I was looking for my puppy."

The woman jabbed an aggressive finger. "Well, you seem to have found him."

"Her," I corrected. "She's a girl."

The suspicious voice took a step closer. Shadows glanced down one side of her face. There was a an irritated glint in her lined narrowed eyes, which were a dazzling shade of lilac. She also possessed thick vanilla-white hair that was secured back off her face. Her chilly gaze travelled from me to Harley and back again. Her tone was accusatory. "Are you looking for someone?"

I shook my head. "Harley spotted a fox back in the field and chased after it. I was trying to find her."

I willed the woman to come a little closer. Being confronted by a shadowy figure in the middle of a dark wood wasn't doing much for my nerves.

She made a clicking noise with her tongue. She didn't believe me.

"This house," I began, sweeping one hand in its direction. "It's very impressive. Do you know who lives here?"

The woman's chin hardened. "Why do you want to know about Merry Wood?"

I blinked. "Merry Wood?"

She rolled her eyes at my apparent stupidity. "That's Merry Wood. The house."

I followed her gaze to a small wooden plaque, which was just visible through a tangle of ivy trailing over it. Sure enough, the words Merry Wood were inscribed on it. I had been so preoccupied by the hypnotic aura of the place that I'd failed to notice.

The woman emerged further out of the shadows. Lines travelled around her wide, flat mouth, which was pulled into a disapproving line. I estimated she must be in her seventies. There was something compelling about her. She had enviable cheekbones too. I bet she was very pretty in her younger years.

Her whole demeanour, however, was almost as buttoned-up as the floral shirt she was wearing. She arched her plucked silvery brows. "You haven't answered my question. Why do you want to know?" She obviously didn't go in for small talk.

Harley sniffed at my walking boots. I bent down to stroke her. It was a relief not to be in the direct line of fire for a few seconds. I straightened up. "I'm just curious." I pushed another smile at her. "I'm from Silver Ness and I never knew there was a house like this out here."

The temperature was dropping further and I didn't just mean the weather. The older woman thrust both her speckled hands into the pockets of her linen trousers. "Why should you know? And why all these questions? Are you some nosey sod from the council?"

"Oh no. Not at all."

She narrowed her eyes at Harley again. "You're not a reporter, are you?" There was an expectant raise of her eyebrows again.

The temptation to lie tugged at my conscience. I knew only too well what the reaction from some people could be when I told them I was a journalist.

Something about this house though was teasing me and it would be great to find out about its background. But it would be wrong to be deceitful.

I set my shoulders and tried to summon up a more confident tone. "As a matter of fact, I am. I work for *The Silver Ness News.*" I heard myself say the words I had repeated over and over for the last couple of years and reality pummelled me. I wouldn't be saying that for much longer.

I pulled my straying thoughts back to the woman. "But the fact I am a reporter is just a coincidence. I really did lose Harley and…"

Before I could elaborate again, she spun round in her flat leather sandals. "I think you should leave. I've got nothing to say to the likes of you."

She tossed a fierce look at me from over her shoulder. "There's no story here. It's an empty house, that's all."

And with that, she marched away back through the trees towards where I could make out a faint and drizzly grey trail of smoke from a chimney.

It was a relief to arrive back at the car, bundle Harley into her seat, and escape back down the now inky-black country lanes.

For a minute I had worried that the woman was going to do a *Hansel and Gretel* on Harley and me and stick us in her cooking pot.

I made myself a cup of tea when we got home and, while Harley snoozed in her basket in the kitchen, I set up my laptop on the kitchen table and prepared to google the name of the mysterious house – Merry Wood.

Her insistence that there was "no story here" invariably meant that there was, going by previous experience. That fanned my curiosity even more.

But any budding hope of finding out some information about the mysterious house soon withered. There was nothing – not even a photograph of the house came up. I entered in various combinations of the name – *MerryWood; Merry Wood; Merry Wood House* – but nothing appeared. It was so strange.

My optimism vanished.

My mind returned to the dusty stillness in those rooms as I looked through the windows and the expectant weary furniture in situ. Then there was that untamed gorgeous front garden. If the rear garden was anything like that, it must have looked spectacular in its heyday.

Where were the occupants? Why on earth would a house be

abandoned like that, if the owner had decided to move away? And why was that strange woman so defensive? It didn't seem like she lived in the house.

She must live not far from Merry Wood though, going by the way she materialised out of nowhere, and that chimney she was headed back to was very close by. She must stay there.

I reached for my notepad and pen and jotted down a plan of action. I would speak to my couple of contacts at the council and ask them if they had any information on Merry Wood. Maybe the Registration Office would have some details on who resided there or had lived there in the past. Perhaps a sift through the births, deaths, and marriages register might throw up something interesting? Might it be worth speaking to my contact at the local police station too?

The anticipation of having stumbled over an intriguing story was diluted by the sobering reminder that in a matter of weeks *The Silver Ness News* would be no more – at least as it is now.

The initial thrill of discovering a possible human-interest story had managed to take my mind off my so far fruitless search for other employment.

I took a mouthful of tea and decided I should have another look at media job vacancies. There would be plenty of time at work tomorrow to check out Merry Wood.

My eyes zipped over a couple of sites to which I had started subscribing. There were a couple of adverts for PR and marketing executives, but nothing in journalism. My chest deflated like a pricked balloon. This was useless.

I was just about to click off the second site, after again reading a series of appeals for advertising representatives, when a striking pink and white advert shimmered up on screen. I didn't remember that being there the other day when I checked.

I leant forward and began to read.

My eyes widened as I processed what it said.

Chapter Five

We are looking for an investigative journalist who can produce sharp, incisive copy and is an excellent communicator. Goddess, the successful weekly Scottish print publication, is seeking a first-rate individual who is keen to make a difference and who isn't afraid of asking the difficult questions. A degree in journalism, together with at least two years' experience of working in a newspaper or magazine environment is desired.

I swallowed and read on:

You will be working directly under editor and Goddess *owner Athena Mayhew. So, if you want to be a part of Scotland's premier magazine for today's independent woman, apply now with your CV and a two-hundred-word article on why you should become the next member of our team.*

My eyes flew to the competitive salary and employment

benefits, but all at once they appeared insignificant when faced with the biting reality that Athena Mayhew would be the successful candidate's boss.

Oh bugger. Athena Mayhew was like the feared lioness of the glossy magazine world. Anybody who worked in journalism knew of her, had heard infamous stories about her or – if you were really unfortunate – had been on the receiving end of one of her tirades.

She was known for not suffering fools gladly and would often take great delight in reminding anyone who cared to listen that she had worked her way up the demanding and competitive ladder of magazine journalism.

There were tales that she had reduced hard-bitten senior executives to quaking jellies prior to staff meetings and instructed her minions to leave their mobiles permanently switched on so that they were never incommunicado.

Athena Mayhew had started at a small weekly publication for women twenty years ago, *Promises*, answering phones and undertaking clerical work in the advertising department. Within a couple of years, she had become the same magazine's senior features editor, before leaving them behind and moving on to become editor of several much higher profile fashion and beauty publications. Now she actually owned her own magazine.

I tried not to dwell on the heart-stopping prospect of working for this tyrant and turned my attention back to the job advert. The deadline for applications closed in one week, on October 15th.

I then clicked on the link to *Goddess* magazine that was

quoted in the advert. It took me to Athena Mayhew's bio. My cursor hovered over her challenging profile:

I have journalism running through my veins and expect the same high standards from my staff as I have for myself. From humble beginnings, I have worked my way up to being in charge of some of the most famous publications on the planet. I believe that women's magazines should not only inform, but challenge, debate, and inspire. Here at Goddess, *we strive to deliver the best journalism to our readers and that will never change. If you want to change, if you want to become a stronger woman, then read us and find your inner* Goddess!

Bloody hell! Her bio read more like a party-political broadcast. At one point I thought I might have to stand up and salute.

I sat up straighter.

Jobs in media were scarce right now, what with online news and various publications shedding rather than recruiting staff. I couldn't afford to be choosy. I had bills to pay.

I set my shoulders. I liked to think I could relate to most people. Perhaps Athena Mayhew wasn't as horrifying as she was reputed to be… yeah and a Bengal tiger was really a cute kitten. I swallowed. She was brilliant, but ruthless.

There was no guarantee I would even get an interview anyway.

Right now, my options were very limited and time was moving on. In a few weeks, *The Silver Ness News* would be no more. Well, not in the form it was now.

I chewed over the prospect of working for an editor like Athena Mayhew, versus having no money coming in.

With Harley curled up and continuing to snooze in her basket, I decided to browse the *Goddess* website.

Images of confident-looking women posing on top of a heather-clotted hill shimmered up on the screen. Previous covers trailed along the bottom of the site with the tagline, *"We don't just find your inner Goddess – we nurture it."*

Photos of polished, pouting members of staff and their impressive bios ran down the right-hand side and heading the pack was Athena Mayhew. She was all buffed, tight white skin and choppy burgundy hair.

I scrolled through the latest edition's headlines. They ranged from "Tartan is the New Black" and "Meet Glasgow's Female Bill Gates" to an exclusive about online scamming sites targeting professional women and an undercover piece on the exploitation of female escorts.

My heart lifted with optimism. It was great to see Athena Mayhew wasn't just focusing her attention on frothy journalism. There were reports about seaweed hair removers and the latest fad for something called Devil Lips, but I wasn't interested in that. It was the juicy, hard-hitting stories that exposed inequality and injustice I wanted to be a part of.

The job was based in their swanky new offices on the north side of Glasgow in Cowcaddens, with its modern apartment blocks, bijoux restaurants, and bustling *Herald* newspaper offices. I took an excited, nervous breath and returned to the investigative reporter job specification.

I read it again.

It sounded like a fantastic opportunity. It was fun covering the school pantomimes and the human-interest angles of the Silver Ness community, but it made my stomach sink to think of this strange new hybrid newspaper they were creating with Drummond. One that I wouldn't be a part of anyway.

I moved the cursor and hovered over the job description as I mulled it all over. There was a good chance I wouldn't even reach the interview stage. There were bound to be young, eager graduates keen for an opportunity like this – poor, naïve, young souls who had probably never heard of Athena Mayhew, unaware of what they could be letting themselves in for.

I glanced down at a slumbering Harley and then around myself at my kitchen, with its daffodil-yellow walls, deep-blue wooden cabinets and rustic beams.

I had come across some difficult characters in my time, working for the ad agency. I couldn't allow Athena Mayhew's fearsome reputation to intimidate me, especially when I had a mortgage to pay.

And I was a good journalist. I had a moral compass; I was hard-working and conscientious…

Before I knew what I was doing or allowed myself any more time to debate it – or even talk myself out of it – I was tapping away at my keyboard, composing my application.

Chapter Six

I sat at my desk the following morning, my thoughts shifting from my *Goddess* job application to Harley's vanishing act and then on to the seemingly abandoned house, Merry Wood.

That cranky lady who had appeared out of the trees... why was she there? She had been so guarded. She must know more than she had been prepared to say.

I glanced over the cork partition at Frances, feeling weary after all the events of last night. She was staring at her computer screen and every so often would offer me an awkward smile. I must have told her twenty times that I didn't blame her for being kept on with Clarity Newspapers while I was being let go, but I don't think she believed me. It was horrible, this weird, artificial atmosphere.

Doug was carrying the same beleaguered bearing too. He ambled over to our kitchen area to make himself a fresh coffee.

We had to accept this was going to be the way of things for the next few weeks. We were doing our best to carry on as usual, producing the paper so many of our locals relied on, but the inevitability of the closure of *The Silver Ness News* in its current guise still stung.

Our loyal readers had no idea yet about the impending amalgamation, so Doug was writing a special editorial for next week's edition.

I didn't envy him that job.

I stared at my screen, not focusing on it. I had decided not to tell either of them about my job application to *Goddess*. I was worried about jinxing it and decided to wait and see how my application was received first.

I forced myself to focus and finished bashing out several hundred words about Silver Ness' oldest fishing boat and pinged it over to Doug. I glanced down at my notebook on which I'd scribbled "Merry Wood" a few times. I pictured the fields and Harley tearing away from me, mingled with images of the grand black and white house with its wild gardens.

"Have either of you heard of an old house situated in the fields on the outskirts of Silver Ness? Well, it's closer to Drummond, actually."

Frances looked up from her desk, startled, as though I had dragged her away from somewhere else. None of the three of us was coping well with what was taking place, but were trying to muddle our way through the best we could. "What's the address?" she asked.

"That's the thing. I don't have an address as such. The house is called Merry Wood but it's in the middle of woodland."

Doug took a thoughtful mouthful of his tar-like coffee as he leant against the sink top "Nope. Never heard of it."

Frances shook her lowlights. "Me neither. Where did you say it was again?"

"In amongst the fields and woodland between here and Drummond."

Frances pulled a face. "Blimey. That's a bit out of the way."

Doug studied me over the rim of his mug. "You onto something, Leonie?"

I shrugged. "I don't know. I took Harley for a walk up there last night. She spotted a fox, chased after it, and I was trying to find her when I came across this strange house."

Frances gave a small smile. "Haunted, maybe?"

I rolled my eyes. "Deserted, more like."

Doug sauntered back to his desk. "I'm a bit confused."

I played with one of my pens. "That's the thing. The house is all furnished, but there doesn't seem to be anyone living there. It's like the place has been abandoned."

Doug rocked backwards and forwards in his chair. "Maybe give your contacts at the council a ring. See if they know anything."

"Births, Deaths, and Marriages too," added Frances. "Check with them as well."

I nodded, chewing over what they were saying. "That's what I was thinking."

Doug shot me a wry look. "It will be some council tax dodge or one of these two-home wealthy types who keeps the place going as a weekend retreat but never uses it." His wide mouth slipped into a despondent smile. "Not that netting some big splash about bodies under the floorboards or haunted mansions will make any difference to us soon, anyway."

I spent the next couple of hours with the office phone clamped to my ear for so long it was turning a fetching shade of puce.

And as I suspected, I would have had more success getting the mobile number of Idris Elba than getting any information about Merry Wood or its occupants.

My main contact at the local police station had no knowledge of the house. There had never been any reports of any disturbances there, let alone missing persons.

As for the council, April, my contact in the press office there, was unable to assist either. "I've asked around and there's nothing on record about this house. Are you sure you got the name right?"

"Absolutely. I saw the name plaque with my own eyes."

April sighed. "Well, even if I were to pass you over to a couple of colleagues in our Housing Section, they couldn't give you information about individual properties or occupants anyway. Data Protection."

I let out a frustrated sigh. "I guessed as much. Thanks anyway, April."

I was about to hang up, when she must have taken pity on me. "Tell you what. Seeing as I'm in such a wonderful mood today, give me half an hour and I'll see what I can find out. I have a friend who works at Registers of Scotland."

"Thanks April. I owe you."

"No luck?" asked Frances, witnessing my dejected expression as I rang off.

I shook my head. "Not a thing. There doesn't seem to be

any information on this house or who lives or has lived there. It's really weird."

Frances chewed the inside of her mouth. "No neighbours close by that you can interrogate?"

I thought back to the frosty woman with the gimlet eyes. "There was one person."

"Then get back there and work your magic on them," she enthused. "If it turns out there is a big enough story with this, one of the nationals might pick up on it and that could lead to a job or some freelance work for you."

Frances coloured at her own words as she realised what she was saying. "I'm so sorry."

I frowned. "What for?"

"For joining the dark side," she half joked. "Honestly, Leonie, I feel terrible about what's happened."

"Then don't," I insisted firmly. "It's not your fault. And anyway, you have the twins to think about."

France's red-slicked mouth trembled. "I still feel like shit about it all."

"Well please don't. I'm sure I'll get something else soon."

Frances agreed. "Of course, you will! You're a great journalist and any publication would be more than lucky to have you." She hesitated. "So, what are you going to do about the Bates Motel then?"

I blinked across the desk at her. "Bates Motel?" It took me a moment to realise she was referring to Merry Wood. I let out a bark of laughter. "It's not that bad. Ok, it's secluded and a bit creepy in the dark…"

Frances smiled. "You're really selling it to me. Have you ever considered becoming an estate agent?"

"Very funny. Seriously though, with a bit of TLC, it could be a stunning house. You should see the front garden and all the wild roses and heather. If the back garden is anything like that, it could be spectacular."

Frances toyed with her mouse. "Very odd though, that it's all still furnished, but no one seems to be about." She smiled over. "Trust your Spidey senses, Leonie. If you think there might be a story there, keep at it."

It was then that April from the council press office rang back. "I haven't had any luck here," she said, "but I did manage to speak to my friend at Registers of Scotland. According to him, it was a couple by the surname of Merry that owned the house in the 1930s. They lived there for forty-odd years, before selling it to a couple by the name of Talbot."

I processed all this. The house must have been named after Mr & Mrs Merry. "Ok, thanks April. That's very helpful. And this Talbot couple still own it?"

"It would seem so. Jerry, my friend at RoS, said that any way."

So, if they owned it, why had they left it sitting there like that, empty?

"Thank you, April. I really appreciate that."

"No worries."

I ended the call. Frances looked over. "Any updates on Amityville?"

I rolled my eyes at her. "That was April from the council. All she can tell me is that Merry Wood's owners are said to be a couple with the surname Talbot."

"Yet they aren't living there?" she puzzled.

"It seems that no one is."

She picked up her Cath Kidston mug and thrust it across at me. "This just gets curiouser and curiouser. Right. Your turn to make another cuppa!"

"You heading straight home now?" asked Frances, sweeping on her fitted jacket. "If not, I thought we could go for a drink?"

I glanced out of the office window. There had been a sudden burst of rain a short while ago and the beach looked like it had been rinsed in diamonds. "Could we do that another evening? I was thinking about trying to speak to the rude woman in the woods about Merry Wood again."

Frances pulled a face. "Once you get your teeth into something, Baxter! Don't you ever switch off?"

I gathered up my notebook. "Well, not all of us have been kept on by Clarity Newspapers." As soon as I made the clumsy remark, I regretted it. Frances's cheeks flared and she dropped her eyes.

"I'm sorry. Really. I didn't mean for it to come out that way."

"No need to apologise. It's true."

She lingered for a few moments by the edge of my desk. "If there's anything you want me to help you with, either story-wise or maybe asking around about other jobs, you just have to say the word. I mean it."

"Thanks. I might take you up on that."

Doug had already left for the evening, having been invited to some local author's latest novel launch at the bookshop.

I locked up the office and made my way round the corner

to my Skoda. I'd had the idea of dropping by Merry Wood again this evening, after Frances's encouragement and so had already texted my parents, telling them I'd be a bit later home tonight to collect Harley. Mum replied, saying not to worry as she would feed her and take her for a play in the garden. *"I bought her a new toy from the pet shop this morning,"* she messaged. *"It's a rope puppy and she went berserk when she saw it!"*

I smiled to myself as I fired up my ignition and began to move off. Mum was always buying Harley treats. Good grief! If she was like this with a ten-month-old puppy, goodness knows what that would be like with grandchildren!

I glanced in my rear-view mirror. My eyebrows shot upwards at the thought. I couldn't have imagined having kids with Miles. Not now anyway. As it turned out, he was far too much of a selfish prick. He thought nothing of letting me down at the last minute for a news story when we were together and if I dared to say I was upset, he would accuse me of not being ambitious like he was.

That wasn't true. It was just I loved him far more than he ever loved me and I was prepared to put our relationship first. The last I heard about him was a couple of months ago in one of the media magazines Doug subscribed to. He was mentioned in the Movers n' Shaker's section, after having been promoted to News Editor at a regional TV station in the Midlands.

We had met when he was working as a news reporter on Musicala Radio, a regional station. Frances had introduced us when she held one of her house parties. I think she's never forgiven herself for the fact that she got us together in the first place.

Things moved quickly and before I knew it, I was staying over in his flat in Glasgow a few nights a week, which overlooked the Clyde. But working for the ad agency was taking its toll and when I decided that I wanted to go for the reporter job at *The Silver Ness News*, he wasn't best pleased. "A parochial little paper," he'd smirked. "Haven't you got loftier ambitions than that, L?"

In time, he was getting the bigger, more prominent stories at the radio station and often moaned that I had taken nine steps back, returning to Silver Ness, rather than moving forward.

In the end, he just announced one snowy night in January over a bottle of Chianti, that he had applied for and been offered a TV news reporter job in the Midlands and that was that. Over. Done.

He had slipped his hand in mine, tipped his head to one side like a pet budgie, and slimed that he would always love me, but he wanted to break into TV and he knew I would understand!

I remember travelling home on the train that same night with random items I'd left over in his flat – toothbrush, shampoo, deodorant, underwear – in a carrier bag and my mascara streaming down my face.

I gave myself a mental shake to loosen the pictures of Miles floating around in there. He didn't deserve the head space.

"That one is all teeth and coiffed hair," remarked Dad not long after we split up. "I was never keen on him. He's got about as much depth as a puddle." He was proved to be right.

As I drove towards Drummond and Merry Wood, I rehearsed in my head what I was planning to say to the bad-tempered woodland woman, if she happened to be on patrol again.

I suspected she wouldn't be forthcoming. She had been off-hand and rude during our first encounter, so I didn't see that changing any time soon. The fact she also knew I was a journalist wouldn't help my case either.

The country lanes slid past in a haze of streaky early evening sunshine. The hedgerows rustled and shimmied in the autumn chill.

The fields Harley had been charging through loomed up ahead on the right-hand side of the road with the trees, some still clinging to their leaves by their fingertips, shadowing them.

I eased my car into the kerb at the picnic area again and clambered out, recalling the house was a good distance ahead and through the woodland facing me.

I began to make my way through the rushing grass, striding with a confident purpose that I didn't feel. I didn't think for one minute that the intimidating woman would be willing to tell me anything, but I wasn't a proper journalist if I didn't at least try.

The element of surprise might work on Mrs Scary. Then again, she might take after me with her hissing black cat and broom.

It was funny how things could turn around. One minute, you're bobbing along with your life and the next you're staring unemployment in the face and creeping through woodland.

I trampled on, my walking boots squashing the grass and

reeds flat before they bounced back up again. If my recollections were correct, Merry Wood was up ahead, past those hillsides with the purple heather.

I propelled myself on until I came face to face with a thicker set of trees. I pushed on through, finding myself staring at Merry Wood again, as it rose up into the pastel sky.

The evening light sifted through the front garden, casting a soupy glow down on the hot-pink and violet clumps of heather growing there. The back garden gave only a tantalising glimpse of fading scarlet leaves over the top of the towering, wooden fence.

I took another look through the windows. Everything was as I remembered it; still, dusty and empty.

I then turned and looked down through the woodland to where I suspected the scary lady lived. It must be down there. I recalled puffs of chimney smoke. There were no other houses around here for miles.

I moved off and away from Merry Wood and it took only a couple of minutes of traipsing through the rustling undergrowth until I was confronted by a small immaculate farmhouse.

It was all pitched roof and stone built, with a rugged façade of sash windows. There was a deep-grey painted front door and assorted potted plants. A white garden bench sat near the entrance.

I made my way up the flagged stone steps and turned around to look over my shoulder. The view from here was straight through the trees and across to Merry Wood. It was just a stone's throw away.

I lifted my hand and although guessing I wouldn't receive a warm welcome, knocked on the door anyway.

I almost fell backwards when a cross face shot up at the nearest window pane. "Who is it? What do you want?"

When she saw me standing there, sporting a hopeful smile, she vanished from the window and yanked open her front door. "Oh. It's you."

I had received more enthusiastic welcomes in my time, it had to be said.

"I'm sorry to trouble you…"

She folded her thin, pale arms across her apron. "Not lost that dog of yours again, have you? You know, you ought to keep her on a lead. She could end up down a fox hole."

"No, I haven't lost my dog again." I cleared my throat. "Look, I'm sorry to bother you but I'm going to be honest. After what happened last week, I'm very curious about Merry Wood and would like to know a bit more about the house." I paused. "I was hoping you might be able to help me."

I noted that the woman's fingers were splattered with flour.

"Oh aye?"

I gestured over my shoulder towards the deserted house. "I think this could have the makings of a very interesting story and I would appreciate it if you could tell me what you know about the house."

Her silver hair wobbled in its haphazard bun. "Do you now? And what makes you say that?"

I squirmed a little on the step. I thought I was supposed to be the one asking all the questions. "The way you reacted when I told you I was a journalist." I cleared my throat. "If you don't mind me saying, you seem rather protective of Merry Wood."

The older woman's lined mouth pinched deeper. A flicker of pain crossed her face. "I don't mean to be rude young lady, but you don't know anything. You don't know anything about me or about that house."

Ouch. Tough crowd.

"That's true," I persisted, "and that's why I'd be very grateful for your help."

She continued to stare me down.

"Look, Ms...?" I allowed the inflection in my voice to rise upwards.

She hesitated, her rinsed-out lilac eyes tense. "It's Mrs," she forced. "Mrs Lily Cruickshank. I'm widowed."

"Mrs Cruickshank," I repeated, relieved that I had managed to at least extract her name. "I'm Leonie Baxter."

She met this information with clear indifference.

"And I'm sorry."

"About what?"

"Losing your husband."

She raised her chin. "Well, *I'm* not."

Okaaaaay...

I shuffled from foot to foot on her step. "I've done some digging on Merry Wood and so far, I haven't been able to come up with anything."

"That's not a surprise," she snorted.

"What makes you say that?"

Her pale lips twitched with self-satisfaction. "That house hasn't been occupied for nearly fifty years now."

"Fifty?" I gasped. "It's been sitting like that for all this time? Why?"

She pinned me to the shadowy step of her home. "Times change. People move on." She swallowed. "Folks do strange things when their heart is broken."

"What do you mean?"

A troubled cloud drifted across her features and stayed there. She didn't answer.

I eyed her. "I was told by a contact that the house is still owned by someone called Talbot. Is that right?"

A distant look passed over her face, followed by something more wistful, before a sudden flurry of activity from a blackbird in a nearby hedgerow made Mrs Cruickshank flinch.

I noticed her flour-dusted fingers reach for the edge of her front door and she clung to it for a few seconds. Her cheeks paled. She wobbled and held the door tighter.

"Mrs Cruickshank? Are you alright?"

She took a couple of deep breaths. "I'm fine. Don't you worry about me."

"You don't look fine…"

She reset her thoughts. The fleeting softness in her expression had vanished, as though it had never been there. "I've told you more than enough, Ms Baxter. You seem to know it all already. Now, if you'll excuse me, I've got to get on."

And with that, she vanished back behind her front door in a flurry of flour and amber apron.

Chapter Seven

I strolled back to my car at the picnic area, giving Merry Wood appreciative but puzzled glances as I passed by.

What had Lily Cruickshank meant about people behaving oddly when their heart was broken? Not to mention that there had been nobody living there for fifty years? What had happened in that house? Had there been some sort of family altercation or falling-out that had festered over the years? Or perhaps a crime had been committed there...?

I stopped and drew myself up. Now I really was allowing my imagination to go into overdrive.

Yet from the way Mrs Cruickshank had been speaking and the preoccupied expression on her face, it was clear something had happened, especially when the house had just been left like that. It was obvious Lily Cruickshank knew far more than she was prepared to say about this Talbot family.

I drove back to my parents' house to collet Harley, my thoughts bombing around my head. It would be worth checking out Lily Cruickshank to see if I could find out anything about her background. Perhaps that might give me the vital starting point I needed.

Once I had fed Harley and thrown on my old jeans and slouchy white knitted jumper, I rustled up a chicken salad for myself and got to work on searching for any information I could find on Lily Cruickshank.

I started to trawl through the internet, finding one grainy photograph of a Mrs Lily Cruickshank pictured locally. That must be her.

It appeared in *The Silver Ness News* on July 3rd 1972 and showed a cluster of dignitaries outside a bakery on Silver Ness High Street.

I leant in closer, savouring a mouthful of crunchy green salad laced with olive oil. There was a caption underneath the photo, which said:

Mrs Lily Cruickshank (centre) who is opening her new bakery, Lily's Loaves, on July 6th.

Surrounding her were a couple of officious-looking local councillors and a few other Silver Ness business owners, whose names were reeled off from left to right. I focused harder on the black and white photograph. Mrs Cruickshank was clutching a couple of loaves in the middle of the semi-circle and she was looking intent. There was a smooth, youthful lightness to her features, her long, thick hair swinging down her back.

I switched my attention to the background. It took me a moment to realise that Lily's Loaves, with its striped awning, was now the handbag shop Bags of Style. I thought it looked familiar.

My mind returned to the memory of Lily Cruickshank's hands as she stood on her doorstep, freckled and doused in flour. Of course! She must still be keeping up her bread-making.

I started to read the accompanying article.

Silver Ness is welcoming a new business into its community, with the launch of a bakery and café in the main street. Lily Cruickshank (26) who is from Perth, trained as a baker under the tutelage of the renowned pastry and bread chef Archibald Strang and worked for him at his bakery, Golden. Mrs Cruickshank, formerly known as Lily Bruce, married local man Bernard Cruickshank and the couple are now settling into their new home on the outskirts of Drummond. She said of her new venture, "Baking bread is one of life's pleasures for me and being able to open my own business, doing what I love, is a dream come true. I feel I have learnt so much whilst working at Golden and from the legendary Mr Strang." She added, "Hopefully I can bring a slice of something warm and delicious to the people of Silver Ness!" Lily's Loaves will open officially on July 6th at 10am.

I studied the photograph of younger Lily again, all big, hopeful eyes and enthusiasm shining out of them.

I decided to ask Mum and Dad about Lily Cruickshank and

her bakery. They might remember her or know a little about her.

While I was speculating about whether they might recall anything about her or about her past business, my inbox pinged.

Harley pushed herself down beside my leg in the kitchen and nuzzled against me. I brushed the top of her head with my fingers, stroking and rubbing the soft downy curls.

I clicked onto my emails on my laptop, half expecting a discount on my favourite shampoo or another offer on the installation of loft insulation.

But it wasn't. It was from *Goddess* magazine, marked *Confidential.*

I made a weird nose – a cross between a gasp and a snort – and scrambled for my mouse. *Oh God. It* must be about my job application. Was it a no? A polite decline?

I felt conflicted as I clicked on it. Time became soupy and lethargic as I waited for the email to appear on my laptop screen. A large part of me wanted the job, while a tiny, apprehensive corner persisted in reminding me who I would be working for.

The email finally pushed its way into view.

My heart juddered in my chest.

Dear Ms Baxter,

Further to your recent job application for the vacancy of Investigative Reporter at Goddess, *I am pleased to invite you to attend an interview on Monday October 22nd at 10am at* Goddess Magazine *HQ…*

I performed a series of frantic blinks at the screen.

I read on, my excitement and trepidation fighting it out:

On the interview panel, will be Barbara McKinnon, Head of HR, Oli Noakes, Deputy Editor of Goddess, and Athena Mayhew, Executive Editor and owner of Goddess.

There were a couple of further paragraphs giving details of directions of where the offices were located and where to park, if travelling by car.

It was a struggle to believe that anyone didn't know where these magazine offices were, seeing as they consisted of rose-gold glass and towered over the Glasgow skyline like the Wicked Queen's mirror.

I sat still for a moment, digesting it all. Then, just to make sure I hadn't imagined the whole thing, I took a breath and scanned over the email again.

Nope. It wasn't an illusion. I was being interviewed. By Athena Mayhew. For a job.

Chapter Eight

I rang my parents first to tell them about my interview in a week's time.

They were delighted, although puzzled by my evident nerves.

"You can do this!" enthused Mum. "They must have received a lot of applications for a job like that, so for you to get through to secure an interview speaks volumes." And off she went with another of her Italian proverbs. "*A caval donato non si guarda in bocca,*" which means "Don't look a gift horse in the mouth."

"It's not so much doubting myself, Mum," I admitted. "It's more that Athena Mayhew is going to be on the interview panel."

"Who?"

I proceeded to explain to her about Athena's reputation in the journalism world.

"You make her sound like a cross between Eva Braun and Margaret Thatcher."

"Then I'm being too complimentary."

Mum laughed into my ear. "I'm sure she's very reasonable, once you get to know her."

"Mmmm." I sighed. "It's a hell of an opportunity though, despite working for DVM."

"DVM?"

"Darth Vader's mother."

Mum laughed again, oblivious to Athena Mayhew's rabid reputation.

I had to go for this job. There was no other option.

I gathered my resolve. I could do this. I knew I could.

Goddess was a gorgeous publication and it was setting itself apart in the world of glossy magazines, with its grittier features and human-interest stories, as well as fluffier pieces on beauty and fashion.

My only reticence was the prospect of having to work for Athena Mayhew. That was, providing I was offered the job.

As though reading my thoughts, Mum spoke again. "Look lovey, you have to succeed at the interview first. Just go and give it everything you've got."

From somewhere in the background, like a flitting ghost, I heard my dad call out, "What's for you won't go by you," which is what he had been saying to me ever since I learnt to walk.

My thoughts were criss-crossing over each other so much about my impending interview, I almost forgot to ask Mum and Dad about Lily Cruickshank.

She pondered the name for a few moments. I didn't think it likely she would know about her but to my surprise, she erupted. "Well, goodness me! That's a blast from the past. Lily Cruickshank. I haven't heard that name for years."

I bent down and rubbed Harley behind her triangular velvet ears, my optimism rising. "So you knew of her then?"

"Well, your grandparents mentioned her but from what they used to say, I don't think anybody really knew Lily Cruickshank. She was friendly enough by all accounts but tended to keep herself to herself. Your Nonna described her as a quiet little thing with gorgeous red hair, if I recall. She said she was very pleasant though."

I processed what Mum was saying. "Lily's Loaves was the name of her business, wasn't it?"

Mum was impressed. "Someone's been doing their research! That's right. How on earth do you know that?"

She dropped her voice, although I wasn't sure why as it was only me and Dad who were able to hear. "Her husband, Bernard, was Silver Ness born and bred. I don't know if the rumours were true, but folks said he was a nasty piece of work. He used to watch her like a hawk."

"And did you know much about him?"

Mum's voice was firm in my ear. "No, but some of the other locals did. He had a reputation for being a prickly bugger. Not the chatty, sociable sort."

I considered this. "Did Nonna ever say if they had a happy marriage, Mum? Lily and Bernard, I mean?"

"I don't recall her saying anything specifically, but from what I heard about him, I would guess he wouldn't have been an easy man to live with."

"What did this Bernard do, Mum? Do you know where he worked?"

She hesitated as she thought about it. "I think he used to work in a shop down by the harbour, selling fishing tackle. He was the manager, if I remember the stories rightly. He used to travel a fair bit to buy new stock as his boss, old Mr Capshaw, didn't keep so well."

Mum again dropped her voice and I had no idea why. "I heard that it was on one of his business trips that he met Lily."

She sounded puzzled. "Nonna used to say she seemed the complete opposite to him though. Lord knows what she saw in him." She murmured away again to herself. "Don't know what happened to her. She hasn't been heard of for years."

"She's still living around here, Mum," I confirmed.

"Really? Are you sure?"

"Absolutely." I then went on to explain about coming across Lily Cruickshank when Harley ran off after the fox.

"Goodness me," remarked Mum, incredulous. "I thought she had moved away, right out of the area, or had passed on. Nobody saw her or heard from her again after Lily's Loaves floundered."

"The business floundered? Are you sure? She just didn't decide to sell up?" From what I read in the newspaper article and the little I'd gleaned from talking to Lily, she didn't come across as the quitting type. To someone like her, I would have thought failure wouldn't have been an option.

"That was the story going around at the time. The rumours were that *Lily's Loaves* was a bit of a five-minute wonder. It started off with a flourish and then when the local supermarket started stocking fresh breads and cakes at cheaper prices, some folks started saying Lily couldn't keep up with the competition. Others said that husband of hers had been syphoning money out of the shop for his gambling addiction, and that he didn't like how successful the business was becoming."

"What, he was jealous of his own wife?" I gasped, struggling to comprehend it.

"Yes. According to the gossip your Nonna heard back in the day, a lot of folks round here said she was making a name for herself; he didn't like it and so he forced her to close down Lily's Loaves and he put out a story that the business wasn't doing so well and so they were cutting their losses and moving on." Mum tutted. "Such a shame. The locals said she was so enthusiastic and put her heart and soul into it too

"So… what happened?"

"My goodness, Leonie," laughed my mum down the line. "What's with all the interest in Lily Cruickshank?"

"I'm looking into a story," I answered. "To do with an old deserted house. I think the place is linked to Lily in some way."

"Well, that is a surprise," breathed Mum down the line. "Where is she living now then?"

"In a cottage on the outskirts of Drummond." I thought again about what Mum had said about Lily's husband. "What happened to him? Bernard?"

"I have no idea. Lily's Loaves started to fail and she couldn't bear to see the business struggling, so the story was that they sold up and moved on. No one knew where or heard from her again after that."

I tried to gather together everything Mum was telling me, mentally sorting it all out and pushing pieces together in the hope they might fit.

Mum sounded pensive down the line. "Nonna commented she always thought that sounded a bit odd though, about the shop failing, as it was always busy whenever she passed by and the girl seemed to love it here. She settled in so quickly and seemed to want to become part of the community." Mum made a grunting noise. "So many folks around here used to say she was far more likeable than that husband of hers." Mum paused. "So, you say you have seen Lily Cruickshank? Here in Silver Ness?"

When I confirmed to Mum again that I had, she relayed what I'd just told her to my dad, who was hovering in the background. "Ross! Wait till you hear this! Do you remember the stories about that red-headed girl who owned the bakery back in the day?"

There was a series of exchanges, Mum sighing at Dad for not recalling fast enough events from years ago when he was small and then Dad confirming that yes, he did recall tales about Lily, her bread was said to be amazing but that my grandparents never had any time for "that vile husband of hers".

"And no one knew what happened to them after they left Silver Ness?"

"Nobody had a clue," Mum sniffed. "When he moved away, there were no tears shed."

My mum let out a little disbelieving chuckle. "She was said to be a damn good bread maker. You know, Silver Ness could be doing with another wee bakery like that. It would go down a storm, not only with the locals but with the tourists too."

I agreed with Mum, still turning over in my head so many

71

questions. "Have you or Dad ever heard of a house called Merry Wood, Mum?"

"Should we have?"

I shrugged, even though Mum couldn't see me. "No. Well, maybe. It's an impressive house, but appears to have been abandoned years ago."

"Where is it?"

"Very close to where Lily Cruickshank is living now."

Mum let out a snort of derision. "Well, that might explain a lot if Bernard Cruickshank was their neighbour. I don't know anyone who would have wanted to live next door to him, if all the awful stories about him are true."

Then she moved the subject on to more familiar territory. "Now, onto far more important matters, *caro*. What are you planning to eat for your dinner, because I have some leftover Italian sausage *polpettina* and macaroni bake?"

———

That evening, I entered Bernard Cruickshank's name into the search engine on my laptop.

A briefly worded obituary emerged from the archives of *The Silver Ness News*. It was dated September 16th 2006.

It read:

> *Bernard Martin Cruickshank. Born January 5th 1947. Died*
> *September 16th 2006, aged 59 years. Husband of Lily*
> *Cruickshank (nee Bruce).*

I sat back and blinked. I had read more passionate and detailed obituaries about a pet passing away.

No beloved or much-missed husband sentiments at all. Then my thoughts travelled to Lily dismissing my sympathy on hearing she had lost Bernard.

I considered what Mum had said earlier about Bernard not being a well-liked figure in the community, too. Perhaps Lily had been relieved at his passing.

An unhappy marriage and a business that didn't survive. That could explain a lot.

Chapter Nine

The next week vanished in a haze of work, visiting Lily's farmhouse again (I'm certain she was at home, but failed to answer the door) and preparing for my interview with *Goddess*, which was screaming up to greet me at an alarming rate.

As soon as I had received that email, informing me that I had secured an interview, I booked the day off as annual leave. I knew I would be too preoccupied before and after it to go to work.

I arranged a taxi to take me so I wouldn't have to concern myself with traffic, flat tyres, or another accident which could befall me. I knew such scenarios would be unlikely, but I didn't want to take any chances.

I was led into the interview room by a buff-cheeked blonde with iron-straight blonde hair and a wide smile.

From what I could see of the other members of staff, stationed at their starched white desks, they too were all groomed and glossy. Shiny skin, dazzling smiles, and gleaming locks were the order of the day and that was just the guys.

I stood out amongst them, with my Mediterranean explosion of hair, curvy bottom, and ample chest.

The room was decked out with huge vases of white and green flower arrangements more in keeping with a glossy wedding and a set of uncomfortable-looking glass furniture.

Barbara McKinnon and Oli Noakes were already seated in front of me at a long table. She was sporting a severe conker-coloured bob and he a buzz cut and a look of faint boredom.

The seat between them was vacant. It was like the opening scene of *The Apprentice*, before Lord Sugar emerges from behind the frosted doors.

I managed a shaky smile and tugged at the hem of my charcoal skirt. The tension was rising at the imminent arrival of Athena Mayhew. I don't know who looked more terrified, me or her two colleagues. The glass doors let out a faint whisper as they opened.

I didn't turn around. I didn't want to fan the flames of trepidation burning away inside of me as it was.

Athena Mayhew swept in and took up her chair. She didn't raise her eyes for a few moments, preferring instead to scan my CV in front of her. After a few more torturous moments, she flipped her charged light-green eyes over me, as though she were bestowing upon me a huge privilege. Raven lowlights glowed around her chin. "Leonie Baxter," she rasped, as though my name were a medical condition.

I straightened the collar of my striped shirt. "That's right, Ms Mayhew."

She grimaced, showing a set of tiny, pearly teeth.

I watched the three of them flick through the papers on the table in front of them.

"Journalism degree. Ad agency employment. Local newspaper. Freelance work." Each word Athena Mayhew said was delivered like a bullet. She steepled her hands together on top of the polished glass table. The gold serpent buttons of her blouse glittered at me. "So why you? Why here?"

I flashed what I hoped was a confident smile at an expectant-faced Barbara and grim-mouthed Oli. "Why not me? I'm a dedicated and hard-working journalist with a solid background in news reporting."

I gestured to my CV on the table. "*Goddess* magazine doesn't just look good. It's making a difference to women's lives and I want to be a part of that. I can produce concise, sharp copy—"

Athena Mayhew remained impassive as she cut me off. "And who do you see as the average *Goddess* reader?"

"In my opinion, there is no such thing," I answered, trying to blank out my protesting toes in my pointed heels. "Anyone who reads a magazine like *Goddess* is insightful, interested in the world around her, and wants to be a part of something bigger." I gathered myself together and ploughed on. "*Goddess* readers are all united by one thing: they want to enrich and better their lives, no matter who they are or where they come from."

I took a breath. All the soundbites and positive compliments were waltzing out of my mouth. "I especially enjoyed the features on female airline pilots and the article highlighting the struggle of female boxing promoters."

One of Athena Mayhew's dark-chocolate brows twitched. She shot an indecipherable sideways glance at her colleagues.

"What would you like to see in the magazine?" piped up Oli Noakes. "What would you wish to report on?"

I sat up straighter, levelling my best professional gaze at each of them in turn. "I'd love to report on the anomalies in women's pay in the media and interview someone like Blaze McGiver, Scotland's answer to Ru Paul."

I gathered myself, discovering my momentum. "Then there's the struggle of women wishing to enter politics, particularly working mothers with families."

Barbara's mouth slid into a brief but appreciative smile and she noted something down.

"Even in today's world, there are still dubieties that exist and there shouldn't be. I think an influential magazine like *Goddess* can really play its part in if not eradicating then certainly dispelling myths about working mothers and making their lives a little easier."

I hesitated, snatching a quick glimpse at each of the three faces of my interviewers. *Oh God.* I didn't want to get ahead of myself, but my Spidey senses were telling me the interview was going rather well. Even Athena Mayhew appeared to be smiling, or at least trying to. Then again, maybe her killer heels were a bit on the snug side for her too.

"Ms Mayhew. I'm so sorry to interrupt."

I spun around in my chair, my chain of thought shattering like broken glass.

It was the young woman with the buffed cheeks. She was shifting from foot to foot in the doorway.

Athena Mayhew narrowed her eyes. "What is it, Orion? We're in the middle of an interview."

Orion swallowed hard. "I'm so sorry Ms Mayhew, but it is urgent."

Oli Noakes muddy eyes bulged out of his head. "Urgent enough to interrupt?"

She flashed me an apologetic look. "I'm afraid it is." She chewed her lip.

Athena Mayhew delivered a disapproving glower at the shrinking Orion and sashayed out in a swish of her strawberry satin suit. She ensured that the door was pulled closed behind her, while the flush-faced Orion explained what was going on.

This was all I needed! Just as I was locating some semblance of confidence and finding my stride too.

After a few more awkward exchanges between me, Barbara, and Oli about my journey here and the weather, Athena stuck her expensive elfin cut back around the door. Orion scurried off.

"We'll have to terminate the interview now. Sorry."

I blinked in surprise. *What?!*

"But… but it's only just started…" I could hear myself bleating.

"I'll liaise with Barbara," replied Athena in her staccato delivery.

Barbara and Oli scooped up their papers and pushed back their futuristic chairs.

I remained seated for a moment, like an errant toddler consigned to the naughty step. *What was going on? Had I said or done something?* No. I was sure I hadn't. There must have been some crisis when that blonde girl came dashing in like that.

I got to my feet, dazed, and snatched up my bag. Disappointment seeped through me.

"We will be in touch," assured Barbara, shaking my hand

Oli backed up her sentiment with an unconvincing nod.

And that was it.

I couldn't believe it.

Why had my interview been brutally cut short like that?

I took a gulp of iced water as I sat inside a café, not far from the *Goddess* offices. The cubes clanked against the side of my glass. It didn't seem like half an hour ago since I'd been summarily dismissed from my interview. My head was still spinning!

That poor receptionist looked like she was going to be physically sick at the prospect of having to tell Athena Mayhew some bad news. She looked like she wished she was anywhere else but there.

I tilted my head back against the quilted chair and stared up at the café's polished mahogany beams and fancy light installation suspended from the ceiling. After my interview fiasco, I felt deflated and irritated. I hadn't wanted to return home straight away, so I'd sought out a cute little café to have some lunch – not that I was very hungry.

I leant my elbows on the circular polished wood table while I absently scrolled through my phone. Should I ask to have the interview rescheduled? Be bolshy about it? It was a reasonable request, surely?

The waitress set down my lunch in front of me and vanished.

I proceeded to poke at my toasted panini with a fork as the lunchtime office workers buzzed past the window. Maybe it wasn't meant to be. Perhaps someone was trying to tell me something.

A chilly unease ran through me. Perhaps I wasn't meant to continue working as a journalist. I took a mournful bite of the panini with its melted Gruyere cheese. Miles used to say he didn't think I had it in me to be a successful journalist; that I wasn't ambitious or ruthless enough.

I cringed at the thought of it; of him holding me at arm's length and speaking to me in that condescending murmur of his. He would often say I was too nice.

I remember relaying his comments to Mum after we split up. "Now you listen to me," she had warned, hugging me close. "You're a terrific reporter with a conscience. You care and want to help people. You're everything he isn't."

My mouth morphed into a watery smile at the memory.

"You don't have to be a selfish knobhead to succeed," Dad had seethed, as he joined in our conversation. "Jesus! He makes it sound like being nice is a criminal offence!"

I took another pensive bite of my lunch. I had to forget about Miles Andrews and concentrate on me. He had been relegated to my past. My thoughts stumbled over one another. Perhaps I *should* give the magazine a ring and ask if I could have my interview rearranged? Miles wouldn't have just rolled over.

I ran my fingers up and down my glass. In a matter of weeks, I wouldn't have a job. The stark realisation hung there in front of me. And it wasn't as if I was exactly flooded with offers at the moment.

Good grief. I had better not decide to go into motivational speaking!

I scooped a hunk of curls back behind my ear.

She had the reputation for being a mardy cow, but working for Athena Mayhew... well, I knew how impressive it would look on my CV.

I couldn't afford to sit back and let someone else swan in and steal that job from under me. If I wanted it, I had to go for it. Would Miles have accepted this morning's events? Like hell he would have! He would have been demanding another interview and compensation for the distress!

Miles.

Guilt and anger charged through me. I was doing it again. Giving him head room when he didn't deserve it. Whenever I thought I was beginning to shrug him off, he'd reappear like some bloody phantom.

I scooped up my glass and gulped down the remainder of my lemon water, determination bubbling away inside of me. Sod it! I decided I would call *Goddess* now and ask for another interview. I would show Athena Mayhew it wasn't just her who had the monopoly on assertiveness.

I attracted the attention of a passing waitress and requested the bill.

"Oh, sorry. I better get that. That's my phone ringing," I said as I was plucking my credit card out of my purse. I quickly paid and then answered it. "Hello?"

I slotted my credit card back into my purse and fished out a tip for the waitress, while an apologetic female voice murmured down the line.

I listened to what she was saying, before my mouth sprang open in surprise and relief. It was Orion, from *Goddess* magazine. They wanted to see me. Straight away.

Chapter Ten

I gawped at Barbara, Oli, and Athena in the same meeting room I had been in earlier, which reminded me even more of a hotel reception area. Talk about Groundhog Day. "Pardon?"

Athena's blood-red lips promised a smile but didn't quite deliver. She shot Barbara and Oli either side of her a knowing glance. "We're offering you a job," she repeated.

My mouth flopped open. "But... but I didn't have a proper interview. I was going to contact you about that, to ask if it could be rearranged."

Good grief! I needed to listen to myself. I was in danger of talking myself out of a job at this rate, even before I started.

Athena flapped her dark talons. "No need. Your solid credentials speak for themselves." She bared her small teeth. "So, when do you think you will be able to join us?"

I took a gulp of the water they'd given me. Was this happening? Was it real?

Bloody hell! My head was scrambling to make sense of it

all. My mind whirred with a combination of surprise and trepidation. They wanted me and a journalism position was being offered. But how could they gauge me as a suitable candidate when they hadn't completed the interview?

I fought to make a coherent decision. They must have just decided that from the brief interview I did have, and my CV, I was suited to the job. But working for Athena Mayhew... I could handle her, couldn't I? I mean, she hadn't seemed that terrifying so far, although I hadn't been on the receiving end of one of her tirades.

I realised with an embarrassed jolt that I wasn't saying anything.

The three faces cross-examined mine across the table. An opportunity with the magazine of the moment, working with Athena Mayhew... It all seemed rather rushed though. But time wasn't on my side to faff around and debate it all. I had to make a choice.

"Yes," I blurted, ignoring a hissing voice in my head, concerned at the speed and unconventionality of it all. "I would be delighted to accept your offer. I'll speak to my editor when I get home. I'm sure he'll be fine about me handing in my notice and leaving a little earlier than anticipated."

"Excellent!" clipped Athena, rising up from her chair. "Barbara here will attend to your contract and the paperwork and have that with you ASAP. If you have any questions about leave and conditions, she can answer them." She clattered away on her thin heels, before whirling back to face me. Her eyes grazed me from head to toe. "As the new beauty reporter here at *Goddess*, I think your... shall we say, more *natural* appearance will be refreshing."

I'd reached down by the side of my chair for my bag, but shot straight up again, as though a bolt of electricity had been fired through me. *Noooo. I must have misheard. Did she just say beauty reporter?*

I stood and fiddled with the strap of my bag. "Pardon?"

Oli gazed everywhere but at me and Barbara's pale cheeks flipped to a heated red.

"You're going to be our new beauty writer," Athena repeated in a matter-of-fact tone. "About time we stopped going for the gormless but well-groomed types."

Her eyes, swept with sparkly coffee shadow, bored into me. "You have more of the earthy, country girl image. You should appeal to a wider audience."

Her words zoomed over my head. No. This was some sort of mistake.

I had stepped into someone else's body. That was it. I was witnessing all this on behalf of someone else. The new beauty writer?

What the hell did I know about beauty? I mean, I did the usual ablutions as every woman does – the odd manicure and pedicure, shaved my legs, went to the hairdresser's every couple of months to have my corkscrew riot tamed – but that was about it.

I thought again about my CV and application. This wasn't the job I had applied for. I had gone for the investigative reporter's job. At least I thought I had. Had I read the spec properly? Maybe I had submitted my application for the wrong one.

Doubts about myself surfaced. No. I had applied for that post. I know I had. So what was going on?

I had all these ideas and plans tumbling around my head for future features. A spotlight on working mothers in the publishing industry. An interview with the latest female football referee. I wanted to write about *Goddess* readers, for *Goddess* readers, not enthusing over stone massages and spa weekends.

"Sorry," I managed through a forced laugh. "I think there has been some sort of mix-up, but I'm sure it can be rectified."

Athena's eyebrows fenced.

"I'm not here about the beauty writer role. I applied for the investigative reporter vacancy."

Athena's hand hovered over the gold door handle of the meeting room. "That post has been filled," she chimed.

I blinked at her. No. This couldn't be right. "Filled? Already? No, there must be some mistake. I was only interviewed for that role this morning." *If you could call that farce an interview.*

Athena pursed her lips. "It transpires we have another applicant who possesses more experience on the ground, as it were."

It felt as if I were trapped in some confusing dream. I waited for Athena to expand but she didn't. They had awarded that role to someone else? Who? When had that happened?

My previous optimism at the job offer deflated like a pricked balloon.

I gripped the strap of my shoulder bag tighter. "Sorry," I stumbled. "I'm a bit confused by all of this."

Athena appraised me. "I don't see what's so confusing about it. You came for a job interview and we are now offering you the job."

"Yes," I faltered, struggling to smile. "But that wasn't the job I applied for and it wasn't the job I was being interviewed for this morning."

Athena propped one brow. "We are still offering you employment. I thought you would be delighted."

"Yes, I am pleased you are offering me a job," I clarified, my panic rising. "But it's not the job I wanted." I cleared my throat. "You're offering me the job of beauty reporter?"

"It has all the same perks and benefits," chimed in Barbara from the corner of the room with her clipboard. "Six weeks annual leave, bank holiday entitlement, company pension scheme…"

She then rattled off a salary that was several thousand pounds more than I had been receiving on *The Silver Ness News*.

Athena, meanwhile, was growing impatient. I noted her right foot was tapping against the polished wooden floor in her lethal heels.

I breathed in as I tried to consolidate my scattered thoughts.

Instead of reporting on injustice, I would be reviewing gold dust facials and vaginal steaming? My stomach pirouetted to the floor. This wasn't what I had planned. But did I have any other option? Jobs on newspapers and magazines in general were thin on the ground at the moment and the three other jobs I'd applied for looked like they were non-starters.

Two hadn't even bothered to reply and the third had responded with a polite decline, saying my application had been unsuccessful.

I needed the money and to sort myself out, and working for

Athena Mayhew would certainly inject a certain pazazz into my CV.

It wasn't what I wanted to do, though.

Athena's smooth jaw was grinding. "Look, Ms Baxter, I don't mean to appear rude, but I am very busy. If you wish to turn down our offer of employment, I can assure you there will be many more journalism graduates more than happy to step up."

I licked my lips and tried to calm my breathing. "I'm afraid I don't have a great deal of knowledge of the beauty industry," I confessed, stalling for more time.

"That's evident," replied Athena, eyeing my hair. "But no matter. You'll have team support and you can learn as you go." Her face adopted a sharper throb of impatience. "We also employ the consultation services of one of the best dermatologists in the business. Ms Susie Calderwood?"

A picture of Susie Calderwood appearing on TV shows, giving advice on skincare, popped into my head. She was a cool, calm, and professional brunette who was always being drafted in to comment on new stories covering dermatological break-throughs and the latest beauty fads.

Then visions of me unemployed, struggling to pay my mortgage and feed Harley and myself took over. They lodged themselves behind the backs of my eyes and refused to budge.

If I turned this opportunity down, I could live to regret it, as would my bank manager. Would I be able to swot up on all things beauty related? I would have to. I had no option.

Was this really what I wanted to do? No, it wasn't. But the post I had originally applied for was gone. Offered to someone else.

Disappointment chimed. What would happen if I said no right this minute? I could be looking for something else for months to come. I might not even secure another job in journalism anyway.

The thought of having to return to somewhere like the advertising agency I worked in before set my anxiety bells into overdrive. I couldn't face the prospect of that. I didn't think my mental health could either.

The three expectant faces of Athena, Barbara, and Oli filled my vision.

"I accept," I gushed, before I could change my mind and pull back the words into my mouth. "I'll take the job. Thank you."

Athena clapped her hands together and purred. "Excellent!"

I was so preoccupied as I departed the rose-gold shard-like offices, debating what the hell I had just done, that I failed to notice the pitying glances of my soon-to-be new work colleagues.

Chapter Eleven

Doug's mouth twitched with amusement. "Are you taking the piss?"

"No! It's true."

Frances folded her arms as she sat at her desk. "So let me get this straight. You applied for a news reporter role with Athena Mayhew and you've ended up as her new beauty writer?"

I picked at my mousepad. "That's about the size of it."

Doug let out a long, low whistle. "How the bloody hell did you let that happen?"

"I don't know," I wailed, flopping my head onto my desk. "She just sprung it on me."

"Well, good luck to you but I have to be honest, Leonie, it's not what I envisaged you doing after here."

"Me neither," I muttered. "But what was I supposed to do? I was staring unemployment or a job offer right in the face and it is Christmas in a couple of months, in case you hadn't noticed."

Frances's eyebrows flexed, encouraging me to elaborate. "So, you didn't actually apply for the beauty writer job then?"

"I applied for the investigative journalist job, submitted what I thought was a good CV, and was granted an interview." I rolled my eyes at the memory. "The interview yesterday turned out to be a bit of a farce, as it only lasted about five minutes until Athena was called away on something urgent."

I leant my arms on the edge of my desk. "My mum is always saying it's easier to go from a job to a job." I hauled one frustrated hand down my face. "And it's not as if I'm drowning in employment offers at the minute."

I pushed and pulled at my mouse pad. "I knew I shouldn't have googled the terms *beauty journalist* and *beauty writer*, but I couldn't help myself." I let out a defeated groan. "A lot of them now have shed loads of experience in beauty blogging or they have qualifications in skincare and haircare... It's not like just commenting on a shampoo."

I flopped my head down again on my desk, closing my eyes for a moment and willing the whole experience to vanish. "What the hell have I done?!"

"You'll soon pick it up," replied Doug, trying to sound encouraging. "Give yourself some time."

"Who has the other job gone to?" asked Frances.

"No idea," I answered. "Someone with more experience on the ground, whatever that means."

Frances angled her head to one side. "I know it's tough out there right now, especially in the media industry. But if you did work for Athena Mayhew, it would be a hell of a boost to your career." She pulled a sympathetic face. "You've got to want it though." She paused. "So, when do you start writing reviews about snake skin moisturiser?"

"Is that a thing?" I asked, screwing up my nose, appalled.

"No idea, but it sounds like the sort of thing the *Goddess* demographic would use."

"Oh don't," I groaned, clasping my hands to my face. "The HR department emailed me last night with a suggested start date of November 5th. Quite apt, really. Fireworks night." I puffed out my cheeks, still unsure of what I was letting myself in for. "Athena is keen to get me installed as soon as possible, before other members of staff start taking their winter leave in the run-up to Christmas."

Doug murmured and checked the dates on his PC. "Today is the 23rd, so that's only a couple of weeks away."

"I know," I gabbled, guilt pressing down on me. "I'm so sorry. It's all happened so fast."

"It's fine," assured Doug. "Don't stress over it."

"And this office will be closed by the end of next month anyway," added Frances. "I'll be working in the Drummond newsroom by then." A resigned look shot across her handsome features.

I stared around, drinking in the gulls dipping and weaving over the choppy waves outside the newsroom window. "What about this place? What's going to happen to it?"

"Clarity Newspapers are going to sell it off," said Doug. "It will probably end up as an ice cream parlour or a charity shop, although I hear they're being greedy, due to its location, and are going to ask a ridiculous amount for it. "

There was a charged silence for a few moments until Doug

thumped the edge of his desk. "Right team, enough of this melancholy. We have Leonie's leaving-do to plan."

I managed to smile, despite the reticence churning around in my stomach. "In other words, where are we going to go for an extended lunch and who is going to get the first round in?"

———

I spent the next two weeks reading up on everything from retinol and hot stone massage, to crystal exfoliation and seaweed wraps. I also threw myself into writing a special piece for the paper about my two years reporting there. That was a task in itself, as every time I reflected on my happy memories there, I would choke up.

My head was such a jumbled mess of beauty products and saying my private farewells to *The Silver Ness News* and its supportive community that I decided to temporarily park any thoughts about further investigations of Merry Wood and Lily Cruickshank.

There would be plenty of time to return to that particular puzzle once I started at *Goddess*.

My leaving lunch on that Friday in October, my last day with the paper, was a tearful event.

Doug, Frances, and I enjoyed delicious seafood overlooking Silver Ness beach, with its chilly water rushing onto the sand and the odd creak of salt-washed boats.

The restaurant, Something Fishy, was all cherry-wood dining tables, with fishing nets artfully draped across the walls and twinkling fairy lights decorating its alcoves.

Doug and Frances presented me with a mocked-up and

framed front page of some of my more memorable news stories. There was the time I got up at silly o'clock to go out on a shift with Silver Ness' most successful fishing trawler and another article I wrote about trying to become a dog behaviourist with Silver Ness' award-winning dog trainer. You only had to look at Harley to see how that turned out!

They also gave me a gorgeous gold and blonde-wood pen, engraved with my initials.

I swallowed hard, tears cluttering up my eyes. The anaemic autumnal sun was flitting across the top of the sea in an almost biblical fashion.

Frances leant forward and bundled me into her arms, before Doug scraped his chair out opposite and gave me a peck on the cheek. He coughed. "Here's to the future of *The Silver Ness News*. Ok, it won't be how we remember it." He sank back down in his chair and picked up his wine glass, forced joviality in abundance. "But here's to new beginnings for all of us."

I felt as if I had been thrown into someone else's life and told to get on with it or drown.

Instead of sitting with Frances and Doug in our cosy little newsroom with its delicious smell of newspaper print and coffee, I was now seated at a baby-pink and white frosted glass desk that would have looked at home inside a doll's house.

Everyone on the *Goddess* team seemed pleasant enough, if a little serious and self-satisfied and once Orion, Athena's PA, had taken me around and made the introductions, she had escorted me to my new desk.

I was surrounded by lethal-looking flowers and glass pillars. My stunned freckled expression stared back.

I mentally ran through the names and faces of my new work colleagues. That was odd. Surely there was a beauty editor on the team who I would be working for? I searched my brain for the colleague introductions I had just received. I didn't remember Orion saying anything about one of them being the beauty editor.

Oh, not to worry. They were probably due in a bit later and I would meet them then.

Athena was expected in at any moment, so there was a charged hush in the air.

I switched on my PC, having been informed by Orion that it was all set up for my use. As it whirred into life, I peered into my in-tray. That seemed to consist of a pile of fancy-looking press releases, promoting everything from smudge-proof mascara to snail slime hand cream.

My chest deflated.

Orion offered me a supportive smile from her corner of the open-plan office and I struggled to return it.

From across the floor, I noticed whispers being exchanged out of the sides of mouths and glances at me over the tops of PC screens.

But the indiscreet asides were interrupted. There was a sudden frisson as the main office doors glided open and Athena swept in, a couple of dayglo folders under one arm. "Team meeting," she barked, looking at none of us. "My office."

I watched my new colleagues delivering discreet eye rolls. I gathered up my notebook and pen and followed them.

Athena's office was like the helm of some futuristic space craft. It was a white-carpeted affair, but with a triangular meeting table and flowing dark blinds at both windows. Even the two potted plants were trapped in angular pots by the door.

I took up the seat next to Orion and shot her an apprehensive glance. I couldn't help but wonder if the other new start – the person who had been appointed to the investigative journalist position – was arriving today too. And the fate of the previous beauty writer nudged the corners of my mind...

Athena was now stationed at the helm. She craned forward in her highbacked chair and opened one of the files. "I take it, Leonie, that you've met everyone already?"

"Yes, thank you, Athena. Although come to think of it, I haven't met—"

I was cut short by Athena's brisk efficiency. "Ursula. How is the feature going on glass thongs?"

I found myself wincing. *Dear God! Seriously? Was that a thing?*

Then it was Dyson's turn. "Where are you at with the interview we were hoping to secure with James McAvoy?"

The speed of the individual conversations was unnerving, like rapid gun fire. Athena appeared either satisfied or would draw in her lips and grind out further instructions. She swivelled her gamine cut to Orion. "Our new investigative reporter starts today. Make sure she has everything she needs."

"Of course, Athena."

A pinch of resentment nipped at me and I tried to brush it off. So, she was starting work here today too. *I wonder who the successful candidate was? Where had she worked before?* Well, wherever that was and whoever she might be, Athena had considered her better suited for the job. It did still smart, but oh well. There was diddly squat I could do about it now and at least I had a job, even if it wasn't the one I had been hankering after...

"Leonie. Are you listening?"

I jumped, bashing my knees against the underside of the glass table. Shit!

Athena was talking to me now. Colour clawed at my cheeks as everyone turned to look at me. I pulled my notebook closer to me. "Yes. Absolutely."

She frowned. *Great.* I'd been here all of five minutes and managed to irritate my new boss already.

I risked a look at the other faces surrounding me, then wished I hadn't. Trixie with her Rapunzel extensions; Cole and his biceps; Ursula sporting a withered expression; and Dyson, who finished examining his manicure, to give me a cool once-over. It was like they were a bunch of schoolkids who had captured a rare insect and were peering it. Guess who was the insect?

"As I was saying," began Athena again with added emphasis, "now that we have a new beauty writer here in Leonie, we can return to our original feature plan." She paused for effect. There was a ripple around the table. "So, Leonie, your fist assigned feature is to arrange the biggest and most prominent beauty feature we have seen here at *Goddess*."

My mouth began to slip open in panic.

"We have signed the three top models of the moment – Esther Drew, Dante, and Carina Salazar – to appear in this feature for our Christmas issue. They will be wearing the latest Avanti cosmetics. I wasn't happy with your predecessor's ideas for location and theme for this. Suggestions, Leonie?"

My heart took off at a gallop. Talk about being thrown into the thick of it. I blinked as a tide of panic threatened to engulf me. Images of the three well-known models paraded in front of my eyes. So, no mentoring period for me then. No induction.

My mouth popped open and closed a few times. The gazes of my fellow magazine colleagues burned into me. Good grief! What was I supposed to say? This was my first morning working here and I was sitting here doing a wonderful impression of a gasping trout. I had to say something. "You mean, you would like some ideas now?" I croaked.

Athena managed to hitch one expectant brow at me, which was a feat in itself. "Yes."

My mouth turned to sandpaper. How the hell could she drop something like this on me and then expect me to reel off an impressive array of ideas?! I wanted to say as much but drew it back.

Whether I liked it or not, I had been thrown in at the deep end without a rubber ring and I had to try and stay afloat. My brain raced to pull up something intelligent to say. I forced my mouth into a rictus smile. "It depends on the fashions."

"Avanti," repeated Athena with growing frustration, "is a brave and bold cosmetics brand. The clothes are secondary, but I envisage wispy, ghostly tunics and shirts. It's all about the make-up." She raked me up and down with a withered smile. "I take it you have heard of them?"

I swallowed, realisation festering. *What the hell was I doing?*

I was out of my depth. *But you need this job*, reminded an echoing voice from the ether.

I pretended to glance at my notebook, even though I only had a doodle of a triangle and a cuddly bear on it. "Oh yes. Of course. Who hasn't?"

"Well then?" she pushed, leaning forward against the table. "Suggestions?"

I had heard of the very expensive, sumptuous brand of cosmetics, favoured by the likes of Jennifer Lopez and Nicole Kidman, but it was somewhat out of my price range. I didn't dare tell Athena that my cosmetic purchases were normally conducted during my weekly supermarket shop, where I would purchase a pretty rose-pink lipstick or my favourite coffee-coloured eye shadow for a fiver.

I raised my chin, hoping that this would make me seem far more confident than I was feeling. Right now, whenever I opened my mouth to say anything, it sounded like I was just saying "Flump".

I scanned the bemused faces of my colleagues, who were clearly relieved it was me and not them making a spectacle of themselves.

There was a painting on the far wall of Athena's office that depicted Glasgow's Queen Street Station in the early 1900s. "Maybe we could have an old hotel lobby or a train station as the setting?" I gabbled, seizing on that sudden idea and clinging onto it like a slippery life raft.

Athena cut me off with a bored look. "Done to death, both of them. Can you come up with something else asap please? Thanks."

Then she moved on to Carter, the graphic designer stationed opposite me.

I felt like slumping back in my chair and begging for oxygen. Bloody hell! The morning had only just begun and yet I was already drained!

When the meeting limped to a close, I hurried back to my desk. It was as if my insides had been tossed around in a blender.

I had read about the three models we were using for that feature and it was widely reported they possessed egos the size of the Grand Canyon. My shoulders disappeared as I thought back to Athena's reaction to my hotel and train station suggestions. She'd looked at me as though I'd thrown up over her shoes.

I sank down into my chair. Talk about a baptism of fire.

I must have looked petrified because Orion stopped in front of my desk and offered me a small smile of understanding. Then she gestured to me to follow her. I reached for my mug and strode towards the breakout area, which was outfitted with a chrome coffee machine and blonde-wood furniture.

She gestured for me to sit down at one of the tables in the far corner. "You, ok? You look like you've just been run over by a double decker."

I let out a sigh. "That's a good description."

I waited until Carter and a girl called Callie with pink bunches had sauntered past.

"It's all rather full-on, isn't it?" she sympathised. "Your first editorial meeting and straight away she's demanding all-singing, all-dancing suggestions."

I let my hands rise and fall. "Maybe I was being a bit naïve.

I just thought I might be allowed a bit of time to settle in before being landed with something like that Avanti feature."

Orion nodded the enormous red polka-dot ribbon in her hair. "Athena doesn't do settling in. Never has done." She lowered her voice to a supportive whisper. "Don't struggle, ok? If you need help, just ask."

I let out a long, low hiss of breath. "Thanks. I appreciate it."

We filled our respective mugs with tea and made our way back to my desk. "Orion, what happened to my predecessor? The previous beauty writer? And when do I get to meet my boss?"

Orion frowned. "Your boss?"

"Yes. You know. The beauty editor."

Orion opened her mouth, but as if on cue, Athena appeared at my desk. Orion flinched at her materialisation.

Athena was clutching a press release. "Leonie, have you heard of Tilly Crabtree at all?"

I flicked Orion a slightly panicked look. "Yes. Isn't she that make-up artist who all the A-listers are clamouring after?"

"The very one," primped Athena. "And she is a very good friend of mine."

She thrust the press release she was clutching towards me. "Tilly is launching her new foundation range this afternoon and I'd like you to pop along and cover it. All the details are on there."

She swivelled on her heel. "Oh, and I told her you would be more than happy to try out the product and give her a review. Thanks!"

Once Athena vanished back into her office, I let out a disgruntled sigh.

Orion shot a kind glance over her frilly shoulder. "I meant what I just said, ok?"

"Ok, Orion, and thanks."

"No problem. Athena has been banging on for ages about what a coup this Avanti spread is going to be for *Goddess*."

"Gee. Thanks. That makes me feel so much better."

Orion grinned, making a dimple erupt in her left cheek. "Don't be hard on yourself. You'll get there."

I'll scream, more like.

She was about to move away when I decided to seize the opportunity again. "Orion, where's my immediate boss?"

Orion didn't say anything. "The beauty editor," I clarified. "I don't remember anyone with that title at the staff meeting. Is she or he on leave at the moment?"

Orion flushed a rose pink. She looked like she wanted to evaporate on the spot. "That's because there isn't one."

I pulled up, a feeling of terror seeping into my veins. "There's no beauty editor? What do you mean? Are you saying it's just me?"

Orion fiddled with her frilly boiler-suit collar. "I'm sure we'll get round to appointing a new one eventually."

A sense of foreboding rose up. "A new one? So, what happened to the previous beauty editor?"

Orion's dark-grey eyes shifted from left to right like a creepy painting in a haunted house. "It's complicated. She and Athena had an exchange of opinions and she decided to move on."

My feeling of growing dread increased. "How long ago was that?"

Orion twitched her nose in recollection. "A few weeks maybe."

She started to move off again at a sharper pace.

"But why hasn't my new boss been appointed? Has the job been advertised? Have you tried to headhunt someone?"

Orion squirmed in her platform trainers.

"What's going on, Orion?"

"It takes time to make these appointments," she answered, not convincing herself or me. "I'm sure it will be filled at some point."

I could feel my worry escalating. It sounded to me like nobody wanted the post or as soon as the prospective candidates found out who they would be working for, they changed their minds about wanting the job.

A thought pinged into my mind. Pictures of a panicky-looking Orion during my interview, summoning Athena to speak to her. "Is that why my interview was interrupted? Why you came in looking all flustered that day? Was it because the previous beauty writer quit?"

Orion looked sheepish. "Maybe."

Ah. The muddled, confused haze in my head was beginning to lift. So, had I been offered the vacancy of beauty writer simply because Athena was so desperate to fill the post?

This unsavoury conclusion clung to me. Not exactly a confidence booster.

I gave myself a mental shake. "And this new investigative reporter who's starting today...?" I allowed the question to hang there between us.

Orion stuffed one hand into her cream boiler-suit pocket. "What about her?"

"Do you know who she is?"

Orion hesitated. "Her name is Kerry Wicks."

I searched my mind to see if I knew her name from another title. It didn't seem familiar. "I don't know of her. What newspaper or magazine was she on before?"

Orion shuffled. "All these questions!" When I arched my brows at her, she sighed. "I'm not sure where she was working."

That didn't ring true. Surely, as Athena's PA, Orion would have all the details about a new recruit?

I shot questioning stares from my desk across at Orion. In the end, she muttered something before suddenly striding back towards me and giving a discreet tug at my sleeve, indicating for me to follow her.

No sooner had we taken a few paces back up the corridor than Orion hauled me into the doorway of an empty meeting room. "Shit, Leonie."

Her kohl-lined eyes did that shifting thing again to make sure the coast was clear. "You're going to find out sooner or later anyway."

"Find out what?"

She stared past my shoulder for a moment. "This is for your ears only just now, ok?"

"Sure. What is it?"

Orion shuffled as she stood there. She looked agonised. "Kerry Wicks... the new investigative reporter... well, it turns out that she is Athena's niece."

Chapter Twelve

What the hell had I done?!

Ok, so I was employed as a writer at one of the biggest magazines of the moment. I was working with the journalistic powerhouse that was Athena Mayhew.

On the other hand, I'd been given the poisoned chalice of working with the fashion industry's three most pretentious models, I didn't have a beauty editor boss to approach for advice, and the job I'd really wanted had been given to Athena's niece.

To top it all off, it also seemed that I had been given the job of beauty writer out of sheer desperation, because there was nobody else.

I set off for Tilly Crabtree's foundation launch on foot, at least grateful that the event was taking place at a plush department store just a few blocks away from the *Goddess* offices and there was no need to take the car or negotiate public transport.

Even though it was only the 5th of November, many of the

shop windows I passed were already decked out with Christmas trees, trailing twinkly lights and an abundance of bows and holly.

My head was cluttered with a myriad of thoughts as I made my way there. I hoped that by walking it might help unscramble them a little.

I glanced down at the press release again that Athena had given me. There was a glorious black and white photograph of Tilly looking glamorous and very pleased with herself in a sharp, dark tailored suit and nothing else underneath.

"Give your skin power with one of the new turbo-charged foundations created by the make-up artist of the moment, Tilly Crabtree," gushed the blurb under her picture.

"As soon as you apply one of the Glorious foundations, you will immediately notice that your skin reacts, creating a glow that can be seen from the heavens…"

What?!

"Watch your complexion transform from dry and dull into a mermaid sheen that will draw gasps and compliments. With thirst-quenching properties and a burst of vitamins, Glorious foundations will revolutionise the way you see yourself – and how others see you…"

Dear me. Could it solve climate change as well?

I turned the corner and made my way down past the stately granite offices and shops. There was an old bridge situated at the end of the road on which was painted one of the legendary Scottish street artist Chandler's pieces of work. It depicted a boat, struggling to get through stormy waves. A couple of gulls were swooshing over the top of the boat, and coming up through the water was a hand, thrusting itself through the foam and clutching a life jacket. Underneath the artwork was painted the caption:

Everybody needs rescuing at one time or another.

Chandler was like the Scottish Banksy, whose array of artwork would appear in a variety of wild and wonderful locations for the masses to enjoy. Everything from satirical sketches of politicians to moody paintings of Glasgow tenements and social commentary images of poverty and deprivation would suddenly appear on the sides of bus stops, dilapidated buildings, and random brick walls.

Chandler was never seen. He would melt away into the dark after painting his latest work. This had been going on since the early 1970s. There was speculation in the media as to who the elusive Chandler might be – everybody from a titled art critic to a museum curator and an old rock star who dabbled in art, had been suggested as the real Chandler but nobody knew for sure. A member of the Royal Family was even rumoured to be the unknown artist.

Chandler was part of Scottish folklore, woven into the fabric of society almost as much as the Loch Ness monster.

He was still an enigma.

I paused to admire the painting on the brickwork as shoppers marched past me and the traffic continued to push along, with the odd irritated beep of a car horn.

It was so lifelike, I felt as though the sea spray was speckling my face.

What an exclusive that would be to find out who Chandler

actually was! Or to even secure an interview with him. He famously never spoke to the press.

I stood for a moment longer, appreciating the white peeling paint and rust of the boat, before reminding myself that I had just started a new job and I had my first journalistic assignment to complete.

I moved on and crossed the road before turning right and drawing up outside the department store, Saskia's, where there was a heavy press presence and lots of overexcited teenage girls with their mobile phones.

I had no option but to make the best of the messy situation I had found myself in. It was a job after all. If I was able to stick it out for even a few months, perhaps something else at another magazine or newspaper might come up?

Good grief! I had landed myself in it this time.

Snapshots of Miles's smug face drifted in front of my eyes and I blinked them away.

I showed the invitation and then my magazine ID card to a dour-faced security guard. He directed me up to the fourth floor.

I caught the lift with a gaggle of other female journalists who were speculating on whether Tilly's latest boyfriend, the actor Dylan McKnight, might be there.

Once we exited the lift, we were greeted by another security guard who welcomed us into a huge suite decked out in purple satin. Enormous Roman urns of purple and white flowers were stationed at the entrance, as well as in each corner of the room.

Images were being played out on a large rectangular screen at the far end, showing a lovely young woman drifting around in a castle, sporting the most glorious transparent skin I had ever seen in my life.

I caught sight of my own preoccupied face in one of the mirrored columns and reached for a glass of water from one of the passing waiters. I could do with some hydration myself.

Just a matter of weeks ago, I was reporting on missing wheelie bins, gulls pinching tourists' chips, and the possible closure of the local library.

There was a sudden burst of enthusiastic applause that made me almost drop my glass of water. When I turned with the assembled throng, I realised that Tilly Crabtree had emerged from behind the purple curtains and was holding court.

She kept tossing back her cloud of dark hair and baring her teeth like she wanted to bite somebody.

She threw her hands wide, like she was about to deliver everyone from salvation. "Welcome to the launch of Glorious!"

Once the excited applause had died down, Tilly reeled off a spiel about what it meant to her to bring such a wonderful product to the masses.

I was more fascinated by how her forehead didn't move, even though her eyebrows did.

"Glorious *is* the new make-up revolution," she breathed, prowling up and down the glittery stage. "No matter how old you are, how young you are, this foundation will bring you joy."

Not as much as a night with Henry Cavill would, I thought to myself.

A waiter meandered past with a tray of champagne flutes

and I decided I needed something like that to keep me going. I had the feeling I would be here for a while yet.

"Here, madam, have a complimentary gift, courtesy of Ms Crabtree," grinned a woman with a swinging ponytail, handing it to me.

"Thank you."

When she vanished in a cloud of heady perfume, I placed my glass of champagne on a nearby high table to take a closer look.

It comprised of a purple satin drawstring bag. Inside, amongst a scattering of flowery confetti, was an array of extravagant freebies: a rose-gold Swarovski powder compact, gold-flecked hand cream, and a silver lipstick holder studded with diamonds. There were also a couple of Tilly Crabtree branded eye shadows.

I let out a gasp, like a child on Christmas morning. Bloody hell! Goodness knows what each of these complimentary bags cost.

"Ms Leonie Baxter?" came a husky female voice across the top of the crowd. "Is there a Ms Leonie Baxter from *Goddess* magazine here please?"

I snatched up my glass of fizz and took a huge gulp. No doubt I would need it. I shoved my goodie bag under my right arm. "Hello. Yes, that's me."

Heads turned as I slid my hand up into the air.

"Can you follow me please?" smiled the ponytailed woman of before. "I was told you have an appointment with Ms Crabtree to experience the revolution that is Glorious?"

"Er… yes. That's right."

"Then please follow me."

We weaved our way through the chattering crowd and passed the still running advert of the woman drifting around the castle. At least her skin was perfect, even if she did appear to be trapped in there.

The swinging ponytailed lady led me to the right, past another swathe of curtains and more security guards and into a separate room set out with indigo furniture and a dazzling showbiz mirror with light bulbs shining around it.

"Welcome! Welcome!" breezed Tilly. "You must be Leonie."

We shook hands.

"Athena is such a great friend of mine. Isn't she a marvel?"

"Isn't she just?" I managed through a rictus grin.

"Coffee? Tea? Merlot? Green tea?"

"I'm fine, thank you," I reassured her, waggling my half-drunk champagne flute, before setting my goodie bag and the flute down on top of the fancy showbiz dressing table.

"Excellent!" said Tilly, scrutinising my face.

She prodded the skin around my nose. "A little dry in places. Not enough water, you naughty girl."

"If I was a dog, that would be more of a worry," I joked.

That didn't illicit much response, except for a polite smile.

"Mediterranean glow," she gasped, taking a step back to evaluate me. "Spanish?"

"Italian. On my mother's side."

"Gorgeous! Gorgeous! Well, we'll soon enhance that," she assured me, reaching for a new-age glass bottle with a bright-purple lid. It contained a gloopy-looking liquid that reminded me of what Harley had produced on the odd occasion after too many treats.

A plastic purple cape was theatrically fluttered by one of

Tilly's minions and secured around my neck and she got to work straight away with a cleanser and toner. Then she squeezed some of the suspicious-looking foundation into her palm, dabbing, blending, and blotting it with a sponge against my skin.

She was jumping about, backwards and forwards, like an artist scrutinising her easel – or a manic glove puppet.

As I sat back, my cape rustling, I struggled not to dwell on my first morning at *Goddess*. It couldn't be described as a runaway success.

It was as I shifted in the chair that I became aware of a sudden, odd sensation in my face. "My skin feels a little tight," I commented after a few minutes.

Tilly ignored me and carried on applying the foundation via a damp sponge.

My complexion continued to protest and the skin around my left ear gave an indignant tingle. *What was going on?* That didn't feel right.

When she had finished, she stood back and revelled in her own work. "Look at you! Look at you!"

I can't look at me, because you are standing in the way of the bloody mirror, I wanted to shout.

"Right. Take a look."

She stepped to one side out of the way of the lightbulb mirror.

I popped one eye open and then the other.

A strange mask-like creature stared back. Where had I gone? I didn't recognise myself. Bloody hell! I looked awful!

I tried to speak but it felt like my whole face had been

dipped in concrete. I was a caricature of myself – a scary waxwork from a Hammer Horror movie.

I tried to smile, to see if I could gain any mobility in my jaw. That was even more terrifying.

"I don't look like me," I managed out of the corner of my mouth, like a second-rate ventriloquist. "What have you done?"

"You look like an even lovelier version," she grinned manically back. "An Italian goddess!"

"More like a Madame Tussauds exhibit," I ground out under my breath.

"Pardon?"

I repeated what I just said, my indignation piquing. "Look, Ms Crabtree, I know you wanted *Goddess* to give you a glowing review of your new foundation, but this…"

I thought of the floaty, dreamy-eyed girl in the advert playing on repeat in the main function suite. I was like the beast to her Belle!

My face felt like it was swathed in several elastic bands!

"What's wrong with it?"

I let out a guffaw. Well, as much as I could with a constricted face. "Are you joking?! I look grotesque – like my whole face has melted." I twisted round in my seat, sending my purple plastic cape rippling. "And it feels like it's sucked all the moisture out of my skin!"

Tilly Crabtree transformed from gushing and giggly to a fire-breathing dragon within a split second. It was unnerving. "Who the hell do you think you are? You've only been working for *Goddess* for five minutes!"

She thrust a couple of cleansing wipes at me. "I shall be

speaking to Athena about this. Where's a proper beauty journalist when you want one?"

I reached for my phone in my bag and took a couple of snaps of my hideous visage. Then with a surge of relief, I attacked my face with the wipes, swiping off every last trace of the hideous foundation.

I angled my face to the right. Where I'd felt the tingling had now erupted into an ugly cluster of pinprick red spots.

A couple of Saskia's department store colleagues watched me gather up my bag, swig down the remainder of my champagne and then march off. Thank goodness I didn't have to be seen in public looking like a gargoyle.

No sooner had I got back to my desk than Athena swooped out of her office like an avenging angel. "Leonie. A word. Now!"

I followed her. She was trussed up in a dogtooth-check suit.

She slammed the glass door behind me, making it shake indignantly. "What the hell do you think you're doing? You've been here for all of five minutes and yet you've managed to offend one of my dearest and closest friends!"

"Athena, she plastered my face in that new foundation of hers and it looked and felt awful."

I swivelled my face to the side. "I didn't have this rash this morning."

Athena narrowed her gaze at the cluster of hot red spots.

Then I held up my mobile and brandished the two photographs of my face at her.

She recoiled. "Good God! What on earth is that?"

"That's me, wearing the Glorious Sun Glow shade from her new range."

She swallowed and eyed me. "You can't have taken those photographs properly."

Oh, give me strength. Never did I want to be back at *The Silver Ness News* more than right now.

Athena folded her spindly arms, sending her dozen bangles clattering up and down. "You need to find a positive. How was the texture? Smooth? Silky? Or what about the price? Competitive in this market?"

"It felt like concrete and the price is extortionate for a 50ml bottle. For what those cost, you could feed a family of four for a week."

She narrowed her eyes at me. "I'm not impressed, Leonie. Not at all."

My stomach rolled but I stood my ground. How could I lie and write up a glowing review of a product like this?

I glanced again at my phone screen and the pictures of me on it. I looked like a bank robber with a pair of American Tan tights pulled over my head.

Athena began ranting about loyalty to her and to *Goddess* and I felt my conscience stand to attention. Surely, she didn't expect me to write lies?

I could still feel the irritated patch of skin close to my ear. I angled my face to the right, pushing a hunk of my curls away so she could see it again. "Athena, please take another look at this."

She peered at the pinprick red spots.

"I didn't have these when I went to the launch. That foundation caused it."

Athena's mouth gave a small wobble. "You must have done. You just didn't notice it."

"I can assure you that I didn't."

Athena's jaw ground with fury and she seemed on the precipice of exploding when Orion appeared at the office door. "Athena..."

"Can't you see Leonie and I are in the middle of something here?"

Orion ignored Athena's thunderous expression. "You need to see this. I've just received an email from two women who were at Tilly Crabtree's launch. They're members of staff at Saskia's department store."

"Yes? And?"

"They both volunteered to have one of Tilly's makeovers too, using her new Glorious foundation."

Athena flapped one hand, irritated. "Well, spit it out, whatever it is."

"Both women's skin flared up within ten minutes of it having been applied. Just like Leonie."

Athena's gaze hardened but she said nothing.

"And before you ask," said Orion calmly, "they've both just emailed me photographs."

Athena barged past Orion and out of her office. "Show me."

Orion curled up her lip in an exaggerated Elvis style at Athena's back and returned to her PC, with me following. "Here."

She clicked on each of the images of the aggrieved women and two photographs shimmied up on screen, showing both of them with the same patchy rash as I had across their cheeks. "Both of these women saw and overheard Leonie talking to Ms Crabtree, found out Leonie works for *Goddess*, and decided to contact us."

Athena continued to hunch over Orion's screen, her jaw jutted out. I noticed her cheek throb with tension.

"It would not be ethical or proper to write a positive review after this," I maintained. "Imagine if we did. We would be putting ourselves and the magazine in a very difficult and dishonest position."

Athena ground her capped teeth together. Her right foot tapped in her pointed kitten heels while she mulled everything over.

She manoeuvred the PC mouse and straightened up. "I'll speak to Tilly. Explain the situation and smooth things over."

She raked me up and down. "I will also suggest she goes back to the drawing board with Glorious."

Orion and I watched her stalk back towards her office. Then she whirled round. "I do hope you are as diligent and take as much interest and care with the Avanti feature. I'm expecting great things from you, Leonie. Don't let me down."

That was a passive-aggressive threat if ever I heard one.

I had now been employed at *Goddess* for three days but it felt more like a painful and joyless six months.

Orion had confided in me about Athena's act of nepotism and I wasn't prepared to betray her trust. From what we could see, no one else appeared to know that Kerry was Athena's niece. Or if they did, they were too frightened to challenge it or say anything.

I carried this piece of information around with me, trying not to let it fester and build into a towering wall of resentment. That wasn't who I usually was and I didn't want to morph into someone like that.

Kerry seemed pleasant enough, if rather clueless and overawed. She spent most of her time cocooned in the Mother Ship (which was my collegues name for Athena's office) than anywhere else.

And as for this beauty feature featuring the three amigos, it was sitting there, growing larger and more prominent; more ominous.

Athena had asked for an update about the feature on Wednesday morning and I had reeled off more ideas but she had batted away my latest suggestions of a space-themed photoshoot and a 1970s disco vibe. "Classy, Leonie. We stay classy."

Does staying classy include employing your own niece too? I thought to myself, sinking back into my chair.

I was so relieved when my first week at *Goddess* limped to a close.

It had disappeared in a sea of reviews and exclamations about everything from anti-aging toothpaste to the latest in Red Sea salt deodorants.

I collected Harley and fobbed off my parents about why I was so subdued. I didn't want to conduct a post-mortem about why I felt such an idiot for jumping into a job I wasn't cut out to do.

The memories of working on *The Silver Ness News*, writing

about people's lives, their achievements, the fight to keep Silver Ness library open, made me want to weep with nostalgia.

I promised to ring my mum and dad later, after dinner, keen to escape from their concern and interrogations.

Once I'd changed out of my fitted shirt and flared pinstriped trousers, I located some salmon in the fridge. My latest copy of *Media World*, a monthly magazine detailing the latest news and job moves in the media industry, had been delivered.

As I made dinner and occupied Harley with her squeaky shoe toy, I browsed through a few pages before stopping dead as the salmon sizzled in the pan behind me.

Miles's triumphant golden smile beamed out at me in full colour.

TV News editor Miles Andrews and his fiancée, TV
journalist Carmel Jennings, are collaborating on a biography
of the late newspaper mogul Sir Russell Stepney. Andrews,
who works for the Central ITV regional station…

My attention lunged at the first couple of sentences. *Fiancée? Miles was engaged? Already?* We only split up ten months ago!

I examined the picture of them cosied up together. Carmel was gorgeous. She reminded me of Thandiwe Newton.

I didn't want to read on. I slapped the magazine shut and shoved it to the other end of the kitchen table. Miles hadn't been prepared to settle down with me. He had been happy enough at the time for me to stay over the odd night at his

Glasgow flat, but as for taking things any further, that had been a non-starter. Whenever we passed by a jeweller and my eyes turned misty at the engagement rings, Miles would bundle me away and assure me we would "look to the future at some point, once we knew where life was taking us." Little did I know that Miles had already decided his life wouldn't include me.

I propped my chin on my hand and observed Harley scoffing down her chicken and kibble as I pushed and poked my dinner around my plate.

I hadn't been enough. What Miles and I had shared hadn't been enough.

When Harley had finished, I jumped up from my kitchen chair. I had to get out of here. The walls were tumbling down, bringing my mood with them. "Come on, sweetheart. Let's go for a lovely walk."

———

I drove on autopilot, away from my house, past the blue ribbon of the sea and out along the thread of fiery-coloured country lanes, where the last remnants of leaves were hanging by a thread to branches. The ones that had already succumbed to the November chill tumbled and pirouetted in front of the car. We pressed on towards Drummond.

Harley sat secured in her dog seat in the back, like a little China ornament.

I slowed down as I glimpsed the couple of wooden picnic tables and found myself parking up. Once I made sure Harley was secured in her pink harness and lead, I locked up the car and we set off through the field.

It had been an odd, discomfiting week and the news about Miles being engaged had bruised and battered my ego. It had only been January when we split up and already he was engaged to someone else for goodness' sake! And he was enjoying a successful career in TV news too.

His life was progressing, moving onwards and upwards and taking a different path, whereas mine was stuck in a quagmire. I was writing about colonic irrigation treatments and teeth whitening, in a job that had been offered to me and which I had accepted out of desperation.

I strode on with Harley, deciding not to allow her to roam free for now. The hedgerows were bustling and I didn't fancy chasing after her again.

I squinted ahead. The milky evening light was surrendering to splashes of sleepy evening sun and darkness was not far away.

I thought again about Athena's demands and her expectations of me. Every suggestion I was making for the Avanti feature was being met with derision and dismissal. It was a bloody mess. I should have listened to my inner voice. I should have declined the offer of the beauty writer job and taken my chances.

I buried myself deeper into my long-knitted scarf and thick winter jacket as my boots trampled through the bursts of grass taking me deeper into the thick haze of woodland. Merry Wood rose up ahead of us, its naked trees and cracked pots of heather waggling in the breeze.

Harley pulled on her lead. She gazed up at me, popping

her dark eyes. "Oh, go on then," I sighed, unclipping her lead. "But no taking off again after Freddie Fox, ok?"

Harley gave a swift waggle of her plume of a tail and made the most of her sudden freedom, gambolling ahead like a baby lamb towards Merry Wood. She reached the towering old fence that concealed the back garden and began to scrabble at a loose plank.

"Harley!" I hissed, glancing around for Lily Cruickshank. "You'll get me into trouble. Stop that!"

We had only just arrived here and already she was desecrating the bloody place!

But she ignored me and continued to paddle her paws at the loose wood and the section of grass underneath it. Brown earth spluttered up behind her. I lunged forward with her lead. "Harley! If the Wicked Witch catches us, we'll both be in big trouble!"

This didn't deter her. She continued to dig, until the fragile section of wood made a cracking groan of surrender and flew off into the earth.

"Oh no! No, Harley!"

I yanked Harley away and made a feeble attempt to prop the broken-off section of wood back into place. I crouched down while Harley reared up on her back legs beside me. "Look at this! Look what you've done!"

I lowered my head and wedged the loose plank back in. Even if I could manage a temporary patch-up, hopefully Lily wouldn't notice it. Maybe if I asked Dad to take a look at the fence for me...

Oh wow.

My jaw grew slack at the sight greeting me through the slender gap in the fence.

The grass was overgrown of course, poking up in long, brave swathes of acid green. But surrounding the lawns was a series of beautiful ivory statues. They depicted young, pensive women in flowing robes and streaming hair gazing at flowers cupped in their hands.

I glanced back over my shoulder to make sure Lily Cruickshank wasn't around. There was no sign of her.

I waggled the section of wood out again for a better view. I couldn't resist. The glossy, festive sight of holly and ivy studded with red berries appeared in front of me. There was a whole bank of it on the other side of the garden.

I stood up, Harley peering at me in confusion. I could see further down the lawns now too.

A sweet garden bench greeted me, surrounded by laces of winter honeysuckle, their creamy-white petals bountiful and fragrant. There was also cyclamen, with its silver-lined green leaves, blooming in bursts of hot pink, red, and vanilla, not to mention more lavender heathers in periwinkle blue and soft pink. A couple more trees, bare but twisting their branches elegantly towards the evening sky, cast looming shadows over the wooden bench. It was like something out of a Renoir painting.

I paused. I was sure I could hear tinkling water.

My curiosity fired up even more, I moved a bit further down the length of the fence, encouraging Harley to go with me. Yes, that was the sound of water. It sounded like a fountain.

I had hoped there might be another section of the fence

further along that had seen better days and which I could dislodge, but no such luck. The rest of the fence looked secure.

I returned to where Harley and I had managed to create a gap. I made a snap decision. We could ease through the space. It would be very uncomfortable squeezing through, but that space would be just wide enough for a twenty-seven-year-old journalist and her Cockapoo puppy to get through.

I gave an uncertain-looking Harley an encouraging smile. "Come on, sweetheart. Let's go and take a look."

Harley wasn't sure. She took a couple of steps backwards.

I clipped her lead on again and stroked her velvet head. "I bet there are lots of lovely birdies in there you can chase."

She considered this for a couple of moments and watched me edge my way through. When I remembered I had a couple of her bone-shaped treats in my jeans pocket and waggled the packet in front of her, she had a change of heart, sped up and slid through the gap behind me.

Oh wow! I didn't know where to look first. I thought the back gardens might be spectacular and they didn't disappoint.

From the splashes of cerise and violet to the imposing trees, the thick hedgerows and the romantic garden bench, it was breath-taking. I turned my attention to the water feature I had heard only moments before, further down the lawn.

It depicted a blossoming lotus flower with a hummingbird drinking from it as it hovered with its wings open. The water was frothing upwards from its centre in a joyous silver stream and even though there were generous chunks of damp moss on its stone base, it didn't detract from the fountain's beauty.

From the water feature to the graceful statues, the whole effect was a magical one. Ok, so the grass could do with a good mow and there were weeds trying to masquerade as flowers, but it was stunning all the same.

I imagined myself lounging on a blanket on a summer's day, lost in a good book as the sun danced across my face...

"What are you doing? You have no right to be in here!"

My skin prickled.

Harley and I whirled round to see an incandescent Lily Cruickshank emerge out of the back door of the house.

"Mrs Cruickshank," I panicked. "I'm so sorry, but Harley had a go at the fence, broke one of the damaged panels and—"

"You seem to be making a habit of hanging about round here."

I thought about the crap day I'd had at work, and self-satisfied Miles and his fiancée. My cheeks flashed. "I just wanted to go somewhere pretty with Harley. Forget about things for a little while." I realised I was at risk of talking too much and stopped.

She gave me an odd look from the doorway. "You do realise I could have you charged with trespassing?"

"I'm sorry. I got a glimpse of this beautiful garden and I couldn't resist coming in to take a look."

Lily Cruickshank's expression, which had verged on the cusp of fury a moment ago, twisted into one of indignation. "You journalists," she ground out, down her regal nose. "You think you have the divine right to interfere in other people's lives."

"Mrs Cruickshank, please."

She cut me off, her long flowing olive skirt flapping around her ankles. "Haven't you got anything better to do than hang around here, sticking your nose into matters that don't concern you?" Her chilled stare ran up and down me. "No husband to go back to? No boyfriend?"

Her words stung. They dredged up more pictures of Miles and his new fiancée.

She folded her arms across her bony chest. "I bet you're one of those hard-nosed young madams who puts her career first, before anything or anyone else."

Her words stung. That wasn't me. That wasn't who I was. I bit back the hurt. "You don't know what you're talking about. You don't know anything about me." Anger was flickering up inside me, like a growing flame, and I was struggling to contain it.

Athena, my new job, Miles… They were piling in on me; stoking my upset and frustration.

Lily Cruickshank smirked. "I've met the likes of you before. You'd deceive your own grandmother to get on."

The hurt twisted itself deeper. I didn't need this. Not now. Not today. On any other day, I would have walked on, shaking it off and dismissing her words with a polite goodbye. "That's not true. And how dare you stand there and make all these assumptions."

She was on a vitriolic roll. She ignored my protests. "Angling for promotion at work, are we? Keen to dig up any dirt you can to impress the boss?"

My stomach sank at the thought of Athena and her withering remarks at my feature suggestions for the Avanti cosmetics spread. They mingled and intertwined with the images of Miles's white grin and the dazzling rock on his bride-to-be's finger. They shimmered and blended with recollections of my happy, contented days at *The Silver Ness*

News; of the banter and camaraderie between Frances, Doug and me.

My life as it was had melted into one giant, messy puddle.

Now, I was standing in the middle of a neglected but romantic garden, with Harley. The chill in the air was beginning to bite deeper and I was being verbally abused by this woman who looked like she wanted to rip my head off.

"Leave this garden now and don't come back," barked Lily Cruickshank. "Do you hear me?"

At any other time, I would have issued an apology and left, cursing the old bag under my breath. But not today. I was feeling lost and bruised, not sure who I was or where my life was heading.

I didn't have the energy to remain composed. That was why I could feel my face crumpling. Tears gathered in my eyes and edged down my cheeks, and I didn't care.

And all Lily Cruickshank could do was stare.

Chapter Thirteen

I dashed the back of my arm against my cheeks. *Come on Leonie!* Don't give this rude woman the satisfaction.

"Sorry," I ground out into the air. "This isn't like me."

Lily Cruickshank didn't say anything. She shot indecipherable glances between me and Harley.

I rooted around inside my jeans pocket and located a tissue. I dabbed at my eyes.

She plunged her hands into the deep pockets of her skirt and shuffled from foot to foot.

Everything had just piled on top of each other and her terse words had sent my emotions skittering. I blew my nose, not making eye contact. I found myself developing a sudden fascination for the grass.

I let out an unladylike sniff. "I'm sorry about the fence. I'm more than happy to contribute to the cost of repairing it."

Lily Cruickshank's silvery brows gathered.

"I had no right to come into the garden, but when I saw all

this…" I flailed around one weary arm. "Well, I couldn't resist."

Lily Cruickshank's eyes followed my hand. They raked over the statues and the little garden bench. There was an agonising pause. "Yes," she admitted. "It is lovely. A very special place."

She seemed lost for a moment, transported somewhere else. "This house… and the garden… it seems to have that effect on people." Then she returned to the present moment. Her gimlet gaze was back.

"Apologies again, Mrs Cruickshank." I rooted around in the back pocket of my jeans where I always stashed a pen and a mini notebook. I dashed down my details. "I meant what I said about the damage to the fence. Please let me know the cost."

The woman accepted the piece of paper and eyed it with an odd look.

I gave a gentle tug on Harley's lead. "Come on, sweetheart. Let's go."

I set off across the lawn, the long grass tickling against my jean-clad legs and started to squeeze Harley and myself back through the gap in the fence. I wanted to get away from her sniping and go home.

I kept my back turned away from Lily Cruickshank. Crikey! How embarrassing was that?! Bursting into tears like that in front of a total stranger. But she had been so spiteful.

"Wait."

Her voice, calling out across the lawn, startled me. I was halfway through the broken section of fence.

I turned around.

Lily Cruickshank pursed her lips. "Did you drive here?"

"Yes."

"Well, you can't drive home like that." Conflict travelled across her features. "I don't want a car accident on my conscience." She pointed at me in a gruff gesture. "You had better come back with me. Pull yourself together first before you go anywhere."

She threw an awkward look over her shoulder. "I'll stick the kettle on."

I straightened up in surprise. I hadn't expected that. Even Harley shot me a look, as if to say, "I didn't see that coming either!"

I blinked and swiped my arm again across my damp cheeks. "Oh. Right. Thank you."

She threw her eyes to Harley by my feet. "And I suppose you had better bring her with you too. Lord only knows what other damage she could inflict if we don't keep an eye on her." She gestured to the back door. "I'll lock up here and see you round at the front." I watched her vanish in a swirl of skirt and a flap of the heavy fleece she was wearing. What was she doing inside Merry Wood? That obviously meant she could gain access to the house, which meant she held keys for the place. That was odd. Why, if the house was sitting deserted, would Lily Cruickshank still possess a set of keys, and what for?

I brushed some hair away from my damp eyes and pulled a curious face at Harley. Bloody hell. And now she was offering to make me a cup of tea. Maybe underneath Lily Cruickshank's concrete exterior beat a heart after all.

I headed round with Harley to the imposing entrance with

its heavy panelled door. Lily locked up and, making no comment, urged us to follow her.

We trailed behind her, like obedient ducklings following their mother.

Lily brushed aside the woodland branches that dipped and weaved like loose shoelaces, crossed the glade, and indicated to her more modest but pretty abode as it emerged through the trees.

The hanging baskets either side of Lily's front door swayed like little boats on a gentle tide.

"Door's open," she barked, as she bustled towards her flapping washing line strung between two ash trees in the back garden. "No need to lock your doors round here. Not like in the city where there are bloody robbers everywhere you turn."

No mugger would dare take you on, I thought to myself. But she still made sure Merry Wood was securely locked up again. I decided not to raise that point though, otherwise it would trigger another exchange of words between us.

"You can't miss the kitchen." She pointed to Harley. "Is she housetrained?"

"Yes. She picked it up very quickly."

"Only I've just mopped my kitchen floor and I don't want her leaving puddles all over it."

I assured her again that Harley wouldn't do that.

"All right. On you go then."

I arched my brows and headed towards Lily's front door. Harley gazed past me, still secured on her lead.

Sure enough, the galley-style kitchen was straight ahead down from the hallway, decked out with red and white gingham curtains and beech-panelled cupboards.

I tried not to stare at Lily's sitting room to my right. It was furnished with a duck-egg-blue sofa and two matching armchairs. Navy cushions and drapes contrasted the biscuit carpet. To the left was her bedroom. The door was pulled almost closed, giving a fleeting glimpse of a poppy-decorated bedspread and a heavy oval standing mirror.

I reached the kitchen and unclipped Harley's lead. "Now, don't let me down," I muttered to her out of the side of my mouth. "No leaving any deposits anywhere." I hadn't lied to Lily when I said she had picked up house training very fast, thanks to Mum and Dad's diligent training whilst I was at work. But if she got excited, she had been known to still emit the odd dribble.

Harley thudded her bottom onto the coffee-coloured laminated floor, as if to say, "Bloody cheek! I hope you're not referring to me!"

I heard Lily thudding down the hallway, cradling a plastic washing basket filled with the clean folded clothes plucked from the line. "Here," I insisted, jumping to my feet. "Let me help you."

She brushed aside my offer. "I may be getting on, but I'm not incapable – at least, not yet."

Lily dumped the plastic washing basket on the sink top, shrugged off her fleece and busied herself with her polka-dot teapot. She cast me a long look over the shoulder of her olive-green jumper. "So why did you get so upset?"

Wow. She didn't go in for small talk or approach a subject with delicacy.

Harley flopped onto her belly.

"It's been a bit of a strange time for me," I admitted after a few moments.

"Milk or sugar?"

"Just milk, thank you."

She nodded her silver head. Another pause. "So, are you going to tell me then or will you mime it and I have to guess?"

I watched her flit between the teapot and a mug tree. Should I tell her? I didn't know her. Was I being propelled into stupid mistakes, after my break-up with Miles? Maybe my head was still scrambled after all that.

It was as Lily was fussing over the teapot that I noticed her pause. She set the teapot to one side by the sink. One hand fluttered up to her chest. Her breathing became a little laboured, just like it had before when she spoke to me from her doorway.

"Mrs Cruickshank? Lily? Are you alright?"

I shot up from the kitchen table and moved towards her.

She dropped her hand back down by her side, drawing a steadying breath. "I'm fine, young lady. No need to make a fuss."

"Are you sure? You've gone rather pale."

Lilly batted her hand in mid-air, like she was swatting an annoying fly. "It's called old age. I'll be fine in a minute or two."

I examined her.

"Stop looking at me as though I'm some old, decrepit museum piece. I might look like one but I don't bloody feel it most of the time."

I wasn't convinced she was all right

She took a couple more breaths. After a few more minutes,

the colour returned to her cheeks and she busied herself with the teapot again.

"Are you sure you're feeling all right now? I could call a doctor…"

Lily rolled her eyes with irritation. "No thank you. I'm fine. So, are you going to tell me why you were getting so upset out there?"

I shook my head. "No. I'm not. Not until you tell me the truth, Mrs Cruickshank. That's twice now I have seen you look frail."

I sat back down at her kitchen table. What a stubborn woman she was.

"Well?"

She pulled an irritated face. "That's blackmail."

"I know."

Lily pressed her lips together in a disapproving way. "All right! All right. I was just recently diagnosed with a heart condition, so I have to take things a little easier."

"I thought as much."

Lily glowered at me. "Since when did you qualify as a doctor?"

Now it was my turn to pull a face at her. "What I mean is, I knew there was something wrong."

"There isn't anything wrong as such," she insisted, glugging some milk into a dinky milk jug. "I've just got to not rush around, that's all."

She eyed me. "My young lady doctor is nice enough, but she's overreacting. They don't know everything."

My lips twitched.

"And I don't want my personal business being spread

around Silver Ness, thank you very much. I've told you in confidence. Well, you literally forced it out of me,"

I tried not to smile. "You have my word that I won't tell anyone."

"Good."

I glanced around, admiring a vase of pretty white lilies on her kitchen windowsill. "How do you manage here on your own?"

"Perfectly well, thank you," she clipped. "They'll have to carry me out of here feet first. I'm not going anywhere." A softer look settled across her face for a few seconds. "This is my home. I belong right here. I always have done." Then she whipped her attention back to me, her tone more officious again.

"Right, young lady, I've confided in you about my minor health issue, so what about you?"

Minor? I thought. I was going to debate the point with her, but decided not to. I probably wouldn't win anyway. I sighed. "Where do you want me to start?"

"At the beginning is always best."

And so, before I could make a decision about what to tell her – or indeed how much to tell her – my concerns poured out of me in a torrent and I couldn't find the barrier. "The newspaper I've been working on for the past two years is being amalgamated and I've been made redundant. I've got another job in journalism, but it's on this intimidating magazine and I've been made the beauty writer, which is not what I wanted to do."

I paused, drawing a ragged breath, while Lily poured a stream of tea into two mugs and listened. "It turns out that the investigative reporter post – that's the one I applied for – has gone to the editor's niece."

Lily still didn't make any comment. She flicked me an unreadable expression.

"And I've just seen a photo of my ex-boyfriend in a media magazine and he's just got engaged to this gorgeous TV reporter." I let my hands flail about in frustration. "He's head of news at a TV station in England." A dry laugh escaped out of my throat. "Whenever I used to hint about us getting engaged, he would come out with a stream of excuses. He was happy enough for us to live together a lot of the time, but didn't want to commit himself. We only broke up earlier this year, so he hasn't wasted any time moving on."

I threw my head back, examining her painted ceiling. The pattern reminded me of whipped cream. "What with losing a job that I love, taking another one I'm not sure about, and then discovering my ex is getting married, life is pretty grotty at the moment."

She got up and fetched a saucer of water for Harley. She eased herself back into the wooden chair opposite. "I can't comment much on your job situation, but regarding your ex-boyfriend... sounds to me like you dodged a bullet there. I bet he's a right dick."

It was like hearing your grandmother reciting gangsta rap. I almost spluttered my mouthful of tea across the kitchen. I swallowed and set my mug back down. "Er, yes. It turns out he was."

"Well then," shrugged Lily. "He's someone else's problem now. Good luck to her. Sounds like she'll need it."

For something to do, I picked up my mug of tea again. I realised I was smiling against the rim. I took another mouthful.

"And the job problem?" she asked. "What's the issue there? Didn't you just say you've got employment elsewhere now?"

I drummed my fingers against the side of my mug. "Yes, but I was getting desperate. I applied for a few other jobs and was getting nowhere. Then I read about this investigative reporter vacancy at *Goddess* magazine. I applied for the job, but got offered the beauty writer post instead."

Lily's thin brows flexed, encouraging me to elaborate.

I let out a resigned sigh. "I've been landed with this difficult feature. I have to come up with this amazing beauty piece, featuring three of the UK's most successful models, for Avanti cosmetics." I rolled my eyes as I bent down to stroke Harley's dozing head. "Every suggestion I've made so far has been treated with disdain by my new boss."

"Like what?"

"Staging it in a train station, a hotel lobby, or on Silver Ness beach."

Lily's deep-set eyes bored into my crestfallen face. "She sounds like a right madam."

I almost spluttered my tea again with the irony. I wanted to say, "It takes one to know one," but seeing as I'd been caught in the garden at Merry Wood and Harley had damaged part of the fence, I didn't think I was in a position to take the high ground on anything.

Looking at Lily now, however, and listening to her no-nonsense approach, I was sure she would give Athena a run for her money in the assertiveness department.

"Do you know what I think?" she asked at length.

"What?"

She pushed her back deeper against her chair. "Give it time with this niece of hers. She's bound to trip over her own feet at some point and make a right cock-up of things."

I nodded and cradled the warm mug between my grateful fingers. My attention shifted out of Lily's kitchen window towards Merry Wood, where its roof was swallowing the sun and becoming a dark silhouette against the trees.

"You just work hard for this Athena woman and don't take any of her old nonsense. She's probably used to riding roughshod over folks, so if you show her you aren't prepared to put up with it, you will gain her respect. You see if you don't."

Lily's glance was stern. "I think if you want a ghost of a chance at success, you just have to buckle down and persuade yourself you can do it." She might not like you for it, but she will respect you."

I listened to her crisp, direct advice. It was funny Lily mentioning the word *ghost*. There was something spiritual and almost ethereal about those statues in the garden over at Merry Wood. I bet they would look amazing in photographs...

An idea pricked me. I pushed myself upwards in my chair. "Ghosts. That's it. That might work."

Lily frowned. "What?"

I thought of the Avanti make-up samples nestling in my desk drawer at work. They were promoting their new shades of eye colours in milk, silver, and gauze. My mind shot towards the statues in Merry Wood's garden again and the captivating water fountain with the hummingbird.

It was shadowy, with the imposing trees and the wintery

shades of white and cream of the flowers, not to mention the overgrown lawn. It would be perfect.

But I had one possible problem: Lily.

I leant forward on the table, my eyes pleading into hers. "Mrs Cruickshank," I began, a desperate waver creeping into my voice.

She blinked at me.

I took a deep breath. "I need to ask you a favour. A big one. Your mention of ghosts has given me a wonderful idea."

Chapter Fourteen

Lily slapped both hands on the edge of her kitchen table. "Are you joking, young lady? No. Perhaps you're pissed. Or have you been smoking something? Absolutely not."

"But Mrs Cruickshank, Merry Wood's garden is gorgeous. There's something ethereal about it and it would make an amazing backdrop for this cosmetics feature."

Lily's lined face closed down harder than a castle portcullis but I was undeterred. "You mentioned ghosts and what with Merry Wood's statues and all those trees, we could run with a ghost and spirits' theme. It's due to run in a special Christmas edition, so that would be perfect."

Her mouth twisted in disagreement. "No one is getting inside that house. I feel responsible for it." Her eyes brimmed with a misty look. "It means a lot to me. You have no idea how much..." Her voice died and she bit her tongue.

The temptation to ask Lily about her link to Merry Wood was pulling harder at me, but I resisted. She would refuse to tell me anything at all if she thought I was being nosey. I decided that could wait until another time. I would have to select my moment.

"Mrs Cruickshank, I'm not asking you to tell me anything you don't want to or to allow me into the house. It would just be access to the gardens for this photoshoot. That's all."

"That's all?" she echoed with incredulity. "You're not expecting much."

"I'm not expecting anything, I promise. That's why I'm asking you if I can use the gardens for the magazine feature." I hesitated, mentally couching how to phrase what to say next. "If you need to speak to the owners of Merry Wood and seek their permission, that's fine."

Lily flinched. She wrapped her arms around herself. "That won't be necessary."

What was going on between Lily and that house?

My fleeting optimism began to deflate as she shook her head. "No. I'm sorry."

She fell silent for a moment before she spoke again. "Leonie," faltered Lily. That was the first time she had used my name. She twisted her hands together on the circular table top. "I don't think Merry Wood appearing in some magazine is a good idea."

I decided to try a different approach. "Mrs Cruickshank, it's not just some magazine. It's *Goddess*. It's a glossy, classy publication that tackles various issues such as child poverty and modern slavery." I offered her a small, cajoling smile. "Unfortunately, I'm not investigating issues like that at the moment, seeing as I've been designated to other duties."

A considered silence settled between us.

"But you have my word that there would be no access allowed to the house. The property would be treated with the utmost respect."

I flicked her a begging look. "You have no idea how much you would be helping me, Mrs Cruickshank." I scrambled around inside my head for further persuasion. Athena was so keen to make this feature a stand-out, she wouldn't hesitate to approve extra expense.

"You would be entitled to payment too of course."

Lily's hooded eyes flicked upwards. "Payment, you say?"

"Yes. Of course. For your co-operation."

Lily's small mouth puckered with deliberation. As she agonised over my request, my attention was drawn to a broken bread maker stashed in the far corner of the kitchen. Lily's gaze followed mine. She stuck her chin out. "What are you looking at?"

"Your bread maker."

Lily laced and unlaced her hands. "What about it?"

"It looks like it might be broken."

Lily sniffed.

"I would make sure you were generously compensated so you could replace that and still have some money left over."

She mentally chewed over my proposition. She glanced down at the slumbering Harley and back up at me. "And you promise there would be no impact on the interior of the house?"

"None at all. I would make it clear that the photoshoot was in the garden and nowhere else."

Lily processed this. I could see conflict waging a war in her expression.

"You can trust me. One hundred percent."

Lily made an agonised sigh. "All right," she agreed after a few more moments, with a stiff nod of her thick silvery head. "You can use the gardens of Merry Wood for your magazine. But the inside of the house remains out of bounds. Is that clear?" She pursed her lips. "If there is so much as one plant trodden on in that garden, I will sue the lot of you and see if I don't."

I was so relieved and bouncing with excitement, I could have hugged her. But I didn't. She wouldn't have liked it. Instead, I thanked her so profusely, she told me to be quiet as I was making her uncomfortable.

Then she informed me she would make a fresh pot of tea.

"So, I thought about the metallic shadow on the models and having them pose like the statues beside them?"

Ebony, the make-up artist, nodded her braided hair at my suggestion. "I'll make sure each of them has bare lips then. Make it all about their eyes and complexions."

The garden of Merry Wood was throbbing with activity. Tall circular lights glowed like inquisitive eyes onto the grass. The three models were languishing in louche poses and the stylist and photographer were engaged in a heated discussion about "what constitutes fluidity and atmosphere".

It was a frosty morning in mid-November with the winter sun spreading her golden paintbrush over the tips of the trees and weaving across the long grass.

The fashion stylist from *Goddess*, Angelica, had brought

with her an array of wispy skirts, shirts, trousers, and tops in the flimsiest gauze and silk, together with long padded coats for the models to shrug on in between photos to stop their teeth chattering. As agreed, we had opted for shades to complement the new Avanti make-up range, so the clothes (such as they were) were all vanillas, steels, ghost grey, and marshmallow colours.

Ebony had slicked each of the three models' hair back from their chiselled faces, so that their mermaid shiny skin did all the talking.

I took a long, charged mouthful of my takeaway coffee. Thank goodness Athena had agreed to run with my idea. I had sold it to her, concentrating on the wild garden/statue vibe, stressing that spooky stories weren't just popular at Halloween, but at Christmas too (think Scrooge) and that it would be a great fit for our festive issue.

I had taken a series of pictures of the gardens on my phone to show her and she had marvelled at the atmosphere of it all.

Now, I was hovering about at 8am on this Monday morning, with the determined frost still glinting on the grass and a raft of sleepless nights worrying about it all still taking their toll on me.

The three models of the moment – Esther Drew, Carina Salazar, and the only male model out of the three, who was known simply as Dante – had been preened and glossed and were strutting backwards and forwards, mumbling to Baz, the photographer.

Like everyone else, I'd seen their faces gracing all the magazines, but having them up close now, in the middle of a sprawling garden early in the morning, was a strange experience. It was also an enlightening one.

Esther Drew never smiled. From what I could see, she didn't possess great teeth, but had a waterfall of dark-blonde hair and legs like a gazelle.

Dante was forever flexing his six-pack under his shirt and reminded me of a show pony. Carina Salazar was a dusky beauty who liked to sit and read self-improvement books between shots.

Baz asked Esther to drape herself around one of the Merry Wood statues. "Now tilt one of your cheese-grater cheeks against the statue, darling. That's it. Look at me. You're killing it! Killing it!"

I glanced up the lawn towards Merry Wood. It was as if the house were watching all the comings and goings, from those unoccupied still rooms of hers.

I promised Lily that the garden would be left how we found it. I had expected her to turn up on some pretext, to make sure no one was taking liberties, but there had been no sign of her so far.

Maybe she did trust me after all.

I hoped she did.

There had been puffs of smoke sailing out of her chimney as usual and a flap of clothes on her washing line when I'd first arrived this morning. At least she appeared to trust me a little more than she had done at the beginning, although that wouldn't have been difficult.

I breathed in a mixture of damp grass, earth, and woodsmoke as Esther strutted past Dante. He grinned, his dark eyes appreciating her.

Now it was Carina's turn to be photographed again.

Ebony finished applying the final touches to her base before Carina ventured over to the garden seat and arranged herself on it, all glossy black skin and dreamy expression.

She was wearing a transparent dress in cream that flowed to the floor. Her dark skin shone like satin.

Baz focused his camera on the glimmers of hammered silver shadow adorning her half-closed lids. "Gorgeous, sweetie!" He angled himself this way and that, leaping about like a demented Jack-in-the-box, snapping more pictures and murmuring.

When he was done and Carina got to her feet to dust herself down, Baz turned to me. "Right. Where's Dante?"

Baz's assistant, a timid-looking young female student in round red spectacles, approached. "Sorry, boss. I haven't seen him."

Baz rolled his eyes up towards the peak of his baseball cap. "Well, where's Esther? I'd like another one of her beside the male statue."

Ebony wiped her make-up-smeared fingers on one of her baby wipes. "No idea. I haven't seen her for a little while either."

Baz shot me an irritated look. "Any ideas, Leonie? We need to get this all wrapped up. I've got a flight to Milan at 3pm."

I scanned the garden. They couldn't have gone far, surely? They were both hardly wearing anything either and this was Scotland in November. "I'll go and have a look for them," I offered, keen for something to do.

I set off across the grass and back towards the house. The sunlight was bouncing off the windows and birdsong chattered from the trees. Had they disappeared together into the woods? Esther had been flirting like crazy with Dante from the off and his tongue had been lolling out like a cartoon wolf every time she so much as spoke to him.

Oh God, don't tell me I was about to discover the two of them in flagrante under a hedgerow!

I moved down the side of the house to take a look but neither of them was there, so I doubled back. I couldn't hear them, let alone see them, which was a blessing at least. Where the hell had they gone?

I took a left and ventured out into the woodland beyond. "Ms Drew? Dante?" There was no reply, except for the trampling of my long boots on twigs.

I returned to the gardens of Merry Wood. Oh, this was ridiculous! How difficult was it to lose two famous six-foot-tall fashion models?

Baz was shifting from foot to foot. "Well?"

I started to say I hadn't been able to find them when Ebony strode towards me. She raised one lacquered nail and pointed towards the house. "I think I know where they are."

Relief swamped me. "Oh great! Where?"

Ebony nodded towards Merry Wood. "They're in the house."

My breath stilled. *What?!*

I swung round, my voice cracking with apprehension. What the hell were they doing inside the house? They knew they weren't allowed in there!

No. They couldn't be. None of us had a key. My nerves jangled.

"They aren't allowed access to the house," I gasped. "It was in the contract. We all agreed to it. There are bloody Portaloos over there if they have a call of nature."

I followed the direction of Ebony's pointing finger, hoping that she had been mistaken.

But sure enough, Esther and Dante were silhouetted in the kitchen window, their tongues stuck down each other's throats.

"Leonie, I don't think they've gone in there to spend a penny," muttered Ebony.

"Shit!" I snarled to anyone that would listen, panic and resentment swilling around inside of me. "How dare they! I gave Lily my word." I whirled back to Ebony. "Do you know how they got in?"

But I didn't give Ebony time to answer. I was already picking up speed, trampling over the grass in wider strides. What would Lily think if she found out? I had made a solemn promise to her. She had trusted me.

White-hot fury burned brighter in my chest. What the hell did they think they were doing?

As I grew closer, I began to realise.

I reached the back door of Merry Wood, furious breath scalding the back of my throat. I had been so preoccupied with locating the pair of them, I failed to notice as I'd passed by the back door a few minutes ago that it had been prized open.

A cacophony of dismay, embarrassment, and guilt erupted inside of me. This was my fault.

What the hell was I going to say to Lily?

I eased myself through the gap in the half-open back door. The house was quiet, cold, and expectant. I moved through the retro-style kitchen, where Esther and Dante had been a few minutes ago. I shoved aside the dangling, multi-coloured beads at the kitchen entrance. They clattered and swung in my wake.

It was so strange being inside Merry Wood, rather than looking in through her giant, sleepy windows. It was like I had been gazing at a snow globe and now found myself inside. I just wished it was under different circumstances.

I drew up in the chintz-carpeted hall. It smelled of mothballs and emptiness. There was the faint rhythmical tick of a clock from somewhere.

A torrent of giggles and male laughter erupted from somewhere. It made me pull up. I could feel my teeth grinding harder with temper.

Where the hell were they and what were they doing?

I followed the direction of the voices. I tried not to imagine the expression on Lily's face if she could see what was happening. I had to get these two selfish idiots out of the house and fast.

There was a closed door to my left, which I guessed was the sitting room. I planted my ear against the heavy oak door. More laugher travelled out.

My jaw tightened. They were both in there.

How rude and inconsiderate! Bad enough they had got inside, but the fact that they had forced their way in fuelled my embarrassment and rage.

I reached for the handle and grasped it, my knuckles flaring white, and yanked it open. I was met with a heavy square stone fireplace, dark furniture, and the sight of Esther Drew and Dante pulling at each other's clothes as they writhed against the far wall.

Esther's half-closed eyes shot open at the sight of me standing there. She let out a shriek and buried her face in Dante's shoulder.

I realised my mouth was opening and closing. I struggled to speak. "What the hell is going on here? What do you think you're doing?"

Dante let go of Esther and began to button up his flapping shirt. "I don't mean to be rude, but what do you think it looks like?"

I folded my arms, my throat dry with boiling tempter. "You know you aren't allowed access to the inside of the house. That was made clear in the brief weeks ago."

Dante flapped one tanned hand. "Chill out, will you? It was just a bit of fun."

"Fun?" I choked. "I was given permission to use the gardens here, based on trust. You all signed that contract. You read the brief. Thank goodness Mrs Cruickshank isn't here."

My heart stilled as Esther's false lashes went rigid. She was staring at something – or someone – past my shoulder. Her cheeks sizzled.

"I am here," ground out a familiar, throaty voice. "And I want an explanation, Leonie. Right now."

Chapter Fifteen

P *lease just let the ground open up and swallow me whole.*
    I spun round, my heart galloping. "Mrs Cruickshank, I'm so sorry. Please let me explain…"

But she wasn't listening. She was too preoccupied by the sight of Esther Drew and Dante, all shiny cheekbones and dishevelled clothes.

She snapped her head back to me. The disappointed pain-filled flecks in her eyes punched me in the stomach. "I thought I could trust you, Leonie. I told you no one was allowed in the house. You promised."

"I had no idea," I protested. "If I had…" My voice vanished.

I whipped my head back to Esther and Dante, who were now standing side by side like a pair of admonished school children.

I wanted to grab both of them by their shirt collars and give them a ruddy good shake. I didn't care that these two were famous fawned-over celebrities. I was far more concerned that Lily thought I'd betrayed her; that I'd thanked her by letting her down. I turned my full ire on Esther and Dante. "Can you leave please? Now!"

Esther Drew opened her rosebud mouth but Dante gave her a fierce dig in the ribs with his elbow to silence her.

He slunk past with an apologetic smile. Esther followed with a belligerent jut of her chin.

When they had vanished back out into the garden, I broke into a series of shame-filled apologies. "I'm so sorry, Mrs Cruickshank. They forced the back door open. If I had known for one minute they would do something like that…"

Her rheumy eyes raked over the tired furniture and curtains. "I should never have said yes to this silly suggestion of yours, Ms Baxter." Resignation settled around her mouth. "More to the point, I should never have trusted you."

Her disappointment in me pulled at her shoulders.

I watched her whirl away from me in her ankle boots, sending the beaded curtain in the kitchen into a crashing frenzy.

"Mrs Cruickshank. Lily. Please. I'm sorry." I started after her, down the narrow hallway. The carriage clock let out its weary, rhythmical ticks.

I was anxious to explain. I wanted her to know that I felt dreadful about what had happened. It had taken a lot for her to place her trust in me. Whatever this house meant to her – and it was clear it meant a great deal – she had entrusted Merry Wood to me for a short time.

A crushing, horrified embarrassment engulfed me as I made an attempt to catch up with her.

I was so anxious that my elbow caught the edge of a rickety bureau as I was dashing past in hot pursuit.

The top drawer was stuffed with papers and my knocking against it sent the whole drawer hurtling towards the russet carpet. "Ow!"

I rubbed my elbow and cursed at the sharp pain, as the drawer contents spilled everywhere, as if in slow motion. Papers slipped and slid on top and across one another.

Great. Just great. Can this day get any better?

I stood there mentally flapping about for a few moments. I knew I should go after Lily and apologise for those two idiots, but I also knew I couldn't walk out and leave this mess in the middle of the hall. What would Lily think, if she returned to see all this?

I had made a monumental cock-up of today as it was.

Releasing a loud and frustrated groan, I dropped down onto my knees and began scooping up the assorted bills, receipts, and correspondence.

As I slapped them back in the drawer, I noticed the letters and bills were all addressed to a Mr & Mrs F Talbot.

My thoughts screeched to a halt.

Talbot. That was the name April from the council mentioned as the owners of Merry Wood.

I rifled through a couple more papers, snatching quick glances at who they were addressed to. Sure enough, the other pieces of correspondence were addressed to a Mr Flynn Talbot. Most of them seemed to be utility bills and gardening invoices from years ago.

I continued to put the papers back, groaning under my breath. I had to speak to Lily again and time was racing.

From the garden, I could hear the plummy vocals of Esther Drew and the sound of Baz packing up his photographic equipment. Then it would be back to the offices of *Goddess* to write up the feature about Avanti's "stunning shades of the latest eye colours. Opt for vanillas and greys that will make your natural beauty sing this festive season."

I was plopping the last few documents back into the drawer and was preparing to pick it up from the floor to slot it back into the bureau when a long, slim white envelope caught my eye. It must have skittered further across the carpet.

I angled the drawer back into place and once it was as secure as I could manage, I retrieved the stray envelope. *Lily* was written in swirling black fountain pen on the front of it.

I turned it over. It wasn't sealed, as I would have expected. Did Lily know there was a letter in that drawer addressed to her? Had she read it?

I would return it to her. Whether she had seen it or not, it would be a good excuse to go to her house and hand it over in person. It would give me the opportunity to try and talk to her again about what had just happened and apologise properly.

I was about to stick it into my back jeans pocket when Baz's irritated voice from the garden made me jump. "Leonie. What the hell are you doing? Stop arsing around in the haunted house, will you? I need to get going."

The letter to Lily slid from the envelope and I just managed to capture it in my flustered fingers. "Ok! Sorry. On my way, Baz."

The writing paper smelled of lavender and had partially unfolded in my hands.

I knew I shouldn't read it. It wasn't mine to read. But the artful handwriting and its opening sentences captured my attention.

And so, I stood there, in the hallway of Merry Wood, and found myself transfixed by this letter.

Chapter Sixteen

13 March 1973

My darling Lily,

I didn't know how to tell you, so please forgive me for writing this letter. It is one I hoped I would never have to write.

Please believe me when I say I knew nothing about this until Astrid told me this morning.

I have spent all day agonising over this. All I know is that I love you with all my heart and always will. I realise we've only known each other less than a year, but I knew from the moment I saw you that you were the only woman I could love.

Astrid's charity has offered to send her to Africa for a year. She's desperate to go and I'm sure you can guess what I'm about to say.

I don't want to go, but I have no option. I can't be parted from my son across the other side of the world for that length of time.

I know you will be angry with me and I don't blame you. But you must know that nothing will change how I feel about you. You are the love of my life and nothing will ever alter that.

It has all happened so quickly, I'm struggling to make sense of it. Final arrangements are being made, but it looks like we will be leaving Scotland for Africa within the next few days. We will arrange for Merry Wood to be rented out for twelve months, until our return.

I know I have no right to ask this of you and that I have no call on you, but I hope you can find it in your heart to forgive me for leaving you for a year – and that you will be prepared to wait for me.

I would love to be able to write to you from Africa, provided that wouldn't cause you any difficulty or awkwardness with Bernard.

I hope you will be happy to write back to me.

My address will be The Sunrise House in Durban but I will give you more details when it is confirmed.

I know our feelings for one another are wrong, but you and I both know that we are trapped in loveless marriages.

We belong together, Lily. You know we do. One day, we will be.

All my love,
Flynn. X

Oh my God. Flynn. Flynn Talbot. Had Lily ever read this letter? Did she even know it existed?

Baz yelled again for me from the garden and I flinched, disturbed by his bellows. "Ok! On my way!"

I folded up the letter and slipped it back into the envelope. I carefully popped it into the back pocket of my jeans. I had to deliver this letter to Lily. It belonged with her.

I stared at my surroundings of embossed old-fashioned

wallpaper, the rattling beaded kitchen curtain and the creaky leather furniture. Was that why Lily was so protective of Merry Wood? Because it was the connection to Flynn and to happy times in her past, and she didn't want to lose them.

But what had happened to the Talbots? Why was the house sitting empty like this?

I was only half listening to Baz prattling on about deadlines. As soon as he packed up and the three models had been swept away in their respective tinted SUVs, I hurried from Merry Wood and across the sun-stippled woodland to Lily's cottage.

My stomach and my heart were swooping. She would know I'd read her letter, but what could I do?

I arrived at her front door, the polished panels of glass capturing the marmalade sun from her windows. I wouldn't blame her if she slammed the door in my face.

As I hovered there, clutching the letter in my apprehensive, charged hands, I quickly came to the realisation Lily wasn't even prepared to do that. I was certain I caught sight of a figure hovering behind her sitting room curtains, but if Lily was home, it soon became clear she wasn't going to answer the door to me.

I lingered for a few moments more. "Lily," I called out. "Mrs Cruickshank. I'm very sorry. If I had thought for one moment that those two cretins were capable of doing something like that…"

There was the faint flutter of towels drying on her washing line.

"Anyway, I have a letter to give to you." I hesitated as I stared down at the delicate paper. Was I doing the right thing?

I'd discovered a letter addressed to her inside Merry Wood. She would be imagining me prowling around with my journalistic hat on. She would wonder how I came to find it.

After a couple more moments of inwardly debating whether to tell Lily about the letter from Flynn Talbot, I knew I had to make a decision. She wouldn't believe I found it by accident. She didn't trust me now as it was.

I lingered at the letterbox.

Then I let out a long, low breath and set my shoulder bag down by my feet. I rummaged inside for my notebook and pen. I leant against one of Lily's garden chairs and scribbled an IOU for £100 to Lily, then I tore another page out of my reporter's notebook and dashed off a note:

Dear Mrs Cruickshank,

My sincere apologies again for what just happened.

I feel awful about it. I shall be making a formal complaint to my editor about the two individuals' behaviour. In the meantime, please accept this IOU for £100 to put towards the cost of the damage of the back door of Merry Wood. Let me know the details, so that I can arrange transfer of the money.

I stress again that I shall be raising this incident with my editor as soon as I return to the office today.

Leonie Baxter.

I wrapped the note around the IOU and slipped it through the letterbox. Then I made my way back to my car, taking Flynn Talbot's letter to Lily with me. I would have to decide what to do about the letter and what was the best way to return it to her.

The lonely figure of Lily Cruickshank was stationed behind her sitting room curtains, watching me leave.

───────────

"Leonie. A word please."

Athena was resplendent in ruffled buttercup-yellow blouse and flared trousers. She jerked her immaculate head, indicating for me to follow her into her office.

The "thank Christ I'm not you" expressions of my magazine colleagues said it all.

I deposited my bag on top of my desk and, returning Orion's supportive smile, did as I was told. I knew what this would be about. It must be to discuss the Esther Drew and Dante scenario.

No sooner had Athena's frosted-glass office door glided shut than she swirled round to face me like a yellow tornado. "What is all this crap I hear about you, Esther, and Dante? She was on the verge of making a complaint."

I blinked at her. "*She* was on the verge of complaining? Are you joking?"

Athena stared me down as she seated herself at her glossy desk, but I remained standing. "She and Dante gained entry to Merry Wood when they were expressly told not to."

She attempted to frown, but her forehead remained immobile and smooth like an egg. "Merry Wood?"

"The house where we did the Avanti shoot this morning."

"Oh yes. Of course. And?"

"And they forced their way in through the back door, so they could have sex in there."

Athena processed this through narrowed eyes. "Are you sure?"

I stared across at her as she slid a gold pen backwards and forwards with her ringed fingers. "Well, they weren't watering the house plants."

When Athena delivered one of her infamous Darth Vader glowers, I cleared my throat.

"Absolutely. I saw them both with my own eyes. Why?"

"Because Esther maintains they just wanted to take a look around the house. She's very interested in architecture."

I snorted. "That's rubbish! She's lying. They weren't in there to appreciate the flocked wallpaper."

Athena studied me.

"They had no right," I managed, my anger peaking again at the memory of Lily's evident disappointment and hurt. "I promised Mrs Cruickshank that nobody would enter the house and yet Esther and Dante went in there when they were clearly instructed not to."

Athena pushed some papers around her desk. "Look Leonie, I know you made a promise to the old dear."

My jaw ground with disapproval at the dismissive way Athena was talking about Lily.

"And what Esther and Dante did was rather naughty, seeing as they were on a shoot, but you have to see it from my point of view."

Rather naughty?

I could feel behind me, even through the panoramic office glass, that my colleagues were doing their best to look busy, but their heads continued to bob up from their screens and then down again like meercats.

Athena steepled her long fingers together under her chin. "*Goddess* is an established magazine, but it does have its competitors. I want us to be the best out there and in order to achieve that, we need the pick of the best models and celebs." She made a frustrated noise. "If we go upsetting and offending people like Esther Drew, it's not going to do our circulation or reputation any good in the longer term."

I pushed myself forward, my nerves biting. Athena was such an intimidating figure, with her razor-sharp nose and perfect lipstick, but this was a load of crap!

"Athena, it took a lot of persuasion on my part to assure Mrs Cruickshank she could trust me. Thanks to those two breaking in through the back door, I'm the one who not only feels she has let this lady down, I'm also one hundred pounds lighter."

"Sorry?"

I flicked her a look. "I wrote an IOU for one hundred pounds and popped it through Mrs Cruickshank's letterbox, to put towards the cost of repairing the damage to the door."

Athena considered all this.

"Mrs Cruickshank came into the house and saw Esther Drew and Dante half-naked, about to have each other against the sitting room wall. I felt awful about it."

Athena kicked out her heeled legs under her desk. "Yes. Well, I'll arrange for a huge bouquet of flowers to be sent to this Mrs Cruickshank. That should do it."

That should do it?

Now it was my turn for my eyebrows to rise up to my hairline. Something was telling me it would take far more than a bunch of orchids to win round Lily Cruickshank.

"In future, Leonie, I ask that you think before you speak. We are working with unpredictable creative types in this industry."

My mouth dropped open. So, the fact that Esther Drew and Dante were about to copulate after having trespassed was because they were "creative types"?

I mentioned this to Athena. "Trespassing is a criminal offence, as I'm sure you are aware, Athena. Mrs Cruickshank would be well within her rights to make a complaint to the police for breaking and entering too, not to mention that she could sue us for violation of our contract."

Athena's hard, green eyes suddenly shone with alarm.

"I think all this is being blown rather out of proportion, don't you?"

I shook my head. "No, in fact, I don't."

Athena's flat mouth indicated she thought I shouldn't have said anything to begin with. So, I should just have left them to it?

"I know you worked on a little local paper before coming here and it must all be a bit of a culture shock for you..."

I struggled to contain my incredulity. All right, perhaps *The Silver Ness News* was a small local paper, but at least the three of us possessed morals!

"But things are done differently here."

You're telling me.

Athena bathed me in one of her self-indulgent smiles that didn't reach her eyes.

"I agree that Esther and Dante shouldn't have done what they did, but there is every chance we will have to use them again in a future issue and we must maintain good relationships with models like them, who are held in such high regard."

I wanted to point out that there were other models out there.

"Yes, well, that's something I've been thinking about," I replied, hovering across from her desk with pent-up frustration. "Why can't we have a future issue where we use real people as models?"

Athena looked like she had just sat on a pin. "I beg your pardon?"

"Real people," I reiterated to her pinched expression. "Real readers, not professional models."

She almost sniggered. "But why on earth would we do that?"

Oh, dear Lord.

"Because it is these women who are actually spending their hard-earned money on our magazine. If they thought there was a chance they could appear between the pages of *Goddess*..."

"*Goddess* is an aspiration," rallied Athena. "It is a way of life. A state of mind. If we start featuring real readers, where will we be? You'll be telling me we should start including makeovers next!"

That had in fact been my next suggestion. I buttoned my lips together. How I longed for the arguments over gull-droppings on the Silver Ness harbour wall and stories of library books being returned thirty years late.

"But that is precisely my point," I answered. "We want *Goddess* readers to feel included—"

Athena rose up snake-like up from her desk and stalked to

her office door. She tugged it open in a flash of cranberry nails. "Thank you, Leonie. We'll consider this matter closed." She bit her lip. "You do, however, seem to have an unfortunate habit of upsetting people. I don't want any more complaints of this nature. Understood?"

Upsetting people? I opened my mouth, my incandescence boiling over, and then thought better of it.

It was obvious Athena was referring to the Tilly Crabtree and Glorious foundation incident.

I marched back to my desk, festering with indignation. If upsetting people meant being honest and not making up bare-faced lies, then she could stick it up her—

"Oh, Leonie," travelled Athena's throaty voice across the sea of heads, as she prepared to retreat back into her office. "I'll make sure you're compensated for that little door."

I sat at my desk for the remainder of the afternoon, seething like a volcano that was about to erupt.

Guilt clung to me about what had happened and not being able to explain it to Lily had made the whole situation take on an even greater and troubling significance.

I made a start on writing up copy for the Avanti cosmetics feature, but I kept throwing out the usual clichés and deleting it. In the end, I parked the article to one side and produced the letter to Lily from my back pocket. My eyes grazed the handwriting again.

I knew I should have returned it to Lily straightaway, whether she knew about it or not. But it hadn't helped that she'd refused to answer her door and a letter like that wasn't something you crammed through someone's letterbox with a, "And oh, yes, I found this. See ya!"

I didn't want her to think any less of me than she already did.

Some of my work colleagues had already slunk off for the evening, proclaiming urgent interviews to conduct or drinky-poos with valuable contacts. There was no sign of Athena either. She had brayed to Orion that she was meeting up with the PR of a high-end fashion house for lunch and hadn't been seen since.

While the Glasgow traffic thrummed outside, I smoothed the passionate letter out and entered the name *Flynn Talbot* into the search engine.

I decided to have a trawl through Facebook first. I suspected it wouldn't be a common name, or at least it didn't sound like it.

How old would this gentleman be now, that's if he was even still alive? Mid-seventies, going by Lily's age when she opened her bakery. Would he use Facebook or social media at all? Was he still living in Scotland? I concluded it was worth a shot.

It transpired from my search that there were three people with the name Flynn Talbot. One was a twenty-five-year-old surfer-type living in Los Angeles. Another was a forty-year-old glass blowing artist based in the South of France. It didn't look like the Flynn Talbot I was searching for could be either of them.

I clicked onto the third and last Flynn Talbot profile, my feelings of pessimism twisting in my stomach.

A profile photo of Loch Lomond for this particular Flynn Talbot glimmered out of the screen. Ok. So, no photo of him. But it was a picture of one of Scotland's most famous landmarks. Could he be Lily's Flynn – or perhaps be able to lead me to him?

Come on, Leonie, I chided myself. Don't get too carried away.

Nevertheless, I took an excited, hopeful breath, prayed I might be onto something, and began to read.

Chapter Seventeen

F lynn Talbot's profile was sparse.

It consisted of beautiful photographs of landscapes and monuments, rather than pictures of himself, family, friends, or even grandchildren. In fact, his personal details were non-existent too, apart from his place of birth, which said Darroch, a little market town about half an hour's drive from Silver Ness.

That gave me an injection of optimism, as I sat there in the now empty office. It must be him, seeing as he was born in the area.

I scrolled down his Facebook posts, hoping for some crumb of information or a photo of him, but they were either more artistic Scottish sunsets or comments about books and films. He seemed to be a huge fan of Clint Eastwood and spaghetti westerns.

Was he married? Divorced? Widowed? Did he have a squad of grandchildren? It seemed unlikely given that, again, there were no photos or proud boasts, but perhaps he just wasn't that type of man?

In his letter to Lily, Flynn Talbot had mentioned a son though.

I sat further back in my desk chair and chewed my lip. What the hell was I going to say to him? "Hi there. I stumbled across a love letter you sent to Lily Cruickshank fifty years ago. Remember her?"

I wound a finger around one of my errant curls. If Flynn Talbot wasn't interested in dredging up the past, then so be it. No harm done. But the way I caught Lily gazing at Merry Wood, lost in days gone by... She was so protective of that house too. Something told me there was unfinished business there and she needed closure.

Whatever had happened between Lily Cruickshank and Flynn Talbot all those years ago, it wasn't healthy for someone to be so preoccupied with an abandoned house. I think her heart went to Africa with him. And it was still with him. Even now.

I thought too about the couple of odd turns she had experienced – her skin growing pale and her breathing becoming laboured. What if she was really ill? This might be the only chance she would have to see him again.

My fingers hovered over the mouse. Was I going to do this? She might be furious with me for interfering, but I was doing it with the best of intentions. It felt like the right thing to do.

Refusing to debate it a second longer, I clicked the cursor on the Message button and began to type, the rattling of my keyboard echoing.

After drafting and deleting several attempts at a short but concise-sounding piece of correspondence, I came up with something I hoped would elicit a response:

Dear Mr Talbot,
Please excuse me for troubling you.
My name is Leonie Baxter. I'm a journalist and a friend of Lily Cruickshank.

Ok, describing myself as her friend was rather an exaggeration.

I accidentally came across a letter you wrote to her a number of years ago and wondered if you might be interested in reaching out to her?

I then quoted my email address and mobile number.

Should you wish to make contact with Lily, please do not hesitate to let me know.
Thank you for your time.
Yours sincerely,
Leonie

I read over the composed message again, my fingers loitering above the keys. I dismissed a stab of hesitancy. Lily couldn't keep living like that, obsessing over that empty house. She had to move on. We all did in the end, I concluded, trying not to conjure up more pictures of Miles.

I pressed *Send* and let out a long, low breath.

Ok, so if anything did come of it, Lily would no doubt want to disembowel me with a teaspoon, but this might just offer her the opportunity to cast off the shackles of years ago.

I admit I was very curious about Merry Wood too and wanted to know more. My journalist's intuition for a story was well and truly piqued.

———

The next few days vanished in a flurry of beauty write-ups, a phone interview I conducted with the new CEO of a skincare company whose packaging was made from recycled paper, and a number of Athena's infamous team meetings, which were really butt-kicking exercises under a different name – whether the staff needed their butts kicked or not.

I dipped into my Facebook messages but there had been no response from Flynn Talbot. Perhaps my optimism had been misplaced. If it was him, maybe he wanted the past to remain where it was and whatever had happened between him and Lily was, as far as he was concerned, confined to history. There was also the subject of his wife, Astrid, to whom he had referred in the letter, and the question of whether she was still alive.

If Flynn Talbot didn't want to revisit those days, what could I do?

I was musing over whether Flynn Talbot was busy, suffering from ill-health, or had simply decided to ignore my message when another dark thought imbedded itself. Oh blimey. What if he had passed away? I checked his account again and saw that it was several weeks since he had posted anything – a photograph of a stream under a mingling sunrise sky of raspberry and gold.

Athena's burgundy lowlights emerged from around her office door, startling me. "Team update folks. In my office now please."

"Not again," groaned Cole over the top of his PC. "We're in and out of that sodding office like it's got a revolving door."

I picked up my notebook and pen and followed the others into Athena's gleaming glass domain.

I noticed her niece, Kerry, was already situated at the oblong meeting table. She delivered an awkward smile and I returned it.

Orion was last to traipse in, once she'd activated the office voicemail system while we were all out of action.

Good grief. How different was all this compared to the casual staff meetings we used to have at *The Silver Ness News*. Doug would saunter back from the cakeshop with glistening Danish pastries and we would devour those over steaming mugs of tea, whilst contemplating life in general and whether the latest issue of the paper could have been improved upon.

Then there would be a running joke about misspellings and grammatical errors. They hadn't happened very often, thank goodness, but when they did, they tended to be real crackers.

We had printed the likes of "Mrs Allison presenting Mr Alcock with his cricket award for his googlies" and "Buy Carpets R Us – perfect for a good, hard shag."

A pang took me unawares. I missed Frances, with her predilection for whacky nail colours, and I missed Doug's dry wit and creased ties. I was so grateful to have another job in journalism. Of course, I was. But I still also longed for the tang of the sea waltzing in through the office windows whilst we worked. The office would be no more in a few weeks' time. I resolved to take Harley for a walk along the beach front and see it again before it closed for good. A melancholy weight pressed down on me, until I realised Athena was staring at me.

I scrambled my brain to attention and pushed myself straighter in my seat.

Athena surveyed us all. "This short meeting is really just to keep you all up to speed and to let you know that Kerry will be investigating the inflated prices of a new skincare range launched by the comedian Lulu Stark."

My brow creased with confusion. Surely, I should be leading on a story like that, seeing as I was the beauty writer? I became aware of several sets of charged eyes zooming in my direction, watching my response. Some of my colleagues must have thought the same.

It was still only Orion and me that were aware that Kerry was Athena's niece, and from the snippets Orion had been able to feed me, Kerry had no training or journalistic background as it was. Lord knows how much longer that little gem could be kept a secret.

I cleared my throat and decided to confront the wrath of Athena.

I pushed my right hand upwards. "Sorry to interrupt, Athena, but seeing as this is a beauty-related story, I would have thought that as the beauty writer here at *Goddess*..."

Athena pinned me to my chair with her laser beam look.

Kerry squirmed beside her. "I appreciate that, Leonie, but seeing as this is an investigative news story, I felt it would be more appropriate for Kerry to take the lead on this one." Her lip sticked mouth bared a few challenging teeth.

Kerry couldn't bring herself to look me in the face. She doodled in her notebook; her chocolate lashes trained downwards.

The meeting rambled on for another ten minutes, covering Cole's suggestion of a pull-out of the best (and presumably most expensive) eateries in Scotland and a brief chat about Brandy's idea of a competition where the top prize was a spa weekend for one reader and their dog.

Sometimes I did feel as if I were inhabiting someone else's hallucination.

Athena dismissed us soon afterwards, swinging her sharp shoulder blades back towards her PC screen.

Resentment burned bright inside of me.

"Leonie?"

I turned around to see a shamefaced Kerry hovering by the breakout area. "Could I have a word please?" She reminded me of a ghostly, awkward schoolgirl loitering there.

"Sure."

My indignation at her aunt's decision to put her on such a prominent story bubbled on. I wasn't proud of it, but Kerry's embarrassment pricked my conscience.

We plonked ourselves down on two uncomfortable white abstract-looking chairs.

"I wanted to apologise," she rushed in a panicked voice. "I promise you that this was not my idea, putting me on this Lulu Stark story."

She didn't give me a chance to comment. She carried on talking in a more urgent tone. "It was all Aunt Athena's... I mean, Athena's idea." Her cheeks lit up. "Shit. I wasn't supposed to..." She clamped her mouth shut.

"It's ok," I assured her. "I know she's your aunt. Orion told me."

The colour in her cheeks deepened. "Oh."

"Don't worry. I won't say anything, but I do think the rest of the team should be told sooner rather than later. It isn't fair keeping something like that from them. If it comes out by accident, it will cause a lot of ill-feeling."

She raised her troubled dark-green gaze up to the textured ceiling. "I agree with you. It's all this cloak and dagger stuff. Aunt Athena insists I need to prove myself first though and then we can tell the rest of the *Goddess* team."

She pulled a face. "She said if we do it that way then nobody can say anything about nepotism... if I prove I can do the job on my own terms."

She rubbed at her eyes. "My parents wish I were more outgoing. I found out they spoke to Athena and she jumped in and said it would do me the world of good to have some responsibility thrust upon me."

Flickers of empathy for this poor young woman reared up in me. "Sink or swim, is that the idea?"

Kerry waited until one of the advertising reps wobbled past in a pair of Perspex platforms. "Something like that, although the way I'm feeling right now, I'm close to drowning."

I offered her a small smile of comfort. That sounded very familiar.

Kerry knotted her fingers together on top of the table.

"Orion told me you were up for the investigative reporter's job."

"Yes. I was."

Her shoulders disappeared into her lacy shirt. "Oh God." She ran an embarrassed hand down her glowing face. "I'm so sorry. I feel awful about it."

I pretended it didn't matter. I didn't want to make Kerry feel any shabbier than she did, but it still smarted.

Kerry looked at me, as though she could tell that was the case and I was trying to bluff it out. "I'm here under false pretences, Leonie. Nepotism is alive and well. I'm not a trained journalist. You might have guessed as much." She chewed her bottom lip. "Athena has put me on this story and I haven't a clue what I'm doing."

I offered her what I hoped was an understanding smile. "What did you do before?"

Kerry's blush deepened, clashing with her straight hazelnut hair. "I got my degree in marketing last year, but was going to take a year out before deciding what I wanted to do with my life." She rolled her eyes. "My parents and my aunt had other ideas."

Poor young woman. If Kerry's mum and dad were anything like Athena, she didn't stand a chance. Shame nipped at me. I had felt so resentful of her; stung and bruised that I'd been passed over, when all the time Kerry hadn't wanted the job of investigative reporter in the first place.

"Will you help me?" she erupted.

I stared at her pleading face. "Sorry?"

"Will you help me investigate these Lulu Stark claims? Please?"

I stuttered, not sure what to say. "Kerry, please don't think I'm being unhelpful here, but I'm not sure about that. Your aunt might not like it. She might think I'm stepping on your toes or trying to side-line you to get my hands on this story myself."

Kerry shook her head of hair fiercely under the breakout area lights. "No, she wouldn't. I'd make it clear to her that I asked you for help." She shot forward in her chair. "Please Leonie. Look, if it would make you any happier, I won't tell Athena you're giving me a hand. Well, not until we have the piece written up. By then it would be too late for her to do anything or complain anyway."

My thoughts leapfrogged over one another. It would be a wonderful story to be involved in, but if Athena thought I'd deceived her, I could be risking my own job. And what with the couple of clashes that had taken place already…

"A shared by-line," burst out Kerry with increasing desperation. "How does that sound?"

Temptation drilled its way deeper. "That's if Athena agrees to it."

Kerry's eyes glittered like jade jewels. "Oh, she would agree to it, otherwise it might come to light about her getting a bit too friendly with her best friend's husband at last year's *Goddess* Christmas party."

My mouth pinged open. "Are you serious?"

"Deadly. My mother was here at the party and saw her." She shot me a look. "It's about time I stood up to her. I've got to start being more assertive, so why not now?"

"You sound like your aunt."

She forced a smiled. "I don't know if that's a good thing or not."

A few seconds ticked past.

"So, Leonie, is that a yes? You'll help me with this story?"

The enticing pull of the opportunity and the tug of Kerry's begging features was too much to handle. "Ok. Ok. Let's do this. Bloody hell, I must be mad."

Kerry let out a long, low, relieved rush of air. "Thank you. Thank you so much. I haven't slept for the last few nights, worrying about it all."

"Well, please don't lose any more sleep," I reassured her. "But not a word to Athena until we're done on this story, ok? And don't mention anything to any of the others, otherwise it could find its way back to your aunt."

Kerry nodded. "I promise." Her features softened. "I owe you one."

I returned to my desk, my head swimming with what I'd just agreed to.

I flicked a guilty look towards Athena's office, but she had her back turned to me and was occupied on the phone. She wouldn't be at all happy that Kerry and I hadn't cleared it with her, but we would deal with the nuclear fallout from that later.

I took up my seat again and resumed typing up my piece about jewel-tipped fake eyelashes. I glanced down at my mobile. Athena wouldn't permit phones in any of her meetings and so they remained on our desks. There was a message alert.

I picked it up and clicked on it. The message was from Facebook. Could it be...?

I couldn't stifle a weird inhaling noise.

"Are you ok, Leonie?" asked Brandy, wandering past with a herbal tea.

I snapped my head up. "Yes. Fine, thanks."

My attention drilled into my phone screen while I clicked on the app and pulled up the message.

Oh my God. It was from him. It was from Flynn Talbot.

Chapter Eighteen

Dear Ms Baxter,

I'm not sure I'm able to help you, but I have an appointment in Glasgow on Friday morning. Perhaps we can meet then?

Regards,

Flynn Talbot

I read over the message a few more times. Wow! Short, concise, and formal. It wasn't buzzing with emotion or sentiment. Bloody hell. Had I done the right thing contacting him after all? Was this in fact the man that Lily appeared to be still thinking about after all these years?

I pressed my lips together, lost in my thoughts. Well, now that he had made contact, it would be ridiculous not to speak to him face-to-face. Did he remember Lily? Was he prepared to acknowledge their past? I sure as hell hoped so!

My apprehensive fingers jabbed my phone keys as I composed a reply:

Thank you for getting back to me, Mr Talbot. I work in the city centre and would be able to meet up for a coffee at 11am this Friday morning in the Sycamore Tea Rooms on Buchanan Street, if that suits?

Seconds later, Flynn Talbot replied through Facebook Messenger, confirming that was fine and he would see me then.

My stomach performed a roll of anticipation. Was I doing the right thing? I would soon find out.

In the meantime, Kerry and I began investigating Lulu Stark's skincare range.

We knew we had to be discreet otherwise Athena would be alerted, so we arranged to meet up at odd times in quiet areas of the office and exchange emails, rather than be seen to be chatting. It suited me too that the majority of our colleagues on *Goddess* thought I was still resentful about Kerry securing the job that I had wanted. That way, they wouldn't even consider the possibility of us working together.

The cost of Lulu Stark's eye cream was ridiculous. A pot the size of a mini jam compote of the kind you get in a bed and breakfast was upwards of £300 – and this from a woman who apart from her witty comedy routines would often use her high profile to promote social inclusion and speak out against poverty.

I advised Kerry to contact the press office of the skincare range, Stardust, for a few quotes. "We can start there and then hopefully speak to Lulu Stark herself. Get her side of the story."

Kerry blushed with gratitude to the roots of her shiny milk-chocolate hair. "I can't thank you enough for your help, Leonie."

I dismissed her thanks with an easy smile. "You can thank me when our investigation is mentioned on the national news."

While Kerry was ringing Lulu's PR people I contacted her agent, but smacked into a brick wall straight away. "Lulu is in the middle of rehearsals for her *It's Not All About Me* tour," snipped one of her management team. "I'll be sure to pass on your interest."

The remainder of the week was proving to be one of mixed fortunes.

Kerry told me she had managed to extract a couple of quotes from Lulu's people about the products "tearing up the rules of skincare and starting a revolution reflecting the stringent research undertaken" and another from a poverty charity that had Lulu as its ambassador who expressed their surprise and concern that "Ms Stark was involved in such a costly enterprise".

"Excellent!" I grinned at Kerry as we hovered by the stairwell. "I'm going to keep pestering Lulu's management. They'll probably resist us for another week or so and then realise they could be doing themselves more damage by not speaking to us."

"And I'll see if I can get anything else from a couple of the other charities Lulu Stark works with," chimed in Kerry.

"Good." I frowned. "It all seems rather odd, though. I've never met Lulu Stark, but she always came across as one of the genuine ones."

"I know what you mean." She swung around in her leather

boots before turning back to me. "You know something, Leonie? I think I'm beginning to enjoy myself working here. That's thanks to you."

I pulled a playful face. "Yes, well don't enjoy yourself too much, otherwise you really will give the game away!"

———————————

Apprehension began to crawl over me about the impending meeting with Flynn Talbot. I tried to dispel the doubts. Something told me I hadn't thought this through as much as I should have done... That should be the inscription on my headstone, I thought to myself.

And so Friday rushed up to greet me and before I knew what I was doing, I was stationed at a table in the impressive surroundings of the Sycamore Tea Rooms, on Glasgow's Buchanan Street.

The atmosphere was one of genteel decadence, emphasising the tea room's stature as the oldest of its kind in the city.

I was sitting at a table across the room, nursing a pot of tea and trying not to look conspicuous – and failing.

I tried not to make it obvious I was staring at the entrance, waiting for Flynn Talbot to arrive. This in itself was crazy, as I didn't even know what the man looked like. I had double and triple checked and there were no photographs of him on his Facebook account and he didn't have a Twitter or Instagram account either.

I had estimated that he must be at least seventy years of age, but had no idea how I might recognise him. The only thing he had said in another Facebook message last night was that he would be wearing a white shirt and a navy waistcoat.

I concluded he might be a bit of a silver fox; one of those lounge lizard types still trying to cling on to the last vestiges of their youth.

The thought made me draw my mouth in with disapproval.

I fought the temptation to make assumptions as I sat there, waiting for Flynn Talbot to arrive. What sort of man was he? Everything pointed to him having upped and left to go to Africa with his wife all those years ago, but having failed to return after a year like he had promised. Is that what happened? Did he break his promise to Lily about coming back?

But he had obviously returned to Scotland at some point, though not to Merry Wood, and poor Lily had been pining for him ever since. In her mind, was Merry Wood like some sort of shrine to him? If so, I was beginning to decide he wasn't worth it. I felt sorry for his wife and for Lily. They no doubt deserved so much better.

I took a sip of my breakfast tea and tried to stem my apprehension and annoyance by appreciating my surroundings.

The Sycamore Tea Rooms were inspired by Charles Rennie McIntosh and consisted of a mix of circular and square tables covered in snow-white table cloths and surrounded by walnut-brown high-backed chairs.

Christmas holly, ribbons, and a white and silver tree decorated with Rennie McIntosh coasters and pens instead of baubles adorned the tea room entrance.

· · ·

The menus were black leather-clad affairs. Straight through from the tea room was a Charles Rennie McIntosh inspired giftshop decked out with white walls and silver cabinets and spotlights, boasting everything from scented candles to pictures, and clocks.

I glanced down at my watch. Flynn Talbot was five minutes late.

My stomach clenched as a couple of well-dressed women arrived and were escorted to their table.

Like composing photo-fit pictures in my head, I imagined him to be all craggy and distinguished, with a sun-kissed complexion and twinkly eyes.

Oh. Hang on! Was that him?

A tall, confident-looking older man with a generous head of silvery hair appeared and stared around himself.

That must be him.

I scraped out my chair, almost knocking over my pot of tea in the process – in time to see him break into a grin at a lady over by the panoramic windows and stride towards her. They embraced.

Ok. So that wasn't him then.

I sank back down, drawing puzzled glances from the waitress.

Had he had second thoughts? Perhaps he had decided not to turn up.

I plunged one hand into my bag dangling down from the side of my chair and reached for the letter he wrote to Lily. He could have at least been honest with her all those years ago, if he had no intention of coming back. But if he was capable of doing that, he would be more than capable of not showing up to see me. Had this been a complete waste of time? I had to return this letter to her, but I knew I would have to carefully consider how to do that. The last thing I wanted was her to suspect me of snooping around Merry Wood.

A few more minutes ticked past.

I poured the remnants of my tea into my cup. I would finish this and then go. Served me right for getting involved. He had stood me up. What a coward.

"Leonie Baxter?"

I snapped my head up from my dainty cup and saucer and came face to face with a man possessing a set of stunning hammered-silver eyes.

He had a camera suspended around his neck. "Sorry about that," he said, not sounding at all sorry.

The man shrugged off the camera around his neck and placed it on the table. He was tall with a halo of wild, dark curls that he had slicked away from his chiselled face. There was the faintest dash of stubble on his chin and a defiant arch to his thick brows. There was something wolfish about his features. On closer inspection, I estimated him to be in his mid-thirties. He was very attractive and I found myself feeling self-conscious.

Who was this? He must have confused me with someone else. I opened my mouth to explain I was waiting for someone. Then I noticed he was wearing a crisp white shirt and a navy-blue waistcoat.

I rose up from my chair, my mouth flopping open.

He extended one hand towards me. His voice was a deep mash-up of Anglified Scottish. "Hi there. I'm Flynn Talbot."

Chapter Nineteen

I continued to stare at him, bewildered. "Flynn Talbot? You're Flynn Talbot?"

He frowned at me from under those thundery brows. "I was the last time I looked. Is that a problem?"

What was going on here? "Yes. No. I mean, I just expected you to be older."

I sank back down in my chair. This didn't make any sense. Who was this? He was nothing like the Flynn Talbot my imagination had conjured up – and he must have been at least forty years younger too.

"Oh, excuse me for a second." He plucked his ringing mobile out of his jacket pocket and proceeded to talk to the caller about something called the "blue hour" and "depth of field".

After a few moments, he rang off. "Sorry about that – a client of mine who's commissioning me to take some shots of his property portfolio."

I tried to push out a polite smile. "Right. I see." I didn't see at all.

There was a tense silence, until Flynn Talbot signalled to the waitress to request a black coffee. "Can I get you anything?" he asked, indicating my pot of tea.

I struggled to answer. "Er. No thanks. I'm fine."

I wasn't fine. My head was scrambled. This wasn't playing out at all like I had expected. Instead of meeting up with what I'd imagined to be a dapper, charming older man with well-cut steely hair and a nice line in Pringle jumpers, I was confronted by a cocksure guy who was aged about thirty-five.

This was all going wrong. I had messed up big time.

I thought about the letter to Lily secreted inside my bag. Now I felt stupid. Why didn't I just let things be, rather than make a stupid tit of myself?

"Ms Baxter? Hello?"

I snapped my head up

"Sorry," I stumbled. "I don't understand what's happened here. I think there's been some sort of mistake."

The waitress set a black coffee down in front of Flynn Talbot and evaporated.

He shifted in his chair. "A mistake?" His brows knotted. "Look, I'm rather busy. What's going on?"

I rubbed at my forehead. Good question. I was wondering the same thing.

"I discovered a letter. It was in a house called Merry Wood, not far from where I live in Silver Ness." I forced out a laugh. "I'm sure it's nothing to do with you."

He shot forward in his seat like he had been punched. His

eyes snapped from me to his coffee and back again. "Sorry. Did you just say Merry Wood?"

I scanned his face. Crikey. The mention of the house had snared his attention. "Yes," I faltered, confused. "And this letter was written to an acquaintance of mine, a Mrs Lily Cruickshank, and was signed by someone also called Flynn Talbot."

An odd expression took over his features. He sat back and folded his arms, a defensive fleck appearing in his eyes. They skewered into me. "Well, that is my name, but whoever this Flynn Talbot is, it's not me. I don't know a Lily Cruickshank. I've never heard of her."

Dear God. This was agony. It was like ripping a plaster from an irritated wound. What the hell was happening here?

He glowered at me again. "Can I see this letter please?"

"No, that wouldn't be right," I explained. "It belongs to Mrs Cruickshank and I don't even know if she is aware of its existence."

Flynn Talbot's light eyes locked with mine. "I see. Well, do you have a photograph of this Lily Cruickshank? Maybe I've taken her picture in the past, but the name doesn't mean anything."

"I don't have a photo, I'm afraid."

"Or perhaps she was a model I've worked with before under a different name."

I reached for the teapot for something to do, only to find a pathetic trickle dissolve into my cup. "No, she isn't a model. She must be in her early seventies."

One of Flynn Talbot's brows rose. He muttered something indecipherable under his breath, before taking a sip of coffee and setting down the cup with a decisive clink. I could sense his shutters were down and refusing to budge. "Right. Look, I have no idea what's going on here. I don't want to appear rude, but I don't have a great deal of time."

He studied me from under his lashes for longer than was necessary.

"Look, I'm going to be honest. I was intrigued when I received your Facebook message. That's why I came here this morning." There was a heated pause until his phone let out an insistent ring. I could see from where I was sitting that the person's image on his phone was a platinum blonde.

Flynn Talbot declined the call.

"Yes, I can see how in-demand you are."

He gave me an indecipherable look.

I thought again about the letter to Lily, nestling in my bag. "Please forgive me but the house – Merry Wood – do you recognise the name of it at all? You gave me the impression that you might."

His clear silver eyes bored into mine. "You were mistaken," he ground out. "In fact, you seem to have been mistaken on several fronts."

My cheeks flared with embarrassment.

I noticed he possessed enviable, spikey lashes. "I'm obviously not the Flynn Talbot you are looking for, whoever he is." His jaw clenched. "Where did you say you found this mysterious letter? In a house?"

"Yes. It's called Merry Wood."

Flynn Talbot looked troubled again

"What is it?" I asked, a kernel of hope unfurling in me at

his odd reaction. "Do you recognise it? The name of the house, I mean?"

A pulse throbbed in his jaw.

"I'm sorry but I can't help you. Now, if you'll excuse me, I have a meeting."

He shot up, fished about in his wallet and tossed a ten pound note down.

I got to my feet. What was going on? He was suddenly very keen to leave. "Do you know the man who wrote that letter?"

Flynn Talbot's eyes flashed.

"Please, Mr Talbot. You happen to share the same name as the man who wrote this letter to Lily. If there is any help at all you think you might be able to give me, I'd very much appreciate it."

He fired his camera back around his neck. "Sharing the same name as someone else isn't uncommon. Sorry, but I'm going to be late as it is."

"Please, Mr Talbot. I could see something in your expression."

"You couldn't see anything!" he growled. "I shouldn't have agreed to meet you." He flicked me a look. "I hope you find the other Flynn Talbot, but this letter is nothing to do with me. I'm sorry I can't help."

"Can't help or won't help?" I called after him, drawing odd looks from surrounding tables. But he ignored me and strode out of the tea room, leaving me staring after his retreating back.

• • •

His reaction, the way he acted, the way he'd batted away my questions and refused to answer…

I sat back down in my chair and fiddled with the handle of the teapot on my table. He'd looked shocked and confused at first. Then defensive.

I drummed my fingers on the edge of the table. I wasn't prepared to give up on finding out who wrote that letter. The fact that Flynn Talbot had reacted to the name of the house told me there was a strong indication he was connected to it somehow. The only conclusion I could come to was that he might have a family member with the same name and that was the person who wrote the letter to Lily. Obviously, it wasn't him. But who was it?

I folded my arms. My emotions had shot from embarrassment that I'd made a mistake to shock and then determination. I would give Flynn Talbot a couple of days to think about things, then I would contact him again.

Around me, there was the clink of cups and polite chatter.

Flynn Talbot wasn't telling me everything. That was obvious.

Chapter Twenty

I returned to the office later that morning and was throwing myself into writing up a feature about New Year ideas for revamping your beauty routine.

Whilst I had been out meeting up with Flynn Talbot, Orion and Cole had been instructed by Athena to put up the *Goddess* office Christmas decorations.

Orion had caught me gawping at the crystal Swarovski Christmas tree at the *Goddess* reception, not to mention the extravagant crystal stars and snowflakes dripping from the ceiling.

"I did suggest to Athena that we get some tinsel and paper chains from the newsagents across the road, but she started hyperventilating," grinned Orion into my ear.

"I wish I had been here to see that."

I returned to my PC but kept recalling Flynn Talbot's face collapsing in shock when I mentioned Merry Wood.

"Leonie? Have you got a minute please?" Kerry's anxious face met mine over the top of my PC.

"Sure."

I saved the feature I was working on and followed her down the office corridor. Her glossy hair was pulled back from her concerned face with some navy ribbon. "It's about Lulu Stark."

"Ok."

She hugged her notebook to her chest. "I made contact with her PR company. She's agreed to do an interview."

"That's great! What angle did you use?"

Kerry struggled to maintain eye contact. "I said we were interviewing three celebs from the world of comedy who take their beauty regimes seriously."

"Good one," I beamed at her. "As a matter of fact, that's a very good idea for a future piece. I like the angle. You should pitch it to Athena."

Kerry forced a smile and nodded. "At least it means now we can see her reaction when we ask her about her products and the cost and testing of them."

"So, when are you going to interview Lulu?"

She pulled her lips into an agonised attempt at a smile and waited until Orion and Cole had retrieved their lunches from the giant Smeg fridge and disappeared again. "Ah. Well, it's not me I said would be interviewing her." Kerry swallowed, "I said you were the reporter who would be conducting the interview with her."

My eyebrows flexed. "Me? But I thought..."

Kerry's mouth wobbled. Tears flickered in her deep green eyes. "I'm not cut out for all of this. Athena is deluding herself, as am I."

"Rubbish! Where is all this coming from?"

Kerry blushed. "She asked me to do a write-up for her this morning about shopaholic therapy, and then proceeded to rip it to bits. She said she's wondering if giving me this job has been one big mistake."

"Don't take any notice. Yes, you have a bit to learn, but you're keen and I see potential in you. I really do."

My mouth sprang open to protest further, but Kerry's expression was crestfallen. "I'm not a project, Leonie."

"I know you're not. I don't think that at all. Who said you were?" I reached out a concerned hand.

"Nobody as such, but it's written all over their faces. It's what they say." She sighed. "It's only a matter of time till they find out Athena is my aunt, so I might as well just tell them all now. They think I'm useless too."

"Who does?"

"Cole, Orion, Tabitha... the whole lot of them. I've seen them giving me pitying looks at the editorial meetings. They don't think I have what it takes either."

"Then prove them wrong and please don't tell anyone you are Athena's niece. At least not yet," I advised. "Why don't you hold off a bit longer and let's see what happens with this Lulu Stark story? It will give you chance to prove your mettle not only to your aunt but to the rest of them in here too. I guarantee you'll do such an excellent job on this story that they'll have to give you credit and you won't just be labelled as the boss's niece when they do find out. You will have earnt their admiration and respect in your own right." I glanced around myself. "It's still only Orion and me that know and we won't tell anyone."

Kerry digested this. She gave a faint nod and an

195

appreciative smile. "Thank you. Ok. And I'm sorry for dropping you in it like this with the interview."

"Don't worry. I am a bit worried what Athena will say though, when she finds out you're not taking on the Lulu Stark story by yourself."

She jutted out her chin. "I'll make it clear all this was my idea and not yours." The prospect of having to confront her scary aunt fluttered across her features and lodged itself there.

Tatiana, one of the advertising team, waggled her fingers in greeting at us as she sauntered past.

I waited until the coast was clear again. An idea sprang into my mind. "Look Kerry, how about you come with me to interview Lulu Stark? We can do it together."

Her expression, rivered with preoccupation, broke into a relieved smile. "Really?"

"Of course. When did you schedule the interview with her for?"

Kerry's cheeks pinged. "I made it for a week on Friday at 2pm."

I screwed up my eyes with concentration. "I think that's ok. I don't remember having anything on then…"

"I've already checked your electronic calendar," she admitted. "You haven't got anything else scheduled for that time."

I cocked one brow at her and her cheeks scorched deeper. "If I could accompany you to the Lulu Stark interview, Leonie, that would be great. It will give me a chance to learn from you."

I rolled my eyes and laughed. "I'm not Joan Bakewell."

Kerry's expression was blank.

"Oh, Yoda then."

She recognised Yoda and laughed.

"You just need to build up your confidence. I think you have all the makings of a very good journalist."

Now it was Kerry's turn to roll her eyes.

"It's all about telling yourself to just put yourself and your questions out there. What's the worst that can happen?" I gave her a wide grin and a wink. "In the meantime, watch and learn from the master."

———————

Christmas was approaching with increasing speed. I realised with a jolt that it was now only a month away.

The shops, not only in Glasgow but back at home in Silver Ness, were all bursting with glitter, dangling decorations, and trees swathed in lights.

The days were drawing to a close quickly, with darkness wrapping itself around everything at four o'clock in the afternoon, but in a way, that added to the growing excitement and anticipation of the festive season being just around the corner.

I had made the decision to contact Flynn Talbot again tomorrow. It had been a few days now since our awkward meet-up in the tea room and although I suspected he still wouldn't be prepared to talk to me about what he knew or was concealing about Lily or Merry Wood, I wouldn't have been doing my job if I didn't possess tenacity.

I had already sent a couple of new Facebook messages to his account, as well as emailing his photographic studio, which

I'd located after a bit of rooting around on social media, but he hadn't replied to any of them.

That hadn't been much of a surprise. He came across as a rude man, rather up-himself, I concluded. Handsome but arrogant.

I stopped by the harbour railings with Harley on our evening walk and surveyed the golden ribbon of sand, illuminated under the throng of street lamps along the pier.

We had just returned from another uneventful trip to try and return the letter to Lily.

Harley and I had stood for a while outside her cosy little cottage, trying to ignore the cold nipping at our extremities and the rhythmical rush of the wind through the woods behind us.

Yet, despite the glow of lamps from behind her closed gingham curtains, she had failed to answer my knocks and pleads on the door.

I could understand her reaction in one way. I had let her down. I'd promised her no one would go inside Merry Wood. Now her trust in me was non-existent.

So, dejected and feeling wretched, we had returned to Silver Ness, I had deposited Lily's letter back at home and then Harley and I had made our way down to the seafront.

The air was punctuated with the bursts of waves hitting the shoreline and the comforting rush as they receded. Stars glittered like shards of glass overhead.

I guided Harley past the steps that led down to the beach and took her by the ice cream shop, Scoops, which was bursting with an impressive window display of sweet pastel flavours and multicoloured Christmas lights. Beside it rippled the striped canopy of the deli, which was closed for the night.

I soon came to the newspaper office.

A garish For Sale/To Rent sign was plastered across the entrance.

I drew up, my heart deflating at the prospect of the once bustling office being reduced to a silent shell. Even the sign proclaiming *The Silver Ness News* had been removed from above the door, leaving a boarded-up gap in its place.

I peered in through one of the windows. The walls were bare and there were empty plastic boxes stacked in one corner, presumably for Doug and Frances to begin the painful task of clearing their desks.

It was a quaint little former cottage with a spectacular view, so I had thought it wouldn't be on the market for very long. However, the local gossip was that the newspaper group were being greedy and Clarity Newspapers were asking a ridiculous amount of money from any potential buyer. If they did sell it, they would make a handsome profit.

Pictures drizzled through my mind of me, Doug, and Frances laughing, rattling off copy and debating who deserved the front-page splash that week.

A longing tugged in my chest. It seemed like an eternity ago now.

Goddess was so clinical in comparison, with its starched white minimalist furniture and staff swathed in designer labels.

Guilt nibbled at me. I was grateful to have another job. Of course, I was. Especially in my beloved field of journalism. But

I missed the familiarity and cosiness of my local newspaper and the warm, easy camaraderie between the three of us.

Harley and I moved further along the promenade of shops, their lit doorways throwing pools of warm amber light onto the pavement. We soon reached the newsagents on the corner.

Sitting outside on the pavement was a billboard proclaiming:

FIRST ISSUE OF THE NEW DRUMMOND & SILVER NESS SENTINEL – BUY NOW!

I hesitated, staring at the headline screaming back at me. It just confirmed that times move on and everything changes.

I hovered for a moment, deliberating whether to buy a copy, when my inquisitiveness won out.

I leant into the doorway of Mrs Bradshaw's newsagent's, ducking out of the way of a couple of beach balls and a display of postcards which she was in the process of bringing back inside for the night as she prepared to close.

She rolled up a copy and handed it to me. She clinked the change into her till. "I bet it's nothing like *The Silver Ness News*," she sniffed. "I bet it's all gossip columns and half-naked models."

I pressed my lips together, stifling a smile. "I think you're getting a bit mixed up with a couple of the tabloids, Mrs Bradshaw."

She sniffed again. "I used to love your paper." She leant against her counter. "Old Andy from the garden centre has read it and he says it's all arty-farty pictures and encouraging readers to get involved with things online." She let out a disgruntled sigh. "Do I look like the type of person who has a TikTok account?"

I made a few sympathetic noises and stuffed the newspaper under my arm.

I encouraged Harley on with a gentle twitch of her lead, debating whether to return to Scoops and treat myself to a double helping of pecan butterscotch. I felt like dollops of creamy, calorific ice cream might just improve my mood a little.

"Nice night for it!"

I squinted along the dark pavement

It was Netta, one of the local doctors. Her charcoal-grey suit was rumpled under her heavy winter coat and she was clutching her briefcase.

"Hard day at the surgery?"

She fired a hunk of dark-blonde bob behind one ear. "You could say that. A very stubborn lady with a recently diagnosed health condition is refusing my help."

"Ah."

Netta lifted her face and sighed as the night sea air washed over her.

"Oh, I'm sure you'll be able to make her see sense."

"I'm glad someone has faith in me." She stooped down and ruffled Harley behind her ears. "Honestly, Leonie, sometimes I feel like I'm fighting a losing battle against an immovable force."

"You're a great doctor," I smiled. "You know you are. All the locals ask to see you."

Netta pulled a face. "That's very nice of you to say so. They might ask to see me, but when it comes to listening to my advice, that's another story."

"You know what some of the locals are like. They can be crochety and stubborn, but they're essentially good people. Your patient will come around."

Netta dumped her case by her feet. "I wish I had your confidence. This patient is an intelligent, independent woman who lives alone. I'd have more luck getting through to her telepathically."

An elderly couple wrapped up against the cold sauntered past, savouring their glistening ice creams and exclaiming at the moody vista of the beach that scooped its way out of the harbour and disappeared into the dark swell of sea.

"Does she have any family who can speak to her?" I suggested.

Netta dragged a hand down her face. Under the streetlights, she looked even more exhausted. "She's lucky if she gives me the time of day, let alone confiding in me about anything. There doesn't seem to be anyone she can rely on." She played with one of the buttons on her vanilla shirt under her coat. "Ah well. I'll stick with it and hope I can get through to her in the end, but I won't hold my breath."

I found my fingers gripping Harley's sparkly pink lead tighter as I mulled over what Netta was saying.

My memory flashed up pictures of a pale, breathless Lily at her front door and then in her kitchen, the teapot set down as she composed herself; her hand flitting to her chest.

Her then reluctantly confiding in me about her heart condition. It was too much of a coincidence. It must be Lily who Netta was talking about.

"This lady," I began, trying to stem my rising tide of concern. "Whereabouts exactly does she live?"

Netta folded her arms and gave me a playful frown. "You know I can't tell you that, Leonie. Patient confidentiality."

She didn't have to. I knew it was Lily she was talking about, and that was why a renewed sense of determination took over.

Chapter Twenty-One

I walked home with Harley, my mind turning over what Netta had told me. It must have been Lily she was talking about. I was convinced of it.

An independent, spirited older lady, living alone with a newly diagnosed health issue? There couldn't be too many of those in this area. Lily had also commented about her GP being a young female doctor, just like Netta. It was too much of a coincidence.

When I arrived back home, I concocted a quick dinner of seabass, chunky fries, and vegetables and fed Harley chicken with her kibble.

Then I set up my laptop at the kitchen table. I couldn't give up on Flynn Talbot, especially not now. This had given me the impetus I needed. If he knew something, I had to find a way to convince him to cooperate.

Ok, so he had chosen to ignore my earlier attempts this week to speak to him again, but the news about Lily's heart condition had fired up my determination. If he knew something about the other Flynn Talbot or about Merry Wood, I would appeal to his conscience to tell me.

I knew enough about Lily to guess that she would resist moving out of her home with every fibre of her being. She wouldn't want to leave. That would mean leaving behind Merry Wood too.

My conscience was screaming in my ear as I considered everything. There was no way I could betray Lily's trust by sharing her private medical information with a stranger. The revelation about Lily's health condition might well change Flynn Talbot's mind about speaking to me, but I felt wretched to be even thinking along those lines. I was not about to betray Lily's faith in me by doing something like that. Her belief in me had taken a hit when those two models decided to trespass inside Merry Wood. I wasn't prepared to put it to the test again.

I would just have to use my persuasive powers to get Flynn Talbot on board some other way.

While my laptop was firing itself up, I hurried into my bedroom and picked up Lily's letter, which I'd put for safekeeping in my jewellery box, and returned to the kitchen.

The expression on Flynn Talbot's face when I had mentioned Merry Wood, and the way he'd marched off, wanting to put distance between himself and what I'd told him, made me even more convinced Flynn Talbot knew more about his namesake or that house than he cared to admit.

I toyed with the idea of shooting off another email to him, but decided I might have more luck trying to speak to him. People could ignore emails whereas if it was a phone call... well, he could of course ignore that too, but I believed the odds of catching him unawares over the phone might be in my favour.

I pulled up his photography website details. It comprised of a minimalist layout and slideshow with horizontal scrolling displaying images one by one. There was a black and white photograph of him in one corner, smouldering at the camera. I jabbed his mobile number into my phone.

Harley watched me as I paced up and down the kitchen floor, mentally couching what I was going to say to him.

He answered after several long rings and let out an irritated sigh when I introduced myself again. "Look, Ms Baxter, I admire your tenacity, but I have nothing to say to you."

"Mr Talbot, you and I both know you reacted the way you did on Friday because you either recognised some detail from the letter I talked about or the mention of Merry Wood gave you a shock. It's one of the two."

There was a bristly pause. "My, we are talented. Telepathic now, are we?"

"No, but in my profession, you learn to read people."

"I'm busy," he barked down the line. "I'm sorry I can't help you."

"Mr Talbot, if you tell yourself that often enough, you might start to believe it." There was a furious growl.

"You share the same name as the man who wrote that letter to Lily. A curious coincidence, don't you think?"

Flynn Talbot didn't say anything for a moment. He gathered himself. "Yes, I recall you saying something like that before, Ms Baxter. A coincidence. They do happen in life, believe it or not. Now, if you'll excuse me, I have an important photography appointment and I'm five minutes late for it as it is."

Frustration gnawed at me. I couldn't tell him about Lily's health condition; it wasn't my information to tell. But he was being so bullish. Hearing something like this might make him reconsider helping me. My brain felt rattled. What I was thinking of doing was wrong. Then images of a pale, tired Lily gazing across at Merry Wood lodged themselves in my head and refused to budge. Shit!

Right. I knew what I was about to say was a breach of confidence, but I was doing it for all the right reasons. This infuriating man was leaving me no other option. I hoped Lily would understand. I sucked in a long breath of air. "Look. I didn't want to say anything as I am breaching a confidence, but you ought to know that Lily Cruickshank – the woman to whom that letter is addressed – has just been diagnosed with a heart problem."

There was a brief frisson of something down the line. An awkward pause ensued. "How do you know that?"

I hesitated. "She told me herself. I wasn't going to betray her trust but you are being so bloody stubborn about this, I feel like I had no choice."

Flynn Talbot chewed this over. "I don't believe you. This all seems rather convenient. You reporters aren't known for your honesty."

His sweeping generalisation stung. "We aren't all underhand, I can assure you, Mr Talbot."

Another jagged, quiet spell ensued between us, until I jumped in to fill it.

"This lady lives alone opposite Merry Wood. I've been told

by a very reliable source that she is refusing to even consider leaving her home and I think I might know why. It's because she doesn't want to be parted from her memories there." I allowed that to sink in for a moment before speaking again. "And these are memories which I think you know more about than you are prepared to say." I dragged a weary hand through my tangle of curls. "Can't you listen to your conscience, Mr Talbot, and do the right thing?"

"It's not as easy as that," he snapped all at once, making my brows zing upwards. *So, I was right. He did know something.*

He let out a ragged sigh down the line. "I do sympathise, but like I told you, I can't help."

What did that mean? *It's not as easy as that?* Frustration flooded through me. "This lady has been loyal to that strange house for goodness knows how many years…"

"Well, more fool her."

"Pardon?"

"People can let you down, Ms Baxter. Even family."

What was he alluding to now?

"Mr Talbot, you have the power to help this lady. I think you know more than you're prepared to say."

He started to gruffly protest, but I carried on. "Even though she has found out she has this heart condition, she is still devoted to looking out for Merry Wood. Don't you want to help her? How can you just refuse to help?"

But before I had the chance to try and persuade him to talk to me, Flynn Talbot cut me off. "I'm sorry, Ms Baxter. I do sympathise. But it's complicated. Now, if you'll excuse me, I've had to break off from a photoshoot with a very prestigious client."

I opened my mouth to appeal to his better side – if he even had one – but he interrupted again. "And no, I can't tell you who that client is. Confidentiality."

Then he issued a sharp goodbye and ended the call.

I made a few more attempts to contact Flynn Talbot over the coming days, but he ignored my voicemail messages and emails to his photography site and to his Facebook account.

All went unanswered. He was like a phantom, vanishing into the ether to attend to his uber important photography clients.

My indignation bubbled. That just showed what sort of a man he was, if he could ignore the plight of a fragile, elderly woman, although Lily would no doubt be appalled at being described like that!

It was clear the Flynn Talbot I met was a self-centred, vacuous bell end.

Why wouldn't he admit he knew something and talk to me? It was obvious he couldn't be the same Flynn Talbot who wrote that love letter to Lily all those years ago, but did he know who the other Flynn Talbot was? If he did, he wasn't prepared to say.

Was there something he didn't want to face up to either?

It was the last week of November.

The Silver Ness Christmas lights switch-on had just taken place and the whole town was now a twinkling sea of illuminated snowflakes, stars, and reindeer. Every shop sparkled with lights and tinsel and the air was brimming with a combination of seaweed, woodsmoke, and building excitement.

It had now been a week since my phone exchange with Flynn Talbot and Kerry and I had our Lulu Stark interview on Friday afternoon.

Maintaining our discreet distance for fear of alerting colleagues, Kerry would happen to sidle up to me in the breakout area when it was empty and extoll her grateful thanks for my help.

Athena was no wiser, of course. If she found out that her niece had recruited me as her "wing woman", her control freak streak wouldn't have been able to compute it. No doubt her burgundy-coiffed head would have exploded.

Instead, I ensured that my electronic diary for that afternoon read: *2pm-4.30pm – Interview with Luna Newman, opera singer.*

I did have an interview with Luna, a twenty-three-year-old opera diva in the making, about her beauty regime scheduled for the following month, so I wasn't telling lies. I was just manipulating the truth a bit about when her interview was actually taking place…

Kerry and I slipped out of the *Goddess* offices within five minutes of each other and met in the car park, citing different reasons to our colleagues for both being out of the office at the same time – just in case there was any suspicion.

She jumped into the passenger side of my car and we set off, like two shamefaced schoolgirls caught skipping double maths.

Kerry played with her tulle skirt. "Thanks for this, Leonie. I owe you one."

I gave her a sideways smile. "I hope we can get this all wrapped up before Athena becomes suspicious. She doesn't miss much."

The interview with Lulu Stark was taking place in the press room of the Gala Theatre in town.

It was a cool, sedate space, all shadowy with a panoramic view of the turrets, spires, and tower blocks of Glasgow and framed by red velvet drapes sliding down to the polished beeswax floor.

Lulu Stark was already seated and waiting for us when we arrived.

She was a Scottish Rebel Wilson with an infectious smile. She indicated to the acid-green armchairs opposite hers.

Once small talk had been exchanged, I began by asking her about her skincare brand.

Lulu enthused about her brand, Stardust, and was about to extoll the virtues of its eco-packaging when I slid a measured side-eye to Kerry. This was her cue.

I noticed her fingers gripping her notebook as though she were about to tear it into shreds. "Ms Stark," she smiled, swallowing. "Sorry to interrupt but I wanted to raise something with you."

From the deep recesses of one corner, her agent Seth Gordon's long, thin face emerged and flickered. He had been so quiet, so obscured, we hadn't realised he was lurking there.

I gave an impromptu start.

"We have been led to believe," faltered Kerry, "that the

Stardust range has been…" Her voice struggled to maintain its level of authority.

I nodded my head at her in an encouraging fashion.

She carried on. "That your skincare range has been cutting some ethical corners, as it were."

Lulu's round, open face was stunned. "Sorry? Like what? Where has this come from?"

Seth Gordon strode out of the shadows like a Machiavellian villain in his slim-cut navy suit. "Ms Stark would be more than happy to discuss any questions about her skincare brand on another occasion. This isn't the time or the place."

"Oh, but I think it is," I explained with a winning smile. "We've been led to believe that a number of the products you are launching will be sold for inflated prices. There's also concern that the eco-friendly packaging isn't as sustainable as you're claiming…"

"This interview is over," barked Seth Gordon, looming over Kerry and me. "This is completely unacceptable. You've come in here to speak to Lulu under false pretences."

"Hang on," said Lulu, at risk of giving herself a crick in the neck as she stared from her agent to me and then to Kerry. "What the hell is going on here? Do you have any evidence of this? Can I see it?"

Kerry dipped into her bucket bag to produce a collection of information she had been sent from a member of Lulu's team, but Seth Gordon was too quick. He fired out a bony hand and grabbed it.

"Hey!"

His cool ice-blue gaze swept over the information he

clutched in his hand. "This is all bollocks! All cooked up by a former employee of Lulu's team."

He gave Lulu a crocodile smile that didn't reach his eyes. "You remember that strange girl we employed eighteen months ago? Simone Wales? I bet it's her that's been bleating a pack of lies to the press."

He let out a dramatic snort. "I knew from day one she couldn't be trusted, but Lulu is a little naïve and trusting when it comes to people. She always has been."

"Can I see it, Seth?" pressed Lulu, ignoring the gentle verbal dig from her agent and craning her neck from her chair.

But Seth swept the papers into his other hand. "No need for you to bother yourself with all this, Lulu. I'll deal with it."

He stalked past Kerry and me and yanked the press room door open. "Thank you for coming, ladies."

"But they only just got here," blustered Lulu.

"They can ask you anything else about your work/life balance over the phone," declared Seth with a shark-like grin. "We can schedule another conversation over the phone or on Zoom."

He leant in to Lulu. "And don't forget, you have that Radio 4 interview for Women's Hour to pre-record today."

Kerry and I swapped knowing, irritated looks and before we knew what was happening, we'd been bundled out of the door and were standing on the other side of it.

It slammed shut behind us.

"Lulu Stark is being manipulated," I hissed to Kerry as we made our way back to my car. "By that slimy creep. She doesn't have a clue what's going on."

Kerry turned around and squinted up at the heavy stone-built theatre glittering in the November light. "So, what do you suggest we do now?"

"You go back to your contact and see what else you and they can come up with. And I can do a bit of digging on our friendly, neighbourhood Seth Gordon, if that would help."

"Oh, that would be brilliant," she breathed. "Thanks."

"It might also be worth making contact with this Simone Wales to get her side of the story. I bet it's the complete opposite to what Seth Gordon is putting out there."

The Friday afternoon sun was shifting across the windscreen as we prepared to make our return journey back to the office. "I think this has all the hallmarks of being one hell of a news story. A famous comedian, known for her ethical business practices, being manipulated by her agent."

Kerry jerked her head towards the backseat where my bag was sitting. "Oh! I think that's your phone ringing."

I killed the engine and reached into the back seat for my phone. A number I didn't recognise, flashed up on the screen.

"Ms Baxter? It's Flynn Talbot." His rumbly voice was guarded.

I sat up straighter in the driver's seat. I wasn't expecting this at all. I thought he had vanished down some photography black hole. "Oh hi. Hello."

"I wondered if we could meet up to talk."

Kerry, sitting beside me, was scanning her own phone.

I blinked in surprise. "Yes. Sure." Talk about a shock. Had he had a crisis of conscience? "Can I ask what this is about?"

Flynn Talbot made a clicking noise with his tongue, as though it were helping him make sense of something. "It's about my grandfather," he managed after a few seconds of pensive silence.

"Your grandfather?"

"Yes."

Another loaded pause.

"Sorry, I don't understand."

There was a breath of irritation. "He's Flynn Talbot too," he revealed. "I'm named after him."

The pieces of the puzzle were beginning to align in front of my eyes., but it took a few moments for my brain to catch up. So, this Flynn Talbot was related to the Flynn Talbot I had been searching for after all. He shared the same name as his grandfather. Oh God. Flynn's grandfather must therefore be the one who wrote the letter to Lily. But why had he been so adamant and quick to deny any connection between them? Why had he lied about the man I was looking for being his grandfather?

My stomach performed an optimistic but stunned cartwheel as Flynn Talbot moved to speak again, cutting through my reeling thoughts. "I think we need to talk."

Chapter Twenty-Two

F lynn Talbot sat opposite me the next morning in Scoops.
Saturday had brought with it drizzly silver rain that still failed to deter the hardened day-trippers to Silver Ness. Some were still quite happy to take in the grey rolling sea and brave the stiff wind, whilst others ducked and dived into the local shops, availing themselves of the opportunity to snap up dinky Christmas gifts, like pirate snow globes embossed with the words *Silver Ness* and jigsaws of the lighthouse depicted with snow swirling around it. The air was a concoction of seaweed and hazelnut hot chocolate.

Flynn had surprised me with his suggestion to meet up, almost as much as his revelation that the Flynn Talbot who had written the letter to Lily was his grandfather.

He had even insisted our rendezvous be local to me, which had taken me aback too. Perhaps he wanted to see a bit of the area his grandfather frequented?

There was a small café area in Scoops which consisted of four tables and a few chairs at the rear of the shop decked out in multicoloured cushions and tie-backs. Christmas lights in a variety of colours flashed around the window frames.

"So, this is the famous Silver Ness?"

"You don't know the area then?"

Flynn Talbot held me to my seat with his unreadable silver gaze. He didn't answer. He could make brooding an Olympic sport.

"So why did you want to speak to me? Why have you changed your mind? You said on the phone the man who wrote this letter is your grandfather?"

He pushed himself forward in his seat, his black curls curling around the base of his neck. He raised both hands up in front of him in a gesture of surrender. "Whoa! One question at a time!"

Flynn looked agonised. Then he folded his arms. His mouth flatlined. "Yes. He is."

I stared across the table at this Flynn Talbot, trying to unravel why he had decided to speak to me now. Flynn had been adamant he didn't know his namesake and had denied having any knowledge of who he might be. He had insisted it was just a coincidence they shared the same name. And now he was confessing that the man who wrote to Lily, was in fact his grandfather?

I allowed this revelation to sink in. "And the son mentioned by your grandfather in the letter?"

"My father, Carl."

I slotted and pieced together these fragments of information. I pinned him to his seat with a disapproving look. "You knew this the first time I told you about the letter. You realised it was your grandfather who wrote it. So why didn't you say anything then? Why did you deny knowing him?"

Why had he just disappeared with these secrets?

Flynn's jaw, dusted with a hint of dark stubble, tightened. "Well, I'm telling you now."

I could feel my irritation burning. "You could have saved me time and hassle by being honest from the beginning."

His level stare back made me prickle in my seat. "I'm not in the habit of speaking to journalists. Well, not anymore."

I arched my brows. *What did that mean?*

"Anyway, that's your job, isn't it? To investigate and uncover things?" He raised one black brow at me and my cheeks flushed. *Arrogant sod!*

"It still would have been appreciated if you had told me this at the start."

I thought back to our previous phone conversation. "So why now? You still haven't explained. Why agree to talk to me?" A thought occurred to me. "It was when I told you about Lily's heart condition, wasn't it?"

His fingers twiddled with the cup of macchiato in front of him.

"Your conscience told you that you had to say something."

His dark lashes dashed against his cheeks as he glanced away. He shrugged and tried to look indifferent. "I knew I wouldn't get any peace if I didn't speak to you. All those Facebook messages and the emails…"

I stared levelly across the table. "And that was the only reason?"

"Does the reason why matter?"

I eyed him. "Your grandfather wrote this letter to Lily in 1973."

"While he was married to my grandmother, no less." Flynn ground his white teeth.

"Is your grandfather still alive?"

Flynn surprised me by breaking into a dry laugh. "Oh yes. He's still alive all right."

I took a considered sip of my tea. "From what the letter says, he and your grandmother moved to Africa because of her charity work?"

Now it was Flynn's turn to take a mouthful of his coffee. "That's what I was told by my parents."

I surveyed him and the tense angle of his shoulders.

"He's not worth it," ground out Flynn, slamming his cup down on its saucer, drawing a couple of curious glances from another occupied table.

I blinked at him in surprise. "What makes you say that?"

He gave me another level stare.

"So, you're not close to your grandfather?"

Flynn's generous mouth twisted up at one corner. "Not exactly. If you mean did he try and win me a goldfish at the fair or play model trains with me, then the answer is no." Flynn gave me a dry smile. "My family are what you might call buttoned-up. They don't go in for public displays of affection."

From the little slivers of information Flynn was revealing, it sounded like he and his grandfather shared the same name but nothing else. They didn't sound like the Waltons, put it that way.

"He keeps the rest of us at arm's length," he added with a bored air.

As if reading the myriad of questions swirling around inside my head, Flynn let out a defeated sigh. "Look, let's just get this over with, shall we? You want to know more details about my grandfather and I have work to do."

"You were the one who contacted me, Mr Talbot. You were the one who initiated this meeting. I didn't force you here."

He took a steady mouthful of his macchiato, his eyes never leaving my face. It was unnerving. For something to do, I reached for my cup of tea and took a sip. It had gone cold.

I grimaced and set my cup back down.

"My grandfather lives in Cairntilloch," he announced out of the blue.

"Cairntilloch?" I repeated, not able to disguise the surprise in my voice. "But that's…"

"Only a matter of miles up the road from here," supplied Flynn. "Yes, I know."

Good grief. The man to whom Lily had lost her heart all those years ago was living a dozen miles away from her. He had left her for Africa fifty years ago but was now just a handful of country lanes away.

Had he never tried to see her again when he returned to Scotland?

I wondered how she would react to that revelation.

"Merry Wood is still furnished but unoccupied," I blurted, as if all the questions I had were breaking apart a dam and spilling out in one big tidal wave.

Now it was Flynn's turn to look blank. "What do you

mean? My grandparents sold it when they returned from Africa."

I shook my head. "They didn't. Your grandparents are still the legal owners of the property."

Flynn stared across the table at me, incredulous. "You're kidding, right?"

"No."

"This is crazy," he half laughed. "Why the hell did they tell everyone that they sold it?"

"I have no idea."

Flynn made a dismissive grunting noise. "I don't get this at all." He flashed me a loaded look. "My grandfather doesn't deserve anyone's loyalty. More fool this Lily woman for believing in him."

He folded his arms. "He's not some romantic hero, so don't be getting any ideas that he is. From what I've been told, he led my grandmother a merry dance during their marriage."

Questions about why he was saying all this, why he was tarnishing his grandfather's reputation, burned bright in my chest and stoked my curiosity even more. "Are your grandparents still together?"

Flynn shook his dark head. "No. They got divorced in the 1970s."

"And where is your grandmother now?"

Flynn cocked one thick brow again. "You're very persistent, Ms Baxter. Nobody would ever guess you were a journalist."

I eyed him. "Are you being sarcastic?"

"Not at all. It was meant as a compliment."

I could feel myself becoming self-conscious under that hypnotic hammered-silver gaze of his. "Thank you, but you're not managing to distract me from my line of questioning, if that was your intention."

Flynn Talbot's mouth hinted at a smile. Then he shrugged. "My grandmother became a bit of a thrill seeker after the divorce. Last I heard, she was investing in a tapas bar in Spain."

We took more sips of our respective drinks as excited children debated over the array of flavours of ice cream, despite it being a grotty winter's day, and the rain finally gave way to watery weekend sunshine.

Flynn's fingers tapped up and down the side of his coffee cup. "I don't mean for this to sound hard-hearted, but I don't have much sympathy for this Lily woman. My grandfather was married to my grandmother at the time."

"I can appreciate things from your point of view, but Lily isn't well," I repeated.

Flynn pulled a face. "Poor, deluded woman."

I flashed him a look. Wow. Well, he really was intent on not cutting his grandfather any slack at all.

"So why contact me again about all this if you have no sympathy at all for Lily?"

Flynn fired out his long legs. "I told you. It was either that or have my inbox seize up with messages from you so I thought meeting up was the best idea." He delivered a charged look across the table. "I can't resist a lovely woman who might need my help."

I folded my arms and smiled. "Another compliment. Oh, it is my lucky day."

Flynn waggled one brow. "It's all meant, I can assure you."

At least the Ice King appeared to be melting a bit more. I had to admit he was very attractive.

I reminded myself why we were sitting in Scoops on a dank November day and returned my attention to Lily's letter. Something told me Flynn Talbot wasn't as cool and detached as he pretended to be. Despite him glossing over my question, I still believed he had experienced a prick of conscience and that was one of the reasons why he had decided to talk to me. "She needs to move on and move away from Merry Wood."

Moving on. *As if it were that simple,* I reminded myself with a small inner smile.

Flynn studied me. "And you're sure that Merry Wood hasn't been sold? There hasn't been some sort of mistake? My parents were told it had been."

"I'm sure. I checked with the council and they confirmed that the property is still owned by a Mr & Mrs Flynn Talbot."

Flynn digested this, a shocked look stealing across his features again. He dragged a hand through his curls. "I can't believe my grandparents' house is still sitting there like that after all these years." A concoction of thoughts drifted through his light eyes. "Even though it pains me to say so, I think it's time I made contact with the old man to find out what the hell has been going on."

He rose up and out of his café chair, insisted on paying, and then vanished to the sound of the gulls swooping over the waves.

Chapter Twenty-Three

"The grumpy old sod wouldn't speak to me," Flynn revealed down the line to me later that day. "He asked his housekeeper to tell me he was busy finishing off his latest piece of work and was indisposed."

"Piece of work?"

"He's an artist," he clarified. "A painter. I think his ego ballooned after all the attention he began receiving after he started this Chandler—" Flynn stopped, his voice withering. "Goddam it!"

I drew myself up at the end of the line. I blinked several times. I was certain I had misheard him at first. "Sorry. Did you just say *Chandler*?"

Flynn fell silent, irritated with himself.

"Let me get this straight," I managed, my heart beginning to gallop. "Are you saying that your grandfather is actually Chandler, the street artist?"

Flynn made a frustrated grunt into my ear.

Excitement flared inside me. "Are you being serious? *The*

Chandler is in fact your grandfather?"

I could hear Flynn was struggling to decide whether to confirm, deny, or just gloss over what he had said. There was a strangulated groan. "Me and my bloody big mouth!" He let out an agonised sigh. "Yes, he is Chandler, but that is strictly off the record, ok?"

"Wow," I squeaked, my thoughts racing. Oh my God! I couldn't process this. I pulled myself together. "Yes, of course you can trust me."

"Oh, since when?"

"Pardon?"

"You're a reporter," he said. "I don't think your profession is big on that."

Incredulity filled up my chest. "Are you always prone to making unsubstantiated statements?"

"No, I leave that to journalists."

Ouch! My teeth gritted together in fury. *Who the hell did this man think he was?!* "You know nothing about me, Mr Talbot, nor about my journalistic career. If you did, you would realise that I am a trustworthy and conscientious reporter."

Flynn Talbot started to reply but I cut him off. "I'm not the one who lied to a journalist."

"I'm sorry," he ground out. "I shouldn't have said that."

"Then why did you?"

Flynn sighed into my ear. "Let's just say my previous experience of journalists hasn't been a positive one."

He then tried to move the conversation on. "It turns out there's enough going on in my family as it is without any more complications and the press camped out on the doorstep, if they found out about the Chandler thing. Present company excepted, of course."

That's big of you, I thought to myself, before my mind took off in another direction with so many questions I wanted to ask and not just about Flynn's grandfather being the infamous artist.

"Flynn, what did you mean when you said you hadn't had a great previous experience with journalists?"

I could hear him considering my question. "Let's just say it was to do with affairs of the heart and a trust issue."

"Ah."

I wanted to ask more, but his deafening silence told me that he wasn't prepared to divulge anything further. At least not for now.

My stunned thoughts careered back to the Chandler revelation. "How long have you known?" I asked, failing to conceal the thrill in my voice.

"That my grandfather was Chandler?"

"Yes."

"Since I was fifteen, so... twenty years now. My father found out by accident when he visited my grandfather one day. They both got a bit pissed and my grandfather told him." Flynn let out a short laugh. "My dad thought he was rambling, but he showed him preparatory images he had been working on that had only just been released into the public domain. He also knew Chandler's secret signature. That's how any forgeries or copycats can be identified, so they know it's a real Chandler piece of art and not a fake."

"It's a black CH in a box," I rambled, my enthusiasm

threatening to spill over. "And it always appears on the image somewhere."

"That's right," faltered Flynn into my ear. "Wow. How do you know that?"

"My ex-boyfriend used to work on one of the Scottish nationals. So, they didn't get caught out by fake artwork purporting to be by Chandler, the artist anonymously contacted the paper, making it known he had started signing his work that way and that all his future paintings would always feature that secret moniker."

I was still fizzing with this revelation. What an exclusive this would be! I was struggling to contain myself, let alone process it. Photos of an interview with Chandler and my by-line underneath scrolled through my head. I gave myself a talking-to. A promise was a promise. "I won't tell anyone what you've just told me," I reassured Flynn. "But if you or your grandfather ever change your mind about revealing his alter-ego, I'm here."

Flynn grunted into my ear. "I doubt that very much, when he wouldn't even talk to me." He made a resigned noise. "That's nothing new. My family are, shall we say, unconventional. I'm sure you got that impression already."

"When was the last time you saw your grandfather?"

There was an awkward hush. "Must be about five years now."

"What?!"

"All right! All right! We can't all have families that bake cakes and reminisce over the piano every Sunday."

Baking cakes and reminiscing over the piano?! My family had never done that and I didn't know any other families that did

227

either. I was tempted to make a joke of it, but something told me that right now, Flynn wouldn't appreciate it.

"My grandfather is like one of those huge, ornate diaries with a padlock," he went on. "Impenetrable and contains so many secrets. He tends to keep people at arm's length."

Just like you, I concluded to myself. I considered his description. "So, in that case, what's the next step?"

Flynn snorted. "There is no next step. My grandfather wouldn't take my call. End of."

"But aren't you curious about Merry Wood and why he told you all it was sold?"

"Nothing that man does surprises me," barbed Flynn. "He's a law unto himself. According to my parents, he holed himself up in Cairntilloch years ago." The frustration was evident in his tone – resigned and irritated. "Look, Ms Baxter, I know you're curious about all this and you want to do right by this Lily friend of yours, but if I were you, I would just forget you ever saw that letter and move on."

I frowned down my phone. "But that seems to be the issue. Lily can't move on, even though she should."

"Sometimes you just have to accept things the way they are," bit back Flynn. "I know you think of yourself as some do-gooding girl-guide—"

I clutched the phone to my ear. "I beg your pardon?"

"You want to go wading in there, solving everyone else's problems and making everything a happy ever after." He made a disgruntled sound. "But life isn't like that."

Anger erupted in my chest. "You might have a very pessimistic view of life and be happy to be part of a buttoned-up family that doesn't communicate, but not everyone else would be."

I scraped my kitchen chair back. "If you haven't forgotten already, this lady isn't keeping well."

Flynn tried to interject but I was so fired up, I carried on. "I can't just turn my back on Lily and I won't."

I took a breath.

"Look, Mr Talbot, I'm sorry. It's just I've grown rather fond of her even if she can be cranky and stubborn and I just want to do what's right by her."

"Flynn? Flynn? Where are you?" I was cut short in my explanation by a female voice drifting into my ear. "We're going to be late!"

I blinked down the phone. He obviously had more pressing matters to attend to. What was it with all the deflections? The pushing away of people? Well, some people...

An odd bout of irritation took over after hearing the voice of a woman with him. "Don't you worry. You sound busy," I said crisply. "I won't be requiring your help from now on, thank you. I can deal with this on my own."

That Saturday night, I looked up the village of Cairntilloch on Google maps and on the Scotland's Villages website. It consisted of a sprinkling of quaint little shops, a post office and a village green with an old-fashioned telephone box. I'd driven past it on a few previous occasions and considered it pretty, but had never had any call to pay it a visit. Until now.

Harley was snoozing by my feet while I balanced my

laptop on the sofa arm. "Guess where I'm taking you for your Sunday morning walkies, Harls?"

I parked my car in an empty lay-by close to the village green. It was a tranquil sea of manicured emerald, laced with the remnants of frost.

A church spire zoomed upwards out of the trees. Rusty bells pealed, denoting it was Sunday morning.

Harley hopped down out of the back seat of the car. I clipped on her lead. "Come on, sweetheart. Let's find this grumpy old man."

My other hand slid into my bag and brushed against Lily's letter.

A woman with an immaculate ball of ash-blonde hair was busy sweeping the steps of the newsagents with a broom. The sound of Christmas carols was coming out of a crackly radio from inside.

Harley and I made our way across the green towards her. "Excuse me. I was wondering if you could help?"

She smiled and bent down to fuss over an appreciative Harley.

"I don't suppose you happen to know where Mr Flynn Talbot lives?"

The woman looked at me as though I had just robbed her of her life savings. "Why on earth are you asking about that cranky old sod?"

I pushed out a polite smile and didn't answer her question. "I understand he lives somewhere here in Cairntilloch?"

She folded her arms. "Aye. He does, more's the pity."

"Why do you say that?"

"You ask any of the folks from around here," she replied

with more than a hint of challenge in her voice. "He's a rude and cantankerous bugger. He never mixes with the likes of us. The only time anyone sees him in the village is if he or that poor housekeeper of his need some groceries."

She leant forward in a conspiratorial fashion. "That Mrs Oates deserves the Victoria Cross, for putting up with the likes of him."

Good grief. Well, he didn't sound like a cuddly Father Christmas type at all. I performed what I hoped was one of my best winning smiles. "His address? Do you know it?"

The woman waggled the broom handle in her hand and turned to point to the other side of the village green. "See those trees over there? Well, there's a posh three-storey house not far from a couple of the holiday homes. That's his. Ostentatious thing it is. You can't miss it."

She jerked her puffball hair. "His house is called Lily Grove. You cut through the trees and take a left. There's a lane that will lead you all the way there. Just watch your footing, pet. It can get a bit icy at this time of year."

My eyes widened at her. Did I hear her correctly? "Sorry," I blinked at her, "did you just say Flynn Talbot's house is called Lily Grove?"

"Aye, that's right. Why?"

"Oh, no reason."

She gave me a quizzical look.

So, Flynn Talbot had named his house after Lily. That threw me. "Thank you very much. You've been very helpful."

The woman turned back to her shop steps. "You're welcome, pet. Just watch yourself, though. That Talbot man is a nasty piece of work."

Harley and I made our way through the woods with the winter sunlight trickling through the bare, gnarled branches.

We soon reached a little pebble lane that opened out to reveal two wood and glass chalet-type holiday homes either side of each other.

Further up the road sat an impressive three-storey townhouse, its garden studded with a variety of evergreen trees and shrubs. There was a black electric gated entrance leading up to it.

Positioned on the gate was a black and white plaque with the words *Lily Grove* painted on it. He hadn't forgotten her after all, despite my earlier reservations. After all these years, she must still be with him.

As I stood there, it was difficult to reconcile that I was standing in front of the mysterious Chandler's house. My stomach gave a flip.

I glanced down at Harley who blinked her hazel eyes back up at me. "Well, here goes."

Chapter Twenty-Four

A twinkle-eyed lady wearing loose-fitting white shirt and flared trousers emerged at the door. Her short hair, although well-cut, was brassy toned.

I felt like I was in prison, talking to her through the wrought-iron teeth of the closed gate.

"Can I help you?"

"I'm looking for Mr Flynn Talbot."

She must be his housekeeper, I surmised. Mrs Oates, was it?

Her navy eyes narrowed. "Can I ask who you are?"

I knew that revealing I was a journalist would likely would kill off any chance of me being able to speak to him, but I wasn't prepared to lie. Flynn's previous words echoed in my head. There seemed to have been enough deception swirling around the Talbot family as it was.

And what if what Flynn had told me about his grandfather being the cult artist Chandler was true? I had no reason to doubt him. If Flynn Talbot senior did decide in the future to tell all, what an exclusive that would be!

"I'm a journalist with *Goddess* magazine."

Mrs Oates eyes narrowed further.

"My name is Leonie Baxter. But I'm not here because I'm a reporter. I'm a friend of a Mrs Lily Cruickshank?"

Mrs Oates's mouth popped open in surprise. She wrapped her arms around herself. "Did you just say Lily Cruickshank?"

Her attention zoomed from me to Harley and back again.

Mrs Oates pushed her hands into the pockets of her charcoal trousers. "Is she alright? Lily, that is?"

"Yes. Well, sort of. Some days are better than others," I commented diplomatically.

Mrs Oates considered this and gave a nod. "I hope she's ok."

I clutched at Harley's lead. "Me too. That's why I'm here. I found a letter addressed to Lily from 1973. It was written by Mr Talbot."

Mrs Oates eyes widened. "Well, I never." She glanced back over her shoulder and into the polished hallway, her expression now tinged with alarm. Then she tapped down the steps and approached me at the gate. She dropped her voice. "Where did you find this letter, Ms Baxter?"

"Please call me Leonie."

"Leonie," she repeated with an awkward smile.

Harley gazed up at me from the pavement, giving Mrs Oates a regular thump of her tail.

"I came across the letter by accident in a house called Merry Wood."

Mrs Oates hand fluttered to her chest. "Are you sure? No. That can't be right. Merry Wood was sold years ago."

Another person who had no idea about Merry Wood's

current status. I shook my head. "But the house wasn't sold. That's the strange thing. Merry Wood is sitting there all furnished and Mr & Mrs Talbot are still the registered owners of the property."

Mrs Oates screwed up her face. "I don't understand. Why on earth would that have happened? It was supposed to have been sold when the Talbots got divorced."

But our hushed conversation was interrupted.

"How dare you!" came an enraged roar from inside the house, making us both flinch with alarm.

Flynn Talbot senior emerged, all wild silvery hair, moustache, and thunderous mouth. He turned his ire on Mrs Oates first. "Having a good gossip about me, were you? I thought I could trust you, Mary."

"Don't be so ridiculous. You know you can."

He growled something incomprehensible and whirled to confront me behind the gate. His pale-blue eyes blazed. "And as for you, I want you to leave my property now and take your mutt with you."

Harley emitted a low bark.

"Mr Talbot, I don't know what you heard—"

"I heard you've been poking your nose in about Merry Wood. My business is mine alone and has nothing to do with anyone else, let alone a bloody reporter." A deeper grimace overtook his mouth. "Did that grandson of mine put you up to this?"

"No. Not at all." I shoved a hand into my shoulder bag and produced Lily's letter. "I have this—"

He cut me off, his attention momentarily transfixed by the letter in my hand. "My grandson tries to speak to me after

Lord knows how long and now you turn up. More than a coincidence, if you ask me."

He folded his arms and glowered. "Leave now, otherwise I'm ringing the police."

"But Mr Talbot—"

His eyes brimmed with fury. "I want you to go. Now!"

Mrs Oates jerked her head in an anxious, encouraging motion for me to leave.

With frustration clawing at my insides, I slid Lily's letter back into my bag and led Harley away.

Kerry cornered me as I made my way to my desk the next morning, inhaling the strong, smoky scent of the takeaway coffee I was clutching.

"Sorry to spring this on you, Leonie, but do you have a minute? It's about the Lulu Stark story."

I switched on my PC and shrugged my jacket onto the back of my chair. "Sure."

Her complexion was pinched.

"Are you ok?" I asked her.

But she didn't have time to reply.

"Leonie, I'm so sorry. I asked this gentleman to wait in reception, but he was insistent that he speak to you."

Orion's voice interrupted us. Behind her appeared Flynn Talbot junior, suited, booted, and harbouring a furious, dark brow.

Kerry shrank back. "I'll catch up with you in a bit."

She vanished.

Flynn stood there, thunderous. "Is there somewhere we can talk in private?"

Heads of my colleagues were raised over the tops of their PCs, appreciating the tall, dark stranger.

I told him to follow me to the breakout area.

No sooner had I set my takeaway coffee on the table than he launched into a frustrated tirade. "What the hell did you think you were doing yesterday? I've just had my grandfather on the phone, telling me a female journalist was hanging about his property and harassing his housekeeper."

He let out a snort of derision. "I knew as soon as I said anything I was making a huge mistake."

"Whoa!" I held up one hand. "Stop right there! I didn't go and see your grandfather about that, nor was I hanging around or harassing anyone."

"Then why rock up at his door like that?"

"I went to Cairntilloch to speak to him about Merry Wood and Lily, but he refused to talk to me."

Flynn stared me down. "Not about anything else?"

"No," I ground out. "I just told you that." I dropped my voice to an irritated hiss. "I know you have a very low opinion of journalists, but when I make a promise, I keep it." How dare he think I would lie?! That I would break a promise and go round to his grandfather's on some pretext in order to get a scoop about him being Chandler?

Flynn folded his arms and jutted out his chin. He looked scolded. "Sorry."

I cupped my hand to my ear in an exaggerated gesture. "Pardon?"

"I said I'm sorry for jumping to the wrong conclusion."

I pursed my lips. "Apology accepted."

There was a stony silence for a few moments. "I bet he doesn't even remember her. Lily, I mean. Based on the stories my grandmother told me, the randy old goat would shag anything with a pulse back in the day."

I couldn't help myself. I let out a dry bark of laughter. One minute he's apologising and the next, he's offending people again!

"And what is that supposed to mean?"

I could feel myself blushing hot. "Well, I hardly think you can comment."

"Pardon?"

I straightened my shoulders, recalling the female voice over the phone from the other night, but bit back any further comment.

Flynn watched my expression and arched a brow. "You seem to be taking rather a keen interest in my love life, Ms Baxter."

I remembered we were in the breakout area and tried to contain the level of temper in my voice. *Talk about having an inflated opinion*! "Oh, don't flatter yourself! And what you just said about your grandfather and Lily doesn't ring true at all."

"What do you mean by that?"

I carried a triumphant smile, pleased that I was about to puncture his ill-conceived confidence. I stared at him levelly. "Lily Grove."

"What?"

"Lily Grove," I repeated with satisfaction. "That's what your grandfather has called his house in Cairntilloch."

Flynn's brows twisted. He fell silent for a moment. "That could just be a coincidence."

"Oh, of course it is."

Flynn glowered at my sarcasm. "And Merry Wood? Did he say anything about that?"

This time I wasn't able to channel the same air of confidence. "No. That was when he ordered me to leave. But his housekeeper knew about Lily."

Flynn hauled a frustrated hand down his face. The spotlights in the office ceiling sifted subtle flecks of burgundy in his hair. "I'm not begging my grandfather to talk to me. It turns out he's deceived me and my parents for years."

"What do you mean?"

"He doesn't give two hoots about family. Money, attention, recognition." He lowered his voice. "That's all he's ever been interested in. He's been so busy playing the part of the people's street artist that he's forgotten where his loyalties should have lain in the first place."

I eyed Flynn, seeing for the first time the clear, sharp pain he was harbouring over the bitterness that existed in his family, not to mention the exhaustion and effort of keeping the secret that his own grandfather was Chandler. Why was he so closed off?

I toyed with the lid of my coffee. "You said your grandmother lives in Spain now."

Flynn made an agonised groan. "Oh, don't tell me you're planning to interrogate her as well?"

Annoyance stirred up inside of me. "I'm not interrogating anyone. I never have done. If someone doesn't want to speak to me, then that's their prerogative."

I shook my curls in disbelief.

"We aren't all monsters, you now. It's like in every walk of life. There are always bad reporters and yet we all get branded the same." I let my hands rise and fall. I found myself using his first name. "Flynn, this is to do with your family. Surely, you're curious?"

He flashed me a hot look out of his striking silvery eyes that made my stomach give a sudden deep flip.

I straightened my shoulders and chose to ignore it. Nope. No way. I wasn't going there. Yes, he was very good-looking, but he had more sides than a Rubik's Cube.

"I want to help Lily," I explained, clearing my throat.

Flynn didn't disagree. He rubbed at his chin. "My grandmother is coming over to Scotland at the weekend on one of her flying visits to see her accountant and meet up with a couple of friends." He paused. "She's booked into a hotel in town."

My optimism burned a little. "Do you have a contact telephone number for her?"

Flynn rolled his eyes. "Why am I not surprised?"

Now it was my turn to sound irritated again. "If you want to get to the bottom of this story with Merry Wood then asking questions is the only way." Pictures of Lily gazing across at the empty, shadowy house skipped through my head. "So, can I have your grandmother's telephone number please?"

The ghost of a brief, admiring smile tugged at the corners of his mouth before vanishing again. "I don't have much choice, do I?"

. . .

Once Flynn had given me his grandmother's mobile telephone number and left, I searched around the office for Kerry.

"Do you know where she is?" I asked Orion.

"She didn't say where she was going. All she said was that she had to pop out." Orion raised her brows in a charged way. "I guess you don't have to worry when you're the editor's niece."

I waited until Monday lunchtime to call, when a few of my colleagues disappeared to the deli across the road to buy their lunch and bring it back to the office.

I requested an Emmental cheese and salad ciabatta and one of their delicious Christmas cinnamon cupcakes to have with my afternoon tea, which Orion said she would bring back for me.

The hush in the office was almost comforting.

I snatched down the post-it that was stuck on the side of my PC terminal with the phone number Flynn had scrawled on it.

It rang for an agonisingly long time until a husky female voice answered with a curt, "Yes?"

"Good afternoon. Is that Ms Astrid Talbot?"

"It is. Who am I speaking to?"

In the background I could hear a rush of waves and the intermittent burst of passionate Spanish from what sounded like a busy taverna. Glasses chimed and chairs scraped.

"I'm Leonie Baxter. I'm a journalist with *Goddess* magazine in Scotland."

"Right. And may I ask why you're calling me?"

"It's about your ex-husband, Mrs Talbot. Flynn."

The line fell silent for a few moments. "Yes, I am aware of who my ex-husband is."

Ok. Knuckles wrapped.

"What about him?" Her voice was prickly. "He's not dead, is he?"

"Oh, it's nothing like that," I assured her. "It's more to do with your former marital home."

"Oh, that place. Merry Wood," she said airily. "We sold that dump donkey's years ago. Flynn dealt with all of that." She hesitated. "Is there a problem, because if so, you'll have to take it up with him."

So, she didn't know that Merry Wood hadn't been sold either.

I pulled my thoughts together. I couldn't drop a bombshell like that over the phone to Spain, let alone mention Lily. It just didn't seem right.

A voice inside my head advised me to keep that bit of information to myself for now. I would hopefully have far more luck if I told her face to face. Gauge her reaction.

"I understand you're travelling to Scotland for a few days on Friday?" I pushed on.

She sounded thrown by my knowledge. "I am. How do you know that?"

I didn't answer her. "Would I be able to meet up with you for a chat please, Mrs Talbot?"

There was the clinking of a glass. "Is that really necessary? I have a busy schedule."

"I wouldn't ask if I didn't think it was important, Mrs

Talbot," I impressed. "I promise I won't take up too much of your time." An idea careered into my head. "You would make a wonderful interview subject for a future issue."

She considered this for a moment. "I would? What, in *Goddess* magazine?"

"Of course. Ex-pat Scot goes to Spain and starts over. It would be wonderful publicity for your new tapas bar."

She hesitated down the line. "How do you know about my tapas bar?"

I scrambled around in my head for what sounded like a plausible explanation. "I hope you don't mind, Mrs Talbot, but I googled you. A prominent Scot like yourself... well, I had to do some research."

The sycophancy seemed to work. She didn't take long to consider that particular carrot being dangled. "Oh, that's sweet of you to say that. All right, but I can't spare too long, I'm afraid."

I heard a tip-tap of her nail on a screen. There were more Spanish exchanges down the line.

"How about we meet at my hotel on Saturday morning, say 11am? I will be staying at The Fontaine."

I confirmed that was fine.

She broke into a burst of rapid Spanish, before turning her attention back to me. "Now, I'm sorry but I must go. I have an appointment for a hot stone massage."

I was still recalling Astrid Talbot's insistence that Merry Wood had been sold years ago as I rang Flynn to tell him.

When I relayed this information to him, he made a dismissive noise. "My grandfather must have fooled her into thinking he sold the house as well. Christ, he's lied to everyone! And what did she say about Lily?"

"I didn't mention her," I admitted. "I just couldn't. Revealing that to someone a thousand miles away in a phone call... it didn't seem right somehow."

"Good grief," teased Flynn. "A journalist with a conscience. You should be knighted."

I stuck my tongue out, even though he couldn't see me. "We aren't all heartless bastards, you know. I keep telling you that."

"Perhaps you're right. I'm beginning to discover that at least one journalist in particular is full of surprises." His voice had become a little softer.

I clamped my phone harder to my ear, not sure that I had heard him correctly.

He broke through my skittering, confused thoughts with a cough. "So, you're meeting my grandmother at 11am on Saturday?"

"Yes. At her hotel. She's staying at The Fontaine."

"Very nice. Well, you won't be going alone."

"Aren't I?"

"No," he growled. "I'm coming with you. I want to know what the hell is going on with my family. There've been enough secrets."

Chapter Twenty-Five

I could see the top of Flynn's dark swept-back curls above the festive shoppers and meandering families, the children pink-faced and jumping about with excitement at the sight of the glittery Glasgow Christmas lights and the shop windows bursting with foil-wrapped presents.

My stomach wriggled, catching me unawares.

I dismissed the sensation and adjusted the collar of my smart brown coat instead. Behind me, the Fontaine Hotel glistened in a maze of buttery brick and mullioned glass.

Flynn stared for longer than necessary at my bottle-green knitted dress and brown ankle boots. I found my cheeks heating up as he studied me.

"You look very pretty."

"Thank you."

In reality, I'd found myself agonising over what to wear, with a bemused Harley watching me from the top of my bed.

I had rifled through everything in my wardrobe, dismissing countless outfit combinations from flared trousers and pussy-bow shirts to one of my ankle-length skirts and a high-necked blouse, before finally settling on this one.

Trying to impress a certain someone? an amused inner voice had tormented me, whilst I'd applied my lipstick and frothed up my curls.

Not at all, I'd hissed back, my cheeks flaring. I was about to meet the ex-wife of one of the country's most iconic artists. I had to look presentable. *Yes, that was it.*

My eyes appreciated Flynn's navy-blue shirt and light trousers under his long military style coat. His hair was still a bit damp from his shower.

I whizzed my attention back to the hotel, determined not to linger on the images of Flynn and showers. All of this – whatever it was – was just an uneasy truce of sorts. He was learning that he could trust me and I had discovered he wasn't quite so much of an arrogant cretin as I first thought.

That was as far as it went. End of.

"When was the last time you saw or spoke to your grandmother?"

"I saw her a couple of months ago, when she came over on one of her flying visits."

"So, you're close to her then?"

Flynn pulled an ironic face. "I don't know if you could ever get close to Astrid."

When I frowned, he ushered me into the hotel reception. "Once you've met her, you'll see what I mean."

It was all white and hessian interior, with sumptuous Christmas decorations and bouquets of festive flowers in deep reds and creams thrusting out of tall gold vases.

A huge white and silver Christmas tree, like something out of Narnia, welcomed guests in the foyer.

My attention was drawn to an immaculately attired willowy lady with a curtain of ghost-grey shoulder-length hair. She was dressed in a long tunic and matching wide-legged trousers, topped with a set of shiny wooden beads.

Her tanned, lined face broke into a surprised smile when she saw Flynn. "Goodness me! What are you doing here? I'm supposed to be meeting some girl reporter."

Flynn shot me an embarrassed look.

"That's me, Mrs Talbot. I'm Leonie Baxter."

"And I'm with Leonie, Grandma."

Astrid Talbot took my hand and shook it, but her attention was taken up with her grandson. "I didn't know you were seeing anyone and a journalist too." She forced a smile but it didn't reach her rheumy powdery-blue eyes.

"Oh, we're not together. I mean, not like that! Good grief, no!" I rushed, letting out an awkward laugh.

Flynn examined me with a quizzical arch of one brow.

I was relieved when he stopped looking at me like that and moved in to embrace his grandmother. Astrid proffered a cheek, on which he grazed a brief kiss.

"Another reporter, eh Flynn? You certainly like to live dangerously."

I almost gave myself a crick in my neck as I turned to look at Flynn. *Another reporter? What was that about?*

Momentary annoyance flickered across his face. Then he shook it off.

Astrid Talbot indicated for us both to sit opposite her in a secluded alcove section of the reception area. She rested her manicured hands on top of one another. "So, what's this all about?"

"It's a bit delicate, Grandma," conceded Flynn beside me. "It's about Merry Wood."

"What about it?" She pursed her pink frosted lips. "You mentioned the house when you rang me the other day." She gave a theatrical shiver. "I was glad to be shot of the place. I never liked it. Goodness knows what your grandfather saw in it." She flicked back her hair. "We were lucky that someone else wanted to take it off our hands."

I frowned at her. Merry Wood must have been a lovely house. It still was. It desperately needed some TLC, but it still had all the hallmarks of being a grand property and the gardens were spectacular. They could be even more wonderful once returned to their groomed, manicured state.

"That's the point," I ventured. "It transpires that Merry Wood was never sold."

Astrid Talbot shook her hair, sending it flying against her cheeks. "No. That's not right. I don't know where you got that nonsense from, young lady."

She pinned me to my seat with a frosty stare. "That house was sold years ago, straight after we returned from Africa." Her expression became more defiant. "I already told you all this on the phone."

"Grandfather led you to believe it had been sold," said Flynn, explaining. "But it wasn't."

She stared across at him. "Don't talk nonsense."

When Flynn continued to stare at her levelly, she shifted in her seat. "You're serious, aren't you?"

I leant forward on the hessian sofa. "Mrs Talbot, do you

remember a lady who lived opposite you when you were at Merry Wood? Lily Cruickshank?"

A strange expression took over her features. She nodded. "Yes, as a matter of fact I do. She was a pleasant but plain little thing with red hair." Her mouth morphed into a smirk. "She was distraught when we left for Africa. I think she had a bit of a thing for your grandfather." She rocked back on the sofa. "Deluded girl!"

I raised my brows. *Oh God. This wasn't going to be easy.* "I discovered a letter," I began, choosing my words. "It was addressed to Lily Cruickshank and written by your husband."

She blinked several times at me. "Why does that not come as a bigger shock. He had a string of women during our marriage. It was all rather embarrassing."

She shot out her hand. "Can I see the letter please?"

I shook my head. "No, I'm afraid not. That letter belongs to Lily. It wouldn't be right for me to pass it around, allowing other people to read what is rightfully hers."

There was a flinty expression charging through her eyes. "How very noble of you."

I bristled but didn't respond. Astrid wasn't coming across as the wronged ex-wife to me.

She performed a theatrical cock of her head. "I wonder if he ever managed to get his leg over with her?"

There was a horrified, strangled gasp from Flynn. "Grandma! Please!"

"Well, it was so obvious she had a thing for him. She used to salivate every time she saw him. All rather common."

Astrid Talbot eyed her grandson. "But onto far more important matters than who your grandfather was sleeping with. You need to tell me what's been going on with Merry Wood."

Flynn opened and closed his mouth. He looked to me and I widened my eyes. She was far more interested in the house than in the news about the letter. How odd.

He cleared his throat. "The house is still sitting there, furnished, from when you and grandfather lived there."

Her eyes hardened like marbles. "I can't believe this." She whipped her head from Flynn to me, making her wooden necklace clack with the motion.

"And is that Lily woman still holed up in that grotty little cottage of hers?"

"Yes, Lily still lives opposite Merry Wood," I clarified, giving her a look.

"I guessed as much. Dear me, don't tell me the poor old dear is still pining for him after all this time! Isn't it all rather pathetic?"

She let out a dry bark of laughter. "He lied to me. Your grandfather lied all those years ago. When we got divorced, he said the proceeds from the sale of Merry Wood would be split. He got some solicitor friend of his to organise it."

"And you believed you received your half?" quizzed Flynn.

"Of course I did. Your grandfather had my proceeds from the house sale paid via some trust he set up. I had no reason to doubt him." She tugged at her floaty tunic. "There was so much money swilling about at the time and I never once suspected he would swindle me."

"I think swindle is rather a strong word," I put in. "We're not sure yet what happened or why." I eyed her. "And you say you did receive your half of the sale proceeds of the house anyway?"

She whirled to confront me. "Well, yes, I did, but it's still deception, isn't it? What would you call it?"

Astrid Talbot didn't give me an opportunity to answer. She paused as a couple of hotel guests tapped past on the polished tiled floor. "I want that house sold. I need the money! Can I rely on you, Flynn?"

"What?"

"Sell that bloody house. Make your grandfather see sense after all these years. It should have been sold there and then, the deceitful old swine!"

She rocked backwards and forwards, fury rising up on her face. "My lifestyle in Spain requires financial support. That tapas bar is eating up more money than I initially envisaged." She grunted under her breath. "It makes me laugh when you consider how successful an artist your grandfather is."

Then she caught sight of my expression, as though she had only just realised I was sitting there. She clamped her lips shut and adopted a guarded glint in her eyes.

"Don't worry, Mrs Talbot. I know about your ex-husband."

She narrowed her gaze and tried to look mysterious. "Know what?"

I lowered my voice in the hotel reception. "I know about him being Chandler."

"Well, I hope you're not planning on broadcasting that!" Her voice was fierce. "The Chandler brand is worth a great deal of money after all these years and the fact that no one knows who he is makes all of his works even more valuable."

She flapped the hem of her tunic again. "If it comes out about who he is, his Chandler work will be worth nothing."

Beside me, I detected Flynn's discreet eye roll.

"You have my word, Mrs Talbot." I could feel Flynn examining me again, with those killer silver eyes of his.

"Well, that's something," she said to no one in particular. She set her shoulders. "But that house needs to be sold, Flynn, and I'm relying on you to persuade your idiot grandfather to do the decent and sensible thing."

She arranged herself on the sofa. "Now, anyone wish to join me in a G&T?"

Chapter Twenty-Six

Flynn and I departed the Fontaine Hotel.

"My ears are scorched," he half joked, giving one of them a playful tug. "I'm fond of my grandmother but she's like Cruella de Vil on steroids when she gets started."

I laughed.

"And now I've been landed with sorting out my divorced grandparents' family home. Whoopee! Just great!"

I thought about Merry Wood again as we weaved between the Saturday shoppers. Illuminated Christmas decorations glowed down onto the pavement and at a nearby kiosk, a young man was busy scooping and shovelling hot chestnuts into bags for a group of hungry customers, the warm, cosy scent adding to the festive atmosphere. "But why though? It still doesn't answer why your grandfather didn't sell Merry Wood, but led Astrid to think he did. And as for his relationship with Lily..."

"What are you doing this afternoon?" asked Flynn, surprising me.

"This afternoon? Oh, nothing much. I was just going to go home, walk Harley, my rescue pup, and take it easy."

Flynn towered over me. "I wondered if you might want to grab some lunch somewhere. Then we could go and visit my grandfather."

I gazed up at him, like a mongoose being hypnotised by a cobra. "What, now?"

Flynn pushed his hands into the pockets of his trousers. "Why not? My magazine photoshoot scheduled for 3pm today has been postponed till next week and you've never struck me as the sort of woman who turns down a challenge."

It was the way he hung on the word *challenge* that sent my heart into a gallop. *What was happening here?* Bloody hell! I was standing here, blushing like a schoolgirl! I locked eyes with him. "I do like a challenge."

A slow smile spread across Flynn's handsome face. "Well then, lunch first, then we tackle the country's most revered street artist about his private life."

So, an easy afternoon ahead then.

We chose an American style place a little further down Byres Road, which served warm pancakes with a variety of delicious toppings.

Its interior was all dark wood and ghost-grey, with huge black and white prints of the Statue of Liberty, the Golden Gate Bridge and the Hollywood sign adorning its walls.

Our cosy booth overlooked the sedate gardens of the Glasgow Royal Botanics, where a choir of children, all decked out in Santa hats, were belting out Christmas favourites for charity.

After some deliberation over the varied menu, I opted for pancakes with strawberries and blueberries, while Flynn couldn't resist the bacon and maple syrup stack.

The waitress set a pot of coffee in the middle of the table and disappeared.

"So, tell me about your family," I said, pouring a stream of hot, black coffee into our mugs. At the back of my mind, Astrid Talbot's remark about him playing with fire and "another reporter" still lurked there.

Flynn let out a groan. "Do I have to?"

That made me laugh. "No, of course you don't have to."

He stirred his coffee and cradled the mug in his hands. "I suppose we're all so guarded in my family because of my grandfather." He set the mug down in front of him. "We've been carrying this secret about who he is for so long that we've forgotten how to open up and trust people."

His face darkened again. "I can remember both my parents warning me not to tell anyone about my grandfather's big secret. Not easy when you're a loud-mouthed teenager, desperate to tell anyone who would listen that your grandfather is the guy who's been painting the Eiffel Tower on the side of bus stops at three in the morning."

"That must have been difficult, keeping that quiet."

"Oh, it was. I was desperate to up my street cred and impress young women, but couldn't."

"I'm sure you didn't have to do anything to impress women…" *Oh shit, Leonie.* It was too late. The words shot out across the table before I could do anything. "What I meant to say," I started, my tongue falling over itself and getting into a tangle, "is that I find it hard to believe you weren't popular with women anyway."

Christ! Everything that was tripping out of my mouth was worse than what came before. I reached for my glass of water and buried my face in it. Pity I couldn't have shoved my head into the whole bloody glass and cooled it down.

He gave me a small smile. "I was warned about journalists in particular."

I grinned back at him, setting down my glass of water. "Oh dear. And yet here we are."

The waitress reappeared and delivered our lunch to us, which we tucked into with gusto.

What was it about this man that sent me into a tongue-twisted spiral of emotion? I was usually a pretty together sort of person, but whenever Flynn looked at me a certain way from under his spikey lashes or spoke to me in that deep rumble of his, I was becoming a blithering wreck.

I composed myself as he began to eat lunch. "You know you can trust me, Flynn."

He sliced up a rasher of bacon. "Do you know something? I think I can."

"Finally!" I joked with an exaggerated eye roll.

My heart juddered as he held my gaze again across the table. "Seriously, Leonie. I do trust you. You could have gone straight to your magazine or a newspaper about my grandfather and yet you didn't. You kept your word. It means a lot."

I busied myself with dissecting a strawberry.

Oh God. Don't let your heart rule your head, Leonie. Look what happened the last time!

I paused as I pricked the strawberry with my fork. "I hope you don't mind me asking, but you've hinted a couple of times before about having had an issue with journalists?" Then I smiled apologetically. "Sorry. I shouldn't have asked. I'm just curious. Goes with the job."

Flynn shot me a look. At first, I wondered if he was going to answer. Then he gave a rueful half-smile.

"I was involved with a journalist a couple of years back. Her name was Rachel. I thought I could trust her, but when she discovered who some of my A-lister photography clients were, she started snooping on them, on the lookout for stories." He shrugged. "She went behind my back, writing up some nasty articles. It lost me a number of real high-profile names and we split."

Flynn heaved a sigh as he reflected on it again. "I felt so gullible and let down at the time. My family have always been so paranoid about reporters anyway, ever since my grandfather started doing all his street art stuff."

"I'm sorry. That must have been hard to deal with. Trusting someone like that and then they let you down."

Miles reared up again in my mind, but I pushed him away.

"Yes, it wasn't a good time. The fact what Rachel did also affected my business and the faith my clients had in me wasn't helpful either."

"What about your parents?" I asked, moving the conversation onto other territory. "What are they like?"

"A bit detached," he admitted. "Don't get me wrong. I know

they love me and I had a happy childhood, but I don't think they were really cut out for all the sacrifice having a kid entails." He chewed on a chunk of pancake. "They never liked me calling them *Mum* and *Dad* either. I've always known them as Diana and Carl."

He explained that he was born in Darroch. He eyed me. "So, what about your parents?"

"My mum, Marina, is Italian and from a little town close to Palermo. She and my late grandparents moved to Scotland when she was small, as my grandfather wanted to seek out new work opportunities in the hospitality industry. My father, Ross, is Silver Ness born and bred. My mum often says he has salt water running through his veins." I speared a strawberry with my fork. "My mum is forever insisting I need to eat more and my dad still thinks I'm eight years old and his little girl."

Flynn smiled at this. "And what do they do?"

"Mum is a mobile hairdresser and Dad is a painter and decorator."

Flynn's attention travelled to my hair. "That explains why you look like one of those Botticelli girls. I wish I had my camera with me right now. The way the light is drizzling through your curls would make a stunning shot."

My hand shot up to my wayward hair. "Your sales pitch is excellent, Mr Talbot."

"Nope. Not a sales pitch at all. It's true."

I trained my attention back on my lunch. This conversation was travelling off in a direction I hadn't envisaged – and it felt lovely.

"My hair is down to my Italian side of the family," I explained. "That and my love of food."

Flynn grinned over the table at me, displaying white even

teeth. "I think a woman who loves her food is very sexy. I can't be bothered with girls who sit and anguish and prod over a lettuce leaf."

I found myself blushing. "I think I know what you mean. A passion for food often indicates a passion for other things."

Flynn's teasing, dark brow made me even more self-conscious when I realised what I'd said and how it could be construed. "Life," I clarified quickly. "You know. Experiences."

Oh, shut up Baxter, before you make even more of a tit of yourself!

I focused all my attention again on my plate in front of me.

This was so ridiculous! I was fine one minute – a perfectly normal, functioning human being. Then when I was in Flynn's company, I was finding more and more that I was morphing into a bumbling, self-conscious sixteen-year-old again.

Flynn delivered a mischievous grin. "I bet you don't call your parents by their first names."

"What makes you say that?"

He gave a shrug. "I don't know. I bet when you get together with them, it's all apple pie and big hugs."

"I don't like apple pie," I teased. "Now if you had said chocolate *torta della nonna*, you would have been on the right track."

"Oh, what's that?"

"A Tuscan tart – dark chocolate with custard filling and sweet pastry. It means *grandmother's cake* in Italian."

"Sounds irresistible."

I flicked him a look and moved the conversation on. "So why photography?"

Flynn set down his knife and fork for a moment. "I've

always wanted to be a photographer. This might sound like a cliché but I love the idea of capturing a moment or a memory." He lifted his glass of water and took a considered sip. "It's being able to let other people see a side to a person or a landscape that they would never normally witness themselves."

Then he told me he had studied for his degree in Photography in Glasgow. "From there, I managed to get some freelance work on a couple of the newspapers, but I always wanted to start my own studio."

He leant across the table in an almost conspiratorial fashion. "The Glasgow skyline, I think, is one of the most beautiful and dramatic there is to photograph. It's all lights and towers and spires." Then he gave a reflective smile. "Golden hour, also commonly referred to as 'magic hour', is my favourite time to go out there and capture something with my camera."

"When is that?" I asked, not failing to notice how enthused he was. It was infectious.

"It's the time right before sunset and after sunrise. The sun is low on the horizon so light takes on a redder shade than when it's higher up in the sky. It can make for a stunning image."

We enjoyed the remainder of our lunch, teasing each other over our respective families and when it was over, he refused to let me pay. "This is on me."

"Thank you. Well, next time..."

I realised what I was about to say and bit it back.

His eyes twinkled, but he didn't say anything.

We returned to the outside world, blinking and sated after

our filling lunch.

"I'll drive to my grandfather's," Flynn insisted. "We'll come back and collect your car from the car park afterwards."

We continued our easy chat as Flynn negotiated our way out of town and towards Cairntilloch. The country lanes were pretty twisting turning roads, bordered by huge swathes of fields and the odd remote cottage. They gave off a sleepy, lazy vibe as we slid past clusters of sheep and the odd grazing cow.

In the distance, the hills were dusted with snow.

After such a generous-sized lunch, I would have been ready for a nap, but seated beside Flynn in his crystal-blue Mazda, I knew I wanted to savour every minute of it.

We laughed about our jobs, regaled each other with tales of work colleges and compared notes on the music drifting out of his car radio.

Part of me didn't want the car journey to end. It was just about us cocooned in there. There were no Chandlers, no prickly grandmothers, no talk of deceitful journalists; no demanding magazine editors or my job pushing its way between us.

"Well, here we are," murmured Flynn, easing his car into the kerb outside his grandfather's house. "This is going to be interesting."

I gazed out of the car window at the balconied bedroom windows. "When was the last time you were here?"

Flynn narrowed his eyes in concentration. "It must be about five years ago since I last came to this house. I think it was for his birthday. He didn't want any fuss, but my parents insisted on getting caterers in." A sardonic smile spread across his face. "He was too busy moving and shaking with his VIP friends and hangers-on to chat to his own family. My grandfather spent the evening complaining about the canapés."

I fetched my bag from the back seat. "You came under duress?"

"In a word, yes."

Flynn pressed the intercom and spoke to Mrs Oates, who came bustling out of the front entrance. There were silver Christmas lights framing the grand entrance and the huge fir tree in the front garden.

She took one look at Flynn, let out a gasp, and then bundled him into her arms. "Look at you! What a handsome young man you are. Oh, my word! I haven't seen you for too long. Much too long!" She beamed up at him. "For a minute there, I thought Aidan Turner had rocked up and my luck was in!"

Flynn laughed. "You need new spectacles, Mary."

Her warm, welcoming face then took on a melancholier edge. "We don't see enough of you, Flynn."

Flynn shrugged. "Well, my grandfather isn't the most welcoming of people, is he?"

Mrs Oates hopped from foot to foot. She looked at me, recognition spreading over her face. "I know you from somewhere. Aren't you the journalist who was here the other day?"

"Yes. That's right."

A cloud of concern took over her features. She turned back

to Flynn. "Your grandfather isn't going to like this, whatever it is."

"We need to speak to him," said Flynn. "It's important."

She let out a resigned sigh. "All right. Come with me, but don't say I didn't warn you. He's working on a landscape of the Queensferry Crossing and is getting rather frustrated with it, so he's not in the best of moods as it is."

I threw an apprehensive glance up at Flynn as we followed Mrs Oates up the paved path and into the house.

The hallway was cool and airy, with a tiled coffee-and-cream floor and a burnished staircase any Hollywood actress would love to descend. A long length of ivy studded with white bows wound its way around the banister. A lavishly decorated Christmas tree stood in the corner, dripping with tear-shaped baubles.

A couple of abstract paintings of cubes and triangles hung from plain white walls.

I could smell the rich aroma of Christmas cake being baked.

"Mr Talbot," called Mrs Oates up the vanishing staircase, offering us an anxious look over her shoulder. "There are a couple of visitors here to see you."

A door handle rattled open somewhere at the top of the stairs. "Who is it? I'm in the middle of the Forth at the moment."

Mrs Oates glanced at both of us. "It's your grandson – and Ms Baxter, the journalist from the other day."

There was a slam of a door. "What the hell?!"

Flynn Talbot senior's feet thundered down the glossy staircase. His silver moustache waggled with fury. "Ah, the cavalry, I see. Now look, I've already said my piece."

But his grandson wasted no time. "May I?" asked Flynn, gesturing to my shoulder bag.

I dipped my hand in and produced the papers I had managed to obtain from the council about Merry Wood's sale – or lack of it – and handed them to him.

"We have proof, Grandfather, that Merry Wood wasn't sold. From the council. I spoke to Grandma this morning and up until today, she was convinced it had been. You even gave her the proceeds, purporting to be from its sale."

The older man's jaw jutted out.

"And Lily Cruickshank still lives in the cottage opposite," I interjected. "Even after all these years."

I thought his eyes were going to fall out of his head. He opened and closed his mouth a couple of times. "Lily?" Then he swallowed and tried to compose himself. "This is ridiculous! You have no right poking around in my private affairs!"

"So, you're not denying it then?" pushed Flynn, folding his arms. "You let my parents think Merry Wood had been sold all those years ago."

Flynn senior's lips ground together harder.

"Well?"

He looked to Mrs Oates for support.

She gave him an awkward smile. "Whatever has been going on here, Mr Talbot, don't you think you ought to be honest?"

He shifted his eyes heavenwards to the corniced hall ceiling.

When it was clear that his grandson and I weren't prepared to leave without answers, he threw his hands up into the air.

"All right! All right. For the love of God! If it means I can return to the peace of my studio, then let's get this over with."

He grunted something else and directed us to the right with a jab of one irritated finger. "I suppose I was deluding myself if I thought I could keep this quiet forever."

The room was an amber and toffee affair, furnished with two marmalade-coloured sofas and an armchair. I imagined sitting there, surrounded by all these rich, autumnal colours, losing myself in a hot chocolate and marshmallows on a dark, chilly evening. A Cary Grant movie would be on TV, the velvet curtains framing dancing leaves out on the lawn.

Flynn senior's voice dragged my attention back. He ordered us to sit down, but Mrs Oates made her way to the door.

"And where do you think you're going, Mary?"

Mrs Oates's hand froze over the door handle. "I thought you would want your privacy, Mr Talbot."

He let out a noise that was a cross between a sigh and a grunt. "For pity's sake, woman! How long have you worked for me now? You know more about me than any other woman I can think of. Now please sit down."

Mrs Oates carried an embarrassed flicker of a smile. She sank down next to Flynn on the other sofa opposite me, while Flynn senior took up residence in the lone armchair.

"So," said Flynn, firing out his long legs in front of him. "Where do you want to start, Grandfather?"

Flynn senior's shoulders sank a little under his checked shirt. He looked as if he wished he were anywhere else than sitting there, confronted by us. He cleared this throat. "It's a cliché, but I suppose at the beginning might be a good idea…"

Chapter Twenty-Seven

"She was the loveliest woman I had ever set eyes on," reminisced Flynn senior.

"It was the 15th of December, 1972 at Merry Wood, and Lily was outside, shovelling snow away from their cottage path. She reminded me of a wood nymph – dainty, pale skin and that lustrous red hair that looked like it was a light, poking out from under her bobble hat."

I smiled over at him. "Please go on."

Flynn senior laced and unlaced his fingers. I could see as I sat across from him what he must have looked like back in the day. Even now, he was a handsome older man, with thick silvery hair and that moustache.

But all those years ago... My eyes drifted to Flynn and I conjured up pictures of his grandfather being tall, dark, and wolfish like him.

Flynn senior resumed his recollection. He glanced at his grandson. "Astrid was occupied on the phone in her office, talking in that strangulated, faux-posh voice she adopted on telephone calls. It sounded nothing like her. And Carl was at school, rehearsing for their school panto, *Aladdin*.

"I saw her move between the snow-drizzled trees, pushing the shovel to create a path out of their cottage."

Flynn senior shook his head. "I remember wondering where that useless, lazy husband of hers was. Bernard. He should have been out there, giving her a helping hand.

"Lily was struggling to push the spade through an obstinate section of icy snow. Behind me and from down the corridor, I could hear your grandmother's forced laughter. It grated against me."

Flynn senior looked at the three of us in turn.

"I couldn't leave her struggling like that, so I moved away from the sitting room window and fetched my gloves, hat, scarf, and coat. My heart was going like a piston as I crunched across that snow towards her. She was puffing out those rosy cheeks of hers, trying to make more headway with the spade."

A warm smile spread over Flynn senior's face as he thought of her. "We said hello and then I insisted on giving her a hand. She told me Bernard wasn't able to help her as his back was playing up again."

Flynn senior's tender smile vanished.

His mouth flatlined with disapproval. "Bernard's back didn't seem to have bothered him in the pub the previous night, when he was hunched over the bar, flirting with the barmaid."

Flynn confirmed that he had kept that piece of information to himself.

Thoughts of Lily being married to someone who didn't

deserve her made me prickle. "So, what happened next, Mr Talbot?"

"We chatted about what we were doing for Christmas and Lily mentioned all the charity work that Astrid did."

Flynn senior's lips hitched into an ironic tilt. "I commented that it was a pity her Lady Bountiful act didn't extend to her own husband."

I shot a look at Flynn, who frowned at his grandfather.

Flynn senior carried on. "Then, while we were talking, Astrid appeared out of nowhere. She virtually ignored Lily and said town would be busy with Christmas shoppers and we had to get going."

Flynn senior let out a pained sigh. "I didn't want to leave. I wanted to stay there, gazing at Lily with her pink-tipped nose and listening to that husky laugh of hers.

"I handed back the shovel to Lily and I remember our gloved hands brushed against each other. All I wanted to do was drink in every curve of that lovely face."

I swallowed, listening to Flynn senior's account. My emotions were whipping backwards and forwards on their behalf. To fall for someone like that and to have them fall for you in the same way... My attention shot back to Flynn and then I forced myself to concentrate.

"I remember Lily mentioning that she had liked the winter woodland painting I had finished a few weeks before. She had spotted me in the woods with my easel, lost in my painting and my thoughts. She said she had heaved a huge sigh of appreciation at the twinkling, crisp snow scene I had created.

"That was when I decided that would be my Christmas

present to her. I made up my mind to drop the painting in to her at her business in Silver Ness. She owned a bakery…"

"Lily's Loaves," I smiled over at him.

Flynn senior blinked at me in surprise. "Yes. That's right. Someone's done their research."

He let his hands rise and fall back down into his lap. "I knew it would be a good excuse to see her again over the Christmas holidays."

Flynn examined his grandfather as we sat there, listening to his recollections.

"Of course, I had seen Lily around and about before then and we had chatted, but that Christmas…" Flynn senior's deep, educated voice tailed off for a few moments. "Something happened between us. It was as though we both realised that we couldn't keep dancing around one another or pretending the attraction we had for one another didn't exist."

I felt Flynn's attention switch from his grandfather to me. We both exchanged heated looks. Then we snapped our attention away from one another.

"When I dropped the painting off to her at her bakery on Christmas Eve, she was thrilled." He paused. "I also secreted a key inside the frame and told her about it."

"A key to get into Merry Wood?" I asked, visions swirling in my head of Lily locking up the house that day that Harley had destroyed part of the fence.

"Yes."

Flynn senior blushed under his dashing moustache. "I wanted to paint her in my studio so much, and just to spend a bit of time alone with her… It meant everything to me." He performed a shadow of a smile. "Having that key meant we could be together and shut out the outside world for a while. When she took it in her hand, I'll never forget the way she looked at me."

Flynn senior's gaze was steady. "What we did was beautiful. It wasn't sordid."

I nodded and gave a small smile of understanding. Some people waited a lifetime for love like that and yet it never comes.

I found my attention drifting to Flynn again.

"Did you feel guilty about Grandma?" asked Flynn.

"Of course, I did," said Flynn senior, clicking his tongue. "But your grandmother... well, I'm sure I don't need to tell you how difficult she can be."

"I know she can be awkward at times, but all the same, Grandfather..."

Flynn senior fired a look at his grandson.

"I'm sorry if I'm going to sound judgemental over this, but while you were flirting with the little redhead across the way, my grandmother was knee-deep in her charity work."

An odd expression gripped Flynn senior's features. He opened and closed his mouth, as though debating what to say. "Still the doyenne of the underprivileged, isn't she?" he managed after a pause. "Good old Astrid Talbot. Bring me your hungry and your oppressed."

"Grandfather..." Flynn's tone was threatening. "There's no need to be sarcastic. Stop it."

Flynn senior swung to look at me, ignoring his grandson. "You have no idea what it's like to be married to a woman like that. It was as if she was living a double life. She had two faces. One for me and our son and one for the public."

"Yes, it must have been awful," drawled Flynn. "Married to a former fashion-model-turned-successful-charity-fundraiser." Flynn shook his head in a sorrowful gesture. "You know, Grandma told me all about the other women. She put up with so much from you." He eyed his grandfather. "I know she can be difficult, but you don't know how lucky you were."

His grandfather swallowed. I noticed he had turned pale. There was sudden apprehension in his eyes.

"Grandma supported you when you were a struggling artist. She was there for you right from the beginning."

Flynn senior's expression grew tighter.

"Do you know," started Flynn, his voice threatening to crack with emotion, "I used to think I was missing out when the other kids would speak about going out to the park with their grandfathers. Sounds like I didn't miss out on much after all."

Flynn senior's expression fell further. "You don't know what you're talking about. You have no idea what it was like!"

"What is it, Mr Talbot?" piped up Mrs Oates. "What's wrong?"

He looked wildly to the three of us, as if trying to focus for a moment. "You don't understand. I thought she might change," said Flynn senior in a dry whisper. "At least, I hoped she would." He leant forward in his armchair. "No one knew. I couldn't tell them. How could I? No one would believe me."

I leant forward now, my concern spiking. "Mr Talbot?"

He stared past us, lost in his memories.

"Mr Talbot," I said again. "What is it?"

Gone was the bluff, enraged man from before.

He agonised for a few moments longer, before his paint-daubed fingers reached for the sleeves of his shirt. He gave each of us in turn a frightened look.

Both of his hands were slow, painstaking, as they began to roll back his shirt sleeves.

Flynn senior lifted his bare arms and twisted them at an angle for us to see. The light from the windows highlighted the sudden, aging planes on his distinguished features.

Mrs Oates gasped and clapped a hand to her mouth.

I let out a small, horrified noise.

Flynn's silvery eyes widened in alarm.

"She did this," croaked the older man, brandishing his marked, disfigured arms to us. "She did this to me for years. Your wonderful, charity-focused grandmother."

Chapter Twenty-Eight

The hush in Flynn Talbot's drawing room was palpable. The ticking from a clock somewhere was the only sound, accompanied by the occasional bird in the garden, flapping its way across the lawns.

Flynn's grandfather sat, his shirt sleeves remaining rolled up his arms, so the three of us could witness the pitted ghosts of cigarette burns, weals, and wounds that cluttered his skin.

"I still look like a bloody pin cushion, even after all these years."

Flynn struggled to speak. He whipped his head to me, then to Mrs Oates, and back to his grandfather. "Jesus." He dragged a hand down his horrified face. "Are you telling me…?"

"These are not self-inflicted," confirmed his grandfather in a hushed voice.

Flynn continued to stare at his grandfather's arms in morbid fascination. "Oh God. You're saying that Grandma did that to you?"

Flynn senior gave the barest nod.

Flynn rubbed at his shocked face. "Oh shit. I had no idea." His silver-grey eyes were pre-occupied. "Who else knows? Did you tell anyone else?"

Flynn senior shook his head. "I told you. I couldn't face telling anyone about it. I was mortified. Too ashamed."

Flynn blinked over at his grandfather, as though he were seeing him for the first time. A thought sprang into his head. "Hang on. Is that why you made excuses not to see me?"

Flynn senior rolled his shirt sleeves down again. Hurt and embarrassment cluttered in his marine-blue eyes. He struggled to answer. "Yes. I didn't want my only grandson to see me like that. I wanted you to think of me as a successful artist, not a victim."

Colour drained away from Flynn's cheeks. "So, you pushed me away. You pushed all the family away."

I rubbed at my forehead, almost causing a friction burn.

Flynn senior spoke again. "That was the last thing I wanted to do, but don't you see? I felt like I had no choice."

He took a deep breath before speaking again. "Astrid received news of her Africa post just after that Christmas. She was so excited." He rocked forwards, his hands rubbing his knees as he spoke. "I actually thought the abuse had stopped by then. She hadn't hurt me for weeks." He emitted a short, ironic laugh. "I convinced myself she was trying to turn a corner and that was why I decided to give our marriage one more chance. I didn't want your father caught in the middle of a messy break-up and divorce and I thought that if she really was trying to change, then I at least owed it to your dad to give things a go."

"So, you decided to go with her to Africa?" asked Mrs Oates, her voice hushed.

"Yes. It was just for twelve months."

"And Lily?" ventured Flynn.

His grandfather's face was torn. "I felt wretched about her. I had made so many promises to her." He shook his silvery head. "Lily was the most beautiful woman, inside and out. She had no idea about the abuse. When we were together, I always made sure I covered my arms or that the lighting was to my advantage. I didn't want her to see." He swallowed back the painful memories. "How could I tell her? It would have made me look pathetic."

"Not at all," I protested. "What happened to you wasn't your fault. Lily would have wanted to know."

Flynn senior raised his brows, questioning that theory. "Lily said she was so in love with me, and I hoped and prayed she would be prepared to wait the year until I came back."

"And what happened then?" asked Flynn, grim-faced.

"Astrid got up to her old tricks again several months after we moved to Africa and it carried on until our return to Scotland." He blinked hard at the memory. He shot each of us a look in turn. "That was when I knew I couldn't do it anymore and asked her for a divorce. I knew she wouldn't change."

"And was that when you were going to sell Merry Wood?" I asked.

"It wasn't my decision," replied Flynn senior. "It was Astrid's."

I could hear the anguish in his chest. "It was like a lot of things in her life. She liked it there at the beginning; kept going on about how grand the house was. Everything was exciting for her at first."

Flynn senior looked resigned. "Then once the novelty started wearing off, Astrid began criticising the house, saying how ugly it was and how boring the area was that we lived in. I think she missed being the centre of attention. She seemed to forget that it was her idea to leave Edinburgh in the first place."

Flynn senior was reflective. "She wanted shot of the house. She was desperate to get her hands on the money from the proceeds of the sale, but I couldn't bear the thought of selling Merry Wood." He gazed at each of us, as though willing us to understand. "It was like I was being torn away from Lily and all the wonderful memories of her."

He paused and composed himself. "That was when I decided to recruit Seb Banks, my accountant friend, to set up this trust under the name of Chandler." He hesitated. "Lily told me her favourite actor was Jeff Chandler."

Ah. That would explain why he chose that name as his alter ego.

There were charged looks swapped when Flynn senior mentioned this. He squirmed in his chair, realising that what he was about to say in front of me would open up a locked box of secrets. He was conflicted and unsure as to whether to say anything else.

"It's ok, Mr Talbot," I assured him. "I know. I know about you being Chandler. You have my word that I won't be revealing anything about that."

He flicked a panicked look at Flynn, who nodded his reassurance.

I turned my attention back to our conversation. "Go on, Mr Talbot," I encouraged him. "I swear your secret is safe with me. What happened then?"

Flynn senior rivered a hand through his hair so that it slipped back off his face in a silvery sweep. "I made sure Astrid received her settlement from the supposed sale of the house – or so she thought. I insisted I deal with the selling off of the furniture, so she wouldn't get suspicious or find out." His mouth flipped into a brief, ironic smile. "Astrid was so greedy and anxious to get her hands on the cash that she wasn't interested in anything else. She didn't want to be bothered with the likes of solicitors or organising the removal of furniture."

"But why?" I asked. "Why didn't you want to sell Merry Wood? Because of Lily?"

"In a word, yes. I had all the plans laid out that we would live there together with Carl. Once Astrid reverted back to her old ways again, I knew I couldn't stay married to her a moment longer. I had been deluding myself that she could change."

He let his shoulders rise and fall. "I loved Lily. I always did."

"So, what happened, Mr Talbot?" asked Mrs Oates, entranced. "Why didn't you end up with Lily?"

A flicker of pain and confusion took over Flynn senior's eyes. "You would have to ask her that. When we returned from Africa and I knew the divorce was going ahead, I went to see Lily straight away, but she refused to speak to me. She told me via her husband that she had decided she wanted to make a go of it with Bernard."

I allowed this revelation to sink in. "Well, she might well have told you that, but it doesn't change the fact that Lily is still living in that cottage opposite Merry Wood."

Flynn senior looked like he had been stung. He made a strangulated noise. "What?! That can't be. Are you sure?"

"Yes. We're sure." I pushed a gentle smile towards him.

All our eyes were trained on Flynn senior's stunned reaction. He let out a long, low breath as he considered this. "I don't believe it. After all these years."

His gaze drifted past my shoulder. "She didn't leave. She stayed there." He flushed a hot pink. "After Bernard told me Lily wanted nothing more to do with me, I couldn't face the prospect of going back there. It meant nothing without her and yet letting go of that house would have meant letting go of her – and I couldn't bring myself to do it."

"Would you like to see her?" I asked.

He stared back at me, his mouth forming a shocked O shape. His attention darted to Flynn and to Mrs Oates.

He took a gulp of air, reconciling this piece of news. Then he gave a brief nod and a shaky smile. "Oh yes, I want to see Lily. My Lily. More than anything."

Flynn senior jumped to his feet, and straightened his shirt. "Right. Let's go."

"What, now?" frowned Flynn. "Are you sure?"

"I've sodded around for too long over the years," replied his grandfather. "I'm not prepared to waste any more precious time."

Flynn looked to me for a reaction and I shrugged.

"Ok, fine," conceded Flynn. "We'll go in my car."

Mrs Oates hung back as the three of us made our way along

the hallway and towards the front door. She eyed Flynn senior as he shrugged on his long black coat and tartan scarf. "Keep an eye on him please, won't you? He likes to make out he's a tough nut, but he is more vulnerable than he cares to admit."

I patted her arm. "Of course."

Chapter Twenty-Nine

T he journey to Merry Wood was a charged expectant one. Flynn senior insisted on sitting in the back seat of his grandson's car. Every so often I would flick down the vanity mirror to check on him. He was sitting behind me, running his fingers through his floppy hair and staring out of the passenger windows with a faraway look.

"How is she?" he blurted; his eyes wide from the back seat of his grandson's car. "How is Lily?"

"She's good," I replied, choosing my words carefully so as not to betray Lily's trust. "A bit frailer on occasion."

Flynn senior nodded and turned his attention back to the landscape sliding past out of the windows to lose himself again.

The December shadows were playing in the intermittent sun as we arrived at the picnic area.

"I always park here," I said. "It's just a short walk."

"I remember," murmured Flynn senior from the back of the car.

Flynn turned to his grandfather as he locked the driver side door. "Is this going to be a bit too far for you? Can you manage?"

Flynn senior snapped his head up to look at his grandson. "I may be knocking on a bit, but I'm not dead yet." He started to stride on ahead. "I would walk over the blazing fires of hell for that woman."

His words made a tiny gasp of emotion escape from the base of my throat. To have someone say that about you…

I believed him too.

We walked in an odd line, almost bumping shoulders, through the wavering grass. Birdsong from a bold little robin fizzed from amongst the trees.

The myriad of leafless branches opened out, revealing the expanse of shadowy glade. We were very close now.

Flynn senior drew up, as if processing it all in his head. Then he moved on ahead of us.

"I hope he knows what he's doing," whispered Flynn.

We crossed through the glade and were met by the sleepy stippled roof of Merry Wood.

I heard Flynn senior take an audible deep breath. "Good God. It's still the same. It hasn't changed." He flicked a look back at us over his shoulder. "It's crazy to think that I haven't been back here since Astrid and I divorced."

"Not even once?" asked Flynn.

"No. I couldn't face the thought of it. Not without Lily."

He turned to face us both. "I had all these great plans and intentions."

"Yes, well, life has a nasty habit of throwing you a curve ball," I smiled back.

"Isn't that the truth."

The three of us drank in the tumble of wild heather in the garden and the misty windows in need of some elbow grease and a dash of vinegar to help them regain their sparkle. It only seemed like minutes ago since the magazine shoot amongst the ghostly statues in the back garden. So much had taken place since then.

I imagined Merry Wood blanketed with snow, like an image on an old Victorian Christmas card.

Flynn senior steeled himself and turned on the spot to face the other way.

Lily's cottage faced him now. There were fluttering clusters of mistletoe bushes and a couple of tea towels billowing on the washing line in the back garden.

"Are you sure you want to do this, Grandfather?" asked Flynn.

Flynn senior didn't speak, but the brief nod of his head told us he was intent on seeing her.

I had intended on knocking on Lily's door first in an attempt to pave the way for what was about to happen and hopefully setting out the stall for an amicable reunion.

But Flynn senior had other ideas.

He picked up his pace and strode up the couple of freshly washed steps to Lily's front door. He raised one hand. It hovered for a brief moment before delivering a hesitant knock.

My stomach reeled on his behalf.

There was a click of the chain and then Lily's quizzical face appeared.

She focused first on Flynn senior standing there, shuffling from foot to foot.

"Lily. It's me."

She eyed him with suspicion for a few seconds and then recognition struck her like a lightning bolt. One of her hands fluttered to her chest and rested there. "Flynn," she stammered. Her skin lost all its colour. "No! Flynn? Is that you?"

"It's so good to see you again."

A myriad of emotions travelled over her confused face. "I don't believe this. This isn't happening."

"I should never have gone to Africa with her," said Flynn, taking in her slim frame and curtain of vanilla-grey hair. "That Christmas was magical. I made the biggest mistake of my life..." He continued to stare up at her, as though terrified she might vanish again. "The years have fallen away, Lily..."

Lily dragged her stunned attention away from Flynn senior as she noticed us hovering a few feet away. She shivered and wrapped her arms around herself. The washed-out winter sun swept across her garden. "You?" she faltered at me. "You arranged this?"

"It's a long story," I admitted. "Flynn would like the opportunity to explain."

But Lily suddenly shook her head, sending her hair flying over her face like a protective veil. The blossoming hope in Flynn senior's face withered and died.

"No. I don't want this. It's all so long ago now."

She fixed Flynn senior with a wounded gaze that seemed to burn down into her soul. "You never came back. I waited for you." Her fingers gripped the edge of the door for support. "I heard you had gone for a year." She swallowed threatening tears. "I spent years hoping I'd see you again. I thought that since you didn't sell Merry Wood, you intended to come back."

"But I did come back," insisted Flynn senior. "I wanted to be with you and Carl and live in Merry Wood, just the three of us... Bernard..." Flynn senior threw me a wild look and carried on. "The letter I wrote to you explaining..."

Lily raised her chin. Pain shone in her eyes. "What letter? You made so many promises to me and broke them all." She swallowed the hurt. "I can't believe you have the audacity to show up again after all these years. I can't do this. I won't."

She shook her head as if to dislodge the emotions swirling around in it. "I want you to leave now, Flynn. And don't bother coming back."

Then she slammed the door.

Chapter Thirty

"Mr Talbot," I called to his hunched back. "Are you alright? Maybe we should leave."

He remained turned away from both of us, like a ghost struggling to decide where its spirit belonged.

"Grandfather," called Flynn. "Maybe you should accept what Lily said…"

Flynn senior didn't reply. He reached his hand to the door and knocked again, more forcefully than before. "Lily! Lily. I need to speak to you. Please!" He banged again. "You don't know the whole story. Please let me explain."

His pleas went unanswered.

I turned to Flynn beside me. "I think we should take him home now. This isn't doing either of them any good."

"I think we should too," agreed Flynn, "but he's an obstinate old man at the best of times."

We looked back to see Flynn senior thumping again on Lily's closed front door. "You have to listen to me. All right, I'm sorry. You don't have to listen to me. But please Lily."

Still the silence continued, apart from a faint rustle in the trees.

Flynn senior steeled himself.

He threw off his heavy coat and scarf and reached for his shirt sleeves. "I don't know if you can see these," he said, raising his voice, unable to maintain a level of calm. "But these wounds on my arms were inflicted by her. Astrid did this to me."

"Grandfather," said Flynn in a warning voice. "You don't have to do this."

Flynn ignored his grandson. His voice crackled with emotion. "At first, I thought she might change. She kept promising she would. When she knew her job was taking her to Africa, she became a different person for a while. Or so I thought."

Flynn senior threw back his head and breathed in a mouthful of air. It smelled of damp moss and burnished December sunshine. "But before we returned to Scotland, the physical abuse started up again. I'd had enough."

I thought I saw the faintest twitch of a curtain inside Lily's cottage.

"When we got back, I told her I wanted a divorce. She insisted we sell Merry Wood as part of the divorce settlement, but I just couldn't."

Flynn senior turned around to stare across the glade at the grand, empty house. "I had hoped you and I could make a life there together with Carl. I knew how much you loved it, especially the garden."

An agonising silence continued, until the three of us jumped as Lily's front door eventually jerked open a notch. She reappeared, sweeping some hair out of her eyes. "Your arms..." she whispered. "What happened? She did that to you?"

Flynn senior's fingertips traced over his damaged skin. "Yes."

Lily's lined, startled eyes brimmed with empathy and then anger. "So why didn't you come back?" she croaked.

"I did. Once. I spoke to Bernard. He knew everything." Flynn senior's face grew haunted at the memory. "He said you were adamant you wanted to make a go of your marriage with him and that you wanted nothing more to do with me."

The heated spots of colour on Lily's face ebbed away. She opened her front door wider. "But that's not true! When was that? I didn't know you spoke to him."

Flynn senior blinked at her from the lower step. "It was on your birthday. February 14th 1974. I've never forgotten it."

A creeping, disturbed realisation dawned on Lily. "Are you sure that was the date?"

"Yes. I remember it all."

Flynn senior's chest heaved as he recalled it. "I deliberately came on your birthday to see you. Bernard stood where you are now. He said that you had changed your mind about being with me and that you had decided you wanted to try for a baby."

Lily's eyes leapt with horror. "He said that to you?" Her breathing grew deeper, stirred up with resentment and rage. "That was lies. All of it. He never wanted children and I didn't want them with him. I wanted them with you."

Flynn senior's throat made a desperate, tiny groan of regret.

Lily screwed up her eyes, shining with the start of tears. "Oh God. That day of my birthday I was visiting my mother who was ill. I stayed over with her at her request, because it was my birthday. When I got back, he never said a word that you had been here."

Lily fiddled with the heavy silver locket around her neck, turning it over and over with her anxious fingers. "I wondered if he knew how I felt about you. He was a sly man. If he did realise, he never said a word to me that he knew."

Her glistening eyes shone with hurt. "I thought you'd forgotten all about me; that you'd abandoned me."

"Never," croaked Flynn senior, gazing up at her.

"Or that you'd decided to make a go of your marriage because of your son."

"I wanted you," managed Flynn senior. "That never changed." He threw his hands up. "I hoped that what I said to you in that letter right before we left for Africa... that would reassure you how much you meant to me..."

Lily looked confused. "What letter?"

"The one I wrote to you just a couple of days before we left Scotland."

"I never received it. The first I heard about Africa was from Astrid." Lily's features misted at the memory. "She couldn't wait to tell me you were leaving."

Cold, hard reality gnawed at Flynn senior. "Then someone stopped you from receiving that letter. Either Bernard or Astrid must have intercepted it."

Lily folded her arms around herself. Pain lodged itself in her features. "And the house, Merry Wood, you never sold it."

Flynn senior swung round and gave his old house an

absent glance. "I couldn't bring myself to sell it. All the happy memories of us together in that garden... I knew how much you loved it." He let out an embarrassed laugh. "It would have been like denying that what we had together ever existed." He shrugged his shoulders. "Bernard told me that you wanted nothing more to do with me and that was bad enough."

He flashed her a look, as if he were begging her to understand.

"I wish I'd tried again to contact you, but he sounded so convincing. I was shocked that he knew."

Flynn senior tried to steady his voice. "When I realised it was over between us, I suppose I thought keeping hold of Merry Wood was the second-best thing. I thought that as long as Merry Wood belonged to me, your heart did too."

My chest heaved in sympathy for the pain both of them had suffered. What a mess. It was a heart-breaking story of deception. Two people who belonged together, kept apart for all these years because of the jealousy and resentment of their partners – partners who never really cared for either of them at all.

Beside me, Flynn reached over and took my hand in his. The sensation of his warm fingers furling around mine sent a bolt of happiness through me. I couldn't fight my feelings for him. It was useless to even try.

I tightened my grip and gave him a shy smile.

"But how on earth could you afford to keep the house?" puzzled Lily, who had emerged onto the top step and was squinting a little in the sun. "You were a struggling artist."

"Thankfully, I didn't have to struggle for much longer at

the time. Not long afterwards, I started selling a lot of my paintings."

Flynn senior hesitated, before posing a question. "Have you heard of the artist Chandler?"

"Yes, of course," replied Lily. "He's that street artist. Nobody knows his identity." She blinked down at Flynn senior. He cocked his head to one side and arched one brow.

A little gasp escaped out of her mouth. Her eyes read his face. "No. Are you trying to tell me that's you? You're Chandler?"

"Yes."

Lily gawped past him at Flynn and me, looking for confirmation.

"It's true, Lily," I nodded.

She made another stunned noise. "Well, I never," she managed, fighting to take it all in. "I don't know what to say." She allowed this revelation to sink in. "Did Astrid ever find out?"

"Oh yes," ground out Flynn senior. "At the beginning, I kept it a secret from her. I was worried she might blab to some of her celebrity friends and then it would end up all over the newspapers."

"But?" I asked.

"But she surprised me. I never knew for certain as she always denied doing it, but I think one day when I wasn't around, she found the key to my studio – I kept it hidden – and had a snoop around. I'm not sure what she was looking for."

"And did she manage to find anything?" asked Lily, curious.

Flynn senior raised his brows at the memory. "She spotted

my Chandler signature in the bottom corner of one of my paintings and put two and two together, what with the speculation in the papers."

"How did she react?" I asked him.

Flynn senior squinted up at Lily through the icy brightness fingering its way through the trees. "She was beside herself with joy. I'm surprised she could see past the pound signs dinging up in her eyes."

He let out a hollow laugh. "If I thought she was planning on broadcasting that her husband was Chandler to the nation, I was very much mistaken. I underestimated even her devious nature."

Flynn shook his head in a disbelieving way. "She soon realised that if she did that, the mystique around me would vanish and so would the value of my work."

The breeze sifted through his generous flop of silvery hair. "So, she did the complete opposite and said nobody was to ever find out Chandler was me. It could ruin everything if they did."

Flynn senior shot me an ironic smile. "Astrid saw me as a cash cow. Up until then, she always looked down on me as her struggling artist of a husband."

He eyed Lily. "That was until her modelling work started to dry up and she realised that my alter ego could keep her in the manner to which she had become accustomed."

His smile widened at her. "Haven't you realised why I chose the name Chandler as my artist persona?"

Lily blushed, wrapping her arms around herself tighter. "I do now."

"It's also how I was able to afford to keep Merry Wood all

these years," explained Flynn senior. "If Chandler hadn't taken off as he did, I don't know what would have happened. My work has been selling so, so well. All that was missing from my life was you."

The charged events unfolding around us meant I almost missed my phone ringing in my bag.

I reluctantly let go of Flynn's hand to answer it. Part of me didn't want to, I was so wrapped up in what was happening in front of us, revealing the truth and banishing the tangle of lies.

My face must have registered surprise when Athena's name and number materialised on the screen.

"Who is it?" asked Flynn.

"My editor. I won't be a second. Sorry about this."

I wandered a few feet away while Flynn carried on observing the exchanges between his grandfather and Lily.

I was still trying to clear my head and unscramble all the painful secrets and revelations that Flynn senior was disclosing, when my editor's voice came screeching down the phone at me at ninety miles per hour.

"Why didn't you tell me?" gushed Athena into my ear, not giving me a chance to speak. "This is such wonderful news! The exclusive of the decade. My goodness, I can scarcely believe it! Well done you!"

I frowned down the line. What was she going on about? I had never heard her so animated. "Sorry? What wonderful news and what exclusive? I don't understand."

"We need to run with this as soon as possible," she breathed, not pausing for air. "I'll make sure we clear a couple of the other features to make way for it. I can stick the piece on female rally drivers and the article about Manuka honey in the next edition."

Her throaty voice then switched from high-pitched, excited squeak to something far syrupier. "Now, I know we've had our disagreements, Leonie. I have to be honest here and say I was very disappointed when you upset Esther Drew and the debacle with Tilly Crabtree. Both most unnecessary."

I opened and closed my mouth. The bloody cheek! "Sorry?"

Athena ploughed on, regardless. "But I have to say a huge congratulations to you. You really have excelled yourself with this story—"

"Athena," I interrupted, struggling to keep the frustration and irritation out of my voice. "I'm sorry, but I have absolutely no idea what you are talking about. What exclusive?"

Her tinkle of indulgent laughter annoyed me further. Had she taken something? Or maybe it was one of her long liquid lunches again.

"Chandler of course," she rasped. "We now know who he is."

The blood in my veins froze. I gripped the phone tighter to my ear.

I snapped my head round in a blind panic to look at an unsuspecting, handsome Flynn only feet away. How the hell did she know? How had she found out? This wasn't happening.

"His alter ego is the artist Flynn Talbot, isn't it?" she giggled. "Oh, go on, stop teasing me!"

She breezed on, ignorant of my horrified, gut-wrenching silence. "It's a bit of a disappointment he isn't someone more high profile to be honest, but we can work with it. Now, I want you to do a write-up about it and how you infiltrated the family." She let out a tinkle of self-indulgent laughter. "You really should have alerted me to this earlier, you naughty girl, but I'll let you off on this occasion."

I felt the colour ebb away from my face. Flynn was grinning at me.

A sick feeling squeezed at my insides. "No. You've got this all wrong. I... I didn't infiltrate anyone," I stammered, my throat dry.

From a few feet away I could see Flynn standing there, observing his grandfather and Lily, oblivious to the mess unfolding on the phone.

My stomach plummeted to the floor as the consequences of all this played out in front of me. Flynn and his grandfather thought they could trust me. They wouldn't now. They would think I had betrayed them to further my career. Nothing could be further from the truth.

Flynn had been involved in a relationship with a reporter before. She had betrayed him. Would he think it was happening again? The idea of Flynn thinking I could do such a thing... My mind churned in panic. "How... how did you find out?"

"Oh, some clever detective work on behalf of my niece."

Athena's answer struck me in the chest like a hot blade. *Kerry?* How the hell had she found out?

Anger and confusion bolted through me. I raised my eyes to look across at Flynn. My heart twisted. What a mess. Oh God. If this came out... No, scrub that. *When* this comes out, Flynn will think I betrayed him. He will think I went behind his back, all for an exclusive.

My heart galloped into overdrive.

"So, see you Monday morning and we can get all this sorted out. Ciao!"

The phone was still hot and pressed to my ear, even though Athena had ended the call.

I slowly lowered the phone, my heart lodged in my throat.

"You ok? Leonie?"

I jerked my head up. Flynn was towering over me, his brow knitted.

Queasiness swirled like a typhoon in my stomach. How the hell had Kerry found out? I hadn't told her anything. I knew I had been so careful. Had someone else in Flynn's family told her?

That seemed very unlikely. What would they gain from doing something like that?

Bewilderment morphed into anger. How could Kerry do this? How could she do this to me after all the help I'd given her? I hadn't told her a thing about Chandler or Flynn Talbot and yet she'd managed to uncover it and had gone straight to Athena, instead of confiding in me about it.

Why would she do that?

"Leonie? What is it?"

I gazed up and into Flynn's light eyes. My heart clattered against my ribs.

I had to tell him. How could I not? The news about his grandfather's secret identity was going to be splashed all over my magazine pages.

My mouth opened and closed for a moment like a ventriloquist's dummy. I didn't want to tell him. I didn't want to shatter what was flourishing and growing between us.

This was like one of those bloody games of Jenga, where you find yourself constructing what you think is a solid tower of brick, only for one of them to dislodge and bring the whole thing crashing down in front of you.

I tried to compose myself. "That was my editor," I managed, wishing I could will away what had just happened.

"Yes, you said it was her a few moments ago."

"Oh, right. Yes, I did, didn't I?" I pressed my lips together, almost suffocating under the despondent, sickening sensation pressing down on my shoulders.

I glanced over at Lily and Flynn senior, still engaged in conversation by the cottage steps.

I was struggling to look Flynn in the eyes.

"Leonie?"

I swallowed a mouthful of woodland air, the words tripping over my tongue as I said them. "Someone's told my editor the identity of Chandler. They know he's your grandfather. They're going to write an exclusive on it."

It took a few agonising moments for this revelation to register in Flynn's handsome face. The soft, gentle way he was looking at me collapsed. His expression contorted. "What? Are you joking?"

"This had nothing to do with me," I insisted, pleading with him to believe me; to understand.

"Then how the hell did they find out?" hissed Flynn, dropping his voice while his grandfather and Lily carried on talking.

"I didn't tell them! Someone must have overheard us talking."

Flynn narrowed his eyes at me. They were swimming with suspicion. "And you expect me to believe that?"

The heavy, wounding realisation that he thought it was me stole the breath from my chest. He still didn't trust me. In a way, I couldn't blame him. I was a journalist who had been told a red-hot exclusive that any magazine or newspaper would have been desperate to scoop.

And I'd told him at the time that if his grandfather ever wanted to reveal his Chandler identity, I would be more than happy to cover it.

But it still didn't change the fact that I hadn't betrayed his trust.

I never would.

I stared up at him through a haze of hurt. The words lodged in my throat. "I knew it. You think it was me who told my editor, don't you?"

"Well how else would your magazine find out? You know my family are really careful around the media." He folded his arms. "What an exclusive, eh? Wasn't that what you said? A real career booster, if ever there was one."

Pain and frustration piled in on me as Flynn threw my earlier words back at me.

"Yes, I admit I did say that. But I didn't tell her about your grandfather." Frustrated tears clotted in my eyes. "You think I could betray you and your grandfather like that? After all I've said?"

Flynn arched one livid brow. Pain clawed at his handsome, dark features. "You're a journalist, Leonie."

"What?" I blurted back. "Like Rachel?"

Flynn's black brows gathered. His Adam's apple rose up and down. "Well, you said it." His voice was heavy with pain.

I took a couple of faltering steps backwards. So that was it. That was why he had struggled to trust me.

Lily had caught sight of our exchange over Flynn senior's shoulder. She switched her attention to us and was now watching.

"Yes, I am a journalist and a bloody good one." I thrust my phone back into my bag and slung it over my shoulder. My heart felt like it had plummeted to the floor. "I also stick by a promise when I make one, but you obviously don't believe that."

I bit my lip, my emotions swirling inside of me. "What Rachel did to you was wrong, but I'm not her."

I tossed my head back, hoping he couldn't detect the jagged tremble in my voice. "The fact that you could even think I would be capable of breaking my promise and doing something like that to you and your family…"

I whirled round and proceeded to march away, tears glittering in the corners of my eyes.

"Where are you going?" Flynn yelled after me.

"Like you care. I'm calling a taxi and going home."

I blundered away from Merry Wood and Lily's cottage, gulping back hot tears. I just wanted to put as much distance between me and Flynn's untrusting, wounded face as possible.

Chapter Thirty-One

I spent an awful Sunday evening seething with injustice and disappointment.

I switched my mobile off too, not expecting Flynn to call and apologise but not wanting to put myself though the agony of looking at my phone on the off chance that he might.

If I left my phone on, I knew I would be checking it every five minutes, mentally willing him to call and apologise; to say that he had reacted on the spur of the moment and that he didn't believe for one minute I could betray him like that.

The twisting sensation of Flynn not believing me made me sink deeper into anger and fury. Well, if he could think so little of me, then it was a good job nothing had happened between us.

In the end, I occupied myself by putting up my Christmas decorations of rose-gold lights and erected my tree in the corner of the sitting room. Harley snuffled and played with the tinsel and baubles, while I fired on my CD player and desperately tried to channel Elton John's joy of stepping into Christmas.

It didn't work.

After we finished, Harley huddled up beside me on the sofa, pushing her curly, warm head into my leg and offering me gentle, loving licks that brought more frustrated tears to my eyes.

I woke up on Monday morning feeling hungover, even though I hadn't had a drink, and robotically got ready for work. I didn't want to go in and face anyone, even though I knew I hadn't done anything wrong.

I dropped Harley round at my parents on the way to the office as fast as I could, citing I had an early meeting as the reason for me not hanging around to chat.

Mum commented that I looked pale and weary. She began quizzing me on what I was eating and whether I was eating enough. "I know a lot of you young working women," she said, appraising me out of her critical eyes. "You're so busy and on the go all the time. You don't eat proper meals. What did you have for dinner last night?"

I mumbled something about lasagne and cited long hours in the office as the reason for me looking like a wax work.

She wasn't convinced by that and called after me that she would make some minestrone soup and drop it round later. Then she ordered me to pace myself.

I pulled up at the rear of the *Goddess* offices and marched in, my chest fizzing with temper and frustration at what Kerry had done. The hurt and disappointment were crumbling, making way for something far bigger and more ferocious.

I wanted to get to the bottom of this mess.

I managed to make some polite conversation with Cole and Orion about the weekend, before Athena popped her smug face out of her glass cage. "Leonie? A moment please?"

Orion frowned over at me with concern as I thumped my bag down on top of my desk and threw my coat over my chair. I picked up my notebook, pen, and phone and strode over to Athena's office.

Kerry was already seated at the new age table with a giant Minnie Mouse style red bow in her hair. I resisted the urge to wrap it around her neck and throttle her with it.

She struggled to look up at me from her notebook. He freckles were buried under scarlet cheeks.

Athena clattered her office door closed and primped to her chair at the top of the table. She clapped her hands together in delight. "So, you've been fraternising with Chandler?"

"I haven't been fraternising with anyone." I struggled to keep my voice calm.

I sat up straighter in my chair, squaring all my attention on Kerry opposite me. How could she do this? She didn't even speak to me about it first. "How did you find out?" I managed to ask her through gritted teeth.

Kerry shrivelled before my eyes. "I overheard you talking to someone in the breakout area."

That was how she found out. Flynn.

I pushed my pen around on the top of the glass table, fighting to keep calm. "Well done you. You must be very proud."

Kerry fidgeted in her seat.

"I'd like the exclusive written up and on my desk ASAP," chirruped Athena, oblivious to the Artic atmosphere. "If you take the lead, Leonie, and perhaps Kerry can assist? It would be good experience for her."

I bit back frissons of fury. I had done all I could to help her. Build her confidence. Yet she does this?

My head blundered around, desperate for something to use as an excuse or at least a delaying tactic. If I could stall this piece for publishing just now, at least it would give Flynn senior and Lily some breathing space until I decided what to do.

They were just getting to know each other again after all these years. This would be the last thing they needed in the glare of publicity.

I pretended to flick through some notes in my reporter's notebook. I couldn't think straight but I had to try and come up with something, albeit a temporary stopgap. I summoned up my most confident-sounding voice. "Would it be possible, Athena, to hold off a little longer on this one before we splash?"

Athena pushed out her Botoxed bottom lip with disapproval. "Why?"

I drew on all my acting skills, which were rather limited. "I don't want to jinx it, but I'm very close to bagging another possible exclusive. Also, I'd like to check out a few contacts about the Chandler story, before we fully commit." I plastered on a big smile. "We want to get all our ducks in a row, don't we?"

I kept my gaze fixed on Athena, pulling on all the confidence and persuasiveness I could muster. I was also aware I was throwing one of her favourite phrases back at her. It was almost like a game of who would dare to blink first.

Athena's brows tangoed. "That sounds intriguing."

"Oh, it is."

Beside Athena, Kerry reminded me of a wobbly deer on ice. She was still struggling to make eye contact with me.

"And you can't give me any more details at the moment?" pushed Athena.

"I'm afraid not. All will be revealed soon though."

As soon as I can come up with a plan.

"I'm not saying we can't go ahead and publish the Chandler story," I clarified. "All I'm asking is for a little more time to tie up a couple of loose ends."

Athena relaxed in her chair and steepled her fingers. "All right. You've got one more week, young lady to get the information and clarification you need. Deal?"

I stifled a sigh of relief. I channelled Athena's coolness. "Deal. Thank you."

I departed Athena's office and exhaled a rush of breath. Now all I had to do was think of an idea that could make this Chandler exclusive dead in the water. *No pressure then.*

"Leonie."

Kerry was shuffling from foot to foot by Orion's desk. She flicked me a look from under her lashes.

I could barely bring myself to speak to her, let alone look at her. "What is it? What do you want?"

"Can I talk to you for a moment please?"

"I don't think so. Whatever we talk about will end up being printed."

Her bottom lip wobbled. "Please, Leonie. I'm so sorry. I need to explain." I offered her a frozen stare. "Look, I don't blame you for being furious with me. Just let me explain

303

what happened and then you don't have to talk to me ever again."

There was another bigger lip wobble. I was also aware of a couple of colleagues beginning to watch us from the office floor.

I rolled my eyes. "Come on then. Let's go to the breakout area. You seem very familiar with it."

Kerry reddened. I knew it was a cheap comment, but I couldn't help it. I sizzled with betrayal and, in turn, Flynn thought I had betrayed him. That thought twisted inside me, like a knife, over and over.

No sooner had we arrived under the spot lit ceiling of the breakout area than Kerry's eyes brimmed with guilty, fearful tears. "I'm sorry! I'm so sorry."

I dragged an exhausted hand through my tangle of curls. "What on earth did you think you were doing? I thought I could trust you."

She gulped back a sob. "I should have told you about Athena, but she was having another go at me, telling me to up my game." She dashed a tear from her cheek. "She started going on about what a mistake she had made giving me this opportunity and that I was letting her down."

She let out a sob-laden breath. "I got so angry. All I kept thinking about was being able to prove her wrong; to show her I wasn't useless." Kerry swallowed. "I happened to be passing by here and I overheard you talking to a good-looking guy with dark hair."

Flynn.

Her chest heaved with guilt at the memory of it. "You were both having a heated discussion and then I heard him say something about his grandfather being the people's artist." Kerry cast her eyes downwards to the petrol-blue carpet. "I couldn't believe what I was hearing. When he'd gone, I checked out the visitor signing-in book down at security and it listed his name as Flynn Talbot." Kerry flushed deeper claret at her deception. "I wasn't going to say anything to Athena at first, but then I kept going over what she had said to me and something snapped." She pulled her watery green eyes away from me. "I just wanted to prove my aunt wrong and show her that I'm not some naïve no-hoper."

"Well, congratulations to you. You've just gone and bagged the exclusive of the year, if not the decade. What a Christmas present. You must be thrilled." She dropped her head and sniffed. "You have indeed managed to find out who the elusive Chandler is and in doing so, you have well and truly dropped me in it now," I whispered, my frustration evident. "Not only does the man I have grown to care so very much about now think I'm a cheap liar who would sell her own granny to get a story, I've got to try and come up with a plan to stop this exclusive being printed." I puffed out my cheeks. "If it does go to print, it's going to damage people that I have grown very fond of."

"I can help," she offered, butting in and sending her sheepish green eyes wide.

I let out a dry laugh. "I don't mean to be rude, Kerry, but I think you've done enough."

Her momentary composure crumpled.

"Oh, please don't cry. If anyone should be in tears, it should be me." Images of Flynn's disappointment and pain at the thought of me deceiving him and his family like that lingered in front of me and refused to move. I couldn't bear the thought of him thinking I had fooled him; lied to him.

I let out another hollow laugh. "But, hey-ho, you got to prove your aunt wrong, so that's all that matters, isn't it?"

Kerry made a gulping noise.

The image of Flynn materialised in front of my eyes again. He had made no attempt to call me last night either and I couldn't say I blamed him. He probably thought I'd got what I wanted now.

"I need to get back to work," I ground out. "I suggest you do the same."

"I'm so sorry, Leonie. I'm going to make it up to you," choked Kerry after my retreating back. "You see if I don't."

I was almost back at my desk with the raindrops chasing each other down the office's windows to fit my despondent grey mood when my mobile startled me with its sudden ring.

I sank down in my swivel chair. I didn't recognise the number.

"Leonie? Leonie Baxter?" came a troubled woman's voice. It was vaguely familiar.

"Yes. Speaking."

There was palpable relief in her sigh. "It's Lulu Stark here. We met the other week."

I sat up straighter. "Yes. Hi. How are you?"

"Not great," she managed, her voice dropping lower.

"What's wrong?"

Her tone was hushed and insistent. "I've recorded a conversation on my phone with my agent Seth Gordon." She breathed into my ear, steeling herself. "I think you'll want to hear it. Can we meet?"

"Of course," I muttered into my mobile. "But can you do me a favour?"

"Yes. Just name it."

"Can you bring along a few samples from your Stardust range? I've had an idea."

Chapter Thirty-Two

"Look, she's too preoccupied with all her corny, right-on comedy to take any notice of what's going on under her nose. I'm her agent, remember? She listens to me."

There was a pause in the phone conversation.

"No, don't do that. It could shoot us in the foot. Go for the packaging that we agreed. It looks the bloody same anyway."

There was a series of mutters and mumbled exchanges.

"We need to be careful. You know how Lulu is with all that hippy crap."

There was another voice, which was difficult to decipher.

"Right, thanks for that Rick. Much appreciated. I owe you one."

The recording fizzled to an end. Lulu Stark jabbed at her phone. "At first, I didn't want to believe it. Seth has been conning me, not only financially but ethically too."

We both stood in the rain-washed car park of *Goddess* after Lulu rang me and we had made a plan to meet.

"How long have you suspected?" I asked her.

"Not long. Just a few weeks," she admitted. "A comedian friend of mine tipped me off about Seth, saying there were rumours about him cutting corners with my brand and being more flash with his cash." She waggled her phone. "As soon as I heard that, I remembered that you and your colleague when you came to interview me alluded to the same thing." She gave her long blonde hair a dismissive shake. "Seth managed to talk me round and assure me it was all idle gossip started by that disgruntled employee and that he would fix it."

Her shoulders slumped under her raincoat. "I wanted to be proved wrong, but there you go."

I huddled into my long coat. Through the silvery, persistent rain, Christmas trees glistened out of shop windows opposite and bursts of festive songs could be heard.

"And Seth assured you that the packaging for your Stardust beauty range was ethical?"

"One hundred percent. I insisted when we were designing it that I wanted one hundred percent post-consumer recycled plastic packaging and that the contents were to be environmentally friendly."

"But?"

Lulu ground her jaw. "But it seems that he's been using some second-rate material that mimics the recycled plastic and passing it off as the real thing."

"And who is this Rick he's talking to on your recording?"

"Rick Askew," replied Lulu with clear disdain. "He's a crony of Seth's. Has been for years. He works in some PR firm, but from what I hear he's been dabbling in a lot of shady businesses on the side."

I glanced at Lulu's rose-gold mobile in her hand. "Can you

send me that recording please? I think I should have a word with our Mr Gordon, and Mr Askew deserves a call too."

Lulu dusted some stray remnants of raindrops from her belted red coat. She looked like a voluptuous 50s film star. Then she delved into her shoulder bag and plucked out a white and gold satin purse embossed with *Stardust.* "Oh, and here are a few of the samples you asked for. I popped in the exfoliator, a body lotion, and hand cream."

"Brilliant. Thank you."

"What else do you need from me?"

"I need you to be careful," I warned her. "Do you think Gordon has any indication that you know what he's been doing?"

Lulu shook her bright-blonde head. "I'm pretty sure he doesn't. He thinks I'm still his ditzy cash cow."

I assured Lulu I would be in touch soon and that I wasn't intending on hanging around with this information.

She vanished off back to her chauffeur-driven car, stationed on the other side of the car park.

"Leonie?"

I jumped at the voice behind me. "Kerry," I gasped, clapping my hand to my chest. "Bloody hell! you gave me such a fright then."

"Sorry."

I frowned at her, decked out in her frilly-necked blouse and slim-fitting trousers. She was huddled under her umbrella. "Did you follow me down here?"

She focused on her chunky heeled shoes. "I thought I saw you talking to Lulu Stark." She gazed past my shoulder. "I was right, wasn't I? It was her."

I didn't answer. I didn't have to. My silence confirmed it.

"I want to help you," she implored. "You have no idea how sorry I am about the Chandler thing."

I heaved a frustrated sigh. "I don't think so, do you? I thought I could trust you and look where that got me."

Kerry's wide mouth trembled. "But that's my point. I've made a terrible cock-up of things. You've been so wonderful and supportive and I need to make it up to you. I want to."

I gazed heavenwards. "It sounds from what Lulu has just told me that this could all get a bit messy and the fewer people that know about it, the better."

Kerry flailed one hand, sending her brolly wobbling around as she clutched it in the other. "Then all the more reason for you to have some help. You can trust me."

I gave her a cool, sceptical look.

"Please, Leonie. Give me a chance to prove to you how sorry I am."

When I still didn't respond, she angled her head to one side. "I'll do all of the legwork and you have my word I won't breathe a word of this to anybody. Please!"

Oh God. She was gazing at me like an abandoned puppy.

It was clear I wouldn't get any peace from her if I said no. My shoulders sank in defeat. "All right! All right! Enough of the guilt trip."

Kerry gave me watery smile. "Does that mean I can work with you on this story after all?"

"Yes. Ok. But you do and say nothing to anyone, including Athena, unless I give you the nod. We need to be careful, otherwise we could blow it." *Like I blew it with Flynn,* whispered a wounded inner voice in my head. I waggled the Stardust goodie bag at her. "Is that a deal?"

"Deal," grinned Kerry, hurrying over to join me as we made our way back into the glistening glass office block. "I won't let you down this time, Leonie. That's a promise. Thanks for giving me a second chance."

I managed a small smile back, in exchange for her relieved glowing one.

Pity that other people weren't so understanding or forgiving.

As we approached the glass-fronted entrance to Goddess, I handed Kerry the bag of Stardust beauty products.

"Can you have these couriered to Susie Calderwood straight away please? She's expecting them."

"Sure."

I smiled at Kerry. "With us both working together, Mr Gordon won't know what's coming to him."

Chapter Thirty-Three

"**B**ut I want to come with you," pleaded Kerry, leaning against the Smeg office fridge that afternoon.

I shook my head. "I need you to work on getting hold of Rick Askew and to speak to that former employee who Seth Gordon was blaming for all of this. Simone Wales."

Kerry looked concerned. "But what if it's dangerous?"

"Seth Gordon will be far too preoccupied with his image and protecting his other showbiz clients to do anything stupid."

She swirled around the tea in her mug. "I suppose you're right." She twitched her freckled nose. "But leave me details of where you're going and what time you expect to be back."

"Now you sound like my mum," I teased.

She laughed. "Ok. I know when I'm not getting anywhere. I'll get back onto Rick Askew's PA and locate Simone Wales."

"Thank you. Remember that being a journalist is often all about the basic ground work and tenacity."

I returned to my desk, reading over again the email from

dermatologist Susie Calderwood with her observations about the Stardust products. Then I printed off a copy to take with me.

A delighted and relieved smile broke across my face as I reflected on what I had just read and scribbled down the phone number and details of Lulu's management. "You probably have these already, but here they are again." I handed the post-it note to her. "I'll take my car. I should be back about half four."

Kerry stuck the post-it to the side of her PC screen. "Please be careful and good luck."

Seth Gordon occupied a glitzy suite of offices on the other side of town.

They were sandblasted brick with a black and gold canopy at the grand entrance and horizontal Japanese-style blinds.

I was directed to the underground car parking area by a stern-faced concierge type in a sharp suit.

"I'm here to speak to Mr Seth Gordon," I told him through the open driver side window of the car.

The man mountain glowered at me and vanished into his booth. "Your name isn't down here to see him."

"No, it's a bit of an impromptu visit." I picked up my phone from the passenger seat and brandished it in the air. "I work for *Goddess* magazine. I have a recording here on my phone that Mr Gordon will definitely want to hear." I might have sounded confident and assured but inside, my stomach was turning to water.

The security guard drew in his lips. He looked uncertain and debated for a few seconds. "Wait there while I speak to Mr Gordon."

He disappeared back into his Perspex booth and made a phone call.

After what seemed like a short, sharp discussion, he emerged again. "Park up to the left," he grunted. "Then take the set of stairs at the rear."

"Thank you. Much appreciated."

Despite my nerves jangling like church bells on Christmas Day, I managed to find a cool smile from somewhere and eased into the parking space.

The set of stairs took me up to a heavy door that was unlocked.

I stepped inside to be met by a sumptuous brandy-coloured carpet and polished burgundy furniture. An ostentatious chandelier dripped from the ceiling.

There was an empty semi-circular reception desk laced with holly and crimson ribbons, and a real Christmas tree lit up like Blackpool illuminations was in the corner.

Inside of me, anticipation and apprehension were battling it out.

From behind one of the closed office doors, I heard Seth Gordon call out. "Take a seat, Ms Baxter."

I arranged myself on a steel chair, taking in the assorted framed photographs of Gordon's glittering showbiz clients. There was everyone from Lulu, her head thrown back in a glamourous black and white Marilyn Monroe style pose, to a young up-and-coming social media influencer, an author-cum-comedy actor, and a TV chef.

After a few more tense moments there was the sound of a door gliding open further up the corridor and Seth Gordon emerged.

He sauntered towards me wearing a charming smile. His hand reached up to smooth down his daffodil-yellow tie. "Ms Baxter. How nice to see you again. How can I help? Lulu isn't here right now. She's on final rehearsals for her tour."

I got to my feet. "I'm not here to see Lulu. I'm here to have a quiet word with you, Mr Gordon."

His hollowed mud-coloured eyes flickered over me. He grinned again. I buried a lump in my throat.

"Then you'd better come this way."

I followed him back up the corridor and into the office from which he had just emerged, phantom-like. The office door glided shut behind me and he took up residence behind his desk. He indicated to me to make myself comfortable.

His office space reflected him. It was all shadowy, with dark panelling.

"So how can I help you?" asked Seth, steepling his fingers.

I decided to just go for it. "I have a recording of you talking to a Mr Rick Askew."

He shifted in his chair. "Sorry. I don't follow."

"It seems to imply that you and Mr Askew are not only conning the public with fraudulent claims about Lulu's Stardust range, you're also conning her too."

Seth's pointed chin quivered. "Apologies, Ms Baxter, but I have no idea what you're talking about."

I reached down into my handbag by my feet and located my phone. I found the recording and pressed *play*. Seth Gordon's greedy, insistent voice bounced around his office.

I observed his reaction, which morphed from charm to arrogant indifference and then to panic. He wriggled in his chair. "Switch it off," he snarled. "I said switch it off!"

I stopped the recording.

"That doesn't prove a thing," he blustered.

"I beg to differ, especially as I now have these."

"Have what?"

I delved into my bag again and plucked out a copy of the email exchanges between me and the dermatologist, concerning the ingredients and quality of Lulu's beauty range.

I handed the papers across the desk to Seth Gordon. His eyes scanned the contents. "Where the hell did you get this?"

"Let's just say it helps to be the beauty writer on a big magazine."

Seth Gordon's face flooded with temper as he read the comments from Susie Calderwood, the dermatologist.

"…these products do not contain environmentally friendly ingredients as claimed. They possess micro-plastic granules which can be very harmful to marine life, as well as acting as an aggressive and abrasive exfoliant against the skin. I would not hesitate in advising consumers not to purchase these products from either an ethical or a healthcare standpoint."

I gestured to the emails as Seth Green rifled through each of them in turn, grinding his teeth.

"The packaging, the ingredients being used, the so-called ethical message… it's all lies. *Your* lies."

He muttered something incomprehensible under his breath.

"You made Lulu think she was attributing her name to a revolutionary range, whereas you've been using sub-standard plastic packaging and cheap ingredients."

Seth Gordon threw the email printouts across his desk, sending them spilling everywhere. "You're making a story out of nothing. You have nothing to corroborate this."

It was then that my phone pinged with a text message from Kerry.

Just spoken to Rick Askew. He caved when I explained the evidence we've collated. I think he's got the wind up about all of this. He's blaming Seth Gordon for being the mastermind behind it all. He says: "I apologise unreservedly for being so naïve as to become involved in what has transpired to be such a fraudulent state of affairs. Showbiz agent Seth Gordon led me to believe that the Stardust packaging and products were revolutionary. If I had learnt of the deception I was becoming embroiled in, I would never have committed my PR services to the campaign..."

Then my phone let out another indignant ping. It was another message from Kerry. This time, she was talking about Simone Wales.

Have managed to locate Simone on holiday in the Algarve. She left Lulu's management company under a cloud a few months back, after discovering that money was being syphoned off from Lulu to Seth Gordon's private accounts. She was going to go to the police, but Gordon threatened her and her family and she was terrified to take it any further.

I started to read Rick Askew's statement aloud, but Seth Gordon cut me off with an infuriated bark. "He knew what he was getting involved in, the sneaky bastard! The pound signs were rattling his eyes from the word go."

I could feel my eyebrows rising. "So, you admit that you knew that the Stardust range wasn't what it was claiming to be?"

He gave his tie an ineffectual flap against his shirt, but said nothing.

"Do I take your silence to mean a yes?"

His hot light-brown eyes flashed.

"Are you prepared to give me a full account of what actually happened, Mr Gordon?"

His frozen gaze locked with mine. "We can talk properly out by reception." His lips flickered into a tight smile. "I've just had a new Jura S8 coffee machine installed."

I examined his face across the desk. An uneasy sense of foreboding crawled over me. "What's wrong with talking in here?"

Seth Gordon made a casual shrug of his bony shoulders. "I could murder a first-rate cappuccino."

The way his lips rolled around the word *murder* made my heart batter harder against my rib cage. Oh, this was ridiculous! I was being ridiculous. He wouldn't be so stupid as to try anything. This was just his pathetic way of trying to frighten me; psyche me out. It was all about intimidation with people like him.

"Ready for a delicious coffee then, Ms Baxter?"

I swallowed back a growing sense of trepidation again. "Yes. All right. Thank you."

He jumped up from behind his desk and pulled open his office door. "Ladies first."

My hand reached for the strap of my shoulder bag and gripped it tighter. The air was still and empty in the silent expanse of the reception area.

"Let's discuss this further down the corridor," he suggested, indicating to an alcove on the right. Talk about smooth.

I started to follow him and then the next few moments morphed into a terrifying blur.

Instead of leading me into the alcove where his coffee machine and squashy seats awaited, Seth Gordon whirled round towards me and grabbed both my arms in a vice-like grip.

It took a few seconds for me to grasp what was happening before adrenalin kicked in. I began to struggle and wriggle, my shoulder bag crashing to the carpet and its contents spinning everywhere. For a slender man he had a powerful grip.

I let out a scream as I realised I was being lifted off my feet. My legs and feet lashed out, trying at first to land back on the carpet. When I realised I couldn't do that, I aimed a series of blows and kicks to his shins. I felt like a cartoon character. I barely landed a blow against his legs; my feet lashed wildly in the air.

"Stop it, you stupid bitch!" he spat into my ear, dragging me backwards towards a fire exit door.

My nails clawed at him as I screamed and yelled again, the noise from my chest ragged and desperate. It sounded like the cries were coming from someone else and not me.

I managed to draw blood across his white knuckles, my nails digging into his skin.

"Ow! Spiteful little cow!"

Panic and bile rose up in my throat as the fire door banged open behind me, bouncing against our two struggling figures.

The empty stairwell loomed below, twisting down into nothing.

He gripped me tighter, before snatching one of my boots from my right foot and snapping off the heel. A dark thought lodged itself in my head.

Oh God. He was going to throw me down the stairs and make it look like an accident.

Chapter Thirty-Four

I squealed like a terrified animal. I couldn't get any traction. Every time I tried to get my feet back onto the floor, Gordon would hoist me back up again. My stomach hurt with his fierce grip.

I threw my head back, jerking in Seth Gordon's arms. "Let me go!"

"With pleasure," he hissed into my ear.

My heart stopped. My breathing rasped in my chest like a snake.

The stairwell was closer now, spinning all the way to the bottom. The air trapped itself in my chest as I wriggled and squirmed, screaming louder, trying not to imagine my broken body lying at the bottom of the set of stairs.

I threw my head back again, trying to land a blow against Seth Gordon's forehead, but he kept moving just out of reach. I pulled and clawed at his arms around my waist, digging my nails in harder.

Then I realised his arms, which had been locked around my

waist, seemed to be loosening. His constricting, vicious grip was losing its strength all of a sudden.

He let out a weird groan, both his arms slithering away from around my crushed waist.

What's happening? What's he doing?

Panic gave way to relief and I let out a series of agonised sobs.

I gasped in more greedy amounts of air and staggered round.

It was like I was drunk, wobbling and weaving around, unable to straighten myself up.

I whirled to see Seth Gordon had now sunk to his knees, an odd look on his face.

What's wrong with him? Why did he let me go?

I saw a flicker of movement behind him and blinked. I couldn't take in what I was seeing.

It was Kerry. She was clutching a fire extinguisher, which she had wrenched off the other wall.

As I watched, open-mouthed and still gasping for breath, she gave Seth Gordon another direct thwack on the back between the shoulder blades with the extinguisher and he flopped forwards, spreadeagled before us like an exhausted starfish.

My mouth flopped open wider, unable to compute what I was seeing. "Kerry? What the hell…?"

She dumped the extinguisher down on the floor. "Shit, Leonie! Are you alright? Did he hurt you?"

I stumbled over Seth Gordon's sprawled and groaning form and Kerry bundled me into her arms. She smelled of camomile shampoo. I struggled to compose myself. "He was going to throw me down the stairs," I gulped into her shoulder, letting out panicked sobs. "He was going to kill me."

"But he didn't," rumbled a male voice.

I looked up through a mist of panic to see Flynn Talbot senior striding towards us both.

"Mr Talbot? What on earth are you doing here?" I wriggled myself out of Kerry's concerned arms, gawping at them both.

"Rick Askew warned me that Seth Gordon was just about capable of anything," said Kerry. "Then when I spoke to Simone Wales, I got really scared. I think Askew was terrified about getting implicated in anything violent, to add to his list of other misdemeanours."

"So, you came along to check I was ok?" I asked, glaring down at the outstretched Seth Gordon at our feet.

"Yes. When Rick Askew and Simone Wales said how ruthless Gordon was, I got worried and wasn't prepared to take any chances."

"Well, thank goodness you did," I mumbled, trying to steady my breath. I rubbed at my aching waist, trying not to think of what could have happened.

My attention focused on Flynn senior again. "But what are you doing here, Mr Talbot? I don't understand." Under my coat, my bruised upper arms gave a dull, painful throb of protest.

Flynn senior shot Kerry a charged look. "I rang your magazine office." He glowered down at Seth Gordon "I asked to speak to you because I was concerned too. I saw you and my grandson exchanging words when we visited Lily."

"Mr Talbot spoke to me instead," explained Kerry in an excited, eager rush. "When he said who he was, I knew I had to tell him the truth; that it wasn't you who revealed to Athena about him being Chandler." She let out a long, embarrassed breath. "It was me. All me."

My stunned expression flicked to Kerry and then to Flynn senior.

"Mr Talbot said he wanted to speak to you not only to apologise but to talk about his grandson, and that was when I told him you were out on a story but that I was getting worried about you."

Flynn senior nodded. "That was when I insisted on coming along with this young lady to make sure you were all right. She flashed her ID at the security chappie downstairs and I made a scene, pretending I was the grandfather of some young starlet this Gordon character was involved with." Then he chuckled. "We were making such a fuss that he let us through."

Flynn senior flashed me a shy smile from under his dashing moustache. "I can't resist a damsel in distress."

His smile evaporated as he watched me. "Seriously, Ms Baxter, I wanted to apologise. I assumed it was you who revealed my Chandler identity, when my grandson warned me that news about my alter ego was set to hit the newsstands. I shouldn't have jumped to conclusions. And neither should that grandson of mine."

From down on the stairwell floor, Seth Gordon let out a self-pitying groan. Flynn senior snorted with derision. He lowered himself down beside him and wrestled off Seth Gordon's yellow tie. "Give me your hands," he snapped to the groaning man, yanking both arms behind his back and securing both his wrists with the tie.

Flynn senior examined me as he checked the knot he had made. "I know a couple of police officers. They're members of the same bridge club as me. I'll give them a ring about this idiot."

Seth Gordon jerked his head up and let out a series of fruity swear words as he struggled ineffectually on the floor like a trussed-up turtle.

Flynn senior extended one hand. "Now I really would appreciate it if either or both of you two lovely ladies could help me to my feet, please? I know I'm incredibly dashing and it's hard to believe, but I'm not in my first flush of youth."

I grabbed one arm, Kerry the other, and we hoisted Flynn senior upright. "Many thanks." He smoothed his flop of silver hair. "And in the meantime, you, young lady, need to go and speak to my stubborn idiot of a grandson. Tell him exactly what's what and clear the air between the two of you. I can't think for the life of me where he gets that stubborn streak from."

I rubbed my upper arms again. Heat flared in my cheeks as I recalled Flynn's wounded expression when he thought I'd betrayed his family secret. "I don't think we have anything to say to one another."

"Crap!" burst out Flynn senior, making Kerry start. "You both have a lot to talk about." He hesitated. "I know what it's like to be so stubborn that you make a life for yourself made up of unhappiness and regret." He jerked his head towards the fire door. "Now, I want both of you ladies to go and explain to my pig-headed grandson about the Chandler issue, once we've spoken to the police." He gave Seth Gordon, trussed up on the floor, an aggressive prod with his foot.

""The sooner we have this waste of space dealt with, the better."

A dark sinking feeling took over. "I'm doing all I can to try and stop my boss revealing who Chandler is," I assured him. "I don't know how successful I will be, Mr Talbot, as it's a huge story with a great deal of public interest and our editor is chomping at the bit."

"I've been giving that a great deal of thought," interrupted Flynn senior, his mobile connecting to the police. "We'll discuss that soon."

His words were cryptic, his eyes unreadable. At the other end of the line, I heard a voice announcing he was through to the police. He clamped his hand over the phone. "I think I might have come up with a suggestion that will solve all our problems."

Flynn senior then explained to the police what had happened and that an attempted murder had taken place.

Much to my relief, a couple of police officers arrived very soon afterwards and took details from the three of us, before handcuffing and preparing to escort a foul-mouthed, dishevelled Seth Gordon away to their vehicle. Flynn senior insisted to the two officers that he would accompany them to the station.

Kerry gave me another reassuring hug as we prepared to leave the stairwell and the empty reception area behind.

Flynn senior noticed we were lingering. "What the hell are you both still standing there for? Chop, chop!"

When I hesitated, Flynn senior grunted with exasperation. "He'll be at his photography studio across town. I checked where he was before I met up with young Kerry here."

Then he asked for my mobile and jabbed his number into my contacts. "I want to know what happens between the two of you."

He handed my phone back to me and folded his arms. "So, what are you waiting for?!"

Chapter Thirty-Five

K erry insisted she drive us to Flynn's photography studio. "You've just had a horrible, traumatic experience and need to recover. You certainly shouldn't be driving."

The prospect of seeing Flynn wasn't doing much for my blood pressure either, but I nodded.

The journey took us across town, down a couple of cobbled streets and into an old Edwardian part of the city, surrounded by stately granite buildings and the waft of money.

Kerry parked her little white Nexus in a vacant space on a side street that sported an old-fashioned barber's sign and an expensive soft-furnishings shop. "Are you feeling ok?" She angled herself round in her driver's seat to look across at me.

"I'm fine, thanks. Just a bit sore." In truth, my insides were like water, but I disguised it. I wanted to clear the air with Flynn and let him know in no uncertain terms that I wasn't the deceitful person he believed me to be.

Then I would whirl on my heels and leave – or at least,

what was left of them after Seth Gordon tore the heel from my right boot.

"I'll come up with you, say my piece, and then leave you two to have your heart-to-heart while I wait in the car," insisted Kerry. "Give you both some privacy."

I chewed my lip. "We won't need any privacy."

Kerry pulled a sceptical expression.

I threw my hands about in an odd, flapping motion. When I realised what I was doing, I stopped. "Once we've explained what really happened and that he shouldn't have been so quick to jump to conclusions, we'll go."

Kerry considered this. "He's very good-looking, isn't he?"

"I suppose he is."

She rolled her eyes up to her car roof. "So, if you aren't bothered about Flynn Talbot, why are you so keen for him to know the truth?"

I shifted in the passenger seat as the barber's canopy opposite us rippled in the wind. "Because I'm a journalist and… and… ethics are important to me."

"Uh-huh."

Kerry stifled a knowing smile. "Come on. I've got some explaining to do."

Flynn's studio shared a suite of office space with other businesses which included a dog behaviourist and a cosmetic surgeon.

Flynn's studio was located at the far end, behind a big black gloss-painted door. A frosted plaque beside it proclaimed *Kaleidoscope Photography – Flynn Talbot.*

Kerry glanced over her shoulder at me. "I'm so sorry, Leonie, for all of this. I've cocked up big time."

"Well, now's your chance to make it right."

She pushed open the door.

We were confronted by an open-plan space with a glass-panelled reception that was currently unmanned, a cream carpet, and an eclectic mix of black and white photographs ranging from a couple of family portraits to a half-dressed model with coltish legs and a stormy lighthouse scene.

Tasteful strands of white and burgundy tinsel were looped around the picture frames and a set of gold lights were draped around a nearby alcove.

All the photographs were entrancing in their own individual way. Flynn's studies of the model were especially haunting. She was gazing down the camera, her lips half-parted.

I turned around to see more pictures of a couple of other models he had taken. They were all hair and attitude.

Kerry dinged an old-fashioned bell stationed on top of the reception desk to attract attention.

Nothing.

"He can't be here at the moment," I said, noting my sudden frisson of disappointment.

"But I'm sure he wouldn't leave the door to his office open when he goes out," disagreed Kerry. "Not when he must have his expensive photography equipment lying around. Come on."

I blinked at her as she made her way past the reception

desk and down towards a couple of closed doors on the right. "What are you doing?"

"Well, he must be here. He's probably on his mobile or has headphones on."

I pursed my lips. "You know what I said about you needing to channel more of your investigative journalism streak?"

"Yep?"

"I wish you'd forgotten that particular piece of advice."

She gave a small smile and headed towards the first door. She knocked on it. There was no reply.

"I don't think he's here," I said again, trying not to acknowledge my growing disappointment.

Kerry stopped in front of me with a swish of her A-line 50s-style skirt. "Listen." She put one finger to her mouth. "Do you hear that?"

"Hear what?"

"Talking. It's coming from inside this room."

Sure enough, I was now able to snatches of conversation coming from the other side of the door. It was Flynn.

Kerry knocked on the door but there was no reply, though we could still hear a chorus of conversation taking place inside the room.

She suddenly appeared hesitant as she hovered there. "I just want to get this over with," she muttered. "I know I've made a mess of things and implicated you and I want to get it all sorted out. Put things right."

When there was no response to another of her sharp, insistent knocks, Kerry steeled herself and reached for the brass door handle. "Mr Talbot? It's Kerry Wicks here, from *Goddess* magazine. I'm sorry to interrupt, but I have to talk to you." She pushed the door wider. "It's about Leonie and the identity of Chandler—" Kerry's voice withered.

She stopped dead in front of me, her brown silky straight hair swishing down her back.

"Kerry? What is it?"

I stepped past her. Now it was my turn to draw to an abrupt halt.

In front of me was Flynn, but in his arms was a young woman draped in a trailing piece of lime-green tulle and nothing else – and they were having an in-depth conversation.

She flicked her wild strawberry-blonde hair back as she laughed at something he was saying. Flynn gave her one of his firework-inducing grins.

Sensing movement, Flynn swung round to look at Kerry and me. I thought his stubbled jaw was about to bounce off the floor.

My heart twisted in on itself.

I turned away, my chest heaving. I wanted to get out of there.

"Leonie?" came Flynn's puzzled voice behind me. "Leonie? What are you doing here?"

But I was already gathering speed, blindly racing back along the office corridor as burning hot tears threatened to spill down my cheeks.

Chapter Thirty-Six

The hypocrite!

It shouldn't have come as a shock, but it did. What else should I have expected?

First Miles and now Flynn.

Anger and pain charged up and down inside of me, spinning around and around like an out-of-control Ferris wheel. Flynn had the audacity to accuse me of deception with his grandfather's street artist identity, compare me to a previous failed relationship and yet when I go to explain, he has a half-naked blonde in his arms!

I blundered out of the entrance to the office suite, my uneven boots slapping along the Glasgow cobbles. All the festive lights and decorations blurred and melted together in front of my tear-cluttered eyes. I found the next street and slumped against the cool white bonnet of Kerry's parked car.

I had been putting myself through torture, agonising over how he was feeling and what his opinion of me was, now that he thought I'd betrayed him and his family. And there he was, grinning like a great white at a half-naked blonde?

How could I have allowed this to happen? After Miles, I had promised myself I wouldn't put my heart out there at the mercy of anyone to trample on it again.

And now look! Here I go again!

I gulped back frustrated tears.

"Leonie?"

Kerry came puffing round the corner, her hair whipping against her flushed cheeks. "Wait up! Are you ok?"

I hoped my voice didn't betray the dull ache inside me. "Let's go, shall we? That man can stew in his own juice." I blinked back fury and hurt. "If he wants to think that I was the one who went to Athena about his grandfather's identity, then that's up to him. What the hell do I care what he thinks anyway? What does it matter what he thinks of me?" I raised my wobbling chin. "He doesn't deserve to know the truth."

"Know the truth about what?"

Flynn emerged, the December sun casting a halo around his swept-back curls. *Ironic really*, I thought. *Devil's horns would be far more apt.*

I could feel my mouth pinching in pain. "Nothing." I knew I sounded petulant but I couldn't help it, and that frustrated me even more.

How on earth had I allowed myself to get into this situation? To have my feelings hurt all over again?

Kerry stood between us in the middle of the cobbled side street, spectating with increasing frustration. She gathered herself up to her full height, which was only about five foot five. "If you don't tell him the truth, Leonie, then I will."

She gulped back any apprehension she might have had as I stared at her.

"Tell me what?" pushed Flynn, eyeing us both. "What the hell is going on?"

"It wasn't Leonie who was going to have your grandfather's alter-ego spread across our magazine. She never told anyone." Kerry whipped her head to me, her cheeks burning. "It was me."

Flynn pushed both hands into the pockets of his black combats and looked from Kerry to me and then back again. "You?"

"My aunt is Athena Mayhew, editor of *Goddess* magazine. I was trying to impress her."

Flynn opened and closed his mouth while the Glasgow afternoon traffic rumbled past and Christmas shoppers negotiated around each other, clutching drawstring gift bags and looking harassed.

A cacophony of emotions travelled through his eyes. "But... but how did you find out?"

Kerry's cheeks burst into a deeper shade of pink. "I overheard both of you in the office. I just happened to be passing and heard you talking about your grandfather being the people's artist. As soon as I heard you say that, I knew he was Chandler."

Kerry appealed to a granite-faced Flynn.

"This had nothing to do with Leonie. She never told anyone about your grandfather, let alone me or my aunt." She let out a sigh. "It was just me trying to prove my aunt wrong about me not making the grade as a journalist. I wanted the brownie points."

Kerry sifted a hand through her hair. "Leonie is the most trustworthy person I know. You shouldn't think any less of her because she doesn't deserve it." She threw her hands up into the air in an exasperated gesture. "All this awful misunderstanding is down to me and I'm so sorry."

I risked a look at Flynn. He was staring across at me. He rubbed at his face. "Oh shit. What a mess. I'm so sorry, Leonie. I should never have jumped to the conclusion that I did. If it's any consolation, I feel awful."

Pictures of the tulle woman shot into my mind. "Right. Thank you, Kerry. I appreciate what you've said. Now, I've got a lot on back at the office…"

In a couple of long strides, Flynn was towering over me. "What do you think you're doing?"

I straightened my shoulders. "I just told you. I'm heading back to work. Now you know what really happened, everything is sorted."

"Is it?"

I avoided his penetrating gaze. "You'd better get yourself back up there. She'll catch her death."

Flynn's mouth twitched. "Are you referring to Courtney, who I was photographing when you came in?"

I arched one brow.

"Courtney is one of my regular models."

I bet she is, snorted an inner voice.

"She also happens to be the partner of my PA, Sorcha."

A flicker of embarrassment stirred inside of me. "Sorry?"

"Courtney is the girlfriend of my PA," he repeated with emphasis. "She's gay."

Flynn folded his arms, amused. "That's right. You and your

337

colleague here are far more her type than I ever could be." He reached for his phone in his pocket and scrolled through a couple of party shots of the two girls gazing at each other and sharing a loving kiss. "It's Sorcha's birthday in a couple of weeks and Courtney wanted to surprise her with a professional portrait of herself."

Oh God. My self-righteousness shrivelled.

"I gave Sorcha the afternoon off to get her out of the way, so she wouldn't find out about Courtney's planned present for her."

As if reading my expression, Kerry started to move away. "I think I'm going to give you two a bit of privacy. I'll be in the car if you need me." She vanished back inside the vehicle and busied herself on her phone from the driver's seat with her head down– or at least pretended to.

Oh, for goodness' sake.

This was such a messy tangle of emotions and unsaids.

"I'm really sorry," said Flynn, making my head snap up to look at him again. "I should never have jumped to the conclusion that I did." He rubbed the back of his neck. "What you said about my ex… well, you were right."

He dragged an awkward hand through his curls. "I should have known you could never do anything like that, but that was why I was so guarded with you – at least at the start."

He gave a wry smile. "I know this is going to sound crazy but I kind of hoped you were the one who was threatening to reveal all about Chandler."

I stared up at him, trying to read his handsome features. "What? Why?"

"Because I wanted to believe it. I wanted to believe you

would do that. Thinking that about you, that you would break a confidence like that, like Rachel did, meant I would have an excuse not to…"

My heart zinged at the way Flynn was examining every inch of my face. "Not to what?"

Flynn's eyes trailed down to my lips and rested there. "Oh, sod it, enough of the talking," he growled, seizing my mouth with his.

We clung to each other, moulding and blending our bodies together as our kisses became greedier, making up for lost time and devouring one another, not wanting to let go.

"Wow," he murmured against my mouth after what seemed like ten minutes. He smiled against my lips, triggering one from me.

My fingers reached up and entwined themselves around the curls furling up at the nape of his neck. "What were you going to say just now?"

"I think it was an observation about the weather."

I playfully slapped him on the arm and he gave me a heart-trembling grin. "Ok, seeing as we're being honest and this is all playing out in the middle of Glasgow…" His face adopted a more pensive expression. "Part of me wanted to think badly of you because I thought it would stop me falling for you. I knew I couldn't go through that deceit again."

I found myself being swallowed up in those heart-stopping silver eyes of his. His lashes flickered.

"Even though you have a little black book that's more like a telephone directory?" I asked him.

"I think that's a bit of an exaggeration. It's more like a copy of *War & Peace*."

I gave him a playful dig with my elbow.

"Ow!

"Yes. Ok," he grinned. "I admit I did play the field a bit up until I met you."

He held me a little tighter and I snuggled into him. "I did date a lot of different women. I suppose being a sexy, handsome, and successful photographer has its advantages."

I pretended to look around. "Well, if you tell me where he is…"

Flynn pulled a comical face that made me laugh. "But then you came along and it made me realise what an empty, vacuous lifestyle I was leading." His gaze softened further. "It's not just because I think you're gorgeous. I love the way you care about other people and how you always want to do the right thing."

I leant up and planted a graze of a kiss on his lips. "Say that again."

Flynn arched one thick, dark brow. "Now you're milking it."

As the sound of the traffic and Christmas crowds echoed around us, we kissed again, lost in each other.

"So, what now?" I asked after a few moments.

Flynn ran one playful finger down the length of my nose before tapping the end of it. "Well, I was going to invite you out to dinner. Something tells me my grandfather will approve."

Oh bugger! I jerked out of Flynn's arms. "Your grandfather!"

Flynn blinked down at me, confused. "What about him? You don't fancy him as well, do you?"

"Very funny." I fished about in my bag by my feet and

dialled Flynn senior, who told me he was en route to the police station with the two arresting officers and a rumpled Seth Gordon who would soon be in the company of one of his detective friends.

"Life with you is never boring," exclaimed Flynn, shaking his head. "Now will you please tell me what's going on? Once I've explained to Courtney back up there where I've got to?"

I took Flynn's hand in mine when he returned from dashing back up to his studio to explain to Courtney what was happening and to apologise for his sudden and prolonged disappearance.

Luckily, she took it in good part, seeing as her photo shoot with Flynn had almost finished by the time I rocked up with Kerry anyway!

I encouraged him to get into Kerry's stationary car. "Come on I'll explain on the way."

Chapter Thirty-Seven

"What the hell did you think you were doing, going to that guy's offices on your own?"

I stared up at Flynn. "I had to find out the truth. Lulu Stark asked Kerry and me for help."

Flynn, his grandfather, Kerry, and I were loitering outside the police station, after Flynn senior, Kerry and I had been questioned further by the police and more statements were taken from us. We all looked and felt mentally and physically exhausted by that afternoon's events – like the three of us had been put through a spin cycle.

We had emerged, blinking, into the early evening which was now all but extinguished by the descending darkness. The lights of the office blocks, shops, and flats intermingled with the festive ones, sparking against one another in a dazzling display. It was as if a box of precious stones had spilled across the city.

Weary office workers shuffled past, ties askew and blouses

crumpled, desperate to get home and wash off the rigours of their working day.

Flynn shook his dark head in exasperation. "You could have been killed."

"But I wasn't and I'm ok. That's thanks to Kerry and your grandfather."

Flynn sighed. "What on earth am I going to do with you, Leonie?"

I gave a small, cheeky smile. He broke into a devastating grin, but we were interrupted by Flynn senior's commanding voice.

"Right, Flynn, I'd like you to give your parents a call and tell them to come over to my place."

Flynn pulled his attention away from me and stared with incredulity at his grandfather. "Are you serious?"

"Of course, I am."

"But why do you want to invite my parents over?" asked Flynn, raising his eyebrows. "I think the last time you had Carl and Diana over, ABBA were at number one."

"Very drole. I can see where you inherited your waspish wit." Flynn senior turned to Kerry and me, presumably because he thought he might have more success at a less pithy conversation. "I've been doing a lot of thinking of late and there are a few things in my life I want to change."

Before either Flynn or I could guess what they might be, Flynn senior turned to Kerry. "Would you be able to take us home, dear girl, and perhaps stop off on the way? There's someone else I want to invite along."

"Merry Wood?" hissed Flynn to me, as Kerry swept her car into the vacated picnic area. "What's the daft old sod up to now?"

"I heard that," said Flynn senior, twisting round in the passenger seat. He ran a hand through his hair and straightened his shirt collar. "I'm going to invite Lily back with us." Then he thrust a finger in the air, as though experiencing a eureka moment. "I just hope she agrees to come along. It's so important that she hears what I have to say. In fact, all of you need to hear it."

He sat up straighter in the passenger seat and fetched his mobile from his trouser pocket. "But first I had better give Mrs Oates a call. Thank goodness she did the weekly shop this morning."

We listened, rapt, in the confines of Kerry's car, as Flynn senior spoke to Mrs Oates. "I'm having a few people back for something to eat," he explained down the phone to her. "No, there's no need to get stressed. Just rustle up some of your famous Cullen skink, if that's all right."

There was a pause. "Oh, not many," he breezed. "There will be seven of us including you… hopefully eight."

Mrs Oates must have exclaimed because Flynn senior flinched. "You've catered for more than that in your time, dear woman!" The he turned on the charm. "Wonderful! Did I ever tell you how fabulous you are?"

He finished the call with a "Thank you, darling." A glimmer of apprehension travelled across his face all of a sudden. "Now to go and speak to Lily again." Flynn senior turned to me. "Would you accompany me please, Leonie? It's obvious you and Lily have grown close and she thinks very highly of you. You seem to have established a bit of a bond with her."

Within the car, I was aware of three expectant faces reading mine and the warm scent of vanilla air freshener. "I have grown very fond of her." I blushed. "She's certainly a very special lady."

Flynn senior's brow arched with optimism. "So, is that a yes?"

"Of course," I answered. "Come on. Let's go."

We arrived at Lily's cottage with the amber lamplight casting a soupy, cosy warmth that splashed out against the dark trees and over her frosty lawn.

Behind us, Merry Wood stood the complete opposite with its dark empty rooms and prickly angled roof. Flynn senior studied it, his expression raking over its peaks and cornices.

"What are you going to say to her?" I whispered to him, as he dragged his attention away from Merry Wood and back to Lily's cottage. He began ascending the front steps.

"I'm still working on that."

Oh God! That didn't sound good. There was every chance after their first encounter here the other day, that Lily would choose to chew him up and spit him out.

Lily had placed a gorgeous blood-red poinsettia in her kitchen window and through a chink in her sitting room curtains, her modest but sparkling Christmas tree throbbed with gold lights.

"Who is it?" called Lily's guarded voice through the closed door. One of her curtains at her sitting room window twitched.

"It's Flynn," he answered, struggling to locate his confidence. "And I have Ms Baxter with me."

Lily's silhouette appeared as the front door eased opened. "Oh. You again."

"Yep. Me again."

Flynn straightened himself. "I'm not prepared to sod about any longer, Lily. Too much of that has happened already and that was down to me." He pinned her to the spot with earnest eyes. "There are things I want to tell you to clear the air. I'm sick of secrets."

He glanced back over his shoulder at me and I widened my eyes, urging him to carry on. "Please come back with me to my house this evening."

"Sorry?"

"My housekeeper is preparing a lovely supper for us all. There will be you, me, Leonie, my grandson, and my son and his wife."

Lily's hand flew to her throat. She looked appalled. "Good grief! Why all these people?"

"Because you all need to hear this. You all need to hear what I have to say. Please."

When Lily's reluctance prickled out of her, I took a tentative step forward. "Lily, please come and hear what Flynn has to say. That's all he's asking of you. Just to hear him out."

She turned over my request in her mind. "But it's been years."

"That's why it's so important for me to speak out now," implored Flynn. "Please Lily."

"But so much time has passed," she said in a whisper. "So many years."

"But they haven't changed how I feel about you," replied Flynn senior. "Not at all."

She reached one hand up to her loose hair, debating whether to accompany us or not. "I look an awful fright."

Flynn senior's expression softened. "You still look as stunning to me today as you did fifty years ago."

Lily shook her head in mock exasperation. "Still the silver-tongued rogue, Flynn Talbot."

Flynn senior smiled hopefully up at her from the cottage steps and all the years that they had been apart seemed to slip away and evaporate in amongst the trees. She let out a defeated sigh. "All right. Just give me a minute to tidy myself up."

The weird atmosphere in Kerry's car was palpable.

It was an eclectic mix of two former star-crossed sweethearts, my work colleague who had stabbed me in the back and then saved my life, and the man who had managed to steal my heart, despite my protestations.

Lily was seated between Flynn and me on the back seat. She appraised him. "At least I'm sitting beside a handsome young man."

Flynn grinned. "You can come again whenever you like."

From the passenger side, Flynn senior glanced around at his grandson. "I used to look like that once, all tall, dark, and devilish."

Lily pulled a face. "Yes, and lacking in confidence, as I remember."

The Drummond scenery gave way to sweeping country lanes before we reached the popular spread of hills that identified Cairntilloch, but which were now sunken in darkness.

There was a crisp woody scent to the evening air.

Kerry eased her car up to the kerb outside Flynn senior's impressively sprawling townhouse.

None of us had even vacated Kerry's Nexus before Mrs Oates appeared at the wrought-iron gated entrance. She stabbed in the code and surveyed us all. She was sporting a wax-coated knee-length apron decorated with sunflowers. Her hair was coiffed. "My word. I never expected this tonight."

Lily disappeared deeper into her stylish shawl. "I'm so sorry about all of this. Flynn said—"

Mrs Oates stepped forward in her gold boat shoes, her dark blue eyes kind. "No need to apologise. This house could be doing with chatter and noise." She extended a warm hand. "I'm Mary, Mr Talbot's housekeeper and jailer."

Lily couldn't stop herself from laughing. "You don't seem to be doing a very good job of the jailer bit."

"Ah. You noticed. Well, if you know the old reprobate at all, you'll realise keeping him on the straight and narrow is easier said than done." She delivered a welcoming smile. "You must be Lily. It's lovely to meet you at last."

A growling engine from another car interrupted the introductions. Mrs Oates peered past Lily's shoulder. "Oh, it's your son and daughter-in-law, Mr Talbot."

A smart bullet-grey Mercedes pulled to a stop behind

Kerry's car and Carl and Diana Talbot stepped out, surveying the cluster of us with bemusement.

"Hi Dad," said Flynn, clutching at my hand. "Surprise!"

Carl Talbot appraised his son and patted him on the back. "Any idea what all this is in aid of? You didn't give much away over the phone."

"I think I might have a rough idea," muttered Flynn, arching his brows at me.

Flynn's mother stepped up and delivered a kiss to his stubbled cheek. "I wish I had."

Flynn senior introduced us all to one another with aplomb and then clapped his hands together in a business-like fashion. "Right. Let's all go inside shall we, before we take root out here."

Flynn leant in to my ear. "Sorry about this. We haven't been out on our first date yet and you've already met my parents."

"Who said I was going to go out with you?"

I returned Flynn's lazy grin.

Ahead of me, Lily was gazing up at the townhouse, with its gorgeous balconied windows. Her attention landed on the gate and the frosted name plate, Lily Grove, as she made her way past. I thought her eyes were going to fall out of her head. I noticed her swallow and gather her shawl tighter to her shoulders.

Meanwhile, I surreptitiously studied Flynn's mum and dad, while Kerry followed up the rear. Then she stopped and angled me to one side. "I'm going to head off home now, Leonie."

I opened my mouth to argue the point, but she shook her

head. "I've got a lot to repent for. You go ahead with the Talbot family. You can give me the lowdown later."

"Are you sure?"

She placed one hand on my coat sleeve. "Positive."

I watched her return to her car and jump in the driver's side. "Kerry?"

She was about to close her car door.

"Thank you for coming to my rescue earlier and for what you did about the Chandler issue."

She gave a small smile. "It was the least I could do."

Her little white car vanished off back down the road in a blaze of headlights.

As they entered Flynn senior's house, Carl and Diana Talbot reminded me of the well-heeled married couples you often see on cruises.

He was like an older, staid version of Flynn, with dark greying hair at his temples and a quizzical look to his Irish features.

Diana was a cool ash-blonde, with a sharp chin and long legs.

Mrs Oates ushered us all towards the end of the hallway, where a closed door to the left revealed a gorgeous dining room with burgundy flocked wallpaper. The table was a sea of sparkling crystal, set atop a dramatic black and white damask tablecloth. Matching napkins poked out of ball glasses.

A Christmas candle table decoration comprised of berries, pinecones and frosted holly sat proudly in the centre.

Fairy lights were strung along the edge of a heavy cabinet at the rear of the room.

Flynn senior directed each of us to our seats. I sat beside

Flynn with Mrs Oates and Flynn senior at opposite ends of the stretching table. Flynn's parents were seated opposite us and Lily sat at Flynn senior's right.

Mrs Oates vanished, moments later returning with a grand silver terrine. Flynn jumped up from beside me to assist her.

She dashed off the ornate lid to reveal the rich, creamy aroma of smoked haddock soup.

While Mrs Oates swooped generous portions of the Cullen skink into each of our soup bowls, I noticed Diana flash her husband a pointed look. "Ask your father what this is all about, Carl," she hissed from the corner of her mouth. "Don't you think it's all rather unnerving?"

I wasn't sure if Flynn senior had heard, but if he did, he didn't react. He appraised each of us from the head of the table, like a dashing moustachioed lord of the manor. "Please eat first, everyone, and then I will explain."

After everything that had taken place today, I was taken aback by how hungry I was. I was sure my run-in with Seth Gordon would have taken its toll on my appetite, but the smoky taste of the Cullen skink, together with the dash of potato and onion, was delicious.

There was a revered hush as soup spoons clinked against the sides of bowls and there were murmurs of appreciation.

When everyone had finished, Mrs Oates moved to gather up the empty soup bowls and I rose to assist her, but Flynn senior indicated for us to leave the clearing up for now and sit back down.

"I didn't sell Merry Wood all those years ago," announced Flynn senior, with an air of resigned calm.

Carl and Diana Talbot's expressions were of stricken bemusement. Their spoons clattered in shock.

Flynn senior glanced down at the table, settling his attention on his son. "When your mother and I decided to divorce, she was desperate for me to sell it, but I just couldn't."

Carl Talbot snapped his head to his father. "Are you joking, Dad?"

"Nope."

"But whyever not?" frowned Diana. "I don't understand."

"I couldn't bear to part with the place," replied Flynn senior.

He turned to Flynn and me. "Before Astrid and I moved into Merry Wood, we lived in Edinburgh. I didn't mind it, but Astrid wasn't keen. She said she kept getting pestered with autograph hunters after her modelling took off and she wanted to live somewhere a bit more rural."

He looked thoughtful. "I believe she had other reasons for wanting to move to a more remote location and that this was just an excuse."

Flynn shot me look of understanding. He looked across the table at his grandfather. "Like keeping you on a tight leash? I mean, she could do what she wanted there and you wouldn't have had the same opportunities to seek help."

"Exactly."

I thought about the struggle I had experienced, trying to get background information on Merry Wood and who lived there. "Is that why I was having issues finding about the history of Merry Wood and who owned it?"

Flynn senior took a gulp of his white wine. "Astrid was paranoid about people finding out where she lived. On one hand she revelled in the publicity, but on the other she wanted her privacy."

I nodded. "When it suited her."

Flynn senior agreed. "She charmed the local authorities into keeping it quiet that we had moved to Merry Wood."

A corner of his mouth flicked upwards in an ironic sort of way. "My ex-wife can be very charming and plausible when it suits her."

Carl looked irritated. "What are you all talking about? What is all this?"

Flynn senior ignored his son for now and carried on. "I thought that if we moved somewhere new, things might improve and Astrid would be calmer. We visited Merry Wood and both fell in love with it."

He turned to Lily beside him. "To this day, Merry Wood does still carry some unpleasant memories for me, I will admit. But then it also had so many more wonderful ones too." He paused and smiled at her. "Thanks to this lady here, the special ones far outweigh the not so pleasant."

Flynn senior stretched out one speckled hand and took a stunned Lily's in his. Carl and Diana's mouths dropped open. Carl's shocked expression twisted into a glower at their entwined hands. "Hang on a second, what do you mean by unpleasant memories? Are you talking about Mum?" He didn't allow Flynn senior enough time to reply. "Do I take it that these wonderful memories you're talking about are connected to this woman?" As if to illustrate the point, Carl lifted a finger and jabbed it at Lily.

Lily shifted in her chair, a pink blush seeping into her cheeks and clashing with her lilac eyes.

"This woman," said Flynn senior with emphasis, "is Lily Cruickshank. She was the love of my life." Now it was Lily's turn to stare wide-eyed at Flynn senior. "And she always will be."

Carl let out a snorting noise that reminded me of a furious bull. "Jesus, Dad! Are you telling me you had an affair behind Mum's back with this old tart?"

"Carl!" barked Flynn, glowering from under his brows at his father. "You don't know the whole story. And please don't talk about Lily like that."

Carl Talbot let out an incredulous bark of laughter. "This just gets better and better. Are you telling me you knew all about this, son?"

"I only found out recently."

"And you didn't think to tell your own father about it?"

Diana glanced across at her son. "I really think you should have told us about this when you found out, darling. I mean, this impacts on your poor grandmother too."

"Yes, well you might not be so sympathetic towards Grandmother when you hear what else Grandfather has to say."

Carl folded his arms. "Oh, I can barely contain myself."

Flynn senior swallowed, aware of the several pairs of eyes scanning him from around the long dining room table.

"Go on," I encouraged him.

Now it was my turn to receive a stony look from Carl Talbot. "How many bloody people around this table know what's going on?"

Flynn senior ignored his son's bark of a question.

"Why are you trashing your marriage to Mum?" probed

Carl Talbot. He slid Lily a spiteful stare. "You and Mum were always so happy together, although she did tell me about the other women you had while you were married and she turned a blind eye to it."

Flynn senior's mouth ground into a taught line. He hesitated, his fingers lingering above his shirt sleeves. Lily reached over and stroked his arm in an act of encouragement.

With growing resolve, Flynn senior's fingers began to roll up his shirt sleeves. Beside me, Flynn reached for my hand and we sat, our fingers locked together in supportive unity.

Flynn senior addressed Carl. "So, this is a sign of a happy marriage, is it?"

Under the dripping chandelier light, Flynn senior's swathe of pitted, abused skin on his arms screamed out.

Carl's pale blue gaze became stricken with horror.

"Your mother did this," stated Flynn senior. "Sometimes it was with a cigarette. Other times with a dripping candle. Then at other times, when she couldn't be bothered to go to the trouble of either of those, she would hit me with anything that came to hand."

Lily's crumpled expression tugged at my chest.

Diana swallowed.

"Your mother would accuse me of all sorts of terrible things and then attack me"," said Flynn senior, training his full attention on his son. "She would say I was ignoring her or that I was being condescending to her; that I was stealing money from her but it wasn't true. None of it. I think she grew jealous of the attention I got and that stoked her temper." Flynn senior then flashed his grandson a look. "I felt ashamed."

Carl looked stricken.

Flynn senior addressed his reeling son. "I know she never laid a finger on you, but I wasn't prepared to take the chance. That's why my intention was for you to live with me and Lily at Merry Wood."

Beside me, I could see Flynn give a brief nod that he understood. He swallowed a ball of emotion and stroked my fingers.

Flynn senior looked softly at Lily beside him. "If it hadn't been for falling in love with this lady at the time, I don't know what would have happened."

Carl cleared his throat. He looked like he was struggling to speak. "So let me get this straight. You're telling me that my mother did that to you?"

"Yes. She did."

Flynn senior rolled his sleeved back down over his offending wounds. "I hoped she might stop. I convinced myself she would, but her violent outbursts just got worse. That was until she got the opportunity to go to Africa."

Flynn senior delivered a small smile to Lily beside him. "But by that time, I had met and fallen in love with Lily."

Lily looked across at me, her eyes softening in her lined but gentle expression. "Was that when you wrote the letter that Leonie found?"

I took my cue and removed the letter from my bag and passed it up the table to Flynn senior.

He took it reverently in his hands, his attention grazing over it. "Yes. My God, after all these years…" Lily shook her head as she watched Flynn senior holding it. "I have no idea what it says."

She gave me an apologetic look. "Leonie tried to return it to me on the day she discovered it in Merry Wood, but I was so stubborn and I wouldn't open the door to her."

Flynn senior's jaw dropped. "But I thought you read it at the time."

"I never even knew that letter existed until you told me about it," clarified Lily. "Like you said, Bernard must have found it and given it to Astrid."

There were meaningful glances exchanged all around the table. Lily's expression cleared with realisation. "They must have concealed it; conspired together to keep us apart."

Lily drank in Flynn senior's features beside her. "I was so hurt, so stunned at the time that you didn't tell me first, Flynn. Now I know why."

Diana's fascination was evident. "So, what happened? Why didn't you go to the police about the abuse?"

Flynn senior shook his head of thick silvery hair. "I was stupid, my dear. I felt ashamed. Domestic abuse wasn't taken seriously in those days; not like it is now. And can you imagine how abuse against a husband, perpetrated by a wife would have been treated back then? Who would have believed me? I went away to Africa with Astrid as you no doubt know, but she fell back into her old ways while we were there."

He scanned us all. "That was when I realised how much I wanted to be with Lily. Even more than before." Flynn senior's attention drifted to Carl. "I had my son to think of too."

Carl swallowed.

"What I didn't know was that Lily waited for me, which I didn't deserve."

Lily clutched and squeezed at his hand again. "That was my decision to make Flynn, not yours."

Flynn senior carried on talking. "When we arrived back in Scotland, I went straight to see Lily, but her husband told me she wanted nothing more to do with me. He knew how we felt about one another."

"And Merry Wood?" asked Carl, the shock still shining out of his face.

Flynn senior's eyes were bursting with the memories of it all. "Lily and I had spent so many happy times wandering around in the garden there. I had even painted her a few times. We always fantasised about the three of us living happily ever after there. You, Lily, and me."

Carl snapped his head to look at Diana beside him. She gave him a soft smile.

"And that was why you couldn't bring yourself to sell it?" surmised Diana, her voice hushed.

"I know it all sounds crazy now, but we were so in love," interrupted Lily. "I lived with my late husband, Bernard, in the cottage opposite Merry Wood and when I thought Flynn had decided not to come back and to try to make his marriage work instead... Well, even though the memories of him hurt so much, it was almost a comfort to still have the house to look at every day."

She let out a dry laugh as we all hung on to every word she was saying. "I had no idea what was happening with Merry Wood but a tiny part of me, even years later, hoped I might see Flynn again and that he would come back."

From around the dining table there hung a heavy, emotional silence.

"Flynn gave me a spare a key that first Christmas, and we would slip out to meet one another." Her eyes clouded over with the memories. "He painted me in his studio a couple of times. He thought that if I had a key, then it would be easier for us to arrange our meetings, if we both had access to the house when Astrid and Bernard weren't around."

I recalled Lily propelling herself out of the back door when Harley and I entered the rear gardens of Merry Wood. "And that's why you could still gain access to the house."

Lily reddened and nodded.

Carl toyed with the cut-crystal wine glass in front of him, not looking at his father. He gathered himself. "Why didn't you go to the police about Mum at the time?"

"Like I said before, I know I should have, but my bloody stupid male pride wouldn't allow it." Flynn senior turned to me. "Back then, I had a fear of what people might think and it was such different times."

"And the fact that Grandma was the doyenne of the fashion and charity circuit?" asked Flynn from beside me.

Flynn senior nodded. "I wondered if anyone would believe me. What? Astrid Talbot? The Scottish Twiggy? Who was raising huge amounts of money for the hungry, needy, and underprivileged? Physically abusing her husband?"

Diana took a gulp of her white wine. "So, what are you going to do now, Flynn? About Astrid, I mean?" She turned to Carl. "I know she's your mother, but she shouldn't be allowed to get away with it."

"I agree," murmured Flynn to his mother.

"I've decided to go public," stated Flynn senior, emboldened. "I'm going to go to the press and reveal what she did to me for years." Now it was his turn to gulp a mouthful of wine. "Something good might come of it. Hopefully any other men or women who are suffering or who have suffered in the past like me, will then feel they can speak out too."

"That's very brave." I smiled up the dining table at him. "And I think it will be the worst thing that could happen to her. I've only met your ex-wife once, but I get the impression her reputation matters a great deal to her and once her charities find out about what she was doing, I'm sure it will only be a matter of time before they disassociate themselves."

There were general murmurs of agreement from around the table.

"No more secrets," exclaimed Flynn senior. "There have been too many for too long and they stop right now."

Carl shuffled in his seat. "Look Dad, I hate to ask but what are you going to do about Merry Wood, now that it still belongs to the family?"

I could see Flynn beside me, rolling his eyes. "Look Carl, I think there will be plenty time for Grandfather to decide what he wants to do, once the air has cleared a bit."

"Oh, no need to procrastinate. I've done enough of that."

We all studied Flynn senior.

"I've made a decision," he said, settling back in his chair and cupping Lily's hand in his. "I'm sick of sneaking around, all secret squirrel. I'm getting too old for all of that nonsense."

"Dad?" frowned Carl. "What are you talking about?"

"I'm talking about my alter ego. Chandler."

More confused glances were swapped between us all as we sat there.

Flynn senior revelled in the questioning looks we were giving him. "I've made up my mind. Enough is enough."

He picked up his wine glass, swished around what was left

of it, and downed the remainder with aplomb. He set it back down on the table. "I've decided to not only go public about Astrid and the abuse I suffered at her hands, but about being Chandler too."

"What?" I asked. "What do you mean?"

"If I'm being honest about Astrid, then it's time I was honest about other things in my life as well." He squeezed Lily's hand again. "All that matters to me now is being with Lily and enjoying the time we have left together."

Flynn beside me shrugged. "So, what does that have to do with Chandler, Grandfather?"

"Everything," he answered, addressing the stillness in the room. He sat back, a palpable relief sweeping away the anxiety, pain, and exhaustion that had been gnawing away at him for years. "It has everything to do with it, dear boy. When you get to my age, you realise what's important and that all the rest of it is a pile of white noise and stuff and nonsense."

Mrs Oates smiled at her irascible employer.

"The true identity of Chandler will be unveiled. It's about time."

"Grandfather, have you thought this through?" asked Flynn. "It's a big deal. You know that once you admit you're Chandler, you will be deluged by the press."

"I have thought about it, dear boy. I've thought about nothing else." He gave a casual shrug. "It's a means to an end. Once the fuss has died down over it, which it inevitability will, Lily and I can relax and enjoy our lives together."

An awkward smile played at his lips. "And I'd like to get to know my grandson properly. So much time has been wasted and I want to rectify that."

Flynn broke into a grin. "I'd like that a lot. First round is on you though, Grandfather."

I squeezed Flynn's hand, which rested on mine. Old wounds were being tended; recognised; addressed. Something told me the Talbot family would be ok.

Epilogue

A thena had been on the verge of spontaneously combusting when I told her about Flynn Talbot senior's revelations about his ex-wife – and that he wanted to reveal exclusively to *Goddess* that he was the secret street artist Chandler.

"He's insisted that he won't speak to anyone else about it, apart from us. We will have the exclusive. All of it."

Athena had sunk behind her desk, her face glowing. She seemed to be hyperventilating. "Oh my God! How quickly can you ladies talk to him? How fast can we get this interview scheduled?"

"Flynn said the sooner the better," beamed Kerry with delight. "He wants to move on with his life."

"Move on?"

"It's a bit of a long story," I clarified, "but that's what Kerry and I are going to write about."

And so, Athena called an impromptu staff meeting, confirming to our magazine colleagues that the Christmas issue would have to be revamped to accommodate something very special.

There had been a chorus of frustrated moans and groans, until she revealed why and then there was an excited chattering and gasps, with the realisation of how many copies the Chandler interview was going to sell.

She instructed that the interview with Flynn Talbot senior would be perfect alongside the Avanti cosmetics feature, photographed at Merry Wood.

Kerry and I conducted the interview, which Athena described as "the scoop of the decade", hoping that our questions would draw out what every reader would want to know: how such an accomplished artist who had become so successful, had also been a victim of domestic abuse before rediscovering the love of his life.

But there had been no need for us to try and get Flynn senior to open up. He had been more than happy to talk about his love of art, and the wonderful Lily who he had loved and lost before finding again. Then there had been Merry Wood, the house he had planned to share with Lily, but then couldn't bear to part with when he thought they couldn't be together.

Finally, there was the subject of his alter ego, Chandler, who for years, had brought the beauty and rich spectacle of art to the streets of Scotland. Everything from empty factory walls to abandoned public toilets had experienced the brush strokes of Flynn.

It had made one very interesting read and I liked to think Kerry and I did Flynn Talbot senior – and Chandler – proud.

So, alongside the glossy feature on Avanti cosmetics, with

its enchanting, ghostly statues and the wild beauty of the gardens of Merry Wood, there was also this:

Goddess magazine, Christmas 2022 edition

Affairs Of The Art

Read our exclusive interview with Flynn Talbot, the debonair artist who reveals that he is elusive street artist Chandler who, for almost fifty years, has brought his brand of rebellious art to the masses, but that he suffered for years in an abusive marriage...

By Leonie Baxter and Kerry Wicks

Flynn Talbot has decided it's time to change things about his life; things that have made him unhappy and regretful for a long time. He has also decided, at the age of seventy-nine, to reveal that he is Chandler, the mysterious and elusive street artist who, for the best part of fifty years, has been painting his dramatic and thought-provoking work on bus stops, brick walls, and derelict buildings.

Billed as "The Scottish Banksy", Talbot has been making social commentary an artform, using his platform to get people to stop and think. "Art is not exclusive to the rich and privileged," he says. "At least, it shouldn't be. It is there to be enjoyed by everyone and that's why I decided to adopt my alter ego of Chandler and put it out there."

Speaking from his gorgeous home, Merry Wood, with his partner, Lily Cruickshank, by his side, Talbot explains that it was the discovery of a letter that he wrote to his long-lost love in 1973 which was the catalyst for his decision to go public with not just his Chandler persona, but also with details of the abusive marriage which has haunted him for the past forty years.

"I would never admit it at the time," confesses the still dashing Flynn Talbot, "but I was being physically and mentally abused by my then wife."

The wife Talbot refers to is willowy former fashion model and fevered charity campaigner Astrid Talbot.

"She would go into these awful rages and I would blame myself. I thought I was behaving in such a way or saying something that would either bring on or fan the flames of her anger. I know now that isn't true."

Confused and embarrassed, Flynn Talbot put up with the abuse inflicted upon him by his now ex-wife. "She was offered an opportunity to work for a charity in Africa," he explains. "I thought our marriage could still be saved, and she would turn a corner." He adds ruefully, "I had my then eight-year-old son to think of too."

Talbot says things improved in Africa for a time, before Astrid reverted back to her old ways. In the meantime, Flynn admits he fell in love with Lily Cruickshank, the flame-haired beauty who lived in a cottage just across the woods from him.

"But it was all a mess, thanks to our respective partners," chimes in Lily, clutching Flynn's hand. "My late husband discovered our feelings for one another and made sure Flynn never returned to Merry Wood or to me."

Goddess approached Astrid Talbot for comment in Spain, where she now resides, but Ms Talbot declined to comment on these allegations…

The truth about Astrid physically abusing Flynn for the duration of their marriage drew a cacophony of cries from every corner of society, from domestic abuse support groups to celebrities and members of the public admitting that they too had experienced the same mental and physical torture at the hands of their partners.

The charities with which Astrid had been associated, from animal welfare groups to overseas fundraisers, seized the opportunity to distance themselves from her, citing disgust and dismay at her behaviour.

Following the publication of the interview, Astrid vanished off-grid. The backers of her proposed tapas bar also pulled the plug on their financial support. One by one, her so-called celebrity friends fell by the wayside too.

Flynn senior refused to raise the historic abuse allegations with the police, instead explaining to Flynn and me that the public shame and loss of her charity spotlight work would be her punishment.

Flynn senior assured us that he and Lily wanted to move on with their lives together and if he pursued Astrid through the courts, they would be unable to do that.

Flynn senior and Lily proceeded with selling her cottage to Mrs Oates and put Lily Grove on the market. Mrs Oates was delighted with Flynn senior's offer of continuing to work as his housekeeper at Merry Wood. After all, an extra pair of hands would be welcome to assist Lily.

Merry Wood was to be adapted to cater for Lily's heart condition, but no problem was ever insurmountable, maintained Flynn senior with his usual air of optimism.

Seth Gordon and Rick Askew were formally arrested and

charged, pending a trial in the New Year, for their part in the Stardust embezzlement, attempted murder and deception.

Lulu Stark's comedy tour was a great success and she found herself a new and trustworthy agent, who suggested they revamp the Stardust range and begin again from scratch with it.

Kerry finally admitted to all of the *Goddess* team that she was Athena's niece. There were a few raised brows, but Kerry adopted the philosophy of Flynn senior and pushed on, working hard to prove she deserved her place there.

I think she'll be ok.

The interview with Flynn senior/Chandler hit the national news headlines, sent the circulation figures for *Goddess* into the stratosphere and earnt me a promotion to the title of features editor.

I also heard that the former newspaper offices of *The Silver Ness News*, had finally found a buyer.

Flynn senior wanted to spend more time on his exhibition work and encourage the talent of young artists, now that it was public knowledge he was Chandler, so he bought our former newspaper office, transforming it into a cosy little art gallery overlooking the sandy smiling Silver Ness beach.

I and the public alike assumed that as Chandler had now been unveiled, that would mean the end of sudden eruptions of art pieces appearing on the streets.

Not so.

Not long after Flynn senior's interview appeared in *Goddess*, a series of stunning, moody, and mysterious photographs began appearing on the sides of wooden fences and old buildings.

Nobody knew who the talented photographer was other than that each of the photographs was autographed by someone calling themselves Strike.

It was only when I mentioned the sudden appearance of the compelling black and white photographs on the streets that Flynn delivered a cheeky wink and said, "Fancy that!"

I guess delivering art to the masses must run in the family.

Doug was enjoying his retirement from *The Silver Ness News*. Whenever I saw him, he would reminisce about the old days and the joviality we shared in the newsroom, but as he and Cheryl now had a campervan, which they called Sophia, they were often touring the country lanes.

Frances meanwhile was still working on a part-time basis as a reporter for the new title. She told me that she would always miss the camaraderie she had with Doug and me, but the new team was a good bunch of people and she was making the most of it.

The new paper had been met with some resistance from the Silver Ness locals, but they were slowly coming around to the changes.

Following feedback from readers, the new editor and his team decided to reflect the wants and desires of their long-established readership, rather than reinvent the wheel.

Gone were the outlandish social media interactions and instead they copied the philosophy of its predecessor. Out went TikTok and back came the local correspondent's news and views, the return of campaigns that were at the heart of Silver Ness and stories about the town's residents' struggles, motivations, and successes.

Nothing ever stays the same, does it?

And as for Flynn and me? Well, his regular appearances at Sea Shell Cottage soon became a winner with Harley.

She adores him. So much so that his occasional overnight stays have turned into a permanent arrangement.

I'm trying to persuade Flynn to give me an exclusive interview as Strike, the elusive street photographer who's taken over where Chandler left off. He keeps insisting he has no idea what I'm talking about and silences me with one of his delicious kisses.

I suppose I'll just have to keep working on him!

Flynn senior and Lily are making up for all the years they lost, creating new memories and treasuring the ones they made in the past, living together in Merry Wood. They really are an example to us all.

Live for today and let tomorrow take care of itself is their motto.

That's what Flynn and I intend to do too.

Now, I'll just ask him again if Strike might consider giving me an interview. He may well silence me again with one of those kisses of his...

If I'm lucky...

The snow was spiralling down, as Flynn and I drove towards Merry Wood.

The air was ripe with Christmas magic and the hills were slick with white.

We parked up in the picnic area as usual and clambered out of Flynn's car. Harley, secured on the back seat, let out an excited ruff and then bounded ahead through the thick layer of snow carpeting the woods and fields as soon as we let her out of the car.

I held on to the wrapped Christmas gifts we had brought them – a new painting palette and brushes for Flynn senior, and a wreath bread-making set for Lily.

As we approached the entrance to Merry Wood, the door opened and Flynn senior and Lily greeted us, sporting wide smiles and beckoning us in.

Harley shot past our legs and into the hallway. There was the delicious, rich scent of warm mulled wine and the cosy aroma of baking wafting out of the kitchen.

I kissed Lily and cocked my head. "What delights are you making now?"

"Cranberry muffins. They shouldn't be much longer."

As Flynn senior guided us into the sitting room, the crackle and spit from the log fire lit up the entire place, like a giant amber smile. Merry Wood was now a welcoming beating heart of a house again. Flynn senior had employed a crack team of cleaners who, prior to him and Lily moving in, had steam-cleaned, polished, and dusted so that their own furniture, as well as some new furnishings and the carpets they had chosen could be installed in time for Christmas.

Gone were the heavy, old, creaky pieces of wooden furniture and in their place was an eclectic mix of Flynn senior's possessions and Lily's too.

The whole house was now a blend of squashy navy sofas and cream cushions, heavy standard lamps, a cream and grey fitted kitchen and bathrooms boasting pine shelves with fluffy towels and non-slip floors. Upstairs, the master bedroom was made up with lemon and jade-green bedding, its views of the garden something to behold.

Flynn and his grandfather were standing at the rear sitting room window as the snow continued to pirouette to the ground.

I watched them laughing together at some joke. Flynn sensed me watching him and gave me a wink.

A hand settled itself on my shoulder and I turned.

It was Lily. Her hair was shiny and falling to her shoulders in a silvery curtain and her lilac eyes brimmed with happiness.

"I just wanted to say thank you, Leonie. For coming into my life."

Emotion rose up inside me. "Oh Lily, there really is no need."

"Oh yes there is. You gave me a second chance of happiness."

She gestured around herself and then towards the two Flynn's. "I thought I was too old to have my happily-ever-after. But you changed all that."

Lily grinned down at Harley, who had bumped her furry little bottom onto the sitting room carpet and was watching both of us avidly. "And thank you to you for chasing a fox!"

Then Lily reached behind her and picked up a small box wrapped in shiny gold paper and topped with a red satin bow. "This is for you."

"Oh no, Lily. There really was no need."

"Hush! Open it."

I pulled a playful face at her and tugged at the ribbon and paper.

Both Flynn's wandered over to see what was happening,

but I could tell by the knowing looks he was giving Lily, Flynn senior already knew what was inside.

I eased open the wooden box. It was an old key. "What's this?"

"It was the key I had for Merry Wood," said Lily, smiling. "I want you to have it."

I opened and closed my mouth. "But Flynn gave it to you all those years ago."

"Yes, he did. But now it's yours."

"That's right," added Flynn senior, moving across to Lily and slipping his arm around her. "You brought us together again and made Merry Wood a real home. You gave this house its heart back."

I smiled through watery eyes at Flynn, who gave me a hug and a gentle kiss.

"So that's why when the time comes, we have arranged for Merry Wood to be inherited by both of you."

Flynn's stubbled jaw dropped. "What? No…"

"Oh yes," insisted his grandfather, making it plain there would be no debate on the matter. "This house deserves to have love inside it."

Lily made her way over to the drinks cabinet. "Mrs Oates is joining us at three o clock for Christmas Eve drinks and to celebrate the occasion."

And as the snow continued to drape itself around the glorious statues in the Merry Wood garden, and Flynn and I shared another lingering kiss, I had the distinct feeling that Christmas magic really did exist after all…

Acknowledgments

Thank you as always to my wonderful editor, Jennie Rothwell, at HarperCollins, for her fabulous editorial advice, guidance, and patience! Thank you too to Sarah Khan for her proof-reading expertise.

Thank you also to my amazing agent, Selwa Anthony, and to Linda Anthony. You are both such strong, inspirational, and determined women.

Love always to Lawrence, Daniel, Ethan, and Cooper.

And to my late grandparents, Ina and George Murray, who I love and miss so much.

This book is dedicated to both of you.

ONE MORE CHAPTER

YOUR NUMBER ONE STOP

FOR PAGETURNING BOOKS

One More Chapter is an
award-winning global
division of HarperCollins.

Sign up to our newsletter to get our
latest eBook deals and stay up to date
with our weekly Book Club!
<u>Subscribe here.</u>

Meet the team at
<u>www.onemorechapter.com</u>

Follow us!
<u>@OneMoreChapter_</u>
<u>@OneMoreChapter</u>
<u>@onemorechapterhc</u>

Do you write unputdownable fiction?
We love to hear from new voices.
Find out how to submit your novel at
<u>www.onemorechapter.com/submissions</u>